AFTER THE STORM OF THE CENTURY rips apart New Orleans, Adele Le Moyne and her father are among the first to return to the city following the mandatory evacuation. Adele wants nothing more than for life to return to normal, but with the silent city resembling a mold-infested war zone, a parish-wide curfew, and mysterious new faces lurking in the abandoned French Quarter, normal will have to be redefined.

Events too unnatural – even for New Orleans – lead Adele to an attic that has been sealed for three hundred years, and the chaos she unleashes threatens not only her life but everyone she knows.

Caught suddenly in a hurricane of eighteenth-century myths and monsters, Adele must quickly untangle a web of magic that links the climbing murder rate back to her own ancestors. But who can you trust in a city where *everyone* has a secret, and where keeping them can be a matter of life and death – unless, that is, you're immortal.

PRAISE FOR THE CASQUETTE GIRLS

★ "In this Southern Gothic love letter to the spookier side of New Orleans's storied past, Arden spins out a moody tale of magic and mystery... a thoroughly satisfying page-turner and a strong debut."

— Publisher's Weekly Starred Review

"Debut author Arden offers readers a full plate of Southern gothic atmospherics and sparkling teen romance in a patiently crafted tale that will best reward careful readers... Satisfying teen entertainment but also a cathartic, uncompromising tribute to New Orleans."

— Kirkus Reviews

"In the way that it fuses the experience of adolescence, the city of New Orleans, history, magic and vampires, *The Casquette Girls* can't help but be a fun adventure, but more than that, it's a smart story with a surprising amount of emotional depth."

— IndieReader

"A slow-burning New Orleans-set vampire novel in the tradition of Anne Rice... that's more intricately woven than your typical supernatural release."

— Rue Morgue Magazine

"An entertaining, engaging story rich in historical detail and lush setting. Readers who love magic and the supernatural will particularly eat up this well-written novel."

— The San Francisco Book Review

"A novel that once I started, I could not put down... the perfect blend of romance and mystery."

— The Paranormal Romance Guild

"The plot is absolutely wonderful, very fresh... like something I've never really seen before."

— ParaJunkee

"A book that will hold your interest from the first page to the last. Each character is important. Each is well defined and well crafted. The ending is thrilling and nearly perfect. This is definitely one of the top books I've read in 2014." ***— Author Alliance***

"A YA tale that intrigued me from the description and did not fail to deliver its share of surprises." ***— Nerd Girl***

"This YA novel will appeal to fans of Divergent and other similar stories that all contain thought-provoking depth and such heart."
— Lucinda Reads

"Horrifying in some spots. Bloody in others. Fabulous in all of it."
— Christina, blogger at Creating Serenity

"The book blends old and new with fact and fiction in a mixture as intoxicating as the witchcraft so integral to the story."
— Blue Ink Reviews

"History, heartbreak, family secrets, monsters, magic powers and mean girls – this book has pretty much everything!"
— Charlotte Ashley, reviewer with Apex Magazine

"The most striking aspect of *The Casquette Girls* is its ability to collapse both time and space, to hold centuries of history together in a few words, and to make magic believable in a modern-world context."
— Laura Perry, author of Ariadne's Thread: Awakening the Wonder of the Ancient Minoans in Our Modern Lives

"Eerie, magical and gritty, getting into the grimy seams of New Orleans in the tradition of Anne Rice or Poppy Z Brite." ***— SPR***

ALYS ARDEN

Published by: fortheARTofit
Cover Design: Lucas Stoffel & Alys Arden
Cover Photo: Christina Deare
Map Illustration: Hellvis

ISBN-13: 978-0-9897577-1-3

This is a work of fiction. Names, character, places and incidents are either the product of the author's imagination or are used fictitiously. Any resemblance to actual events, locales, or persons, living, or dead is coincidental.

CONTENTS

AUTHOR'S NOTE

This book is dedicated to the people of New Orleans – past, present and future. To the people who inspired the myths and the legends, to the people who continue to tell them, and to the people who continue to believe them.

Which ones are true?
Well, that depends on what *you* believe in.

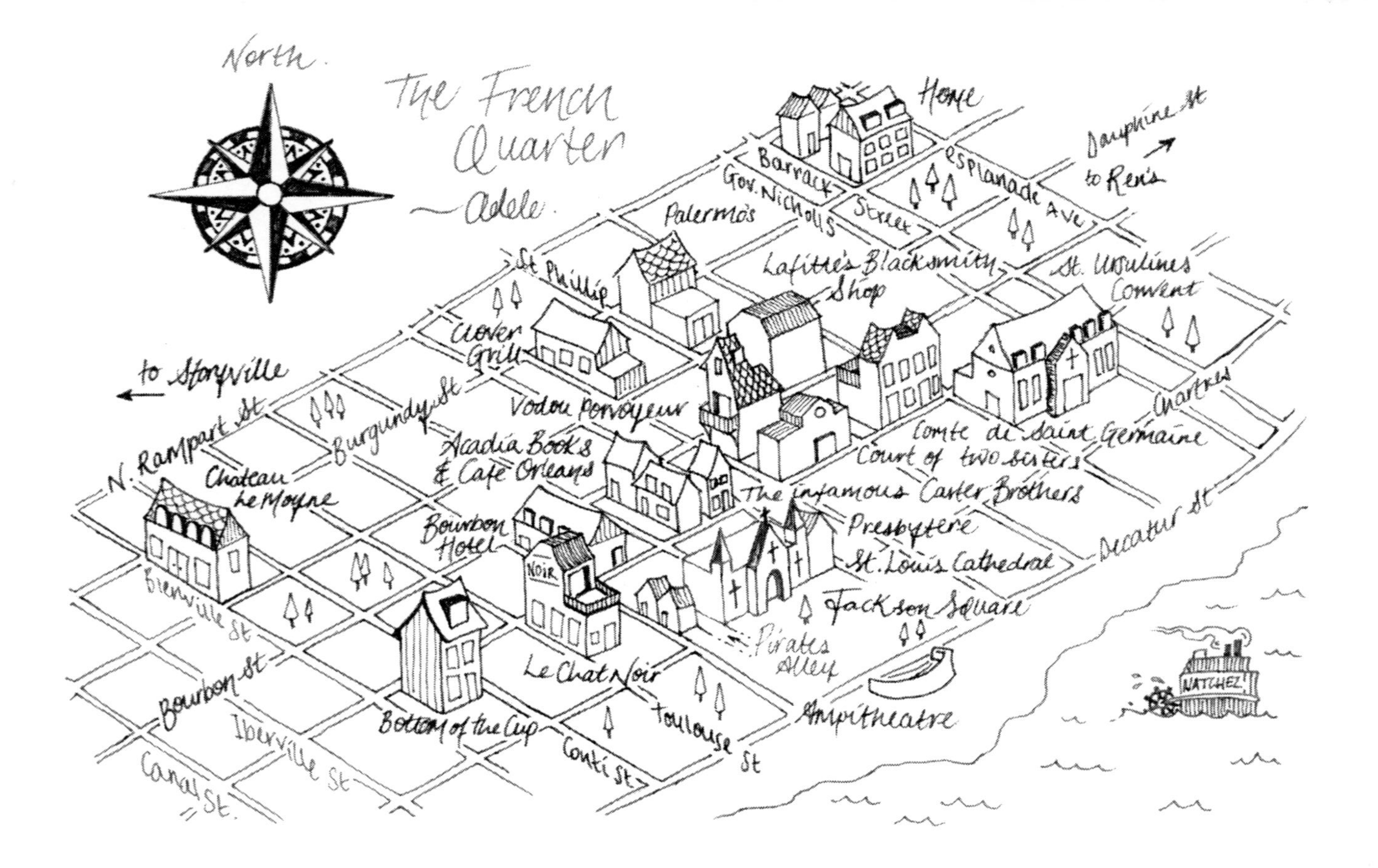
North
The French Quarter
~Adele
Home
Dauphine St → to Reni's
Barrack Street
Gov. Nicholls
Esplanade Ave
Palermo's
St Phillip
Lafitte's Blacksmith Shop
St. Ursulines Convent
Clover Grill
to Storyville ←
Burgundy St
Vodou Porvoyeur
N. Rampart St
Chateau Le Moyne
Acadia Books & Cafe Orleans
Comte de Saint Germaine
Court of two sisters
Chartres
The infamous Carter Brothers
Bourbon Hotel
Presbytere
St. Louis Cathedral
Decatur St
NOIR
Jackson Square
Bienville St
Pirates Alley
Le Chat Noir
Bourbon St
Amphitheatre
NATCHEZ
Iberville St
Bottom of the Cup
Toulouse St
Conti St
Canal St.

THE CASQUETTE GIRLS

part 1

adele

"The city where imagination takes precedent over fact."

William Faulkner

1

on the road

October 9th

THE DAY HAD FINALLY COME. The feeling coursed through my head, my chest, my stomach – until the tips of my fingers tingled, as if the sensation were trying to escape the confines of my nervous system.

My father and I were finally on our way home.

Trying not to let the anticipation drive me crazy, I leaned back in the passenger seat and took deep breaths, inhaling the smells of worn black leather and bubble gum. The combination always reminded me of sitting in the front seat as a child. I had always been up for a ride in my father's prized possession because I knew there would be a sugary pink stick waiting for me in the glove box.

The city wasn't exactly encouraging people to come home yet, but my father had always been a bit of a rebel. This fact, topped with endless nights of me begging and pleading, had finally made those four little words slip out of his mouth: "Okay, let's go home."

As soon as he caved, I fled the Parisian boarding school my French mother had dumped me in while my father and I were "displaced." She didn't tell me goodbye. And I never looked back. *I wonder if she even knows that I left?* I landed in Miami late last night, and we were on the road by six this morning. I didn't want to give my father the chance to renege.

Ten hours later, we were still purring down the interstate in his 1981 BMW.

But I didn't mind the long drive. I had never been away from my father for that long. I had never been away from New Orleans for that long. It felt like years since the mandatory evacuation, but in reality it had only been two months – two months, two days, and nine hours since the Storm touched ground.

The Storm was the largest hurricane in the history of the United States. Scientists were still debating whether it should even be considered a hurricane because it smashed all previous parameters used for classification. They didn't even name it. Everyone simply referred to it as "the Storm."

Economists were predicting it would end up being the greatest natural disaster in the Western world, and there were even rumors flying around that the U.S. federal government was considering constituting the area uninhabitable and not rebuilding the city. That idea was incomprehensible to me.

The media was all over the place about the devastation. We had heard such conflicting stories that there was really no telling what would be awaiting us (or not awaiting us) upon our arrival. Had our home been damaged, flooded, ransacked, robbed – or any combination of those things? Was it now just rotting away? I fiddled with the sun-shaped charm hanging from the silver necklace that nearly reached my waist, wrapping and unwrapping the thin chain around my fingers.

My phone buzzed.

Brooke	**5:12 p.m.**	Are you close? Text me as soon as you get home. I want to know everything, ASAP! xoxo

I quickly pecked,

Adele	**5:13 p.m.**	I will! How is La La land? <3

I didn't exactly have a laundry list of close friends, but Brooke Jones and I had been attached at the hip since the second grade. The Joneses had been stuck in Los Angeles since the evacuation, and Brooke was freaking out on a daily basis because her parents were adjusting to the West Coast lifestyle at an alarming rate. Even the *thought* that her parents might permanently relocate to California made me cringe.

"Waffle House?" my father asked as we sped past the Florida State line into Alabama. He proceeded down the exit ramp before I could respond.

A BELL DINGED when I opened the door of the infamous southern chain, causing all of the employees to shout a welcome without looking up from what they were doing. My father headed to the bathroom, and I jumped into a booth, grabbing a napkin to wipe pancake-syrup residue off the table.

"I'll be with ya in a second, darlin'," a waitress yelled from across the narrow diner.

Johnny Cash blared on the jukebox, the air reeked of grease, and the fluorescent bulb in the overhead light gave everything a sickly tint. I couldn't help but chuckle thinking about the stark contrast of this scene compared to my life just two nights ago: sitting in a café on the *Champs-*

Élysées, eating a *Crêpe Suzette* with my mother. Well, *I* had been eating a *crêpe*. She would never have allowed herself to eat something as appalling as sugar.

Mid-chuckle, my eyes caught the gaze of a guy sitting solo in a booth across the aisle, slowly stirring a cup of coffee. Our eyes locked momentarily, and my cheeks started to burn. I let my long waves of espresso-colored hair fall in front of my face and grabbed a menu so I could pretend to focus on something. I tried to recall the last time I'd taken a shower – I'd been in transit for more than twenty-four hours at this point. *Oof.*

I lifted one eye to find him still looking intensely at me.

He was probably a little older than me… and far too sophisticated to be sitting in this particular establishment among the tall hairdos and flip-flops. His black leather jacket was not the biker kind you might find in a diner in the Deep South – it was softer-looking, more fashionable. Possibly custom made. The jacket, along with his dark, slicked hair, made him appear part-James Dean, part-*Italian Vogue.* For a split second I forgot where I was, as if stuck in some kind of Paris-Mississippi-time-continuum hiccup.

When I realized I was staring at him, I became instantly flustered. His eyes didn't move, but the corners of his mouth slowly spread upward into an innocent smile. *Or maybe it was deceptively innocent?* Just as my heart began to speed up at the prospect of finding out, my fork slid across the table, flew halfway across the room, and clanked against his ceramic mug. I had been so caught up in the moment I hadn't even noticed myself flick it.

"Sorry!" I covered my face, mortified, and considered crawling underneath the table.

"Don't worry, honey, I'll bring ya a new one," the waitress yelled.

As if I was worried about the fork. I'd nearly taken out the eye of the hottest guy within a fifty-mile radius.

I finally mustered the courage to raise my head and try to catch another glimpse of him, but all I saw was his mug on top of a ten-dollar bill. When I realized I'd been hiding my gaze from no one, I became even more embarrassed.

Of course he ran. I am obviously hazardous.

"You okay?" my father asked as he slid across the orange leather into the booth.

"Yep, the jet lag must have just kicked in," I blurted out, "but I'm super excited for cheesy eggs."

"I thought you hated American cheese?" he asked suspiciously. "You always called it plastic."

"Yeah, well, I guess something becomes more desirable when you can't have it." There were certainly no American-cheese-like products in France. My heart rate began to drop back to a normal rhythm.

We ordered and then sat in silence while we waited for our food. My father turned his head to stare out the window. I knew he was too nervous to ask me about Paris, and I was not readily volunteering up any information. It was weird to spend your entire life with someone, be suddenly separated for two months, and then reunite. It felt strange that it felt strange being together.

AFTER HE POLISHED OFF a stack of waffles and I forced myself to choke back eggs smothered in plastic cheese, we headed back to the car.

"How about I drive for a while?" I asked.

"How about I drive and you study?"

"Why should I study? I'm not even technically enrolled in a school right now."

"You are enrolled in a school right now, Adele…"

I unintentionally slammed the passenger door behind me.

"You are *technically* still enrolled in Notre-Dame International."

As he pulled out of the deserted parking lot, he added in his best I-am-serious voice, "And if we get to New Orleans and find out you can't get into a school, then you are going to be on the first plane back to Paris. Back to school. That was the deal."

"I am *not* going back to Paris. *Non, je déteste Notre-Dame International!"* I said in my most dramatic French accent, hoping he would still be able to understand the juvenile words. He had only himself to blame for my speaking French; he was the one who'd forced me to take private lessons since I was five, a year after my mother skipped town – as if he thought my ability to speak her native language might bring her back. "I can't believe you shipped me off there in the first place. I belong here, not with rich kids in boarding school. Not with her." My eyes began to well. I knew my reaction would upset him, but just the thought of having to go back to Paris made me want to jump out of the moving car and run away.

The old Beamer filled up with awkward tension because he didn't know what to do or say next – any sign of teenage-girl tears made my father uncomfortable. He always tried his best to be paternal, but it never really seemed natural for him, not even after all this time of just the two of us living together.

In my sixteen years, he had never once said anything bad about my mother to me, but I could tell he felt a tiny bit relieved that I'd fight to return to New Orleans with him instead of staying in Paris with her. He was simultaneously terrified and proud that I had inherited his rebellious streak rather than her need for refinement.

He patted my hand. "Don't get upset. You know school comes first."

My father, Macalister Le Moyne, lived with a perpetually tired look. He had inherited a popular bar from his father at around the same time my mother left us, making him an artist-turned-business-owner and single parent all at once. Since then, he kept mostly nocturnal hours, waking at midday to give himself enough time to work in his metal shop on sculptures and furniture before going back to the bar. Now he was unshaven and a bit shaggier than usual, appearing to have aged a few years in the last couple of months, just like all the other displaced citizens of New Orleans.

The Storm had been peculiar not just because of the suddenness with which it had grown but because its target had been so unexpected. The day before it hit, the Storm was a routine Category 2 hurricane – not something to shrug off but something people knew how to handle – predicted to make landfall somewhere around Galveston, Texas. Eighteen hours prior to hitting land, for no reason scientists could explain, the hurricane changed course and headed straight for New Orleans.

Everyone trying to clear the city at such short notice caused total mayhem. We ended up evacuating to Miami with a few of Dad's bartenders, never dreaming we'd be gone for more than a few days. But before the Storm left the Gulf of Mexico, it tipped the Saffir-Simpson scale, and once it hit land, like most folks upon arrival in New Orleans, it didn't want to leave. We watched on in horror as it hovered. And hovered. And hovered. All we could do was stare at the television from afar and wait for our unwelcome houseguest to take a hint.

That was before the levees broke and turned the city into a fishbowl.

When reality kicked in and we were suddenly unable to return home for an undetermined period, my father decided that I would be better off in Paris with my mother rather than in Miami with a bunch of vagabonds looking for bar work. I wasn't sure if he really believed that or if he'd just cracked under post-Storm pressure, either way, he shipped me off to France as soon as he managed to get in touch with her. As far as I knew, that was the first time they'd had contact in all those twelve years.

I refused to let my eyes get blurry as I looked out the window. *I'm not going back to live with her. I won't let it happen. New Orleans is my home.*

THINKING ABOUT GOING BACK to Paris made me immediately self-conscious. Up until eight weeks ago, I had always thought of myself as just a normal teenager – not the head-cheerleader type but not being shoved into lockers either. I did pretty well in school but was certainly not in the running for valedictorian. I had inherited my father's artistic tendencies, but (to my curatorial mother's *high-art* dismay) I channeled them mostly through designing clothes. Despite all of this, I had hardly tipped average by Paris-standards. During the last two months, I couldn't have felt more plain, more uncultured, and more *passé*. My Parisian classmates were like ballerinas in three-inch heels, born to analyze *haute couture* and recite Baudelaire, making my skinny jeans and DIY dresses seem childish and unsophisticated.

I sighed and attempted to push the French memories out of my consciousness: the sparkling Eiffel Tower, the macarons from *Ladurée,* and most of all, Émile.

My stomach twisted.

I definitely didn't want to think about Émile. Not the way he tilted his head when he looked at me. Not the way his slight smile always made me wonder what he was thinking. Not his Vespa, or his sexy French accent. I'd be kidding myself if I said a small part of me hadn't wanted to stay in Paris because of him, which was pathetic; it's not like anything ever really happened between us. It's not like he was my boyfriend.

The car went over a bump, and I realized that trying not to think about Émile was actually making me think about Émile. *Ugh.*

2

the final stretch

THIRTY MINUTES LATER, we detoured from I-10 onto Highway 90 to drive the scenic route along the Gulf of Mexico, or what *used* to be the scenic route. The damage to the Mississippi coastline was insurmountable. I didn't know what to feel, only that nothing felt real.

Every single one of the behemoth antebellum homes that had lined the beach was gone. The humungous casino barges previously anchored in the Gulf had been slammed onto the other side of the highway and shattered. The souvenir shop with the monstrous shark-mouth entrance, where Dad had taken me and Brooke to buy rubber rafts when we were kids, was gone. The mom-and-pop places, the national franchises, the historic landmarks – all gone.

Waves crashed over an enormous pair of golden arches lying in the sand near the tide. I felt like I was floating outside of my body and peering down at the beach from some transcendental reality. *Was I really ready to handle the havoc wreaked by the Storm at home?*

"The media's been so focused on Louisiana, we didn't hear much about the damage in Mississippi," my father said, attempting to hide his own shock.

"How bad do you think it is in New Orleans?"

"I don't know, but you should prepare yourself for the worst."

Soon there was too much destruction blocking the highway to drive at a decent speed. Getting frustrated, my father threw the car into reverse until he had enough room to whip it around, and we went back to the interstate. The desire for the truth about the condition of the city became unbearable.

"ROLLERS...," MY FATHER SAID, taking his foot off of the accelerator. We hadn't passed another moving car since Alabama but now approached some kind of roadblock.

"An army tank? Really?" I muttered. The combat vehicle was parked among five police cars with flashing lights. We slowed to a halt, and my father rolled down his window.

"Evening, officer."

"Evening, sir," said a stocky African-American man of the law. He leaned in the window and took a good look at us. "Where y'all headed tonight?"

"Just heading home. Haven't been back since the Storm."

"You got some ID? We're only letting residents of the city back in."

My father fished his license out of his wallet and handed it over.

"And what about you, young lady?"

"She's my *daughter*," my father said, trying not to sound too perturbed. "She doesn't even drive yet."

"It's okay, Dad." I leaned over him and handed the cop my passport.

After carefully examining the documents with a flashlight, he gave them back. "Thank you, Mr. Le Moyne. You can never be too careful in times like this. Are you aware of the mandatory curfew?"

"Yes, sir, nine p.m. lockdown."

It was nearly impossible for me to imagine a citywide curfew in New Orleans, or anywhere, really. It was supposedly meant to keep people safe while the infrastructure was so poor and crime was so high. I wondered if they were really enforcing it.

"If I can offer some unsolicited advice," the cop said, "go straight home, and lock all the doors behind you. Assuming you have doors to lock."

"Thank you, officer. We'll do just that."

The cops moved the wooden barricades to let us pass, and we drove into the sunset, careful to not go over the speed limit while still within view of the fuzz.

"The bridges going over Lake Pontchartrain are out, so we are going to have to take the long route," my father said. I plugged my phone into the old tape-deck console and put on a special New Orleans mix I had made for Émile in an attempt at cultural exchange. We both settled deeper into our seats.

The familiar tunes made my desire to be home grow more and more intense. I cranked the window handle, letting the humidity roll in, along with that unexplainable presence – the *je ne sais quoi* of the city. The muggy air hit my face, making me smile with nervous anticipation as I watched the cypress trees go by. They had once been tall enough to hide the swampy marshes, but now they were mostly snapped in half like twigs.

A brassy version of "When the Saints Come Marching In" came on. My father turned up the volume and sped across the Louisiana State line, and the foliage whipped past my window until it was nothing but a blur.

I had probably heard the song a thousand times in my life – it was an unofficial anthem of our city – but I don't think I'd ever paid attention to the lyrics until then.

It felt like we were marching in.

THE BACK WAY, THROUGH THE RIGOLETS, was oddly serene. When I looked out towards the horizon of the lagoon, it seemed like any other day – birds swooped in and out of frame, and the setting sun made the muddy tributaries sparkle. But once we crossed the parish line, the residential neighborhood looked more like a war zone. My father and I simultaneously reached for the power button to turn off the music, for there was suddenly an overwhelming need for reverence, as if we were passing a funeral procession.

The closer we got to our final destination, the slower we had to drive.

The streets in New Orleans had already been some of the worst in the country before the Storm, but now there were potholes that could swallow a small car. The massive roots of two-hundred-year-old oak trees had torn through the sidewalks like rippling waves, and the fallen trees now lay lifelessly against houses. Overturned SUVs, boats, broken glass and mountains of unidentifiable debris caused the roads to appear as if they hadn't been driven on for decades. Nothing seemed to have escaped the fury of the Storm.

I stared hard out the windshield, trying to figure out what was out of place, and then horror struck me: I was looking at a house that the Storm had moved to the opposite side of the street, as if some omnipotent giant's finger had slid it like a toy. By some miracle it was still standing, but it appeared so fragile that the weight of a resting bird might have caused the whole thing to collapse. We bumped in our seats as the car went over the crumbled slab smeared across the road behind it.

"Looks like the electricity is still out," my father said, slowing to a halt at an inactive stoplight.

Observing the desolate intersection, I wished I hadn't watched *The Night of the Living Dead* only a week before (another attempt at cultural exchange with Émile). The approaching twilight sky and the thin mist rolling in made me feel sympathetic towards those post-apocalyptic zombie victims. Concerned that an arm of the living dead might reach in for my face, I quickly cranked up my window and pushed the lock button on the door.

My overactive imagination stopped bombarding me as we approached the Lower Ninth Ward. Other than the occasional cop car silently patrolling the streets, there wasn't a soul around. We had known the neighborhood would be bad – it had been getting the most press due to the levee breaches – but nothing could have prepared us for the reality of the destruction. The streets looked as if they had been bombed out.

It took me several blocks to realize that the very distinct line drawn across all the abandoned houses was an indicator of where the standing water had sat for days. The mark of the Storm.

Tears rolled down my face.

AS THE NIGHT SKY DREW IN and the last slither of sun slipped behind the horizon, it became harder to see the horrific details, especially without the aid of working streetlights. It gave us a little peace – a peace that was abruptly interrupted by screeching tires when my father slammed on the brakes.

I lurched forward.

My seatbelt snapped against my chest, and my eyes smashed shut, awaiting impact. We swerved to a stop, and there was an aggressive smack to the hood of the car.

"Dammit!" my father yelled.

With short breaths, I opened my eyes and pushed his bracing hand from my chest.

"Did you see that?" he quickly asked.

"See what?"

"A silhouette? A guy who came out of nowhere?" He yanked up the emergency brake and opened his door.

"No! Dad—"

"Stay in the car," he ordered. "And lock the doors." He gently slammed the door behind him.

Instinct brought my fingers to his lock button, but I refused to press it with him outside. I unclipped my taut seatbelt and felt an immediate release when my lungs were able to fully expand.

The whole incident replayed in my mind. The screech. The thud to the hood. It hadn't felt like we'd hit something – it felt like something had hit *us*.

Despite being only a few minutes from our house, I had the distinct feeling that we were trespassing.

My fingers tapped nervously on the door handle.

"Hello?" my father shouted out into the darkness.

I silenced my strumming fingers, and listened for a response.

"Hello? Is anyone there?"

The dead quiet made all the hairs on my arms shoot up. The tingle crawled up my neck to my scalp and clutched the back of my head. My father's boots clicked against the pavement as he circled the car a couple of times, searching for the figure. Whoever it was seemed to have disappeared into thin air.

In the beam of the headlights, my father looked back at me and shrugged.

We drove away without finding a trace of evidence that anything had even occurred.

Eager to get home and assess the damage, I pushed the incident to the back of my mind, and the only noises for the remainder of the ride came from beneath the slow-moving tires as the rubber crunched over leaves, sticks, and glass from broken windows.

My heart pounded with anticipation by the time the car finally edged onto Esplanade Avenue, the border of the *Faubourg Marigny* and our neighborhood – the *Vieux Carré*. The historic French Quarter had burnt down to the ground in 1788 and again in 1794. Since then it's drowned more times than anyone could count and has been a haven for eccentrics and freaks for more than three centuries. It's a place where strange things have been known to happen, but locals learn not to think twice about every little unexplainable detail; otherwise they'd go mad.

The enormous oak trees bent over both sides of the wide avenue, as if in agreement with the night sky to hide the current state of the gigantic old homes. I became relieved we had arrived by only the light of the moon, so we didn't have to take in all the damage at once.

Everything felt surreal – the scenery seemed familiar, but nothing looked the same.

With each turn, my anxiety levels rose higher. I wanted to jump out of the car to get a better view. I wanted to cry out, and then I wanted to cry. Instead, I sat perfectly still, was perfectly quiet, and looked straight ahead through the dusty windshield.

"Breathe," said my father.

And I did.

"HOME SWEET HOME." He pulled in front of the Creole cottage, which had been in the Le Moyne family ever since its construction in the mid-eighteenth century. The small flames in the gas lamps on either side of the entrance wished us welcome, but our home still felt strange, especially with the salmon-colored, floor-to-ceiling shutters now covered by long protective panels.

But it wasn't just the storm boards that made things creepy. It wasn't even the near total darkness. The most disturbing thing by far was the lack of noise, which normally would have drowned out the car's rumbling engine. *Usually* the Big Easy never sleeps. In our part of town in particular, a mere two blocks from the nefarious Bourbon Street, any random night usually boasted a gamut of sounds from people gradually losing their inhibitions: broad-shouldered barkers in suits luring people into gentlemen's clubs, middle-aged women belting out karaoke, frat boys hazing each other, underage teenagers squealing with mischievous delight, theatrical tour guides shouting out ghost stories, and jazz pounding out of antique pianos.

Tonight, there was only the hum of our old car. My father cut the engine.

Silence.

The car door opened loudly, and I stood, stretching my legs. Chills crept up my spine when I realized there weren't any other cars around. The historical commission enforced strict rules over maintaining the building façades, so without the cars there was little to suggest we were even in modern times. My mind got lost in the fog and the gas lamps and the granite-stoned sidewalks, wondering if this was what the street had looked like three hundred years ago.

My head suddenly whipped as I thought I saw someone dash across the street. I squinted to focus better through the haze but didn't see any movement.

"Get a grip," I whispered to myself.

"We're gonna have to leave the car on the street," my father said, pointing to the tree lying in the driveway on the other side of the iron gate.

"Well, I don't think we have to worry about parking violations."

"It's not parking that I'm worried about," he said. "Crime has been record high since the Storm. I need you to be extra careful."

"I know, Dad. You already told me, like, ten times."

"I'm serious, Adele. I will—"

"Dad! Please, don't threaten to send me back to Brigitte's every time you need to emphasize the severity of this situation. I get it. Crime is up. I will keep my street-smart meter dialed up to level orange—"

"Adele, don't call your mother Brigitte."

Neither of us could really blame the other for the intensity of our moods. Besides our home and possessions, we had no idea what the future had in store. School? Jobs? Displaced friends and loved ones? The death count was already in the thousands, and tens of thousands were still reported missing. There were too many *what-ifs* to think about.

"We'll get through this, Dad. We always do." I gave his shoulder a little squeeze and then hopped the steps to hold the gate open. He followed up the stoop with my luggage.

The heavy bolt clicked as he turned the key. The original cedar door was temperamental on a good day, but after sitting still for two months in this humidity, it had swollen into its frame even more than usual.

"Okay, the moment of truth," he said, leaning his shoulder against it. With one final shove, the door swung open.

3

home, sweet, home

THE WARM AIR LINGERED, and dampness wrapped around my skin as if we had entered a gym locker room. I flicked the light switch just to be certain. Nothing. We both reached for our phones. That feeling of peculiarity versus familiarity swept over me once again.

The total silence had crept into the house with us, but after sixteen years of hearing the pendulum swings of the old grandfather clock in the foyer, an impression of the sound was left burned in my mind. The phantom ticks became louder in my head as we crept through the foyer and into the living room. My father walked a few feet ahead of me with his makeshift flashlight thrust forward and his right arm extended over me in a protective stance. There had been countless reports of people breaking into homes and squatting in the less-flooded neighborhoods.

By the glow of our phones, nothing appeared to be out of place – not that either of us could remember exactly how we had left it.

No signs of water or mold. My father exhaled loudly.

"I'm going to get the hurricane box," I said, already halfway through the dormant dining room when he yelled my name in protest. The thick, old walls muffled his voice.

Despite the long journey, I felt incredibly alert – my eyes darted back and forth like an animal's as I surveyed each room – and, now that I was alone, I became very aware of the beating of my own heart. The deeper I moved into the house, the harder it pounded, until the beating reverberated in my ears.

When I entered the kitchen, I couldn't shake the feeling that something was very wrong. And yet everything seemed okay…

My hair lifted from my shoulders, sending waves of shivers down my back. A delicate touch brushed my neck.

"Who's there?" My body twisted around, and I ducked away.

A slow creak answered.

I spun towards the noise, dropping my phone in the process. I bent to find it on the tile floor, and when I rose, my head collided with something soft but solid, nearly knocking me back down.

"What the—?"

My hair yanked backwards.

"Who's there?" I yelled, thrashing my head.

I screamed in pain when something small and sharp pierced the skin at the base of my neck and clawed all the way up to my cheekbone.

High-pitched screams assaulted me. Blood smeared from my neck to my face as I covered my ears, screaming back. I continued to flail wildly in the dark – the intruder's wings flapped frantically in my face.

"Adele!"

"Dad! Kitchen!" My head jerked backwards again as my hair became entangled with the bird's talons and ripped from my scalp.

"Get away!"

Each time its feathers touched my skin, a wave of shudders went down my spine, making my feet dance. My arms got scratched up shielding my face. I fell to my knees, ripping the last of my tangled hair free from the bird's claws. Tears poured.

"Adele! Where are you?"

I crouched in a ball next to a cabinet as glassware began to fall from the counter and smash onto the tile floor around me.

"Down here!"

"What the hell?" he yelled over the ruckus, sliding onto the floor. "Are you okay?" He pulled me close.

His heart raced against his chest. In the illumination of his phone, I saw the crow's giant black wings open and close, breaking everything they came into contact with.

He helped me up, then swiftly grabbed a broom from behind the refrigerator and shooed the trespasser out the kitchen door. I followed and slammed the door shut.

"Are you hurt?" He held the light of his phone up to my face. My hand and arm covered the wound, but his eyes still bulged, causing me to look down. Red covered most of my right shoulder. I wiped more blood off my face with the back of my other hand.

"It looks worse than it is," I lied, my throat raw from screaming. The wound throbbed, but I kept it covered so he would calm down. "All of this over a bird?" I tried to joke, fighting the tears.

He still clutched the broom in one hand and his lit phone in the other. I don't know if it was the anxiety, the weariness, or just how ridiculous we both must have looked, but I started laughing, and soon he did too.

He put the broom down and wrapped his arms around me. "Home sweet home."

"Never a dull moment." My voice was muffled into his shoulder. I squirmed trying not to get blood on his shirt. "Wait a second." I raised my head. "That door must have been open."

"What?"

"The kitchen door… I never opened it for the crow to fly out."

He held his phone up to shine the light on the old brass doorknob. Someone had definitely smashed the lock to force the door open. He tapped the keypad on his phone three times and brought it to his ear.

"Dammit! No service."

They had warned everyone not to come home yet…

He gave up on the call, went to the pantry, and lifted out a large cardboard box onto the kitchen counter. I didn't need my phone light to know it was appropriately labeled "Hurricane Box" in my six-year-old scribble. On the side, written in a range of green Crayola to Sharpie, was a list of every hurricane it had been used in, along with the date. We were pretty diligent about keeping it fully stocked because we weren't the type who evacuated every time bad weather brewed in the Atlantic.

He pulled out a robust first-aid kit.

I nervously removed my sticky fingers from the wound.

"Dammit, Adele!"

"What?"

"I'm taking you to the hospital."

"Dad, there *aren't* any hospitals."

"Dammit." He hesitated for a second before he managed his manly-dad-poker-face.

"Dad!" The tears began to well again.

"I'm sorry, baby, it's not that bad. I didn't mean to scare you," he lied. "It's just a lot of blood."

He pressed the gauze against my face. "Damn bird."

When the bleeding subsided, he spun the lid off the bottle of rubbing alcohol. My face scrunched at the chemical smell. "It's gonna burn," he said gently and poured a generous stream of the clear liquid down my face and neck.

My limbs twisted into each other. I tried not to yelp as the solvent spidered into the wound, burning like fire. He covered the clean wound with new gauze and pressed my hand over it.

"Stay here, and I'll check out the rest of the house."

"No, I want to see!"

"Okay, but just stay put for two minutes. Keep applying pressure. I'll be right back. I promise."

Something about his exit made me suspicious. I attached the gauze to my skin with some medical tape and dug through the remaining contents of the supply box: a transistor radio, an assortment of nonperishable food items, various kinds of batteries. *Voilà.* Two flashlights. I flicked them on and off to test the batteries.

When he returned, the beams of light revealed a small black object in his hand. I did a double-take. "What is *that?*" I exclaimed in a loud whisper. "You own a gun? Do you even know how to use that thing?"

"Calm down, sweetheart. It was Grandpa's, and it's always been locked up in the safe." He seemed oddly at ease holding the weapon, as if it was something he used on a daily basis. *Who is this guy?* I gently placed the second flashlight into his free hand. *And what else had Grandpa locked up?*

"Let's go," I said and filed behind him.

He led the way back down the hall and into his bedroom, waving his light around to check out the state of his things. I continued to the rear of the room and opened the large pocket doors that separated his bedroom from his studio.

My brain refused to register what I saw in front of me. I hastily moved my flashlight from one thing to the next.

No.

No.

No.

"I'm so sorry, Dad." I couldn't think of anything else to say.

He rushed over, slid the wooden doors completely open, and stepped into the workspace.

"Stay here."

Most of my father's life work was in total disarray, strewn about the large, open room. I focused my light on the rear wall and gasped. My flashlight was shining straight into the back courtyard – a humungous Greek-revival-style column from a neighboring house had smashed through the exterior brick wall and created a gaping hole at least seven feet tall and ten feet wide. *Does it still constitute as a hole if a giant could walk through it?* Wind, rain, and Lord knows what else had poured in. I thought of the crow as I slowly approached the gap and wondered if there were any other animals lurking in the house.

"Adele, *stay back.* There might be structural damage."

Backing away from the hole, I picked up two unstretched canvases and tried to separate them, but they had fused upon drying. I put them down to avoid any further damage.

"Come on, Dad, there isn't much we can do tonight." My hand rested on his shoulder as I pulled him away from the acetylene tank he was examining. "We'll get a better look in the morning."

We did a quick run-through of the rest of the house and ended back in the kitchen. To our relief, everything else appeared unscathed.

"No crows, squatters, gaping holes or pools of standing water," my father said, dodging broken glass on the floor as he brought a chair to the kitchen door. He jammed it under the broken knob, securing the door for the evening. "Anything else can wait until the morning as far as I am concerned. Can you get through the night without electricity? I can set up the generator in the morning."

I nodded with a jet-lag-induced yawn. "Definitely." It was only 8:30 p.m. (3:30 a.m. Paris time), but I was so tired I could have slept through another hurricane.

I agreed to sleep in the living room to appease my father's fear that the back of the house might have structural damage, although I'm not sure it would have made a difference where we slept if the house did cave in. I didn't mind, though – after the crow incident, I was still kind of spooked. Not that I would have admitted it.

By the time I got back from a bottled-water tooth brushing, my father was snoring on the love seat. I sniffed an old afghan; when the smell didn't make me scowl, I pulled it over him.

Lying in a heap of blankets and cushions on the floor, I felt better than I had in weeks. Just being home brought on a small smile. Although it quickly faded when I thought about Dad's studio. His schedule was erratic because of the bar, so it was hard for him to meet people outside of the nightlife, who he tried to avoid since he was solely responsible for me. The only thing that truly seemed to make him happy was his art.

Why couldn't that column have fallen into any other room in the house? Even my own bedroom would have been better. I wondered if any of his paintings or charcoals had survived. A sinking feeling inside told me, *unlikely*. At least his main medium was metal…

I pulled out my phone and hoped a quick text to Brooke would go through.

Adele	**8:57 p.m.**	Made it home. Able to sleep in the house. Full report tomorrow. xo.

I was out cold before she had a chance to respond.

4

gris-gris

October 10th

MY FACE STUNG. As soon as I became conscious of the muggy air around me, I remembered I was home.

The storm boards on the windows blocked even the slightest crack of light from entering, masking any hints about what time it was. Based on the stiffness in my body, I guessed I had slept for at least ten hours. My phone told me twelve. *Nice.*

The quick glow from the screen had also showed me that I was alone. *How had I slept later than my father, especially considering I was on Paris time?*

Curiosity finally pulled me up and to the front door.

I squinted as the morning light poured into the cave-like foyer, and then stepped onto the stoop and let my forehead rest on the iron gate. The metal was cool. A breeze pricked my skin. *Had the season already turned? Maybe we'd have a cold Halloween...? If we even have*

Halloween this year. The only thing harder for me to imagine would be a year without carnival season.

A wave of guilt swept over me. There were tens of thousands of families who had lost everything, including each other, and I was worrying whether all the hours I had put into my costume would be in vain. I pushed the thought away, double-checked the bolt on the gate, and left the door open to maximize the natural light.

THE SLIDING DOORS SEPARATING my father's bedroom and studio were wide open. A squirrel bounced across the room, scavenging through the wreckage. I chased it out into the courtyard. His studio was now an open-air space, thanks to the damage to the back wall.

It looked like a tornado had spun through. I guess one kind of had.

Hundreds of sketches, inks, paintings, and brushes littered the studio space. Colorful dried pools of paint, resin, and other chemicals patched the wooden floor. A large oxygen tank had smashed into a wall and cracked the plaster all the way up to the ceiling. Iron patio furniture and a mass of leaves and other garden debris had blown inside through the hole. Then there was the culprit: the giant column lying in the middle. *How the hell are we going to move this thing?* I wondered, failing to roll it even an inch with my foot.

"Zeus, I think you dropped something," I joked halfheartedly. The small smile made my claw-wound sting beneath the bandage.

My father was sleeping on an old couch in the corner. My nose turned up, considering how the upholstery had surely been drenched. At least he had bothered to put a blanket down first. He rolled his back to me, revealing a half-drunk bottle of whiskey wedged between the cushion cracks.

"Ugh, Dad…" I yanked the bottle free.

He barely stirred. Looking around the room again, I felt more sympathetic and decided to let him sleep it off. I tiptoed back to the kitchen to sort more pressing things. Coffee.

Thank God we had a gas stove, and thank God we used a French press. No electricity required.

Waiting for the grinds to steep, I quietly cleaned up the mess of broken glass and bird feathers.

Just as the rich smells of coffee 'n chicory filled the air, in walked my father like a perfectly timed commercial. Only in this version the cheery tone of his voice served to overcompensate for his hangover. He broke from rubbing his head to kiss my cheek.

"Morning. It's almost like being a normal person, being awake at this hour."

"I know. I'm so used to your vampire hours." That was the moment I realized how much I'd missed him. "It's nice." I wiped down a mug and poured him the first cup. He took a giant swig and nearly choked.

"Jeez, Adele, trying to put more hair on my chest?"

"Sorry, I forgot we wouldn't have milk to steam." Chuckling, I added more hot water to both our cups. "What's the plan for today?"

He took another sip before answering. "Hunt down Eddie. Have him look at the back wall and fix the kitchen door. If he's not back in town, I'll try to get someone else to come out and assess the damage. Sort through what is salvageable in my studio, take photos, and begin the mountain of paperwork to file an insurance claim. Exciting stuff. Oh, then I'll go down to the bar and start the process all over. How 'bout you?"

"The house needs to be aired out ASAP, so can you take down the storm boards first?"

He nodded.

"Oh, and set up the generator?"

A yawn interrupted his second nod.

"I'll do an inventory of our food and water," I continued, "and find out which grocers are back in business. Then I have school stuff. And I want to stop by Café Orléans to see if the Michels are back in town—"

"You've obviously had more coffee than me." He drained his cup.

"Oh, and I was thinking I'd move all of my stuff to the room upstairs, but I'll have to clean it out first." Before our quick inspection last night, I hadn't been up there in ages.

"Why would you move your stuff upstairs?"

"So you can move into my bedroom."

"You don't have to do that, sweetheart. I want you to get settled. I can move the studio to the second floor."

"No, it just makes more sense for me to move upstairs. This way your studio can be right next to your bedroom, and if you decide to work when you get home from the bar, you won't wake me up going up and down the stairs."

"You're the best." He kissed my forehead. "I am going to start unboarding the windows."

I STEPPED OUT OF THE BATHROOM, hair dripping, candle in hand. It's amazing what a hot shower can do, even if beforehand I had to wait for the brown water to run clear and was subsequently freaked out the entire time because, in the candlelight, I couldn't tell whether it had turned murky again.

When I got to my bedroom, I blew out the candle excitedly – the boards were gone from the ten-foot-high windows. A small win for normalcy.

Everything got a sniff test for mustiness as I dug through my closet. After tossing four different dresses on the floor, I decided that everything needed to be washed.

Thanks to *ma grand-mère* (who I had just met for the first time in Paris), there was certainly no shortage of things to wear. She had been appalled by the lack of designer names in my wardrobe and had not held back on our shopping spree. I pulled out the simplest thing from my suitcase: a plain black Chanel frock. The idea of walking through a heavily devastated area wearing a six-hundred-euro dress nauseated me, but there weren't really any better options. At least it was lacking embellishments.

I tied the matching silk sash around my waist and dug through my luggage for shoes. Thinking about the amount of rubble and broken glass we had seen the night before, I tossed aside ballet flats and dainty booties and went back to my closet for my deep-burgundy Doc Martens – my shit-kickers, as Brooke called them. My feet slipped easily into the molds of the worn boots, making me instantly happy. *Familiarity.*

I rebandaged my wound, grabbed a small blue-fringed bag, keys, and sunglasses, and was out the door.

The shrill of a power tool unscrewing the boards came from the side of the house.

"Dad, I'm going for a walk! Be back soon!"

The drill stopped, and my father's head popped through the side gate. "Please be careful. Call me if you need anything, and be back before lunchtime."

"Uh, okay." My father hadn't told me to be back home by lunchtime since I was about nine years old. In fact, he was rarely awake before lunchtime.

Two blocks later, signs of life began to emerge: a lady walking her dog, a couple of gutter punks kicking a can, an elderly man shouting expletives while taking photos of his property damage. I turned onto another residential block and came across a shop hidden among the boarded-up homes. The doors were propped open, and the sign for Vodou Pourvoyeur gently swung in the breeze, making a faint creaking sound. Incense wafted out to the street. I'd never been inside the shop, but I'd referred many tourists from the café where I worked part time. Now, for no real reason, I found myself crossing the threshold.

Inside, everything was so bright, colorful and foreign, I couldn't decide what to focus on first. The front room was filled with tourist thrills: make-your-own-Voodoo-doll kits, spell books, premixed bottles labeled "Love Potion #9," vintage Ouija Boards and bright rabbit-foot key chains. To the right was a painting of Marie Laveau affixed atop an altar of flowers, melted candles and prayer cards. Visitors had adorned it with cigarettes, coins, candies, and a plethora of other small tokens to please the Voodoo Queen of New Orleans.

The smell of incense grew more pungent. I couldn't pinpoint the earthy scent – floral, with a hint of something sweet like vanilla. The shop was very long, probably a former shotgun house, and the deeper I walked, the more exotic the inventory became. Alligator skulls. Necklaces made of cowrie shells, bones and claws. Statues of Catholic saints carved from wax, wood, and ivory. A variety of other oddities that appeared to have originated from the local swampland, the Caribbean, or Africa. Both walls of the next room were covered by a sea of rainbow-colored Voodoo dolls decorated with neon feathers, sequins, and Spanish moss. The back of the shop was lit by candles and reminded me of an old apothecary.

How have I never been inside this place before?

I stood mesmerized by the floor-to-ceiling shelves of antique books and jars of all shapes and sizes, filled with herbs, powders, salts and oils. *Indigo. Ylang Ylang. Wormwood.* I recognized some of the names on the labels, but most completely escaped me.

Two women were near the rear of the room: one, a very old lady in a sleeveless, white, linen dress, sat behind the wooden counter. The old woman's wild gray curls were half-tied up into a traditional head wrap. It was obvious she had been a beauty in her time. A tall girl with straight, black hair stood in front of the counter, her back turned to me. She was trying to coax the old woman into eating something from a bowl and was growing increasingly impatient.

To give them some privacy, I shifted my gaze to a shelf displaying an assortment of gemstone-encrusted daggers next to a *"Do Not Touch"* sign.

"Fine, Gran, don't eat. I'm still not going to the gathering."

So as not to listen to their private conversation, I tried to focus on the small daggers – when suddenly, without warning, two of the weapons near my elbow shifted and clattered onto the floor.

The girl dropped the bowl onto the counter and spun around.

"I swear I didn't touch anything!" I mumbled, double-checking the proximity of my elbows. The girl shot me a glare that meant either she was embarrassed or that I should leave. Probably both.

"Child," the old woman called out to me. "Child, you need to protect yourself. You need protection."

The girl let out an exasperated sigh.

I brought the daggers to her and placed them gently in her hands. "It's okay. My dad is a broken record about the crime in the city these days." She rolled her eyes with annoyance and left them on the counter for the old woman to deal with. To say she was stunning was a major understatement. Long, black, pin-straight hair hung past her waist, and her toffee-colored skin was flawless. She towered over my average frame and could have easily passed for twenty-three, but judging from the private-school uniform and her attitude she must have been closer to my age. Immediately, I became self-conscious about the giant bandage across my cheek.

"So, your school has reopened?" I asked. The words came out rushed and slightly desperate sounding. "Do you go to school down here?"

"As if. I attend the Academy of the Sacred Heart. *Uptown*."

Historically, Americans who had migrated down the Mississippi River had settled uptown, away from the wilder and more superstitious European, African and Caribbean Creoles who ruled downtown.

The Academy of the Sacred Heart was the most prestigious all-girls school in the city, possibly in the entire South. The campus was only a couple of miles away, in the uptown Garden District, but it might as well have been a world away. Supposedly, couples put their progeny on the Sacred Heart waiting list as soon as the birth certificates were inked. The school was chock-full of carefully curated pedigree – a mix of old money and *nouveau riche,* southern debutantes, daughters of politicians and oil tycoons, and even the offspring of celebrities who made New Orleans their home to escape the limelight of Hollywood.

"So Sacred Heart has reopened?"

"Obviously. In fact, it's better than ever. Holy Cross flooded, and we graciously took in their all-male student body." She was now fully scoping me out. Her blatant gaze started at my feet, where my worn boots got her utter disapproval, and then moved up to my dress, where her disapproval faded to befuddlement. Perhaps she recognized it from this season's runway?

"Nice dress," she muttered.

After navigating Parisian boarding school for the last two months, I was a professional in these kinds of situations. "*Merci beaucoup*, I bought it in Paris. Just got back in town late last night," I said, as if I flew to Paris every Saturday for shopping and croissants. As soon as the words came out of my mouth I wanted to slap myself, but I had her attention now. Her left eyebrow raised, perplexed.

"I'm late." She flipped her hair and grabbed her bag.

"How did your family make out with the Storm?" I tried to change the subject but had maxed the quota of attention she was willing to allocate to me.

"We don't have problems with storms." She smirked and pivoted to the front door.

I stood, a little stunned by her resolute manner.

"Don't worry about Désirée, my dear. She doesn't understand yet."

I turned to the old woman. "Understand what?"

"Her importance in the world," she answered tenderly, as if it was the most obvious thing in the universe.

The comment caught me off guard. My paternal grandmother had died when I was little, and *ma grand-mère* certainly didn't think I had any importance in the world. All she cared about was my French accent and cramming me into smaller and smaller dress sizes.

The old woman began to open and close jars, making meticulous selections. She held one under my nose.

"Lavender, my favorite." I inhaled deeply. "By the way, I'm Adele—"

"Le Moyne," a resonant female voice finished for me.

I turned to find a middle-aged woman standing behind me. She had the same long hair and almond-shaped brown eyes as Désirée, but she exuded authority. With her tailored turquoise dress, navy blazer and gold bangles, she was way more Jackie-O than new-agey Voodoo priestess.

"You are Mac and Gidget's daughter," she said.

"Gidget?" Trying to imagine my mother with a girlish nickname almost made me snicker. Even hearing the Americanized version of her name, Bridget, sounded weird. To me, she was only *Madame Brigitte Dupré.*

"Your mother was— *is* an amazing woman."

"Ugh…," I fumbled.

Everyone in the French Quarter knew my father, and most knew me, but very few people knew my mother. She had lived here for only a few years before her sudden departure more than a decade ago. *Or maybe people did know her and just never spoke about her? At least not to me.*

"I'm Ana Marie Borges, Désirée's mother, and this is my mother-in-law, Ritha."

The old woman came from behind the counter.

"Borges? As in Morgan Borges?"

Ritha smiled in the way only a mother could. Lost in the moment, I didn't notice she had drawn close behind me. "Ow!" I flinched when she plucked a few strands of hair from my head; my scalp was still sore from the bird attack.

She quickly retreated behind the counter to her herbs, muttering something indiscernible under her breath.

Borges was a household name in Louisiana, with deep roots in the political history of New Orleans, and like most political families, people tended to love or hate them. Morgan Borges had been elected mayor of the city of New Orleans earlier that year. Most of his campaign had revolved around bridging the socioeconomic divide. *It was pretty apparent which side of the divide his daughter stood on.* It made sense that Désirée would attend the Academy of the Sacred Heart, being the mayor's daughter and all. I wasn't old enough to vote, but I had always thought the mayor seemed like a genuine guy, for a politician.

"It's nice to see you again, honey," old Ritha said. *Again?* "Take this." She leaned over the counter and curled my fingers around something soft. She had a wide grin and seemed a little kooky. I liked her.

Ana Marie moved directly in front of me and examined my face. Before I could protest, she peeled back the bandage and smeared something across my cut. I winced as it tingled.

Overcome with awkwardness from all the matriarchal attention, I searched for purpose by inspecting a basket on the floor at my feet, and grabbing a few bundles of herbs.

"Sage," said Ana Marie. "Smart choice. Wards off evil."

"Right…" I produced a few dollars, which they refused to accept. "Well, it was nice to meet the both of you."

"Send our regards to your father," said Ana Marie. "It's been far too long."

Was she just being polite? I hoped she meant it.

I exited the shop and paused out front to examine the object Ritha had slipped me. There was a small muslin satchel attached in the middle of the long white ribbon. When I pressed my fingers against the little fabric pouch, I could feel dried herbs and stones. *And apparently my hair*, I thought, rubbing my scalp. Ritha's warning about protection echoed in my head.

"What's the harm?" I whispered as I tied the ribbon around my neck and hid the *gris-gris* underneath my dress.

5

blue eyes

THE CONDITIONS OF HOUSES significantly worsened after I crossed Esplanade Avenue. The change was so sudden, it almost seemed like it had been purposely engineered. Once I left the French Quarter, signs of life went from slim to none.

Historically, the *Faubourg Marigny* was a neighborhood where immigrants had settled to build homes and chase the American Dream. In more recent years, artists and bohemian types had moved into the neighborhood because it was cheaper than other parts of the city but still well located. Post-Storm, one could beg to differ whether it was really so well located – in between the Mississippi River and the Industrial Canal.

Pre-Storm, this neighborhood had been one of the most colorful in the city, literally. The cultural diversity of its inhabitants brought a distinct flavor to each one of the old Creole cottages. Chartreuse, orange, magenta – pick any Crayon from the box and you could have found it here. Now it felt like I was looking at everything through a dirty gray lens. Rust and mold were the new accent colors, and the neighborhood was more akin to a junkyard: tricycles, hi-tops, ceiling fans, and bunk beds were sprinkled on the lawns. The contents strewn about varied from block to block, but every street looked exactly the same – like it had drowned and then been left out to bake and rot in the Indian summer sun. Flipped cars and boats, some smashed into houses and storefronts, had become a common sight. The sidewalk lifted in various places, reminding me of colliding plate tectonics from seventh-grade social studies.

A cloud of flies swarmed an overturned refrigerator, and an accidental glimpse of the maggot-infested mystery meat inside made me gag uncontrollably. I tried to move away quickly, but there were still puddles the size of ponds and no clear paths. I took a giant step, barely avoiding a drowned rat, and said a quick thank you for my Doc Martens.

A bad feeling crept up as my school came into view; all the windows of the old factory-converted building had been blown out. I approached the nearest one and peered in. The ground level was still filled with stagnant water. My heart sank.

The warm familiar feeling I usually had on campus had been replaced with the strange sense that I was trespassing. I circled around to the front and found a piece of paper inside a plastic sheath nailed to the front door:

New Orleans School of Arts
Closed — Indefinitely
Contact the office of the
School Board Superintendent
for current status updates.

I snapped a photo and texted it to Brooke, adding only a sad-face.

Despite the official stamp on the paper, there was something so *unofficial* about the posting that it looked piteous: the handwriting, the nail. For the first time in my life, the lack of bureaucracy made me *un*comfortable. School and bureaucracy went hand in hand.

NOSA was an audition-only art high school where we were taught that creativity was in everything, even in trigonometry, which I struggled to believe. After my audition, my father had sat me down and very seriously explained that the greatest lesson an artist could learn was how to deal with rejection. I think the day I got my acceptance letter was the best day of both our lives.

Now I wondered if this would be it for NOSA.

As I approached the corner where I would normally see my father's beautiful ballerina sculpture, I tried to brace myself for the possibility that she would be mangled, vandalized or missing altogether. He'd donated the sculpture for the school's twenty-fifth anniversary. She was who I'd hidden behind, crying, after Johnnie West robbed me of my *very first kiss* during a scene-study class freshman year, and she'd always been there to listen to my nervous banter before my juries. I'd grown attached to seeing her every morning. *Please be there. Please be—*

"Thank God!"

I nearly skipped when I saw that she was still mid-pirouette. Her metal tutu, thin as paper, still created that amazing sense of movement, even the mask that covered the top half of her face was still intact – a metal version of the ones traditionally worn during Mardi Gras. She had always been one of my favorite pieces of his, and now she glimmered bronze against the sad spectrum of gray, almost begging me to not worry. I would have hugged her if she hadn't been smeared in rotting foliage.

At least I'd have some good news for my father – his work withstood the strength of the Storm.

My father sometimes taught weekend metalsmithing workshops for adults at NOSA. I wished the school would allow him to teach us classes, but they weren't too keen on allowing students to use blowtorches. Fair enough. Luckily, he'd been teaching me the art of harnessing fire since age six, after I snuck into his studio and burned off a pigtail (which gave me a very punk-rock haircut for a summer and nearly gave him a stroke). No matter what lengths he took to childproof his workspace, I had always managed to get in and meddle. Teaching me to correctly use the tools was his way of being better safe than sorry.

My eyes teared at the thought of not being able to spend my junior and senior years at NOSA. Most kids hated school, but I'd always felt strong and confident here.

Adele, think about how much more other people lost. I wiped my eyes and started the trek back.

Large orange X's had been spray-painted directly onto the exteriors of the now-abandoned old homes. I'd seen images of them on TV, but they were so much more upsetting in person. The numbers sprayed into each quadrant of the X indicated when the premise had been searched and how many dead bodies had been found. The dilapidated houses, formerly as vibrant as the Caribbean, encouraged me to flee, but I couldn't help but pause outside one house: next to the X, a rescuer had taken the time to spray out the words *"1 dead in attic."*

The looming eeriness was suffocating.

Glass crunched under my feet as I walked away – it had come from the shattered window of a black town car parked next to me. There was a man in the driver's seat.

I froze and stammered, "Hello?"

He didn't stir.

I moved to see his face. His neatly groomed blond head was resting in the open window amongst a scattering of shiny glass fragments – his empty blue eyes looked straight through me.

"Sir? Sir, are you okay?" Southern hospitality took over, even though I knew there was only one explanation for the stillness of his body and for his head to be turned at that unnatural angle. I extended my hand towards his neck to check his pulse.

A bird squawked loudly, and I ripped my arm back in fright, barely aware of the broken glass grazing my hand as I spun around and broke into a full-on sprint. I ran through the remaining blocks of the Marigny, past Esplanade Avenue and back into the French Quarter. I kept running until sucking in the humid air became so difficult I had to stop and lean against a wooden fence.

Panting, I pulled out my cell phone and dialed 9-1-1.

The sound of the busy signal made me burst into tears. *How many other people were trying to call the police at this exact moment?* I'd never seen a dead body before much less touched one. Now, all I could picture were those blue eyes. I felt his dead skin on my fingers. My chest tightened, and an asthmatic noise croaked from my throat.

Breathe, Adele.

Tears dripped.

I threw my arms over my head, determined to pull it together.

The imposing concrete wall surrounding the old Ursuline Convent was directly across the street, which meant I was on Chartres Street, only about six blocks from home. My hand throbbed, and I felt liquid dripping down my arm, but before I could inspect it, a rattling noise caught my attention. I held my breath to create perfect silence, and heard the noise again.

From my vantage, all I could see were the five attic windows protruding from the slope of the convent roof – two left of center and three on the right. (Blame my father for teaching me to always notice symmetry.) One shutter had become detached and was hanging loosely, rattling in the wind.

I watched the shutter methodically flap open and snap shut again, but the man's dead blue eyes stained my mind. *What had happened to him? A car accident?* The rhythm of the knocking wood put me into a meditative state. My tears stopped, and my breathing evened. The claps gradually became louder and louder, drawing my focus back to the window.

A rusty smell pinched my nostrils, and only then did I realize the cut in my palm was now bleeding profusely. I untied the sash from around my waist and wrapped it tightly around my hand. *Back less than a day and I already have two injuries. Dad is going to freak.* I silently mourned the death of the Chanel as the blood soaked through it.

Sweat dripped down my back. *Gross.* I tugged at my now-damp dress and wiped the tears from my face with the back of my bandaged hand, all the while watching the attic window. The heat was incredible, rippling down my torso in waves, almost feverish. *Was it wrong to pray for a cool front,* I wondered, staring at the convent. *Maybe just a little breeze?*

The shutter snapped back shut. Something bothered me about it... and then I realized what it was.

I stopped and stood perfectly still. There was no breeze; the air was dead. The shutter flapped back open and snapped shut again, as if demanding my attention.

My pulse picked up.

I squinted as the shutter flapped open – there was a flash of movement behind the panes before it swung shut again. *What the hell?* I blinked the remaining water from my eyelids.

When I looked back up, the shutter swung open.

Faint clinking sounds came from the convent courtyard, like metal raindrops hitting the pavement. Curious, I crossed the street and approached the convent's iron gate, trying to keep my eyes on the dark window behind the shutter.

Through the bars, the overgrown garden looked as if it had been abandoned years ago, but then again, that's how most of the city looked presently. I reached for the ornate handle, but the fixture turned downwards before I touched it. The loud clank made me jump back, and the gate creaked open just enough to let me pass through.

A little voice inside pleaded with me to bail, but instinct led me through the maze of overgrown hedges as if I'd been there a hundred times before. My eyes went back to the window and refused to look away. As I drew closer, the wooden shutter continued to open and close – slowly and precisely. Once I was directly underneath, I could see the nails popping out of the joining shutter, which was still closed. I glanced at my feet. The ground was covered in long black carpenter nails – clearly the work of a blacksmith, not a modern machine. *Had it really been necessary to use so many nails to secure the shutters?* A tiny raindrop hit my face.

The shutter flapped twice more, faster and faster.

It was slowly pulling itself off the building. Only a single stake in the center hinge kept it from falling, but it, too, was protruding, as if being pulled by some invisible force. The cut on my hand throbbed; the blood had soaked completely through the sash.

A loud clap of thunder made my pulse race, but my feet still wouldn't carry me away. I stood motionless, neck craned, watching the shutter wrench itself free until it was suspended by just the very tip of the stake.

For a brief moment, the world seemed to freeze.

Then gravity prevailed.

My arms flew over my head as the dangling shutter crashed three stories to the ground – just a few inches from my feet.

The speed with which the sky became dark felt wholly unnatural. Bigger droplets of rain began to fall. Too stunned to move, I tried to make sense of what had just happened.

Suddenly, the remaining wooden shutter slammed open, and the windowpane blew outward in an explosion of showering glass. I fell to the ground and curled into a tight ball, shielding my face. A whoosh of wind whipped around me, and there was a loud whistle that faded into what sounded like sardonic laughter.

This is not happening right now. This is a dream.

The clank of metal nearby forced me to release my tense muscles and unwrap my arms from my head. I peeked out with one eye. The thick iron stake that had held the shutter was rolling along the cement towards my face, as if pulled by a magnetic force. It stopped right before it touched my nose.

I quickly sat up and grabbed it. The metal felt strangely powerful in my hand, a thick, giant nail, twice the width of my palm.

My eyes told me I was alone, but my gut told me I wasn't. Every ounce of my being screamed, *Get out!* Now I really was trespassing, and on the private grounds of the archdiocese.

Another loud crack of thunder made me scramble to my feet.

The wrought-iron gate banged shut behind me, just as the chapel bells began to clang.

6

busy signal

I SPRINTED THE REMAINING SIX BLOCKS home and slammed the front gate behind me, pausing on the stoop to catch my breath. I grasped the slick, wet bars and looked both ways down the street.

No one. Nothing.

Safe behind the iron gate, my pulse mellowed, but then I remembered only a chair held the kitchen door closed and that there was a giant hole in the back of our house – not exactly high security.

Rain dripped from my dress and weighed down my Docs as I stormed to my room. I kicked off the boots and flopped onto my bed, not caring that my hair would soak the pillow. My head spun.

What the hell just happened?

The stake was still clutched tightly across my chest. I loosened my grip, allowing blood to flow back to my white knuckles, and examined the piece of iron. I turned it over and over, but there was nothing to give me a clue.

Blue eyes. Dead, blue eyes. I exhaled loudly, trying not to cry. *Why had that man's eyes still been so blue? He had shown no signs of decay, but the Storm had hit over two months ago.* My hands began to shake. I set the stake down on the bed as I tried to recall the scene in exact detail.

The black sedan seemed undamaged, except for the smashed driver's side window. Gray suit, blond hair, blue eyes. My breathing picked up. *What if the man hadn't actually been dead, and I had neglected to help him?*

No, his neck had been contorted into a position allowed to no living person. He could *not* have still been alive. And yet, he certainly couldn't have died two months ago. *Had I discovered a recently deceased man?*

I sat up quickly, knocking the stake off the bed, and dug my phone out of my bag. My heart pumped faster as I pushed the three numbers we were schooled to never dial unless in case of a real emergency.

Busy signal.

I dialed four more times until I finally heard ringing. The line picked up:

"Hello."

"Hello! I need to report a murder!"

"You have reached the New Orleans Police Department automated hotline. If you are calling to report a missing person, please visit our website at www.nopd.gov._If you are calling to report a crime or another emergency, please stay on the line."

"Oh, you have got to be kidding! Who in this city has Internet right now?"

An instrumental version of "Mardi Gras Mambo" started playing.

From the ground next to my bed came a gentle scraping sound. I glanced down.

"What the...?"

The stake was standing upright on its point. As the hold music droned on, the stake slowly started to turn, grinding itself into the floorboard. I blinked several times, totally perplexed.

"To report a dead body, press one. To report a dead animal, press two. To report a non-Storm-related violent crime, press three."

I pressed the number three without looking at my phone.

"Please state the nature of your call. You can use phrases like, 'My house has been robbed.'"

"Um, I'd like to report a crime. A dead body, possibly a murder—"

"Thank you for calling the N.O.P.D. Who am I speaking with?" asked a despondent female voice.

The stake stopped turning.

"Hi, my name is Adele Le Moyne." My tongue garbled the words.

"Ms. Le Moyne, what's the incident you'd like to report?"

"I was walking on Chartres Street around Franklin. And there was—there *is* a dead body in a black car on the side of the street… It's not from the Storm… his eyes were still normal, so he couldn't have been dead for that long, right?"

"Calm down. Slow down. Did you witness any acts of violence?"

"No, I was just walking and found him, about forty minutes ago. I tried to call earlier but the line was busy." Talking about the corpse brought the reality of a post-Storm New Orleans to a whole new level. Chills shuddered through my shoulders. My father and I had been driving down that street less than twenty-four hours ago.

"And you have reason to believe this was a homicide?"

"Yes. I mean, I don't know. His neck looked really… wrong, like he had fallen down stairs or something. But he was in a car."

"Did you see any other distinctive wounds or unusual markings?"

A splinter of wood cracked. I glanced down to the ground to find the stake turning itself again.

"Um, no, but I was only there for a minute before I ran away."

"Okay, Ms. Le Moyne, are there any other details you would like to report?"

"No, I don't think so."

"All right, we'll send a unit over to investigate. I just need your contact information; an officer will reach out to you for an official statement."

I gave her my contact info and hung up the phone.

"What the heck?" I tugged the stake out of the floor.

It felt hot.

I flung it into the nightstand as if it had some contagious disease, slammed the drawer, and fell back onto the mattress with an incredulous headshake. My chest tightened. "I'm losing my mind."

WHEN I WOKE, the sheets were damp. I was unsure whether it was from the rain-soaked clothes I had fallen asleep in, or from the layer of sweat coating me, thanks to the humidity and lack of air-conditioning. My face throbbed from accidentally rolling over on it, and my left palm ached. The silk sash wrapped around my hand was now encrusted with dried blood. I pushed it over enough to reveal my watch.

Nine o'clock? I sat up a little too quickly, and the room spun. *Had I really slept for sixteen hours?* The overhead light was still on, and the curtains were still open, but it was pitch black outside.

"Nine *p.m.*," I said out loud. It had only been four hours. "Ugh, jet lag." I fell back on the pillows. Immediately, those dead, blue eyes popped into my mind, and memories of the nonsensical events at the Ursuline Convent followed. I groaned and got out of bed with illusions of productivity to avoid the vivid memories. There was still the daunting task of moving the entire contents of my sixteen years of existence upstairs. *Perfect.*

First, I retrieved the first-aid kit. The alcohol stung, but the cut on my hand wasn't that bad; the blood made it seem far worse. I wrapped it tightly and then stripped off my wrinkled dress. The *gris-gris* necklace Ritha Borges had given me was stuck to my chest. I peeled it from my skin but then decided it could stay.

THE STAIRCASE LED to a small open space, which we lazily used for storage. I flashed my light as I stepped over sacks of Mardi Gras beads from years past, crates of bulk art supplies, and a box of winter clothes I would soon pull down for the two months a year that allowed for wool blends. The second level was an attic my great-grandparents had converted. I could count the number of times I'd been upstairs on one hand; the ground level had always been plenty big enough for the two of us.

I pushed the simple wooden door, and it swung open.

The air on the other side was thin and stale. A flip of the light switch got me nothing. *Ugh. Had Dad not connected the attic breakers to the generator?*

I slowly scanned the unkept bedroom with my flashlight. In the darkness, the room was unassuming, and the furniture was covered up with old drop cloths. I bumped into a tall, slender object and pulled off the sheet, revealing a lamp. When I toggled the switch, a muted light shone through the old linen shade.

"Success!" The bulb in the ceiling fixture must have burnt out. I removed the lampshade to amplify the light. "Good enough for tonight."

The room was quite large, covering the width of the downstairs. The ceiling sloped at various heights due to the roof's slant, and four dormer windows protruded over the front of the house. There was a small fireplace and two doors on opposite walls.

The first door revealed a small room, about ten feet by ten feet, with mountains of stuff piled up to the ceiling. I flicked my flashlight around for a few seconds. *Whoa. I could have my own little studio... or a walk-in closet.* Suddenly the task of cleaning everything out didn't seem so arduous. I nearly skipped as I closed the door and crossed the room to door number two.

I pulled the long ball 'n chain dangling from the ceiling. A single bulb flickered on, and I shrieked, "WHY have I been sharing a bathroom with my father for all of these years when there is one up here?" I pressed the flusher on the toilet and marveled at the working plumbing.

The dust was so thick on the oval mirror above the pedestal sink that I struggled to see my own reflection. Feeling slightly nosey, I opened the glass door of a tall, narrow cabinet, disrupting the long-settled dust, which in turn disrupted my sinuses and caused me to sneeze three times.

Stacks of towels long past their prime. A heavy, silver hairbrush. An assortment of vintage cosmetics. I ogled at a collection of perfume bottles made of multicolored, unlabeled glass. A few were marked with the word "Paris."

Who did you all belong to? They were way too old to have belonged to my mother. The little objects begged me to make them shiny again.

I pulled out the rotting linens. They were far from salvageable, but my affinity for fabric caused me to poke through them anyway. A misplaced square of lace lay among the tattered terrycloth. The dry-rotted Chantilly fell apart at my touch, revealing a piece of silver. At a glance, it looked like an old coin, but on further inspection it seemed to be a medallion of some sort. One side was rough, as if something had broken off and left behind a scar in the metal. There was something familiar about the shape – an eight-pointed star. The other side was flat and smooth except for an ornate border. It looked sad. Unfinished. Like a canvas someone had given up on. I wondered if something was missing from the piece or if this was the artist's intended design.

I slipped it into my pocket and sighed at the tragic state of the disintegrated loops of lace. After another minute mourning the textiles, I started a trash pile, telling myself I couldn't get attached to every inch of vintage something-or-the-other I found while cleaning.

THE SMELL OF BLEACH permeated the air as I wrung the mop into the sink. My fingers ached from scrubbing. I caught a glimpse of my watch and was surprised to find more than two hours had passed.

Break time.

The air in the lamp-lit bedroom wasn't any better. I struck a wooden match and lit one of the Voodoo shop's sage bundles, unsure whether it would help or hinder the dusty and now chemical-filled air.

At least now the room will be free of evil spirits.

Chuckling, I left the smoking herbs in a glass dish on the fireplace mantle. The dust began to tickle the back of my throat, making me cough.

With some force, I managed to wriggle open one of the windows. In the darkness, there was nothing to look at but the moon, but I rested my elbows on the sill and breathed in some of the cooler, cleaner air.

No tourists, no screaming drag queens, no horse hooves clacking down the street. The perfect still of the night – this was something I would never get used to. Not in New Orleans. The quietness freaked me out.

My mind drifted back to the Ursuline Convent. I could almost feel the swoosh of energy that had moved past me after the shutter burst open and glass rained down in sparkling shards. *It was a miracle I had walked away unscathed.*

A trapped breath escaped.

I leaned out the window and tugged at the shutters. Neither budged; both were securely fastened open. I'm not sure what else I expected to happen. With my upper body still hanging outside, I noticed a bird perched on our neighbor's balcony: a large black crow, staring. I yanked myself back inside, banging my head, and slammed the window shut.

Touching the bandage on my face, I looked back through the glass with a little spite, but only the moon stared back at me. "Come on, Adele, it's just a stupid bird."

I shoved the window open and turned back around, ready to clean.

"Dad! Are you trying to scare me to death?"

My hands went to my knees, pulse exploding.

"I'm sorry, sweetheart. I called your name when I walked through the front door, but I guess you couldn't hear me all the way up here. I didn't mean to scare you." He pulled me up. "What's wrong?"

I hesitated as the day's events sped through my head. There was no real need to tell him about the dead body. It would only make him worry, and might even result in stricter attempts at parenting, an experiment in which I didn't want to be a test subject. And there was no way to explain the bizarre events I had seen in the convent courtyard; I felt insane just thinking about them.

"Nothing's wrong. You just startled me. How was your day?"

"Okay, considering all things. No leads on finding someone to fix the wall. The supply and demand ratio for labor is already way out of whack. It's going to be mayhem when the masses return."

"And the bar?"

"Looks like it got a couple inches of water, just enough to damage anything that was resting on the floor."

"Oof, that's good? I guess?"

"Yeah, it could have been a lot worse, I suppose. The smell was the worst part, but I managed to drag most of the rank furniture outside. Did you make it to school?"

"Uh, no." I braced myself for the onslaught of guilt after lying to my father, but I didn't want to open that can of worms tonight. I moved my bandaged hand behind my back.

"What's that smell?"

"It's sage. Oh, I ran into an old friend of yours… and Mom's."

His left eyebrow raised into a question mark.

"Ana Marie Borges."

"Wow, that's a name I haven't heard in a long time. Where did you run into her?"

"In their shop. That place is so cool! I can't believe you've never taken me there before."

"What were you doing in Vodou Pourvoyeur?"

"Nothing, really. I moseyed in because it was actually open."

He looked a little more uncomfortable than usual.

"It was kinda weird."

"How so?"

"Just, they kinda acted like they knew me."

"Ana and Morgan have a daughter about your age."

"Désirée. We met. She's *delightful*."

He laughed. "Well, I'm sure she's grown up wanting for nothing."

"That's an understatement."

"Let me guess, the Storm went easy on their shop?"

"To quote Désirée, the Borges 'don't have problems with Storms.' Oh, I have some more sage if you want to bring a bundle to the bar."

He gave me a funny look.

"You know, for the rank smell?" I looked down at my watch. "Whoa, where have you been all night, Dad? It's after midnight."

"I told you, at the bar—"

"But what about the curfew?"

"It's not like I was out loitering or looting, Adele. People have lives; people have to work. Damn curfew."

"Jeez, sorry I asked."

"And that doesn't give you permission to be out past curfew."

"All right."

"We should go to bed. It's late."

"I took an epic nap, so I'm not really tired."

He moved to the window and pushed it shut.

I sighed, switched off the light, and followed him down the stairs to my bedroom door.

"Try to sleep. It's the only way you'll get back on Central Time." He kissed my cheek. "Goodnight."

"G'night."

I kicked off my flip-flops, playing back our conversation in my head. Something about the casual way he had mentioned Ana Marie struck me as odd.

7

ciao, bella

October 11th

WITH THE CURTAINS OPEN, I sat at the antique vanity, under the natural light. I leaned so close to the mirror, my nose nearly touched it. The advantage to listening to my father and not staying up all night was that the signs of life were slowly coming back to my face: the puffy dark circles from switching time zones had mostly faded, and the crow wound was slowly starting to scab over. *Gross. But at least now I could lose the giant bandage.*

I slathered on an assortment of fancy French *crèmes* my mother had stocked my dorm room with. *She must be doing something right, to stay so young-looking.* As I breathed in the lavender moisturizer, I wondered if she used the same scent. Too lazy to do much else, I ripped a comb through my tangles, spritzed in some product, and hoped my mop of brown waves would dry in a decent manner.

Black leggings. Grey T-shirt. Shit-kickers.

It was unsettling that my old routine felt only vaguely familiar. *When would things start to feel normal again?*

I reached for my chain on the vanity and also found the silver medallion from the disintegrating lace. I moved closer to the window and held it under the morning light – there was something underneath the burned star. Initials. I breathed heavily on it and rubbed it with my towel, vowing to clean it properly later, in my father's studio. The letters were difficult to make out at first, but then became clearer: A.S.G., etched in sweeping calligraphy. I flipped it over to see if I had missed anything else last night. There was nothing special on the other side – just the ornate border.

Something about the medallion felt old, and I found myself slipping it onto the silver chain next to the sun charm my father had made.

I looped the long, thin necklace over my head. My collar slouched off one shoulder, revealing the *gris-gris* ribbon. *Who was A.S.G.?*

I BROUGHT MY SECOND *café au* (powdered) *lait* with me into my father's room. He looked depressed, blindly dumping stuff into a large garbage can. I wondered if I should stay and help him.

"Morning," I said and decided that having to unexpectedly throw away piles of your own work was something an artist would want to do alone. "I'm gonna go for a walk, check out the grocery situation, and swing by Café Orléans."

"All right, let's go for a run when you get back, before it gets too hot?"

"Ugh, sure." It had been months since I had done any real physical activity.

"That's the spirit, honey."

I smiled and left the coffee for him on his workbench.

On the way to the front door, I grabbed my bag and reached for my keys. They shot up into my palm.

I stopped short.

Quickly, I looked around to see if anyone else had just witnessed the strange occurrence, knowing full well that no one was there. My fingers tightened around the keys into a fist.

Breathe.

The metal felt warm, and my fingers began to tingle. My heart started skipping as I racked my brain for a reasonable explanation, but nothing came to mind. I felt strangely at odds, like my subconscious was trying to fight back – fighting the part of me that was desperately trying to suppress yesterday's memories as if they were a bad dream.

Trying not to go into a full-on panic attack, I dropped the keys into my bag and did what any reasonable person would do: ignored it and hustled out the door.

My nervousness transferred from my shoulders down to my feet, which carried me down the block at a non-Southern pace. I misjudged the hop onto the curb and stumbled, but caught myself before falling.

"Adele? You okay?" Felix Palermo yelled, witnessing my spastic moment. He sure had good eyesight for someone pushing eighty. The old man was hunched over a broom, next to a large pile of window shards. I hurried across the street, eager for the distraction.

"Hi, Mr. Felix!"

"If it isn't little Miss Adele."

Behind him, a couple of younger guys I didn't recognize exited Palermo's deli, carrying a moldy refrigerator. The little corner store was not in good shape, but I tried not to let the shock show on my face. Palermo's was one of the many Italian delicatessens that had opened after a huge influx of Southern Italians migrated to the city in the late nineteenth century. They have mountains and the Mediterranean, and we have marshes and the Mississippi – I'm not sure I see the appeal – the climate's similar, I suppose.

The guys dropped the fridge near the curb and quickly retreated back into the deli.

"When did you and Mrs. Rosaria get back?" I asked, giving the old man a hug.

"We snuck back a few days ago, but it wasn't 'til yesterday that I found a couple of boys to help us start haulin' the trash out. They're staying in the top-floor apartment, trading rent for labor. If ya ask me, I'm getting the better end of the deal – the apartment doesn't even have electricity. But they're over from the motherland, lookin' for some missing relatives, so they've got bigger problems."

"We're running a generator," I said. "I don't think anyone in the Quarter has electricity, yet."

"We got a few feet of water. It poured in the storefront window where an old Chevy had pushed through. The boys managed to get the car out last night, and we were still mopping water out this morning. Looters trashed the place." He sighed. "I suppose I can't really blame them. People need to eat. This hurricane, Addie, I don't know. I've been through Betsy and Camille and at least a couple dozen more, but something's just not right about this one."

I didn't know why, but I understood what he meant. Something just felt off. I had tried to convince myself that the feeling was just due to being away for so long, combined with the shock at the level of destruction, but I couldn't shake the feeling that something else was different. That something had changed.

He gestured to the store. "You go in there and take anything you and your pop need. That is, if there's anything left."

"I'm not taking anything from you without paying—"

"Adele, you go salvage anything you can. And don't you worry about it; I'm filin' an insurance claim tomorrow. *Capisce?*" He gave me an exaggerated wink.

"*Capisce.*" I smiled and walked towards the entrance.

"And be careful in there, Adele! It's a goddamn mess."

I yelled, "Okay," over my shoulder and stopped in the entrance. The store's enormous retro sign had been split in half. The half with "PAL" still seemed secure, but "ERMO'S" now hung at a dangerous ninety-degree angle. I hurried underneath to enter the store. The whole city was starting to feel like one giant booby-trapped obstacle course.

FLIES BUZZED AROUND MOUNDS of brown-colored mush that used to be fruit but now reeked like rotten grass. I covered my nose and mouth to mask the smell, attempting to control my jerking stomach muscles, and then hurried to the other side of the store, being extra careful not to step on anything that would require a tetanus shot after.

Sauntering down the remaining aisles, I assessed my options, scared of anything not preserved in glass, aluminum, or a vacuum-sealed bag. Most of the nonperishables had already been cleared out. I grabbed a can of steel-cut oats as if it was gold, and then a couple sacks of red beans and rice. *Would bigger supermarket chains look like this too – empty shelves with a rotting inventory? Would we have to ration these oats? Surely the government would intervene if it came to that... right?*

I quickly scooped up two cans of tomato soup, and, through the empty space they opened up, got a view to the other side of the room, where Mr. Felix's two workers were ripping the commercial freezers from the wall. Neither seemed to be breaking a sweat.

Impressive.

One had light-blond hair, and the other's was nearly black, but there was something very similar about them. *They must be brothers*, I thought, watching them from between jars of pepper jelly and dusty cans of New England clam chowder. Even their movements were synced; each carried out the manual labor with a strange amount of grace. Mr. Felix had said they were from the motherland; he must have meant Italy; their slickly styled hair seemed very Italian to me. Flashbacks to my European days suddenly made me feel very underdressed.

The dark-haired guy was closest to me, but all I could see was the back of his head. He wore dark jeans and a black leather jacket, and even from behind, seemed more focused on the task at hand than the blond, who appeared bored, his thin lips in a near pout.

The blond looked to be in his mid-twenties. The cuffs of his pale-blue denim jeans were turned up, and his suspenders hung lose at his sides. He had the most perfect skin I had ever seen, but his aquiline features combined with his lackadaisical demeanor made him come across as some kind of naughty prince.

"How long do we have to do this, brother?" he asked.

"Until we've acclimated. Or until everyone is reunited, I suppose." His English had only a hint of foreign accent, while the blond's was much thicker.

"I assumed finding everyone would require some brute force, but this wasn't exactly what I had in mind," the blond said as he jerked the refrigeration system from the wall.

"Stop whining. Like you couldn't do this in your sleep."

"Don't mention sleep around me," said the blond. His brother softly chuckled.

My chest stung. The Storm had turned so many people into insomniacs. *How could you sleep if you were missing loved ones?*

Out of nowhere, the cans of chowder betrayed me by flying off the shelf and onto the floor in a series of loud crashes. I watched in horror as one rolled all the way over to the boot of the blond.

"Well, whom do we have here?" he asked, overjoyed to have a distraction from the labor.

I was mortified, caught spying on a private conversation. And not just any conversation but one between two hot guys. I suddenly wished I had taken the time to put on makeup, but what were the odds of meeting two beautiful foreigners at Palermo's? I tried to walk casually to the other side of the shelf, as if I was just doing the daily shopping.

"Hi, I'm Adele. I live around the corner."

"Adele?" He looked at me with an eagerness that made me slightly uncomfortable.

"Yeah, Adele Le Moyne." My attempt to offer a hand failed because I was holding too many things, so I resorted to a half-nod, half-curtsey. Blood rose in my cheeks.

"*Buongiorno*, Adele. I am Gabe." The blond's light-green eyes sparkled against the grim backdrop of the store. "And this is my younger brother, Niccolò."

Niccolò nodded at me and then casually leaned against the wall with one foot up, his hands stuffed deep into his pockets.

"Nice to meet you both. *Bienvenue?*" *Is welcoming appropriate under these circumstances?*

"The pleasure is entirely ours," Gabe said, looking down at me with a dramatic smile. From my hiding spot, I hadn't realized how tall they were, both over six feet. The outline of Gabe's well-defined chest was easy to see through his fitted white T-shirt, which he had somehow managed not to dirty at all.

I scrambled to think of something to say. "Mr. Felix said you are over from Europe. Italy?" I placed my bags on the ground.

"*Si*," Gabe said quickly. "We are looking for our cousins. We have three missing in action. Maybe you know them?"

There was something strange about the way he had asked. Like the way a Mafioso would casually inquire about his next victim. My knowledge of the Mafia, of course, came only from watching the *Godfather* movies repeatedly with my father.

As I listened to Gabe describe their missing relatives, I couldn't help notice that Niccolò's gaze still hadn't shifted from me. He had the same light-green eyes as Gabe, only his made me think of a cat preparing to pounce on a toy. My fingers went to the chain around my neck as my eyes flicked to his – never for more than a few seconds at a time. He was just as attractive as his brother, but with more of a James Dean vibe about him. *Wait, did I know this guy?* I blushed when I realized there was no way I could have met a guy *this* attractive and then simply forgotten about him.

His lips moved into a slight smile, as if he knew I was trying to figure it out.

Then I noticed the silence. Gabe had stopped talking and was looking at me, obviously expecting me to answer a question.

"I'm sorry," I stuttered. "What was the name?"

"Me-di-ci," he repeated slowly, as if I was having trouble comprehending him and was not just absorbed by the way his brother was looking at me.

"Leave her alone, Gabriel." Niccolò finally spoke. "She obviously doesn't know anything." The softness of his voice surprised me.

"It's fine," I squeaked, dropping the chain. The charms bounced against my stomach as I turned back to Gabe. "I'm sorry, I was paying attention. I just… got distracted." I tried not to smile, knowing Niccolò was still looking at me. "I don't know any Medicis. I'm sorry." I desperately wished I knew something, anything, about their family. "Three people missing – that's horrible."

Gabe let out an exasperated sigh. "Don't worry, little lamb, we aren't going to rest until we find them." He walked across the room and stood right outside the doorway, staring down the street like a posted guard.

"What happened to your face?" Niccolò asked, obviously trying to change the subject.

"Um, a bird clawed me." I was not thrilled that the attention now focused on my giant scab.

"A bird? What kind of bird?" he probed in a serious tone. I had a hunch it was only a slight variation from his natural disposition.

"I'm pretty sure it was a crow, but it was really dark in the kitchen so I can't be certain. Everyone around here has so many horror stories from the last couple of months, but all I got was a crow attack. Not that I'm complaining," I quickly added.

"A crow? In your home?"

He seemed to mull over the idea as he slowly approached me.

My mouth moved, but I no longer heard the sounds coming out… something about how great the city was under different circumstances. My brain ping-ponged between wondering where I knew him from and wondering whether I should stay and continue embarrassing myself with my pathetic attempts at conversation. Unfortunately, he said nothing to interrupt my rambling as he moved closer, although, his focus was so attentive on my wounded cheek, I questioned whether he was even listening.

He stopped directly in front of me, forcing my fluttering eyes to focus on him. "It is an amazing city. Luckily we've been here before."

My throat tightened. "Oh, good."

He was so close I could smell him over the lingering stench of putrid produce: leather and soap. The scent reminded me of Émile. Probably because Émile was one of my few points of reference when it came to male scents.

He raised his hand to my face, and I prayed that I wasn't showing any outward signs that my knees were about to buckle. Careful not to touch the wound, his fingertips grazed my cheek, sending chills up my head and into my hairline. Surely he must have noticed.

He took a deep breath and whispered, "Lavender."

His hand swept my neck as he delicately picked up the thin silver chain, following the tightly woven links all the way down to the two charms dangling at my waist. He brought the medallion up to his face, pulling me even closer. My chest bobbed against his leather jacket. I strained my legs to keep my balance and not fall into him as he flipped it over, keenly examining both sides. My gaze nervously wandered to the broken Palermo's sign hanging over the door, where Gabe was still standing sentry.

"Pretty necklace. Where did you get it?"

We were standing so close, I could barely breathe. I tried to turn sounds into words, but nothing came out of my mouth easily, for a change.

"My dad— Gabe!" I screamed as a loud screech of scraping metal interrupted us.

The latter half of the massive sign tore free and plummeted toward him. My eyes smashed shut, and I covered my ears, anticipating the loud crash… but a few beats of silence went by instead.

In that fraction of a second before I closed my eyes, had I really seen the sign momentarily freeze in midair?

I cautiously opened my eyes to find the two modelesque brothers each holding one end of the broken neon namesake. The sign was so old, it must have been extraordinarily heavy, but they rested it on the floor as if it was as light as a kitten. They both brushed their hands and turned to me with a look of bewilderment plus a hint of suspicion. Which was strange, because that's exactly how I was looking at them.

"Are you okay?" I asked, hurrying over to them. My hand instinctually went to Gabe's shoulder, but then I quickly pulled it back, not that he seemed to mind the physical touch.

"You saved me," he said.

I balked at the very idea.

"Your warning scream… I am forever in your debt." He gallantly kissed my hand.

The metal screeched again.

I looked up just in time to see the lonely letter L dropping from above us.

Before I could blink, Gabe jumped up and knocked it aside. Niccolò jerked my arm, pulling me out of the way as it crashed onto the brick floor in an explosion of glass and plastic.

A wheeze escaped my throat. Gabe looked straight in my eyes and smiled.

"I guess you're even now," Niccolò said.

They both just stared at me, seemingly undisturbed. The silence quickly became deafening. Rampant insecurity took over. I wasn't sure what to do or say next, so I fled back for my bag and gathered up my loot. Their gazes continued to burn through me – whether it was with disbelief, admiration, or scorn I had no idea.

Trying to be nonchalant on the way out, I grabbed a bottle of rubbing alcohol, a large box of salt, and a couple boxes of baking soda.

"Well, it was nice to meet you both."

"Until we meet again," said Gabe. "*Arrivederci.*"

"And welcome to the neighborhood." I looked at Niccolò. "I wish it were under better circumstances."

"Me too." The corner of his mouth crooked. *"Ciao, bella."*

8

bisous, bisous

COMPLETELY FRAZZLED, I took off in the wrong direction. Luckily, I only covered one block before I came to my senses and detoured onto Bourbon Street.

Usually at this hour, employees would be receiving truckloads of inventory and hosing out the proof of last night's vices from barroom floors. Usually I had to hold my breath because of the rank aromatic meld of stale beer, ashtrays, bleach, and garbage baking in the end of summer heat. But this morning that was not necessary. Today there was only one man in view, and he wasn't hosing. He was just leaning against the entranceway of the Court of Two Sisters, smoking a cigarette, shaking his head.

I looped onto Orleans Avenue and sped up, partly out of excitement and partly because my bag of nonperishables was getting heavy.

This particular block, where Café Orléans is located, is one of my favorite streets in the city – I loved its duality. At the far end is one of the loudest blocks of Bourbon, home of the infamous hand-grenade: a toxic-green melon cocktail served in a plastic yard-glass shaped like an explosive device – touted as the world's most powerful drink. The opposite end of the short block dead-ends in St. Anthony's Garden, the back courtyard of the St. Louis Cathedral. New Orleans, like this street block, was a place of contradictions. Especially in the French Quarter, you could never guess what you'd find.

I stopped in front of the used bookshop next to the café, one of my most frequented locales. It was closed, but the shutters were open, indicating that someone had been back since the evacuation. I leaned my head against the windowpane to look inside.

The tiny shop didn't appear to have any damage. *Thank God,* I thought selfishly. This bookstore had provided me with far more important knowledge than my school textbooks.

The hanging wooden sign for Café Orléans caused a rush of excitement to fill my chest – I had helped Sébastien climb up and take the sign down before his family evacuated, so they must have returned.

Sébastien Michel and his twin sister, Jeanne, were the closest things to siblings I ever had. The Michels had been like a surrogate family to me ever since my mother left, so practically my whole life. Ever since they were small children, the twins had been raised by their grandparents, Bertrand and Sabine, who were originally from France. Since they had a French-speaking household, my father wouldn't allow anyone else to babysit me when I was a child. It was his version of language immersion/torturing me. French is not widely spoken in New Orleans anymore, so it's not particularly useful, but he did it because it was supposedly important to my mother. He always seemed sad when he reminded me of that, so I never fought him on it.

I stood in the doorway and watched as the four of them bustled about, each of them wrapped up in their duties. The old couple was wiping down the furniture with spritzer that smelled like pine. Jeanne was tugging on her blonde hair while meticulously recording inventory on a clipboard, and Sébastien was lugging in giant sacks of coffee beans from the back alley.

I tried to put my bag down gently, but the weight of the canned goods made a clank. Everyone paused and turned their heads in unison.

"Adele!" cried the twins, cueing everyone to hustle over and make a fuss. French, English, everyone talking over each other: after spending so much time alone recently, it felt like a party.

Jeanne threw her arms around me. *"Comment était Paris?* I want to know everything!"

"*Misérable,"* I replied. *"Tout le monde parle français à Paris!"*

She laughed. "Well, it's a good thing you have such a brilliant French tutor!"

When I was nine, my father had decided immersion wasn't enough, and started paying Jeanne to teach me things like grammar.

"Wow, your accent is better than mine now! *Très impressionnant.*"

"*J'en doute.* I *seriously* doubt it." I couldn't imagine myself ever being better than Jeanne at *anything.* The twins were only four years older than me, but she was about to finish her master's degree in biochemistry, was engaged to a med student, had the confidence of a beauty queen, and all of this before she was legally able to drink. *Maybe that's what happens when you get to skip the formidable high school years?* Yes, the twins were both some kind of super-geniuses.

Sébastien leaned forward to gently kiss both of my cheeks. "*Salut, Adele, bienvenue.*" His voice was quiet, but I could tell he was just as excited as his sister. His shyness caused us both to blush a little. "What happened to your face?" He pushed his black-rimmed glasses closer to his baby-blues.

I sighed. "It's an embarrassing story involving a bird. How long have you guys been back?" I felt kind of bad. I'd been so wrapped up in trying to navigate the heinous waters of Parisian boarding school, I'd done a crummy job keeping in touch with the people I actually cared about.

"We just got back from Cambridge yesterday." Jeanne pulled my arm and whisked me down to a café table. "I thought being displaced would be terrible, Adele, but M.I.T. was SO amazing. I got to work with—"

"*We,*" Sébastien corrected. "*We* got to work with three different Nobel Laureates."

"And they even put Mémé and Pépé up in this adorable little colonial house. It was so beautiful, all the xanthophylls, carotenoids and anthocyanins—"

"She's referring to the different colors of the changing leaves," Sébastien translated. "They actually have four seasons in Massachusetts."

I gave him my all-too-familiar "*thank you for explaining her craziness*" look.

"But thank goodness we were able to leave before winter," their grandmother interjected from across the room. "They got thirty inches of snow in one blizzard last year! Can you imagine? These old bones do not shovel snow."

"Adele! I can't believe I forgot to ask." Jeanne's usual scrutinizing, aquamarine eyes grew wide with concern. "*Ta mère?* What was she like?"

Everyone else pretended to go back to work as I scrambled to figure out what to say about my mother.

All the way across the Atlantic, I had imagined one hundred different scenarios for my joyful reunion with my mother, wherein she would tell me a complicated, heartbreaking story explaining how she had been forced to abandon me and my father and had lived in agony ever since. In some versions I cried, in others I yelled, in most we ended up drinking tea next to a fireplace and talking for hours.

But any pathetic fantasies I had entertained about finally rebuilding a relationship with my mother burst upon arrival in Paris when the only person who came to greet me at *Aéroport Paris–Charles de Gaulle* was her driver, Paul-Louis, who took me directly to boarding school. There was no trace of her cold-blooded heart other than a small bottle of champagne in the car with a beautiful card that said,

Bienvenue à Paris, mon amour.
Bisous,
Brigitte

It was probably the standard greeting she used for all of her acquaintances arriving at the airport. Not that I was surprised by my mother's epic fail. I had just thought that maybe with the Storm and all, she might suddenly have started caring that I was alive. There had been a basket of luxurious French beauty products and boxes and boxes of Chanel dresses waiting for me in my dorm room, but I had to wait another week before even hearing from Brigitte. I was in full-on rage mode by the time our first meeting had occurred.

"What was she like?" I repeated. "I wouldn't really know. I saw her three times over the course of two months. We had approximately seventeen interactions, if you include voicemail, text, and email. I did, however, see *ma grand-mère* a few times. She was appalled by my French but bought me racks of fancy clothes to make up for it."

"To make up for being appalled, or to make up for your appalling French?"

"Hmm. *Je ne sais pas,* both maybe?" We both laughed. "Whatever." I forced a smile and tried not to roll my eyes. "I'm over it."

"I'm sure her intentions were good, Adele," Mrs. Michel said loudly from across the room. "And now you are back home where you belong, safe and sound."

I smiled back at her and, for a moment, pretended she really was *ma grand-mère.*

"So, are you coming back to work?" asked Jeanne, wagging her eyebrows.

"Yes, please!"

"Thank God," she said, looking at her grandparents. "I *need* to get back to my lab."

"So do I!" chimed Sébastien from behind the counter.

"No problem. I can hold down the fort. NOSA is closed indefinitely, so I've got nothing but time."

"I don't see your papa letting that stand for too long," said Mrs. Michel without turning from the window she was spritzing.

"*Oui, oui.* He says I have to go back to my *mother's* if I can't get into a school pronto."

"Don't worry, we'll homeschool you before we let that happen, right, Sebby?"

Jeanne and I both looked up at him with big eyes. He walked over, leaned on the back of my chair, but looked at his sister. "Why do I see that turning into *me* tutoring Adele in *all* of her subjects while you conveniently get stuck at school?"

I flicked his arm as hard as I could, even though he was right; Jeanne didn't have the attention span to tutor me in subjects as elementary as pre-cal and chemistry. At this point, I was more her practice partner with French.

"Ouch! You know I'm kidding! Don't worry, *mon chou,* we won't let your dad send you back to Paris. Whatever you need—"

"Pre-cal!"

"You cover my shift tomorrow, and I will teach you everything I know about function derivatives."

"Deal!"

"No, cover my shift tomorrow afternoon!" Jeanne yelled, grabbing my arm.

"Too late!" he said.

"Don't worry. I'll cover both of your shifts. I have to get into a school first before I can attend one. And for the record, I don't need to know *everything* you know about function derivatives, just enough to get, like, a B."

"Slacker," they said simultaneously.

I turned to Sébastien. "So, I'll come by tomorrow morning?"

"*Oui.* But I'm not sure if we'll be open for business, so don't wake up early on account of the café."

"I'm still waking up early on account of crossing the Atlantic."

I was so excited to be back in action, I kissed all of their cheeks goodbye before skipping out the door. "*À demain!*"

"DAD?" I YELLED AS I ENTERED THE HOUSE through the broken kitchen door. "Dad, are you home?" I tried a little louder; sometimes he wore protective earphones if he was using loud equipment in his studio.

"In the living room, Adele," he responded, his voice beckoning me to come hither.

My hand froze as I dropped my heavy bag on the kitchen counter. We never used the living room. It was usually reserved for formal circumstances, like Christmas morning or the occasional spot of tea with a wealthy patron of the arts who was viewing my dad's work.

As I walked down the hallway, I heard a second, vaguely familiar male voice talking about the curfew, and then the electronic beep of a walkie-talkie. I stopped short in the doorway. *Oh, shit.*

Thank God the words hadn't slipped out of my mouth.

My father was sitting on the couch, tapping his foot, and Officer Terry Matthews was sitting in a wingtip chair, sipping coffee from the strawberry-shaped mug I had scored at a thrift store last year.

"Hi, Officer Matthews." My voice reached an unusual octave. I sat on the couch next to my father but directed all of my attention towards the uniformed man.

"Actually, Adele, it's detective now; just got the promotion this morning," he said sheepishly.

The New Orleans Police Department lost a lot of officers to the Storm… meaning many fled with the evacuees and then stayed in greener pastures. I had to give credit to the ones who stayed behind to defend the city and its inhabitants.

"Adele, Detective Matthews is here to follow up on the police report you filed yesterday. Remember, the dead body you found?" His tone indicated that I had some serious explaining to do once the detective left.

"Congratulations on the promotion!" I smiled as innocently as I could.

"Thank you, young lady. Wow, are you looking more like your mama every year." He leaned in and gave me an awkward, one-armed hug.

Whenever I met someone who actually knew my mother, they were never able to resist mentioning how we could be twins. Even though

Brigitte and I do share an uncanny resemblance, it grated my nerves. I tried not to let my jaw clench as I asked him how his family was.

"The family is good. The kids' school was wiped out, so they're in Houston right now with their mom. We're waiting on a timeline from our insurance agent…" Just when I hoped he might ramble for a while, he stopped and asked, "So, what's this business about a body you reported?"

"Well…"

"Don't be afraid to mention every tiny detail. What may seem insignificant to you might be a clue to the trained mind." He flipped open a small pad.

"Right." I could see the protocol running through his head as he clicked the pen. I guessed his promotion had been unexpected.

I avoided my father's gaze as I recounted my run-in with the blue-eyed corpse.

"And where were you coming from?"

I cringed and questioned whether telling the truth about this next bit was critical. Lying to a cop didn't seem like a good idea. I sighed.

"I was coming from NOSA. I went to see if there was any information about school reopening."

I refused to look my father's way but imagined wisps of smoke coming out of his ears. *I knew I shouldn't have lied last night. Paris threats or not.*

"And he was dead upon arrival?"

My mind wandered back to the street scene. "His blue eyes just stared at me… like he had died horrified." And then my own eyes began to sting as I waited for the next question. I quickly wiped them and felt my dad's hand on the top of my back.

"So, I'm going to take that as a yes?"

I nodded, and the detective handed me a folded handkerchief from his pocket.

"Were there any visible signs of violence? A wound? Blood?"

"Not that I could tell, but I didn't hang around for very long."

"Did you see any other people, any other witnesses?"

"No, I didn't see a single person on my walk, not once I crossed Esplanade into the Marigny. Except for him."

"And this was around 11 a.m.?"

"Yes, right before it started raining. I got soaked. I tried to call the police right away, but the line was busy, so I kept calling when I got home."

"And you went straight home from the crime scene?"

I contemplated telling him about the strange shutter incident, but an image of me being dragged to Charity Hospital in a straightjacket popped into my head.

"Yes, I went straight home."

"Did you witness anything else that might be strange, unusual, or bring further evidence to this case?"

"No, that's it." My throat tightened.

"Well, thanks for calling in the body, Adele. The longer these things sit in the heat, the more evidence we lose." There was something too complacent about the way he said 'these things.' *How many dead bodies had he seen in the last couple of months?*

"Has there been other news about the case?" I asked.

"These things are complicated, but we're ruling it as a homicide for now."

Great, my dad was definitely going to put a lock on my door.

"That neck certainly didn't snap itself," he finished. "It's crazy out there, Mac. This is the twelfth body we've found in the past three days, most of them in the last twenty-four hours."

"What?" my father softly yelled.

That did seem excessive, even for New Orleans.

"All the same. Necks snapped and—"

"Have you identified him yet?" I interrupted before my father decided to never let me out of the house again.

"We don't have any suspects yet. The crime scenes have been completely clean, but…" He stopped himself, probably realizing he was giving away more information than he should.

"No, I mean the dead man."

"Oh, Jarod O'Connell. He had a local driver's license. We haven't been able to locate any family, yet, so we don't know much else." He downed the last sip from the strawberry and stood up. "Thanks for the coffee, Mac. I'll keep you posted about the curfew. I understand it's gonna cramp your biz when people get back into town."

"Much obliged." Dad gruffly shook his hand, and we followed our guest to the front steps. My father put his hand on my shoulder, as if I might take off running down the street.

Detective Matthews climbed back into an unmarked Crown Vic. No wonder I hadn't noticed it when I walked up. *I really need to start paying better attention.*

He cranked the engine, rolled down the passenger window, and yelled out, "I hope it won't happen, but if any reporters start sniffing around, can you kindly tell them to buzz off?"

"Don't worry, Officer Matthews— I mean, Detective Matthews." I dragged out the last two words.

"Not sure I'll ever get used to that," he said with a goofy expression. "Oh, and Mac, I'll file a report about your kitchen break-in. It's always better to have everything on record."

"Thanks, Terry, I appreciate it. Stop by the bar soon."

We waved as the car pulled away, and then stood in silence for a few seconds. I braced myself for one of my father's painfully awkward lectures.

"Dammit, Adele."

Here it comes, I thought.

Instead he went silent again. I didn't know if he was pausing for emphasis or taking a moment to suppress his temper, but it confused me – and my father rarely confused me. *Maybe being apart for so long was throwing off my game?*

"Go put on your running shoes."

"What?"

"Go get changed. We're going for a run before it gets too hot. Remember?"

"Um, okay." I was no longer in any position to argue about the run.

9

run, run, run

I WAS BOTH CURIOUS AND MILDLY DISCONCERTED that my father was just ignoring the fact that I had lied to him. I mean, it wasn't a major lie or anything, but he was so tense about the crime in the city, I couldn't imagine him just letting it slide. Each second it took me to lace up my running shoes and loop my hair into a ponytail built my dread of the upcoming interrogation. I traded my silver chain for a house key on a knotted shoestring and hurried through the kitchen to get it over with.

He was already waiting outside, rolling his ankles. I bent over next to him and became momentarily woozy as the blood rushed to my head, and the stretch moved up my hamstrings.

"When's the last time you ran?" he asked.

"Uh, I think I ran twice in Paris, in the very beginning."

"I ran every day in Miami."

Good for you. Normally, I would have said it, but something about this trite conversation warned me to proceed with caution, so I held back on the sarcasm. "My dad the fitness buff – who would have known?"

He did his best not to crack a smile. "Well, what else was I supposed to do without you around to bug me all the time?" He tossed me his second bottle of water and took off jogging.

So we're joking now? My father could never stay mad at me for long, but this was a record. Something else was up.

"Wait up!"

"Catch up!"

"Oh, this is going to be loads of fun."

The quick sprint left me panting. I took his right side; my father was adamant about the man's position always being on the street side. He seriously watched too many Mafia movies.

We jogged in silence through Jackson Square, up the cement stairs of the amphitheater, over the two sets of nonfunctioning tracks (one for the train and the other for the streetcar) and finally arrived at the Moonwalk, as the riverfront is called, downtown.

The Toulouse Street Wharf was annihilated. Pieces of it bobbed on the river along with a mass of other buoyant debris, and heaps of floating trash occupied the large empty space where the S.S. *Natchez* had been docked since the early 1800s.

Just as my breathing began to even out, he broke the silence. "Up or down?"

"Up," I answered, and that was the end of our conversation for several more minutes.

The murky Mississippi was calm. I pretended the paddleboat was just out on the river, lazily taking mint-julep-drinking tourists on leisurely rides. The absence of the old riverboat was another reason the city now felt so eerily silent. If I concentrated hard enough, I could hear the steam shooting out of the whistling calliope – I had heard that pipe organ at 11 a.m. and 2 p.m., like clockwork, almost every day of my life. Its whistling tunes were deeply woven into the fabric of the French Quarter. My eyes burned, and I had to tell myself not to cry over a missing riverboat. *Pathetic.*

"I heard the *Natchez* is docked somewhere in Baton Rouge," my father informed me, as if he knew it was bothering me.

"Oh, good." I sucked in a breath of air, and then we were back to silence. The muscles in my legs eased from a deep hibernation, remembering what physical activity was, and side by side, we fell into a steady rhythm. I spaced out for a while.

We passed the open-air French Market, which was now a ghost town, and crossed the border into the Faubourg Marigny. When we approached NOSA, just a few blocks from where I had found the body, my father said, "So, we need to talk about school."

I picked up the pace. He followed suit.

"Dad, I am not going back to Paris just because I found a dead body and didn't tell you. I'm sorry I lied about going down to school. I was just scared you were going to freak out and try to send me back to live with Brigitte!"

"Adele— I'm not sending you back to Paris... Not yet, at least. Although, you have one more encounter with a dead person and I will quickly change my mind."

My brow momentarily unfurled.

"I got a call from your guidance counselor. NOSA is in line for the city-state-fed-whatever government to allocate funds for rebuilding, so who knows when they will reopen."

I had guessed that based on the state of the campus, but my chest tightened anyway. I could already see where this was leading: *my father was going to try to send me away again.*

"In the meantime, students have been placed in arts high schools around the country, including the Houston School for Visual Arts, and some place in Florida. A couple even went to New York City."

I could easily have listed the students who would have gone to NYC. I had many Broadway-bound classmates working night and day to become triple threats.

"She told me about a program you might be interested in, a high school that agreed to auto-admit a few displaced Storm kids. They have a textiles program; you'd get to meet real designers and work with real fashion labels."

I jogged faster. His longer stride easily kept up.

"And where is this dream school located?" I mumbled.

He took a deep breath. "It's in California. Los Angeles."

My eyes welled.

"I already talked to the Joneses, and they would love to have you stay with them."

My stored tears began to drip. *I shouldn't be upset.* There were thousands of kids out there who had been crammed into schools in Baton Rouge and Texas, without books, friends, or routines... But I couldn't help it; I had just gotten home, and I didn't want to leave.

"Sounds like a cool opportunity, Dad," I choked out.

He stopped running. As did I, gasping at the ground.

"Then why are you crying?" He sucked in a couple breaths of air.

I did everything I could to hold in the tears, which made the words come out in a near-scream. "Why do you keep trying to get rid of me?"

"Sweetheart, that is *ludicrous.* I am *not* trying to get rid of you. How can you say that? I just don't want you to miss out on any opportunities because of the Storm. You have to be in school, so I figured you'd like this way better than going back to your mother's, although I wish you would consider that option."

I scowled.

"You'll be with Brooke, and you can come home for Christmas."

It was a perfectly rational justification, but I still didn't want to hear it. I stayed hunched over my knees, unable to look up at him. My lack of response made him anxious.

"I don't care about school, Dad. I am NOT leaving New Orleans again."

He put his hand on my shoulder. "Well, I thought you might feel that way... and I may have a happy medium. Do you want the good news or the bad news first?"

I smeared away the tears with the back of my hand. *Was my father actually executing a classic bait and switch?* I filed a mental note to use the tactic on him in the future.

He continued with caution. "So, I made some arrangements."

My back shot straight up. "Some *arrangements*?" The last time my father had made some *arrangements*, I ended up on a plane, flying across the Atlantic, only four hours later.

"If you want to stay in New Orleans… then the Academy of the Sacred Heart has agreed to permit you a seat."

I covered my mouth as a small cough wheezed from my throat. He must be confused.

"Surely you don't mean *the* Academy of the Sacred Heart? As in uptown*?* As in Désirée Borges's *Academy?* As in Bradgelina's future kids' *Academy*?"

"The one and only."

"They agreed to permit me a seat? What does that even mean?"

"It means they are taking in three displaced students per grade, and they agreed to offer you one of the slots."

"So, I'm a charity case?"

"Well, it's not exactly charity."

"Dad, what are you talking about? There is not a chance in hell we can afford something like that."

"Don't curse, Adele!"

"Don't be evasive!"

"Well…" He looked behind me, up at the sky. "Your mother made a call."

"*What?* Since when does Brigitte get to take part in making decisions about my life?"

"Well, I'm sure your *mother* didn't make the call. I'm sure she had her assistant do it," he said, trying to make me laugh.

But the thought of Émile helping my mother plan my little high-school life only made my jaw clinch.

I started jogging again, back the way we came. *Do not overreact, Adele. Surely he has just mixed up the school's name.*

He quickly caught up. "Adele, if you want to stay in New Orleans, then you are going to Sacred Heart, because I know you'll be safe there – and that's final. Take it or leave it. It's your choice."

"So my choices are imprisonment in my own personal hell of cotillion balls or banishment to the land of Barbie dolls?"

"Well, there is a third choice," he said with a curt smile.

I looked at him with a glimmer of hope. After all, he had said there was good news too.

"You can always go back to Paris with your mother." He laughed and took off running.

"Ugh, I hate you!" I yelled, chasing him back down the river.

"Oh, don't be so melodramatic," he called over his shoulder. "Whatever you choose, it's just temporary."

I had less than two years of high school left, but at the rate aid was coming to the city, 'temporary' might as well have been 'forever.'

He slowed his pace until we were back together.

"So, what part was supposed to be the good news?"

"Well... in order to keep your status at NOSA, you'll have to continue your mentorship training, so you only have to attend Sacred Heart for half the day."

At NOSA, we spent the mornings doing regular classes like biology and literature, and then spent the afternoons doing intensive workshop-style training in our focus area. I had spent my sophomore year apprenticing with the head seamstress at the University of New Orleans's theatre department, working on the school's spring production of Shakespeare's *A Midsummer Night's Dream.* I was dying to show her my Halloween costume. I had spent every weekend in Paris working my fingers to the bone, hand-stitching embellishments. The *haute couture* Master Classes had been the highlight of my trip. Not to mention they were also how I met Émile. Those were the only times my mother parted with her assistant – so he could escort me to and from my dormitory to class every Saturday and Sunday. On week two, we had moved from her car to the back of his Vespa. On week three, he was lying to her about what time my class ended.

"Does that mean I get to work at UNO again?" This situation was starting to appear slightly more tolerable.

"Not exactly. All the current mentors are scrambling to sort out their own affairs. Actually, NOSA is making this exception just for you, sweetheart, since Sacred Heart isn't an art school."

"Why? I don't understand."

"On account of you knowing an amazing local artist willing to mentor you. One of the best in the city if you ask me." His lips tightened into a wiry smile, waiting for a reaction. I tried my best to remain poised, but my words became short as I struggled to run, breathe, and speak at the time.

"Let me get this straight… You want me to go to the Academy of the Sacred Heart, and then spend every afternoon apprenticing with you in the metal shop?"

"Jeez, do you have to put me in the same category with your disdain for Sacred Heart?"

"That's not what I meant, Dad, I'm just trying to process all of this. It's making my brain hurt."

"Well, I'm sorry that the idea of working with me makes your brain hurt."

"Ugh, Dad, stop. That's not what I meant. I just…" A seagull squawked as it dipped low to investigate a pile of floating wreckage. "I mean, I'm supposed to be apprenticing in fashion. What would we work on together?" I tried my best not to sound as though there was nothing he could teach me.

"What do you mean? There's tons of cool stuff we could do. You could create a jewelry line. We could focus on your fashion illustrations, which you and I both know need serious work if you are ever going to put together a decent portfolio."

That stung a little, but he was right.

"You've been talking for ages about wanting to learn how to make your own hardware for your pieces."

He'd obviously been thinking about this a lot. His pitch was starting to sound pretty convincing.

"We could do chainmaille, or something really avant-garde or conceptual."

My mind raced with possibilities as he rattled off more and more ideas.

"Dad, stop!" I couldn't keep the giant grin from spreading across my face. "You had me at chainmaille."

His shoulders relaxed, and I saw a little excitement in his eyes. "Really? You'd choose Sacred Heart and me over Brooke and a real *atelier*? I never thought I'd see this day."

I really, really wanted to be with my best friend, but how could I leave this place? There was so much to do, to rebuild. It was utterly overwhelming. My father put his arm around me and pulled me close. I concentrated on my feet so I didn't stumble in the awkward runner's embrace.

"Gross, you're sweaty, Dad."

"So are you!" He squirted water in my face. Sometimes he really was a child.

"All right, let's go home," I said, letting the water run down my neck. It actually felt pretty good; the noon sun was in full blaze.

"Home? We are just getting warmed up."

"Warmed up! Maybe you are, but not all of us vacationed in Miami for the last two months," I teased. "My legs are like jelly. I am going home." I veered onto Esplanade Avenue as he continued down the river.

"Going to let your old man show you up?" he yelled over his shoulder.

"*Oui!*"

"And don't think I forgot about you lying to my face yesterday."

"Yeah, yeah, yeah…." There was now too much distance between us to yell back and forth. *What was he going to do, ground me?* The whole city was already on lock-down. None of my friends were back. There was no Internet and barely any cellphone reception.

I slowed down to pace myself for the remaining ten blocks home. *Had I really just agreed to go to the Academy of the Sacred Heart? "The Academy," as they called it.* Images of Catholic schoolgirl uniforms, sweet sixteens and hundreds of cookie-cutter copies of Désirée Borges popped in my head. I cut across the neutral ground onto

Chartres Street and began to count down the blocks when an unfamiliar sight caught my attention.

People.

Three of them standing in the middle of the road on the next block. A little old lady leaning on a cane was looking up with her hand shielding her eyes from the sun. Behind her were two goth guys, who appeared to be either elated or scowling; between the makeup and facial piercings it was hard to tell. As I slowly approached them, I realized they were standing outside the cement wall behind the Ursuline Convent, in almost the exact spot where yesterday's crying fit had begun. I suddenly had a sinking feeling that I knew what they were all looking at.

The taller goth with the twelve-inch bleached spikes was Theis, the boyfriend of one of my favorite coffee-shop regulars. He was contorting himself into various positions to snap photos with his cell phone. Before I even reached them, his aperture led my gaze straight to the attic window.

It looked exactly as I had left it yesterday: glass blown out and one shutter missing. The remaining shutter now swayed, although today there was actually a decent breeze to push it back and forth – so there was nothing peculiar about the motion. Anxiety pricked my stomach, warning me not to incriminate myself. For what, exactly, I had no clue.

"They definitely escaped," Theis said dryly to his shorter, *Manic-Panic*-red-haired companion.

I ducked my head as I jogged past them, but the old lady turned to me anyway. "Even all those nails from the Vatican couldn't hold a candle to the power of the Storm."

I had no idea what she was talking about, but I craned my neck back to her, nodded, and mumbled, "Mother Nature."

"You got it, baby. Lord, help us."

I picked up my pace.

The crazies are sure out in full force this morning, I thought, shaking my head. *What did Theis mean, escaped?*

10

lady stardust

BY THE TIME I DRAGGED MY LUGGAGE UPSTAIRS, I felt like I'd had a total body workout, but whenever I rested for more than a minute, my mind bounced back and forth between the convent and Sacred Heart, until I felt like I was going to explode.

Focus on something, Adele. Anything.

I stood with my hands on my hips, trying to figure out where to start.

The afternoon sun illuminated the dust, making everything in my new bedroom sparkle in a strange, dirty way; the sheeted furniture cast oddly-shaped shadows, reminding me of a modern art exhibit.

Cool. I snapped a photo of the nearest mystery sculpture's oblong silhouette on the wall, and then tucked the phone into my back pocket, held my breath and pulled the first sheet off, sending dust sparkles everywhere.

Whoa, an upright piano. Maybe everything isn't just old junk.

I started tearing off the sheets like a kid on Christmas morning. A rocking chair. A beautifully carved vanity with a tri-folding mirror. A rose-colored chaise lounge. And a large oak wardrobe. The perfect little setup from the past. In the middle of the room was a large bed with four ornate brass posts that would have once held a delicate canopy, but from which now hung a couple of limp drop cloths. Without thinking, I yanked them off and plopped down onto the mattress.

"Ow!" I yelped, getting a whack to my hipbone. The ancient mattress would have to go.

Lying on the bed, my gaze settled on the last drop-cloth sculpture. It was an incredibly odd shape. *Tuba?* I jumped up and ripped off the cover, revealing a Victrola.

"Cool."

The case over the turntable had been sealed tight, so it wasn't even that dusty. "Do you still work?"

I raced down to my father's studio and then, breathing heavily, ran back up the stairs with an armful of records I'd randomly grabbed: the soundtrack to *Jesus Christ Superstar*, a classic Louis Armstrong, a Led Zeppelin, and a David Bowie. I carefully looked over the cardboard case protecting *The Rise and Fall of Ziggy Stardust and the Spiders from Mars.* I didn't know much about David Bowie, but something about the bright gas lamp on the cover attracted me. I gently pulled the record from the sleeve, placed the old vinyl on the turntable, and moved the needle.

My fingers searched for a power switch – until I remembered how old the machine was. *Idiot,* I thought, reaching for the manual power source. But I couldn't get the hand-crank to budge. *Mental note: get the WD-40 from Dad's studio.*

I gave the Victrola a little pep talk and exerted some force.

It gradually started to turn.

The record spun, and the music started playing, all without the power of electricity. "Just like magic," I whispered.

The glam-rock beats sounded raw and scratchy coming from the large flower-shaped cone, and the slow start of the opening song crept over me with the grip of a soon-to-be obsession. I spritzed dusting cleanser with the downbeats of the tune, and wiped the rag over the piano as if I was performing on stage. By the time the next track began, I had moved on to the vanity mirror and decided that I loved Bowie.

When the third track began to crescendo, my fingers picked an air-guitar, but just as I started to shred, the music suddenly cut off, and the room became completely still. I caught sight of my frozen pose in the mirror and quickly dropped the imaginary instrument.

I glanced at the Victrola, hoping I hadn't broken it. Blaming the spiders from Mars, I forced myself to keep cleaning, but it wasn't the same. Even though we had only just been introduced, I was already having *Ziggy Stardust* withdrawal.

"Ugh, the crank!" I yelped, having a second mini-revelation over the machine's need for manual power.

Finish the mirror first...

Without even the slightest ambient street noise coming in through the open windows, the swooshes from my rag seemed loud. I worked fast, eager to get back into David Bowie's spaceship, but then a wave of tingles jettisoning down my spine made me freeze mid-scrub.

A faint rattle was coming from behind me.

I strained to listen. *It's just the old pipes,* I told myself. But the rattling sounded way too close to be coming from behind a wall.

Scrubbing again, my nerves began to fry, but I refused to look back, feeling safety in not knowing the truth. The noise grew louder and louder, chipping at my curiosity like an ice pick. Chip. Chip.

Breathe.

Without moving my head, I slowly raised my eyes to the mirror and blinked a couple of times at the reflection. Across the room, the metal hand-crank was aggressively jerking, causing the entire music box to shake. I spun around, dropping the rag.

As I gaped at the machine, the handle slowly began to turn itself, and the music started up again.

"What the...?"

Am I losing my mind? I wondered as I went back to cleaning. *Experiencing some kind of Storm-induced post-traumatic stress disorder?*

The next time the volume died, the sounds of my own heartbeat pounding were interrupted only by the sound of creaking metal. I knew what was making the noises, but my brain could not adjust to the idea.

Breathe.

Creak.

Breathe.

Creak.

Bowie's voice warbled back to full volume, and the room was back to feeling like a 1970s rock opera.

I bent and swooshed the rag around the bucket of soapy water, racking my brain for logical explanations, never landing on anything scientific. *Maybe it's a ghost?* A lost spirit who really, really wanted to listen to "Ziggy Stardust." I couldn't blame it. *Wait, do I even believe in ghosts?*

The volume died again.

Getting annoyed by the start and stop, I whipped around to the machine. The metal handle flew around so quickly that the album hardly skipped a beat. David Bowie's voice parachuted in to keep me from going into panic mode.

I had no idea if I was dreaming, awake, crazy, or sane, but as the B-side repeated, I began to relax, and my thoughts moved from a recently grayed-out New Orleans to Mr. Bowie's fantastical world.

I hadn't realized that I was full-on rocking out with the mop until my father appeared and spun me around, but I was loving it too much to be embarrassed.

"There is absolutely no denying that you are my daughter," he yelled over the music, twirling me around.

He grabbed the shadeless floor lamp and belted out the "Lady Stardust" lyrics, doing his best David Bowie impression. I burst out laughing.

"Oh my God, Dad, stop. You're ridiculous."

He sang even louder.

The more I laughed, the more dramatic he became. I hadn't seen him act this silly since I was a kid. *Maybe we were both going loopy?* He slid across the piano bench and banged out the chords on the long-dormant instrument.

His ridiculousness escalated until I was doubled over with tears pouring down my cheeks. I couldn't remember the last time I had laughed so hard. My ribs hurt, my cheeks hurt, and I was gasping for air.

A really good laugh could change everything.

He jumped up from the piano bench just in time for the last verse, twirled me around a few times, and then slowly rocked me back and forth. As the song finished, so did the crank, and the music stopped.

"Everything's going to be all right, Adele." He kissed the top of my head. "I promise."

I willed myself to believe him, but when I opened my eyes, I saw the metal crank vibrating, as if it was trying to figure out what I wanted it to do. And then, even stranger – I felt myself commanding it to stay still.

11

absinthe vs. wheatgrass

DANCING TURNED INTO A DINNER DATE. My father cooked a bland feast of plain red beans 'n rice (all the while playing *Hunky Dory* loudly to further my Bowie indoctrination), while I took on the gag-inducing task of cleaning out the fridge. It was funny experiencing such a domestic scene in our home. Usually we just sort of coexisted, sharing the occasional cup of coffee and discussion about art when our schedules overlapped.

After dinner, he hurried off to Le Chat Noir, and I was left alone, trying to change the overhead light bulb in my bedroom. Even standing on my toes on top of the piano bench, with my arms fully extended, I wasn't close to reaching the ceiling fan.

I sighed. "What were you thinking, Adele? You are way taller in your mind than in actuality."

Fetching the ladder wasn't an appealing task after having hauled all of my clothing, books, sewing paraphernalia, and sixteen years' worth of God-only-knows-what else up the stairs, but, unless a bottle of potion labeled *"Drink Me"* was suddenly going to appear and make me grow, there were no other options.

With one foot out the door, a ridiculous idea entered my mind. I stepped back onto the bench, looked up at the old bulb, and imagined it turning.

Nothing happened.

"This is insane," I said, before realizing that talking to myself only confirmed the statement. The old bulb shook a little. My heart skipped. I had this strange feeling that it *wanted* to move.

Focus. Who knows when the light bulb had last been touched? Maybe it's stuck. I concentrated explicitly on the metal ridges of the bulb's base, picturing it moving in a slow circular motion.

"Come on, you can do it!"

It budged a millimeter. This time, instead of fear, I felt exhilarated.

"That's it. Slow and steady."

I watched in amazement as the bulb slowly unscrewed itself and then plopped into my cupped palms.

My hand shook as I pulled the new bulb from its box and extended it upward. When my arm reached its full length, the bulb left my hand, gracefully floated up to the fixture, and slowly began to turn itself into place. My shoulders tingled with excitement as the base of the bulb was swallowed, and the bright light popped on.

"And then there was light," I whispered and looked around, almost fearful that someone had witnessed me bend the laws of nature.

My pocket vibrated before I could further freak out.

"PLEASE, PLEASE, PLEASE tell me you are moving to L.A.!" Brooke screamed before I could even say hello.

"It's so weird here without you! How is Los Angeles? How are your parents?"

"Oh no, girlfriend. Don't think I am letting you off the hook that easily. Are you moving to L.A. or what?"

"Well..."

"What? Nooooo! I already cleared out half of my closet for you. I mean, it's not like I really have any stuff, so it wasn't that hard, but still. Adele, this school is uh-mazing. Last year they worked with Rodarte, Chanel and *Project Runway*."

I tried to pay attention as she rattled on about the fashion program, but I was stuck on how casually she had mentioned having no stuff. In New Orleans, Brooke cleaning out half of her closet would have been a major feat.

"The program sounds cool."

"Cool? Adele, it's *Chanel*, as in the empire built by Coco Chanel, your idol! This is your future we are talking about—"

"I know! It's just that... everything is so messed up here. I don't really know how to explain it. I can't abandon the city, not unless I absolutely have to... I mean... not that I think y'all abandoned the city. We just had something to come home to..."

She didn't say anything.

I turned off the light and headed downstairs to snuggle into the quilt on my bed. "So... have your parents been back?" I asked. "Has anyone been to your house?"

She remained silent, which was usually impossible for Brooke, so I knew she was crying, which was also unusual for her. I was usually the crier of the two of us.

I didn't know what to say, so I just waited.

"We don't know anything for sure, but there's not much hope – our whole neighborhood was obliterated. Dad's going home next week to see if anything is salvageable, and to speak with our insurance agent. The settlement has already turned into a big battle. I begged him to let me go with him, but he refused." She paused again. "He says there's nothing left there for us anymore."

I knew it was selfish of me, considering the circumstances, but I couldn't imagine spending the rest of high school without my best friend.

And I couldn't imagine Brooke's father actually feeling that way. Alphonse Jones was— *is* a part of this city. His horns could be heard on most of the major records to come out of the Big Easy in the last decade.

A giant lump formed in my throat. There was no way I would be able to get words out. *Do not cry, Adele.*

"I'm sure it will only be temporary," I said, choking back tears. "No one is back yet, I promise. Seriously, the streets are empty. It's deathly quiet."

"Quiet?"

"Yeah… it's creepy."

There was another long pause and a wet sniffle.

"Enough of this mopey stuff," said Brooke. "We haven't talked in like two months… tell me a story. *Bonjour*, how was Paris? And don't say anything about it being lame, or I will jump through this phone and smack you!"

Classic Brooke. This was why I loved her.

"Well, Paris was…" I struggled to find the words to describe the raw magnificence of the city. "Paris is amazing. It's Paris." Giddiness rushed over me as I curled into the covers. "It's so hard to describe it without sounding like a sappy cliché."

"Well, I already know you're a sappy cliché, so try."

"'There are only two places in the world where we can live happy: at home and in Paris.'"

"Whoa, that's deep, Adele."

"*Oui,* but I can't take credit; it's Hemingway."

Émile had turned me on to Hemingway, yelling in a fiery fit, *"How iz it possible zhat you've never read Hemingway? He's even American!"* Mortified, I had spent the rest of my stay devouring all the Hemingway I could get my hands on. Luckily, Émile was totally right (about Hemingway, anyway).

"Again, in your own words, please."

"Hmm… It has this *joie de vivre* that devours you. Kind of like New Orleans, but times a hundred. My feelings were heightened just by walking down the street. If I was happy, I wanted to dance. If I was sad, I wanted to weep openly in the street."

"And if you wanted to love...?"

"God, shut up! Do you ever think about anything but guys, Brooke?"

"Uh huh... sore subject, much? Go on, but don't think I'm going to let you keep the Émile saga a secret forever."

It was exponentially harder to focus now that I was thinking about Émile again. I dug deep for words.

"There are so many emotional things on every street corner – a café where a poor Toulouse-Lautrec used to drink absinthe, a scene from a Baudelaire sonnet, a street Marie Antoinette once rode down, a corner where a revolution sparked. Hugo, Sartre, Piaf, and not to mention Coco – the list is endless! Everyone says you fall in love with Paris, but sometimes I had this burning jealousy of her." I paused to take a breath, astonished by how much I had been suppressing over the last couple of months – burying anything good that had happened in Paris out of fear I wouldn't want to return home to help rebuild.

"And?"

"And what?"

"And tell me about the boy!"

"Hello, it's your turn! What's L.A. like?"

"Mmm... hmmm..."

"I mean, besides celebrities and wheatgrass shots?" I pushed.

"Fine. It's not New Orleans, but I get why people love it here. The weather is perfect – like, always perfect. From the Santa Monica Pier, you can listen to the ocean and see mountains in the background at the same time."

"Wow, mountains?" I laughed. "I don't think I've ever seen a mountain in real life."

"Yeah, the nature in California is out of control. It's the polar opposite of home. Everything is clean; no one smokes – well, not cigarettes, at least. Everyone is beautiful, and everyone is always on, from their hair to their clothes to their cars – like they need to be ready for a magazine shoot at any given moment." She paused. "The hardest part is my mom. She's upset about the Storm, but she just seems so happy here. She's totally back in her element. We were here for like a day before she was offered this high-powered position at Capitol, and my dad's been getting all these gigs and recording sessions. She thinks it might be his big chance to 'break out of the New Orleans scene,' whatever that means."

Brooke's mother, Klara, was a California girl more akin to a Russian supermodel. She had met Mr. Jones when he was on a West Coast tour. They got married when the tour stopped in Vegas, and she had been running her own entertainment public relations firm in New Orleans ever since. Brooke always joked that she got the best of both worlds from her parents, and I tended to agree. She had a totally exotic look and a voice that could silence a stadium. No surprise she focused on music at NOSA. There was no doubt in my mind that she would become a famous singer one day.

"Adele, I'm gonna freak if I have to stay here!"

"Don't worry. When NOSA reopens, you can come and stay with us if your parents end up relocating." I didn't tell her how bad a shape our school was in.

"Wait a second, if you aren't coming to L.A. and NOSA isn't reopening for a while, why isn't Mac sending you back to Paris?"

The inevitable question I had been dreading.

"Apparently, the Academy of the Sacred Heart has reserved a seat for me." I moved the phone away from my ear.

"What! Oh, hardy-har. Good one, Adele."

"Yeah… I'm not joking."

"What? What does that even mean, they reserved a seat for you?"

"That's exactly what I asked." I explained the situation as best as I could, realizing how few details I actually knew, but once Brooke started ranting about prissy girls and Catholic schoolgirl uniforms, my nerves began firing up. "Next thing you know," I said, "my picture is going to appear in the society column of the *Times Picayune*—"

"Okay, spill it. What are you hiding? Did you do it with him?"

"Jeez, Brooke, we didn't do it!" My face burned red through the phone. Thank God I hadn't slept with Émile. I couldn't imagine thinking about him more than I already was. "I'm not hiding anything. I just don't really know what to say about him. He's very hot and very French."

"What exactly is the problem?"

"He's very much my mother's assistant! And very confusing. It was almost like he was too perfect. He was kind of the bad boy, but he always managed to say the right thing. Loved art! Always knew how to cheer me up even with everything going on." I didn't know how to explain that he always made me feel like he had some unfair advantage, like he had read an operating manual on me before we met.

"Oh my God, Adele! Can't you ever just let something good happen to you without sabotaging it?"

"See! This is why I didn't want to talk about him. He made me feel crazy all the time! He was fascinated with my banal existence – always wanting to know more about me but never revealing anything about himself. It started to seem like he was hiding something."

I was still spending countless woeful hours trying to figure out if he had been genuinely interested in me or had some ulterior motive for trying to pry information out of me, like spying for my mother. Every time I had let him get closer, a million tiny warning bells had exploded throughout my body.

A sigh came from the other end of the line. My eyes rolled in return.

"What does it matter, now? He's in Paris. With my *mother*."

"Have you heard from him since you left?"

"No."

"Jerk."

"Have you heard from her?"

"No."

"Jerk."

"And I'm starting to feel like it was all in my head, like I just read into him too much—"

"Adele, are you still there?"

"Yeah, can you hear me?"

"Are you there?"

I hung up and tried to ring her back, but the call wouldn't connect. I can't say the idea of ending the Émile conversation broke my heart. I pecked a text and prayed it would go through.

Adele	**11:09 p.m.**	Call dropped. Can't reconnect. Reception here is abysmal. Talk *mañana*! xoxo

11:10 p.m. Dad is out past curfew again.

Worried, I aggressively fluffed my pillow.

Before the Storm, there wasn't a waking hour in which Brooke and I hadn't communicated in some way, shape or form. It's so strange how an external event can suddenly change all of that. We had barely spoken since I left Miami two months ago and put a nine-hour time difference between us. My heart told me Brooke would stay in L.A., and I hated that idea.

I felt myself drifting off to sleep as I lay there staring at the ceiling, thinking about the little things that were slipping away. Things I had taken for granted before the Storm. But I couldn't muster my lead-like muscles to get up and turn off the light. The long ball 'n chain dangling down from the ceiling-fan started swaying back and forth.

Tension spread through my body until I was stiff as a board.

The chain slowly gained momentum until it swung in a small circular pattern. I was so tired, it was difficult to focus on the blur. I imagined a forceful pulling motion.

Click.

Darkness.

Breathe.

12

the truth

October 12th

MY FINGERS TAPPED THE KITCHEN COUNTER, waiting for the pot of water to boil, and my eyes kept moving to the clock on the wall – it wasn't even 7 a.m. yet. I was starting to like the residual effects of jet lag. Before the Storm, I had certainly never gotten excited about waking up early for work, but now I was just eager for life to return to normal. My eagerness, however, was no match for my muscles, every inch of which were sore.

I groaned as I bent over to stretch. My legs immediately started to shake. "Thirty more seconds," I whispered and began to analyze my afternoon with *Ziggy Stardust* to distract myself from the pain. I barely made it to the half-minute marker before my torso flung up. The head-rush made the magic music box incident seem even more surreal. It wasn't just the Victrola, and the keys, and the shutter – *everything* was different now. And it all felt like a dream.

"There is a logical explanation for all of this. You just have to figure it out." I extended my arm across the counter towards the box of oatmeal and imagined it coming to my hand.

Nothing happened. I felt like a clown.

"Ugh, boil, already!" I snapped at the pot.

The fire under the pot pulsed bigger. *Maybe I am going crazy after all?*

The water began to gently bubble. "Finally…"

When the oats had formed a hot mush, I sprinkled cinnamon and sugar on top, wishing we had milk. I grabbed the nondairy creamer and then stopped myself. Too disgusting. Without looking, I reached for the cutlery drawer, but before I could grasp the handle, it shot open and crashed into my hip. My yelp faded as a spoon jumped out of the drawer and landed in my hand.

I unclenched my fingers from around the utensil, and it vibrated in my palm. My heart felt like it was going to pound out of my chest.

"It's too early for this."

On a whim, I popped the spoon into the air. A smile slipped out as it dove into my oatmeal and stirred in the auburn swirls. The scent of cinnamon danced around the kitchen, reminding me of what our home used to feel like. Lived in.

WITHOUT THE AIR-CONDITIONING, there was no discernible difference in the temperature when I walked out of the steamy bathroom and into the hallway. It was an odd feeling. My father used to keep the house freezing because it got so hot in his studio with all the torches he worked with.

As I walked up the stairs, a breeze pricked my naked skin; I wrapped my towel tighter. *I know I didn't leave the bedroom windows open, last night.*

Under the lingering aroma of burnt sage, there was a chemical twinge in the air. Something was different. The place looked magnificent, almost shiny, and all the posters I had hung were nowhere to be seen. The ceiling fan, which I knew I had turned off, was now on high.

"Dad, you are the best," I whispered, realizing he must have stayed up late when he got home and put a fresh coat of white paint on the walls. I was well on my way to forgiving him for shipping me to Paris.

Craving the connection to the outside world I usually got via the Internet, I pushed the plug of an old-school boom-box into an electrical socket, and was immediately assaulted by voices of varying levels of hysteria. I stopped twisting the dial when I heard a woman with a more grounded tone replying to the disc jockey.

"The real question is why isn't anyone talking about the fact that people are still dying around here? Are we all really this desensitized to death? And what is the mayor really doing about the crime? This curfew doesn't seem to be helping anything; in fact, I would suggest it's making the city even more unsafe. The empty streets are becoming easy target zones for predators."

Evidently, the early hour wasn't keeping people from going at it. I sat at the vanity and attempted to put moisturizer on my face, but I was already beginning to sweat. *Don't even think of complaining about the lack of air-conditioning. At least you have a home, unlike Brooke's family.*

"Thanks for calling in, ma'am. Do we have our next caller on the line?"

"Hello? Hello? Am I on the air?"

"Yes, ma'am, you are live on the air."

"Oh, good, my name is Nora Murphy. My boyfriend, James Manale, is missing, and I want to ask whether anyone out there has seen him—"

"Excuse me, ma'am, this is just a morning radio show," the DJ said gently, "but I can give you our hotline number to report missing Storm victims—"

"He's not a missing Storm victim! We've been back from Memphis for over a week. Two days ago, he went out to try to find groceries, and he hasn't been back since." She broke down in sobs. "The cops just tell me that he probably bailed on the situation, on New Orleans..."

"Do you hear that, folks? Something is going on in this city. Fourteen people reported dead and countless reported missing in the last couple weeks."

The woman's sobs became hysterical.

"Ma'am, please stay on the line; we'll collect your information and do whatever we can to help."

I squirted a cloud of mousse into my palms and rubbed it through my quickly drying waves. Without even trying, a flick of my mind twisted the tuner dial.

"Recent figures show that only about twenty-five thousand inhabitants of Orleans Parish have returned. Electricity has been fully restored in Baton Rouge, but there is no timeline yet for Orleans, Jefferson, St. Charles or the surrounding parishes. We also have reports that all gas stations in Orleans Parish are wiped clean, so make sure to fill up outside the city limits. There's still no news on when any of the major supermarkets will reopen."

I put one leg into a pair of jeans, but then, immediately suffocated by the denim, kicked them off and dug through the mountain of clothes on the bed until I found a lilac cotton sundress I had made at the beginning of the summer. It had a large sash that tied into a bow in the back – a tad dressy for work, but at least my legs and back would be free to breathe. I slipped on black Converse sneakers to tone it down.

Three commercials came on in a row, each one with different attorneys claiming they could help get your insurance settlement. When I couldn't get the radio to turn off on its own, I sprang from my seat and snapped the plastic power button before I could hear the empty promise of another lawyer.

Desperate to be out of the hot attic room, I quickly pulled a souvenir T-shirt from my suitcase – a small velvet sack I didn't recognize came flying out with it.

"What…?"

Inside the drawstrings was a matching velvet box with a tiny folded note. *Could it possibly be from Émile?* I paused, wondering whether to open the box or the note first, and then feverishly unfolded the stationary.

My heart fluttered, pushing my lagging brain to translate the handwritten French faster.

Dearest Adele,

Even though your visit was short, I hope you were able to find joy in the streets of Paris, in the way that I do every day. Enclosed you'll find a ring that has been in your father's family for many generations, and now it belongs to you.

I do long for the day when we can be friends.

Bisous,
Brigitte

I was stunned.

Oh Jesus. What if this was her passive way of returning her wedding ring to my father? I popped the box open, and a wave of relief washed over me – it contained a ring of an entirely different sort.

Regardless, the little rush of stress caused me to slam the box down on the vanity. *She hadn't even told me goodbye in person! How had she slipped the little sack into my suitcase?* I had only stayed at her house – my grandmother's estate – for one night before my early-morning flight home. I hadn't even seen her. She had simply left me yet another two-sentence note with a basket of brioche, and had her driver whisk me to the airport.

My subconscious gnawed at me.

Are you really upset to find a note from her? Or just disappointed that it wasn't from Émile?

I slipped on my standard silver chain and roughly knotted my hair into a loose bun on top of my head. "He's not your boyfriend. Don't let this ruin the morning."

As I approached Café Orléans, I now realized how much the little outdoor tables resembled any quaint corner of the *Faubourg-Montmartre* in Paris. Usually I could smell the coffee beans half a block away. Today, not even close. I could, however, hear Louis Armstrong sounding through the open doors, which meant Sébastien must have opened up. Jeanne usually blared Beethoven concertos.

It was sad, but not surprising, to see the place void of customers.

This hour of the morning was usually the peak time due to the overlap of the day-job crowd on their way to work and the service crowd retiring from the night shift. This morning there was only one guy, maybe in his late teens, sitting by himself at the corner table in the front window, sketching on a pad of paper. Messy, light-brown hair hung in his face, and large headphones hugged his ears.

"Sébastien?" I yelled, looking for him. *"Tu es là?"*

I must have startled the customer because he appeared a little shocked to see me when he looked up from his pad. As soon as I smiled, his wide eyes went back to his pencil.

A head of perfectly combed blond hair popped up from underneath the counter. "*Bonjour!*"

"Jesus!"

"Désolé!" Sébastien said, laughing. "I didn't mean to scare you."

"Shouldn't you be behind a microscope, Mr. Neuroscientist?"

"Ha ha." He blushed and pushed his glasses up his nose. "Mémé's been on the phone with our insurance agent for the last two hours, so I told her I would come downstairs and open up."

I joined him behind the wooden counter, where the espresso machine was laid out in a million pieces.

"I want to make sure there was no mold on any of the parts...."

I scavenged elsewhere for caffeine. Usually, we kept several different industrial-sized vats of coffee brewed at once. Today there was only one lonely pot of standard coffee 'n chicory. I poured myself a cup.

"No milk, eh?"

"*Non.* No dairy. Nothing fresh, really." He nodded to the empty pastry case.

"I wonder how long it will be before things go back to normal?"

"I have a feeling we will be redefining what constitutes normal." Always the pragmatist.

I stirred in a spoonful of nondairy creamer.

"Oh!" I pulled out three boxes of macarons. "I brought something for *la famille*."

"*Ladurée?*" He kissed my cheeks, tore open a box, and stuffed one of the pistachio confectionaries in his mouth. *"Merci, Adele."*

"Anything for you." I sipped the light-brown coffee, trying not to cringe from the taste of the fake milk. "So, where should I start?"

He gave me an apologetic look as he eyed the pile of cleaning supplies in the corner.

"Don't worry, I'm a professional at this point."

AN HOUR LATER, I had finished the mopping and was at the front of the store dusting the floor-to-ceiling shelves of jars that usually contained fifty different varieties of coffee beans but were now mostly empty. I climbed onto a chair to try to reach the top shelves. My biceps shook when I raised my arms overhead for even a few moments at a time. Just as it became difficult not to complain, a booming voice filled the room.

"*Ma chérie!* You're back!"

"Ren!" I jumped down and ran to greet my favorite customer. His giant arms squeezed me into a bear hug, lifting me into the air.

"Ren… crushing ribs… can't breathe."

He gently dropped me to the ground. "Sorry about that. It's just been so long."

"No worries." I smiled, having forgotten the magnitude of the man's hugs.

René Simoneaux was what people call "a character." He was born and raised somewhere south of New Orleans in the bayou but had been a permanent fixture of the French Quarter for as long as I could remember.

At six feet, seven inches, Ren was a pale-skinned giant with black curls that rippled down his back and a Cajun accent as thick as molasses. With his collection of white peasant shirts, red velvet jackets (in winter), black leather pants (all year round) and boots with shiny brass buckles (also all year round), he reminded me of one of those models from the covers of cheesy romance novels. The women on his tours fawned over him, never guessing that he went home and curled up next to Theis – a pasty, Scandinavian DJ who had fangs that had been surgically implanted by a dentist or, as I had once heard him say, by a fangsmith. The tall, blond-spiked guy from the convent yesterday.

"I have something for you, Ren!" I scooted behind the counter and rummaged through my bag.

"For *moi*?"

I pulled out a large white T-shirt with black gothic script that read, "*Equipe Edward!*"

"Adele, how many times do I have to tell you?" he said in a very serious tone. "Vampires do *not* sparkle."

"Okay, fine." I pretended to pout. "I'll give it to someone else."

"No, you will not!" He yanked the T-shirt out of my reach. "Sparkles or not, I am still Team Edward." We both laughed, and he hugged me again.

"*Ça va?* How was Paris? I missed you."

"I missed you, too. I hated being away for so long."

"At least you were back in the mothership."

"I know, that's what everyone keeps saying. And everyone is right, *j'adore Paris*!"

I poured him a coffee, slid him the powdered milk, and told him the twenty-minute version of my French adventures. "And you? Where did you guys end up?"

"Theis and I drove to Austin with Fluffy, thinking we'd only be there for a couple of days." Fluffy was their white Persian cat. "But once the media frenzy turned into a circus act, we kept driving through New Mexico and into the Grand Canyon. We camped there for a couple of weeks. When things still looked grim, we drove north and stayed with friends in San Francisco for a month. Just got back last night."

"Back last night and already working?"

"I've done enough waiting around in the last two months to last a lifetime."

Every morning, starting at Café Orléans, Ren led crowds of tourists through the trials and tribulations of the streets of "Naw'lins." There was also a special evening version of the tour, which he touted by promising to spill the secrets hidden in the dark crannies of the Quarter. The odds of even a single tourist being in town were slim to none, but he had still showed up at the rendezvous-point, just in case. Admirable.

But waiting we would do. An hour went by without anyone coming through the door. After cleaning everything I could reach, I took my place on the stool behind the counter. It was sad to see Ren, who was normally polished to perfection, with droopy bags under his eyes and rumpled clothes.

"Ren, tell me a story, *s'il te plaît.*" It was a request I usually reserved for slow summer afternoons, when people stayed inside to hide from the heat.

"Hmm…" He carefully twirled the end of his waxed mustache. "Do you know the story of the Carter brothers?"

I shook my head and leaned on the counter. I could tell that even though Sébastien was meticulously putting the espresso machine back together, he was listening too.

Never able to pass up the opportunity to take center stage, Ren walked to the middle of the café and brought his fingers to a point. His flair for the dramatic always led me to question how much truth there was to his stories, but their accuracy didn't really matter because his entertainment value was ace.

"The year was 1930. Huey Long was two years into his infamous reign as the governor of Louisiana. The country was still recovering from World War I, and the stock market had crashed less than a year prior. With the breakneck decline in foreign trade, warehouses on the Port of New Orleans emptied, and activity on the docks hushed. Times were hard all throughout the city, and the French Quarter was in dire straits. The buildings were in deplorable condition, and many of the historic establishments had been temporarily closed or abandoned. The prohibition had created a swell of illegal underground activity, and debauchery ran rampant, even more than usual." He paused to give me a giant wink.

I rested my head on my hands to get comfortable. He was just getting warmed up.

"John and Wayne Carter were two brothers who lived just around the corner from here on St. Ann and Royal Street. Other than the charm that was expected of Southern gentlemen, they appeared to be just your average men with labor jobs down by the river.

"One cool autumn afternoon, while the Carter brothers were down at the docks, a nine-year-old girl escaped from their apartment and ran all the way to the local precinct. Her face was gaunt, her eyes were sunken in, and her hair was thin where patches had fallen out. At a first glance, she appeared sickly, but uninjured. That was until she held out her arms, palms up. The authorities thought that her wounds were a botched suicide attempt, but upon further examination, they discovered that the cuts had been made in a very precise way – with the skill of a surgeon – as if to drain her blood slowly over time. The little girl was in such a state of shock that she was unable to tell her tale, but she kept repeating the words 'help them' over and over again. When the policemen raided the brothers' third-story apartment, they found—"

"Ahem," a female voice interrupted. "Is anyone here actually working?" The voice belonged to Désirée Borges.

When had she walked in? I'd never seen her in the café before, but, as far as I knew, we were the only coffee shop in the neighborhood open for business. If you could call it that.

"I'd like a nonfat, vanilla granita. Extra whip."

I stared at her, puzzled by how she thought we could accommodate her request.

"Please?" she added, trying to get me to hustle.

"Um… We can't make granitas right now. We're barely operational."

"Fine, I'll just have a sugar-free vanilla iced coffee, lots of room for soy milk."

"We don't have iced coffee or—"

"It's still summer! Why are you open if you don't have iced coffee?"

I considered mentioning my new Sacred Heart status in hopes that knowing someone as lowly as me would be attending her school might cause her head to explode, but Sébastien intervened.

"We just reopened today. Like most places in the city, our iced coffee takes twenty-four hours to cold drip. We should have some tomorrow." He was far more diplomatic than I would have been.

"Oh, then I'll just take whatever you've got, as long as it's got caffeine in it." She obnoxiously batted her eyelashes. I had to keep myself from making gagging noises. Of course, Sébastien was completely oblivious to her flirtation.

I poured her coffee in a paper cup, hoping she wouldn't stay, splashed in some sugar-free vanilla syrup, and slid it across the counter with a smile as fake as hers. *How the hell am I going to survive Sacred Heart?*

Her heels clicking the pavement outside cued Ren to reclaim the stage. This time, Sébastien stopped fiddling with the machine and leaned on the counter next to me.

"*Procéde, s'il te plaît,*" I said.

Ren pretended to ponder. "Where was I?"

"The policemen were just getting to the apartment of the Carter brothers," Sébastien reminded him.

"*Oui, oui, merci beaucoup.* The policemen raided the third-story apartment and, to their horror, found seven other people held captive, all with their wrists sliced open in the same fashion as the little girl's. Most of the victims praised God for the miracle of being rescued, but those who had been there for more than a few days begged for death. They screamed that they would never be able to escape the Carter brothers or all the horror they had witnessed.

"None of the victims reported having been taken to the grandiose apartment against their will. It was when they tried to leave that the brothers demanded the party never end! They tied each one up and held them prisoner. The victims claimed that every night, when John and Wayne arrived home from work, the brothers would slice open their flesh and drink their blood directly from the pierced veins.

"The cops found only two dead bodies, but the survivors claimed to have witnessed at least six others come through the front door and never leave. They said that once a victim's blood had been completely drained, the Carter brothers would dispose of the body by shoving them through a trash chute into a bath of acid below. No traces of these bodies were ever found.

"The policemen waited for John and Wayne Carter to return from work, and ambushed them right outside their apartment. Even though the brothers should have been exhausted after their day of manual labor, it still took over a dozen men to hold them down. As you can imagine, there was a media frenzy after the arrests. The Carter brothers photographed well and were charming enough to gain a surprising swell of sympathizers – but despite their charisma and good looks, the sadistic killers were sentenced to be hanged. Post-execution, their bodies were laid to rest in St. Louis Cemetery No. 1.

"Now, here is where it gets interesting."

Sébastien and I exchanged looks.

"I'm sure you know that if you live, or more specifically die, in New Orleans, you're probably gonna end up buried in an oven tomb, since the high water table makes earth inhumation difficult. You'll spend your eternal slumber in something that not only looks like an oven but literally roasts you, like a slow-cooker. In times when the body count outnumbered the tombs available, resting bodies got exactly one year to roast in peace – not a day more, not a day less. Then the crypt-keepers would push the crumbling remains to the back and slip in a fresh corpse.

"When the Carter brothers' remains were scheduled to be pushed to the back, the crypt-keeper found the tomb empty of bone fragments. There was not a trace of John or Wayne Carter ever having been laid to rest."

Ren took a deep breath, allowing his audience a moment to ponder the strangeness of his story.

"In all the decades since, no one has been able to explain how two corpses could simply vanish without a trace. The mystery is all that remains."

He paused again and then took a dramatic bow.

I clapped loudly, and Sébastien joined me for a moment before returning to the espresso machine with a smile on his face.

Ren took another bow. Despite the meager audience and the events of the last couple of months, nothing had affected his ability to tell a story.

"John and Wayne?" came an unfamiliar voice from the corner. The sketcher. "As in John Wayne? Do people in this town believe this crap?" His headphones were still on, but he must have turned his music off and listened in on the story. I scowled, annoyed by his blatant skepticism, but the questions didn't faze Ren in the slightest. On the contrary, the naysaying seemed to enliven him. There was nothing Ren loved more than a debate about the supernatural.

"Oh, people in this town believe far crazier things than the tale of the Carter brothers, young man. But you are probably correct that the brothers were likely living under false names. Even so, that's who they claimed to be, so that's how the story goes."

"Blood-drinkers? And do people in this town believe in vampires?" the guy asked, pushing his hair behind his ears.

"The truth is relative," Ren answered, being purposefully vague.

The scientist in the room interjected, "A logical truth is a statement that is true in *all* possible worlds. As opposed to a fact, which is only true in this world, as it has historically unfolded." Sébastien made my brain hurt.

"Don't bring logic into a discussion about the truth, my boy!" Ren yelled.

Sébastien raised one eyebrow, but knew that arguing would be an exercise in futility.

Ren looked back at the sketcher. "The truth depends on what you believe in."

"I believe if I ever came across a vampire, I would stake it." He gathered up his things.

"Them are fighting words, son!"

"You have no idea," he mumbled, walking out the door.

The three of us looked at each other with blank expressions and then burst out laughing.

"Testy young fellow!"

Suppressing giggles, I looked at Ren. "Sorry about that."

"Miss Le Moyne, if you remember only one thing I have ever taught you, let it be this: you can never please everyone. As an artist, if your work doesn't inflame at least part of the audience, then you might as well call it quits and sell insurance. And that goes for you too, Mr. Scientist. The world needs more boundary pushers, not more boundary creators."

"Ha ha. I'll keep that in mind."

Ren nudged my elbow and motioned towards the window table. "Anyway, he was cute."

"Yeah, Adele, maybe you two could go vampire hunting together," Sébastien teased.

I rolled my eyes.

"Speaking of dead… I have a brilliant idea. We've only had two customers today: the prissy, sugar-free-vanilla girl, and the disgruntled artist. Let's close up early and call it a day."

"Hey, what am I, chopped liver? You've had *three* customers."

"Let me rephrase, two *paying* customers," Sébastien countered. "What year was it the last time you paid for your caffeine fix, Ren?"

"You know I leave the math to you and your sister." He headed for the door. *"Au revoir!"*

"Bye, Ren!" I yelled.

"À demain, ma chérie!"

13

the unexpected muse

October 19th

SEVEN DAYS WENT BY with nearly the exact same routine. I woke up to a silent house, showered, listened to the radio while getting ready, and then went to Café Orléans.

The thrill of going back to work had quickly worn thin – there was barely anything to serve and hardly anyone to serve it to. I never saw more than a handful of customers a day, most of whom were cops or government recovery workers. Sébastien had returned to his lab rats. I hadn't seen Jeanne; she was practically sleeping in her lab, trying to get it back to full capacity. Mr. Michel spent most of his time at the roasters, and Mrs. Michel spent most of her time upstairs on the phone with insurance agents, lawyers and vendors. There wasn't really a point in opening the coffee shop, but it gave us hope that one day things would return to normal.

After I finished the post-Storm cleaning, there was nothing to do but watch the clock tick away the remaining days of my plaid-skirt-free life. My anxiety over starting at Sacred Heart had grown so intense I began to feel sick. I attempted every persuasive argument I could think of to get out of going to school, but my father, who I had barely seen all week, wasn't budging.

Every day, he disappeared, driving out of the city to find groceries, or gasoline for the generator, or construction supplies. Between the broken infrastructure and the scarcity of goods, this endeavor sometimes took the entire afternoon. Then he went straight to the bar "to get things in order," or so he said, not to return until after I was asleep. Always after curfew.

We hadn't been able to find anyone to fix the wall, but my father had managed to get a government-issued blue tarp. The blue plastic patches were becoming a frequent sight all around the city – a marker of someone who'd returned home. After moving his bed into my old room, my father now said that his studio was finally *well ventilated.* He joked, but I knew he was desperate to get the wall fixed because the crime in the city was out of control (two more dead bodies had been found). Every day, I worried more and more that he would send me back to my mother's.

The physical destruction didn't hold a candle to the mental damage the Storm was doing to the city's inhabitants. For me, the worst part of the aftermath was the guilt. I felt guilty all the time. I felt guilty to have survived when so many others hadn't. I felt guilty that we still had our home. I felt guilty that our most frustrating problem was finding gasoline for the generator. Bouncing between the guilt and trying not to feel sorry for myself was maddening.

The lack of interaction with people forced me into an even deeper state of introversion than usual. At times, I felt like an empty shell of myself, staring blankly at things I was supposed to recognize. Everyone else appeared zombie-like as well, but the solidarity only brought temporary comfort. It was as if we had all gone to war together.

Little did I know, the war hadn't even begun.

I HAD TWO DISTRACTIONS from the dystopia that was real life. The first was Arcadian, the used bookshop next door to the café. Even though they hadn't reopened yet, Mr. Mauer let me borrow books like he always had. I helped him clean, and together we mourned several trash cans worth of pages that had drench 'n dried, but seventeen feet of water had poured into the neighborhood where he lived, so the ruined books were the least of his problems.

Maybe the solitude was a good thing since I was becoming a walking hazard, leading me to my second great distraction – tinkering with my new, er, talent.

I attempted to use it *only* when no one was around *and* I had reached the peak of absolute boredom with everything else. I don't know if this was because it scared the hell out of me or if I was hoarding it, like saving the last bite of your favorite food on the plate until everything else was gone. A cherished treasure to give me something to do when I felt like I was on the brink of solitude-induced insanity. Sometimes it worked, and sometimes it didn't. The random freak occurrences were making me a frazzled wreck.

Yesterday, at the café, I had been in such a deep Émile-daydream that I hadn't realized I was stirring my *Americano* with a floating spoon. Not until Ren walked in and it clanked down onto the rim of the cup. I'm not sure whether he saw, but he did look at me a bit suspiciously after that.

Note to self: BE MORE DISCREET.

Regardless, Ren was the highlight of my days. He came into the café every morning and patiently waited, just in case people showed up for a tour. No one ever came, although he mentioned that two or three customers usually showed up at night for his ghost tour.

The only other people I consistently saw were the uniform-clad mayor's daughter, Désirée, and the naysaying vampire-hater, whose name I had learned was Isaac. Désirée came in early morning. I still wasn't sure why she came downtown every morning just to turn around and go back uptown for school, but we had gained her patronage. At least we now had iced coffee, so I didn't have to deal with her stink-eye (at least, not regarding the coffee). Isaac always came in at around ten and stayed for at least two hours, always with headphones on and sketchpad in hand. Besides his name, the only other piece of information I had garnered was that he was from New York City, which was apparently superior to New Orleans in every way, and which possibly explained his too-cool-for-school attitude. I had grown immensely curious as to why he was in town – the city being far from tourist friendly. Other than ordering his coffee (plain black, not that we had much else to offer), the only time he ever spoke was to openly complain about something.

His condescending air was the reason I had *initially* disliked him. The reason I *continued* to dislike him was that whenever I broke from my book, I caught him looking at me. He'd always quickly lower his gaze when our eyes met, but I had a sneaking suspicion he was sketching me, which made me extremely self-conscious. And extremely annoyed. And feel even more trapped in this bizarre reality. It's not like I could ask him to stop without seeming totally presumptuous and vain, because I didn't have any real evidence that he was actually doing it, but each day I caught him glancing at me more frequently, and each day playing the role of unexpected muse made me loathe his presence. I racked my brain to think of a way to catch a glimpse of his sketchpad and vindicate my suspicion. Luckily, I had a lot of time on my hands to plot.

The only good news was the heat had finally broken, and the dreadfully long, unair-conditioned summer was over. But the electricity in the fall air that I usually loved, now only amplified the feeling that each day was a ticking time bomb.

14

t-minus one

October 20th

"WHY DON'T YOU GUYS JUST HAVE plain New York coffee?" Isaac asked, pushing the tips of his light-brown hair out of his face and over his head. The sleeves of his dirty gray T-shirt hiked up just enough to reveal that the tops of his arms were not as tanned as his forearms. The hair fell back in his face as soon as his shoulders relaxed. He pushed it behind his ears again as if by autopilot.

Today was really no different from the last eight; only today I was having trouble suppressing the urge to dropkick him as he asked for a refill.

"Oh, I know where you can get some plain New York coffee..."

His big brown eyes lit up.

"In *New York*. I'm sure they would *love* to have you back."

He started laughing. His fingers scratched the result of not having shaven in a few days. “Are you sure you’re from around here? Aren’t Southern girls supposed to be hospitable?”

I wanted to jump across the counter and strangle him.

Instead of getting angry, he was actually being congenial for the first time. *Is this how New Yorkers are? Be mean to them, and they like you back?*

“So, where *are* you from?” he asked.

I was still a little taken aback by his prompt of nonobligatory chatter.

“I’m from around the corner.”

I knew exactly where this conversation was going. I’d had it a hundred times with tourists over the years, but it had never truly annoyed me until the question came from him.

“You were born around the corner?”

“Well, technically, I was born in a hospital a couple of miles away, but I was raised my whole life, minus the last two months, around the corner from here.”

“You don’t sound Southern,” he replied in his usual know-it-all tone.

Films and television shows almost always got the New Orleans dialect wrong, further perpetuating the incorrect assumption that we all have a twang. It was a pet peeve of mine, my father’s, and all native New Orleanians. Even though Isaac was correct – my accent did sound nearly identical to his – I scowled, not wanting to be disassociated from my hometown, especially not now.

“Are you some kind of expert on Southern dialects?”

“Ugh, no. I just thought—”

“You just thought we would all sound like Scarlett O’Hara?”

“I guess. I don’t know… You seem to really love this place.”

“Well, yeah. It’s messed up right now, but you’re an idiot if you can’t see why I love this place.”

His smile cocked. *I call him an idiot and he smiles?*

“Maybe you could show me around sometime? Take me to see some of the things that were so great?”

“Are!” I yelled. “Are so great. The city isn’t dead.”

"Right… I guess I've only seen the dead parts." He was not helping his cause. "So how about it?"

Was this some coy way of asking me out? My defensiveness flipped into nervousness. I slammed his coffee mug down. The contents sloshed over the rim. "Sorry, I don't have time. Too busy trying to keep things from dying."

"Fine, sorry I asked."

He went back to his table, jammed his headphones on, and started furiously moving his pencil.

Great, now he's probably turning me into a monster.

Luckily, before the guilt could set in for being unnecessarily mean, Sébastien walked through the door with his hands behind his back.

"M'aimes-tu?" he asked as he approached the counter. The heavy-looking bags he was attempting to hide swayed into my sightline.

"Of course I love you," I answered, eying a red plastic top jutting out the top of a bag. "Is that what I think it is?"

"Well, that depends on—"

"Oh my God, is that milk?"

"*Oui*!" He smiled. "Pépé found a place two hours outside of the city. He bought as much as they would allow."

"We're going to be the cat's meow around here," I said, mouth salivating as I ripped the plastic ring from one of the jugs.

I steamed the milk into a creamy white foam and poured it over my chicory coffee. The first sip burned my tongue, but I didn't care. I greedily took another. The mixture tasted like New Orleans. I attempted to savor the third sip, hanging on to every flavor.

"Things are on the up and up," I said, making another *café au lait* for him. "First milk, then who knows? Maybe the government will get its act together and fix this place."

"Baby steps… *Merci.*" He gently kissed my cheeks and poured his coffee into a paper cup. "I have to get back to school. Pépé just asked me to run the milk over because there are no working refrigerators at the roasters."

"No!" I grabbed his arm. "You just got here! I am dying of boredom. Please!"

"I have to go. *Je suis désolé, Adele.* I am so far behind, I have no idea how to catch up." He grabbed a book from my stack on the counter and tossed it at me. "Plus, it looks like you have plenty to keep you occupied. *À bientôt!*"

I tried not to sulk as he walked out the door.

It was back to just me and Isaac, who, if I wasn't mistaken, was smiling at Sébastien's departure. I cranked some classical music, hoping to scare him off, and picked up the loaner copy of Franz Kafka's *The Metamorphosis.* The deceivingly thin paperback was the only book on the Sacred Heart reading list that I hadn't already read. I sighed, shuffled the pages to my folded earmark, and read the first three sentences.

Then I read the first three sentences again. And again.

Despite not retaining much, I turned the page, trying to prompt my brain into a reading rhythm.

Read.

Read.

Read.

My eyes kept moving from the page to the two lonely nickels sitting in the tip jar – they were begging me to play with them.

Unlike the reading progress, it took only a little mental focus before the coins were dancing around the jar to the Tchaikovsky overture blaring in the background. Careful not to let them clink on the glass and bring attention to what I was doing, I smiled as a dime did a swan-dive to join the pirouetting nickels. The motion was hypnotizing.

When the song ended, I glanced up and saw Isaac staring at me from his table. The nickels clanked back to the base of the jar. *There was no way he could have seen the tiny coins from across the room, right?* This time his gaze didn't break away as quickly as usual. My cheeks flushed, and I ducked under the counter to have a moment to myself.

Ugh. I need to focus my energy on something productive, or I am going to end up doing something stupid.

I took a deep breath while I searched for a less dramatic song on the radio and then grabbed a small black notebook from my bag. When I stood back up, his gaze had returned to the felt tip of his marker. I daydreamed the marker floating from his hand and inking a mustache across his upper lip. Thank God it didn't actually happen, but trying to contain the giggle made me snort.

He looked up. My hand flew to my forehead to hide my smile as I flipped open the notebook.

I tried my best to ignore him as I drew a line down the middle of a new page. On the left side I listed all the items I had tried to move but couldn't: box of oatmeal, ceramic bowl, sponge, tennis shoe, bag of coffee beans, single coffee bean, toilette paper, broom, towel, stick of gum, book.

There must be some kind of pattern.

I forced myself not to chew on the pen while I recalled more items.

A cool gust of air came through the doors, making my arm hairs stand up. Without looking up from the notebook, I tugged the short sleeves of my coffee-stained V-neck and rubbed my arms, fingers landing on the thin *gris-gris* ribbon.

"Your cut is getting better—"

I slammed the notebook shut, jumping an inch off the stool.

The voice had come from lips just a few inches from my forehead. Niccolò Medici, the *Italiano.* I felt my eyes grow wide as I suddenly wondered if I had actually *caused* the Palermo's sign to fall, nearly crushing his brother. "*Scusa,*" he said softly, trying not to laugh. "I didn't mean to scare you."

I'd been hearing that a lot lately. *I really need to stop moping around and start being more alert.*

"No worries." I attempted to resume my casual position on the counter, but it now felt awkward – he was still staring at my face.

My hand went over the claw mark, which was now a pinkish-purple, raised line from the base of my neck to my cheekbone. He pushed my fingers away and softly touched the tender mark. His touch was cool on my warm skin; he must have been working outside this morning. Our eyes locked. I tried my best not to let my nervousness transfer from my pulse, to my cheek, to his fingertips. He *did not* need to know how intimidated I was by the close proximity of his ridiculous good looks.

If this had been a scene from a French film, it would have been the perfect opportunity for two almost-strangers to kiss – it was exactly the bold kind of thing Émile would have done.

Ugh, get over him, Adele. He's gone. Focus on the guy in front of you.

But it was too late; Niccolò shifted back, probably sensing my emotional spiral.

"Absurdist fiction?" he asked, picking up the tattered paperback. "So, you are into Kafka?" His accent slightly dragged the first vowel in the author's name.

My brain begged me not to lie. It had barely retained part one of the German novella.

"Well, I'm reading it for school. The jury is still out on whether I'm into it or not." My brain thanked me, but then I immediately wanted to choke myself to stop the next words from flying out. "But generally I like the absurd."

He laughed. "Me too." His expression briefly scrunched, probably trying to figure out whether I was alluding to Ionesco or just trying to be abstract. "Although, I've learned to appreciate when things are simple, more straightforward." He leaned on the counter, his hands nearly touching mine. I had no clue if we were still talking about literature. I nodded, even though "simple" was not the vibe I got from him. Something about him exuded double entendre – not in an indecent way, but in a cryptic way – and for some twisted reason, I think I was attracted to the confusion it caused me.

Don't overanalyze everything, as per usual, Adele.

Before I could respond, Isaac butted in with his empty mug. I quickly refilled it.

He gave Niccolò a hard stare before going back to his seat, and with that, our moment was over. I sighed internally. "Can I get you something?"

"No, I'm good."

"Are you sure?" I asked, not wanting him to leave. "I know we aren't in Rome, but I can pull a pretty decent shot of espresso."

"*No, grazie.* I just came to see you."

"Oh." My stomach did a back flip.

"And I wanted a break from work," he quickly added, "and from my brother."

"Gabe seems pretty full-on."

He let out a deep laugh and leaned a back on the counter. "That is a drastic understatement." His lips pressed into a tight smile. Then, as if beckoned, his older brother walked through the door.

"*Bella*, my heroine! We meet again."

Gabriel Medici was the type of guy who commanded the attention of a room simply by walking in and being beautiful. I remember thinking the same thing about Émile, only Émile was far more subtle. *Ugh. Stop!* It was strange to think about a man being beautiful, but it really was the most fitting word to accurately describe the blond – well, both of the brothers, really, but Gabe had the unabashed personality to go along with it.

Niccolò retreated to a table, and his brother kissed my hand in a dramatic fashion, which I assumed was his norm.

"Why do you look so sad, *bella*? A beautiful woman should never look so sad." He raised my arm over the empty pastry case, guiding me around the counter, and then spun me around, just as a Louis Armstrong and Billie Holiday duet started. I cracked a smile remembering the "Lady Stardust" night with my father, which already seemed like a month ago.

Gabe was as good at dancing as he was at posing – he led me around the floor in perfect time with the music, turning me at all the appropriate moments. It was totally over the top, but I can't say I didn't enjoy the attention, especially since he was doing it right in front of Isaac, which for some reason delighted me. Gabe seemed to pick up on this and further taunted him by bending me into a low dip directly in front of his table. I shot the Northerner a look that meant, *Take note,* as Gabe held the pose for another measure. He must have gotten the hint because he grabbed his stuff and huffed out the door.

When my attention turned back to my partner, his eyes were stuck on my chest. *Jeez, he could at least be a little more discreet.* Instead of attempting to hide his overt behavior, he looked up at me with an inquisitive expression and then back down at my chest.

That's when I realized he was just looking at my necklace. The medallion had slipped out of the V-neck. *Innocent enough, I suppose.* He pulled me up with such excitement, my feet couldn't keep up with the spin. I flung towards the door, where I was caught in the arms of Désirée Borges. My momentum knocked us both over, because, of course, she was wearing six-inch heels. She was cursing my name before we even hit the ground.

In a flash, Niccolò put himself in between me and Désirée's line of venomous lashes. He helped me up, while Gabe extended his hand to her. As Désirée's gaze went from his fingers to his face, her slanderous rage dwindled to silence. I tried to contain it but couldn't help let out a quiet giggle, witnessing Gabe's mere presence shut her up.

"Please accept my apology, *signorina.* I am entirely at fault." He helped her up with one fell swoop. She looked from Gabe to me and then to Niccolò as she adjusted the micro-miniskirt over her perfect stems.

She seemed rendered speechless by the idea of me fraternizing with not only one but two older, stylish guys. I couldn't say I blamed her. "No harm, no foul," she finally managed.

I walked back behind the counter to get a better view of whatever was about to unfold.

"Adele, aren't you going to introduce me to your friends?"

She knows my name? The title "friends" was a bit of a stretch, given this was my second run-in with the foreigners, but there was no way I was going to let an opportunity like this pass me by. "Désirée Borges, meet Gabe and Niccolò Medici. They're over from Italy, looking for some missing relatives and staying with the Palermos."

"That's so terrible," she said. I couldn't help but wonder if she cared at all or if she just wanted to jump Gabe. "Anyway, it's nice to meet you."

"The pleasure is entirely ours," Gabe said as he kissed her hand.

Niccolò stood in the background, looking my way. He rolled his eyes at his brother's dramatic gesture. I got the impression this was something he'd heard a thousand times before. Another quiet chuckle escaped my lips.

"We're not staying with the Palermos anymore," he said to me. "We managed to get our own place around the corner."

"So, how do you ladies know each other?" Gabe asked Désirée.

The look in her eyes showed that she was falling fast. "Well... um... our parents..."

I intercepted. "We don't actually know each other that well." She appeared grateful to no longer be on the spot but seemed alarmed I might blow the fact that we weren't BFFs. "Which is kind of odd, considering our parents go way back. But we're going to be spending a lot of time together soon..."

She looked at me with suspicion.

"Because we'll be attending the same school, as of tomorrow, right?" I flashed her a beaming smile.

Her eyes bugged. "Right," she said through gritted teeth.

I guess she hadn't known I was the Academy's newest recruit.

"*Eccellente*!" Gabe said. "Adele is my absolute favorite person in New Orleans. Promise me you'll take good care of her."

"Really?" she asked, flabbergasted.

I tried not to show my own surprise. I owed Gabe for this. *Big time.*

"*Si*, she saved my life, but that's another story for another time."

"I promise," she said. "And you can tell me the whole story, *next* time."

I had no idea if Gabe was really interested in Désirée, but she was eating it up. While she continued to flirt relentlessly, I realized Niccolò had disappeared. My disappointment surprised me, but I couldn't blame him for wanting to bail on this nauseating display of high school flirtation. I wished I could have.

I made Désirée her sugar-free vanilla iced-coffee so I didn't have to watch every move as she threw herself at the elder Medici. When I slid the cup across the counter, she happily grabbed it and seductively sucked on the straw, ogling.

Vomit.

"Burgundy, right?" she asked as she flipped her hair and sashayed to the door. The question had been directed at me.

"Huh?"

"You live on Burgundy Street, right? Tomorrow. Seven a.m. sharp. Bring coffee." Before committing to the exit, she turned back and winked at Gabe. He returned a small wave.

I was stunned. *Did Désirée Borges really just offer me a ride to school? Maybe she isn't so bad after all?*

Gabe leaned on the counter, posing, and turned to me. "Well, she seems like trouble."

"*Si*, she scares me."

We both laughed, and then he looked me straight in the eyes. "She's nothing that you can't handle, Adele." It felt genuine, like he had finally stopped performing.

"Grazie, Gabriel."

"*Prego*. Until we meet again."

15

walk of shame

October 22nd

CLEANING OUT MY NEW ROOM was a constant treasure hunt, always ending with something beautiful and vintage as a reward. I had been excited when I first found the little brass clock hidden amongst the junk in the closet, but now, as I lay in the dark, the ticking noises felt like the prelude to my execution. I imagined myself smashing the alarm clock against the wall.

Breathe.

Most of the night had been spent like this – suffering the first-day jitters for the third time in one semester. It wasn't humane. My mind time-warped to Paris and reminded me of how pathetic I had felt lying in my dorm room, terrified of the sun rising. I had been so jealous of my Romanian roommate, who lay peacefully asleep while my pulse raced. But Paris was different: over there, everyone had just cause to prejudge me; I was the foreigner invading their land of wealth and glamour. Feeling like a foreigner in my hometown was so much worse.

I rolled over. 5:12 a.m.

As soon as I groaned, the cute little alarm clock went flying into the fresh paint job.

"Shit!" I sat up. All three lamps snapped on.

I hope the clock isn't broken.

I looked over at the small pile of things I'd destroyed in the last week. This parlor trick – ability, whatever you call it – was out of control, and one more reason I had new-school anxiety.

Now that my nerves were fired up, I conceded to the day's events. Stood and stretched, forcing my skin to embrace the chill in the air.

LEGS SHAVED, SKIN MOISTURIZED, AND HAIR TAMED, I pressed the power button on the boom-box, not caring if it was too loud for six in the morning. I didn't care if it woke my father; he had no reason to be out all night given the curfew. Plus, as far as I was concerned, having to go to Sacred Heart was entirely his fault.

"Add one more tally to the dead-body count," came the DJ's voice through the speaker. I turned to look at it as he continued: "The N.O.P.D. still doesn't have anything to say about these recently reported crimes." He went on about the lack of aid from the federal government.

Ugh. Listening to people rant about our demise wasn't going to help my anxiety. The tuner knob spun until the voices of people shouting were drowned out by a boy band crooning about how beautiful I was. I walked to the full-length dressing mirror for a self-assessment.

I looked a little skinnier than usual, easily attributed to my meager diet of oatmeal, red beans 'n rice, and coffee. I hadn't eaten a piece of meat or a vegetable since my transatlantic meal on the plane, if that even counted as real food. My loose waves fell several inches past my shoulders now, much longer than they had been at the beginning of summer – before the Storm, when life was normal. Back when Brooke and I were still planning out our entire junior and senior years.

I moved to the metal garment rack usually reserved for in-progress designs. Now there were just two hangers: on one hung layers of tulle covered in hand-stitched beading, and on the other were various layers of blue, white and gray. Three months ago I would have had trouble guessing which one was my Halloween costume. *We couldn't buy milk or find someone to fix our wall, but Sacred Heart had managed to get me monogrammed uniforms.*

I shimmied on the scratchy polyester skirt and buttoned up the collared shirt. My white bra easily showed through the thin, white cotton.

"That doesn't seem very Catholic schoolgirl-like to me."

Over went the navy-blue cardigan with A.L.M. embroidered over my heart.

I had never worn a uniform in my life. Even my boarding school in Paris didn't require them, hence the multiple shopping sprees with *ma grand-mère*. On the bright side, the uniform should make it easier to blend in. Taking cues from an old Britney Spears video, I pulled on a pair of white knee socks and laced up the saddle Oxfords. I actually kind of liked the contrasting black and white leather shoes.

No amount of concealer dabbing was going to cover the dark circles under my eyes, nor had my prayers been answered about my battle wound miraculously fading overnight. Self-consciousness made my hand shake as I swept powder over the ugly pink line on my cheek. Two layers of black mascara. Light pink lip-gloss. Silver chain. I knotted my hair up into a messy bun on top of my head and started to feel more like myself.

Am I even allowed to wear jewelry? I wondered as I tucked the *gris-gris* underneath my shirt. I picked up the box my mother had stealthily hidden in my suitcase and tried to suppress the angst that rose whenever I thought about her. *It's an heirloom from your paternal side*, I reminded myself and popped the box open. The ring's style was unlike anything I had ever seen: an opaline stone nested into a thick silver medallion, like a giant pearl in an oyster shell, encircled by an intricately engraved border.

Light caught the milky, iridescent stone as I slid the ring on my middle finger. The metal was warm against my skin. For a moment, I wondered what era it was from and suddenly found myself silently thanking my mother. Maybe it was the pop music (I never would have admitted it, if it was), or maybe it was residual effects from the warm bath, but I felt a bit better. *Maybe I would actually make friends? Maybe I would forget about Émile...* I drew the navy-blue tie under my collar and snapped it into an X.

When I went back to the mirror, I waved my hand just to make sure the reflection belonged to me, and then texted a photo to Brooke so she could get a good laugh upon waking – maybe it would get her to call me back. I hadn't heard from her since our initial call, which felt strange since there was no longer an ocean and several time zones between us. She was probably mad at me for not moving to L.A., or she had adjusted to her new life and was out living it up every day. Or she had already forgotten about me....

I tossed my notebook, Kafka, and some pens into a black canvas tote bag and felt unusually light not being weighed down with art supplies. My keys flew from across the room and fell gently into my palm. That was it. There was nothing else I could procrastinate with. The day was officially starting. I slipped out the front door to hold up my end of the carpool deal. Coffee.

SMALL FLAMES FLICKERING in the gas lamps on houses led the way through the low-hanging fog, not that I needed them. I could do the walk to Café Orléans in my sleep. Regardless, it felt strange to be out in the semi-dark after being cooped up every night. A glance at my watch assured me the sun would soon make an appearance. The silence contributed to freak me out – no bars closing up, no drunken idiots yelling, no sounds of garbage trucks disposing last night's glut. My usual sense of familiarity with the route was lost.

Chills invaded my body like a virus, giving me the sense that I wasn't alone. I pulled my cardigan closed and hustled down the last two blocks. By the time I fumbled the keys into the lock and shoved the door closed, paranoia had engulfed me.

Chill out. You're just nervous about school.

I dropped my stuff on the floor and went straight to the giant wall of beans. While I contemplated which type to brew, the gas lamp's soft light flooding in through the window flickered, as if temporarily obstructed. A quick glance showed nothing suspicious outside.

I focused back on the task at hand and carefully lifted the jar of dark-roasted Kenyan beans, but another break in the light made my heart freeze. I walked to the large bay window and scanned the street in both directions. No one, not even a rat.

With one look at the door, the brass deadbolt snapped into the locked position. I hurried through the process of measuring, grinding and filtering the beans, and then the machine hummed on, leaving me with nothing to do but wait for the coffee to drip.

I glanced out the window repeatedly.

It wasn't until the first rays of morning sun peeked underneath the door and the delicious scent of freshly brewed dark roast filled the air that the knot in my stomach began to untangle.

6:42 a.m. Perfect. Plenty of time before seven. *Wait, what if Désirée doesn't turn up? What if she had only offered the ride to score brownie points with Gabe*? I really didn't want to have to wake up my father to get a ride. I didn't want to start the day begging him to reconsider.

Quickly, I glugged sugar-free vanilla syrup into one of the cups, as if getting Désirée's coffee order correct might give me some kind of good juju, and then proceeded out the front door. Between my bag and the two warm cups, my hands were full. I willed my keys out of my cardigan pocket and into the lock.

"*Voilà!*" The door locked, and the keys dropped back into my sweater. "*Merci beaucoup*."

Each click of my heels made by the brand-new saddle Oxfords seemed to echo louder and louder down the desolate street. My pace quickened as the thought of Désirée arriving early and leaving without me chewed at my nerves.

One block later, I suddenly wasn't so sure if the clicking on the pavement was coming from my shoes alone.

I glanced behind me.

No one.

But as I continued to walk, the sounds seemed a little sharp for my flats. I stopped short to convince myself it was in my head, but the staccato click lasted an extra step.

I started walking again. Faster.

The second set of steps followed suit, no longer trying to hide under the cover of my loud shoes. I contemplated breaking into a run but worried it would make me appear more victimlike.

The rising sun forced me to squint.

Lost in my escalating hysteria, I turned the corner sharply and smacked right into a tall, hooded figure. I fell backwards, but before I hit the ground, his arm swept underneath my back. My arms reflexively shot around his shoulders as he aggressively yanked me into his chest to keep me from falling.

I tried to regain my balance and back away, but his arms enclosed me, trapping me in the awkward embrace. "Let me g—"

"Shhh!" he hissed.

All I could see was the blinding dawn over his shoulder. Again, I tried to break away, "get off," but his hand slipped tightly over my mouth, muffling my words. That's when I realized he was listening.

Like a hunter.

The sharp clicking of heels against cement was still approaching.

My heart pounded with fear, but his intense interest in the person following me brought an unexplainable sense of relief.

I craned my neck sideways and caught the silhouette of a woman with a hooded cloak passing us on the other side of the street.

She turned back and flashed a twisted smile, like she meant to taunt him, and a low growl came from the back of his throat. Just when I thought he might drop me and go after her, his grip tightened once more. His fingers dug into my ribcage, making me wince.

The sounds of her clicking heels faded into total silence, leaving just him and me. My fingers clutched the back of his leather jacket so tightly I began to shake.

I couldn't breathe. He didn't stir.

I forced myself to suck in air, and felt my lungs push against his chest. The breath brought in a vaguely familiar scent: leather and soap. His head shifted inward towards me.

"*Scusa*," he whispered. His soft words ricocheted off my neck. "Are you okay?"

All I could do was nod. He retracted from around me, but his cold fingers paused at the back of my neck. Chills radiated throughout my entire body as Niccolò's face showed from underneath the hood.

"Fancy running into you here," I squeaked.

His shoulders tightened when I spoke, but he just looked down at me with a blank stare. I couldn't get my eyes to unlock from his.

A memory flashed in my head, too fast for me to catch it. Or déjà vu. Or something. Again, I had an overwhelming feeling that I'd seen him before.

He inched closer, until our bodies were practically touching again.

Is he actually going to kiss me?

His eyes looked peculiar, almost as if he was in some kind of trance. Something in his expression made him seem uneasy. Him being uneasy made me uneasy.

"Yesterday..." My voice shook. "I forgot to ask, have you had any luck finding your family?"

He pressed his incredibly red lips together until they became white. I immediately regretted asking. If he had had good news, he would have mentioned it.

"I shouldn't have brought it up. I'm sorry... What are you doing up so early?"

He opened his mouth to answer, but, before a word could come out, he snapped it shut again.

"Are you okay?" I quickly asked, catching a glimpse of his mouth.

He nodded. The bright morning light washed out his pale face.

"Your mouth… I think it's bleeding?"

His jaw tightened. *Is my close proximity making him nervous? Maybe he just doesn't want to admit that he's hurt?* Beneath his pinched lips, I saw his tongue circle over his teeth. He looked like he was struggling not to implode.

"Um, are you sure you're okay?" I raised my hand to his jawline, but he swatted it away and licked his lips.

"Oh my God, you *are* bleeding." I stood on my toes to investigate. "What happened?"

This time when my hand touched his face, he covered it with his own. I trembled, unsure whether I was terrified or excited by his touch. His head lowered closer to mine.

A loud squawk broke the silence.

He blinked. His gaze slid over to the crow flapping on top of a street sign. He stared at it for a long beat, again like a hunter. The moment… our moment, whatever it was, was over.

"Do you think that is your crow?" He finally spoke. "The one who attacked you?"

"Ha. How could I tell?"

He forgot to snap his mouth closed – the lines of his gums were stained with blood – when his attention turned back to me, I was staring.

"I bit my tongue, and it won't stop bleeding," he mumbled. "It's not a big deal." He picked up the one cup of coffee from the ground that, miraculously, had not been destroyed in the tumble.

Lights flashed, and a loud horn honked.

"Do you want a ride or not?" yelled a voice from the driver's-side window. Désirée had followed through after all.

"That's my ride, I have to—"

But he was gone. As was the crow. Just me with the single cup of coffee in hand.

My hands shook as I wiped the drips on the cup with the cuff of my sweater and then hustled to the passenger-side door. I prayed that the surviving coffee was the one with the vanilla as I stepped over a giant java puddle.

"Was that who I think it was?" Désirée asked as soon as I opened the door.

"Uh, Niccolò?" I handed her the cup of coffee.

She looked at me with one eyebrow raised as I climbed into the giant SUV.

"What?"

"Oh, don't look at me with those doe eyes, sister. Parting ways with one of the hottest guys on this side of town before seven o'clock in the morning?" A wicked smile spread across her face. "I just might have underestimated you, little Miss Adele Le Moyne."

My face burned. "It's not what you're thinking, if that's what you're thinking."

"Riiiight." She tapped her perfectly manicured nails on the steering wheel.

"Well, I'm sure you're going to believe whatever you want to believe," I snapped. The quickness with which I had slipped back into Parisian boarding-school mode startled me, but my defenses were sky high after the bizarre run-in.

"Hmm, maybe I really did underestimate you." She put the car into drive. "Whatever, I don't really care if the two of you were having an early-morning romp."

I caught sight of my reflection in the window – a small smile fought my lips. Just the idea that Désirée thought I stood a chance with Niccolò boosted my ego. But it also made me wonder why he had been out so early. *Had I busted him in a walk of shame, coming home from a late-night fling?*

It was certainly plausible. In the city's current state, there was nothing else to do before sunrise, and nothing was open that early. He was hot enough to have met someone so quickly. A twinge of jealousy bubbled. *What the hell, Adele? You don't even know this guy.*

"What's the deal with his brother?" Désirée asked. "Does Gabe have a girlfriend?"

As happy as I was for the conversation to move from me to her, I worried that I didn't have enough intel on Gabe to satisfy. "I don't really know."

Her face scrunched.

"If he does have a girlfriend, I'd assume she's in Italy. He and Niccolò have only been here about a week."

Her expression relaxed, and she turned on the radio. "I'm going to take Claiborne; it'll be a lot faster."

"Traffic?"

"There is no traffic, Adele. No one is back in the city. They've cleared most of Claiborne, so it's faster to drive down. How do you not know this? Don't you drive?"

"No, I was in Paris for my sixteenth birthday." I refrained from telling her I didn't even have a learner's permit.

"Don't you ever leave downtown?"

"Not really."

When we pulled onto Claiborne, I quickly understood what she meant. The multilane avenue was almost completely empty. Despite it being rush hour, we were one of only a handful of cars on the road.

"Jesus, is that…?"

"Yep, the water line."

Everything we drove past—an abandoned supermarket, a dilapidated bank, a gym, a hamburger chain, a laundry mat, a pizza joint, a housing project—everything had the same distinct mark of the Storm left on it: the water line. As we moved from block to block, the five-foot-high line continued alongside us.

Neither of us said another word for the duration of the ten-minute ride.

Eventually the houses became bigger, the cars became fancier, and everything became shinier. It was like we had entered another world.

NO MATTER HOW MANY TIMES I'd been uptown, its beauty never escaped me. Even in the aftermath of the Storm, St. Charles looked like a scene from an oil painting. Giant oak trees created a canopy over the long avenue of historic mansions, further preserving the feeling of exclusion.

Most of the damage on this side of town had been from the wind tossing cars around or ripping roofs off, and since St. Charles sat atop a natural levee, there had been less flooding, and more people had been able to return home. Uptown being far livelier than downtown was a weird role reversal – the lack of damage to the Lower Garden District shocked me almost as much as seeing the damaged areas of the city. I was overjoyed for these residents, but it was frustrating that the people with the most money seemed to have experienced the least amount of damage. I was going to have to bury that thought if I wanted to survive my junior year at *the Academy.*

Désirée easily maneuvered the sprawling SUV into the school parking lot and cut the engine.

"So, do you have any advice for me?"

"You only need to remember one thing to survive at Sacred Heart," she said without looking my way. "Stay away from Annabelle Lee Drake."

"Who is Annabelle Lee Drake?"

"My bestie." Her fake tone was back to accompany her fake smile. It was as if she had switched on her uptown persona. She grabbed her bag and exited the car, slamming the door behind her.

As soon as I shut my door, a sharp noise signaled the activated alarm. I took it as a sign that I was now on my own. My heart sank a little, but what had I been expecting? That Désirée Borges and I would walk onto campus, arms locked, as she shouted introductions to all her friends? I took a peek at my reflection in the car window and tried to wipe the terrified expression off my face.

"Here goes nothing," I whispered and followed the gaggles of uniformed teenagers towards the large iron gate that surrounded the campus, protecting the city's finest youth from the proletariat.

16

uptown girls

THERE WAS NO DENYING that the school grounds were magnificent. The Greek-revival estate had a connected wing on each side and a white balcony that wrapped around the entire second floor. A large crucifix that had a green patina sat atop the small cupola on the roof. Workers bustled about, busy getting the courtyard landscaping back to its pre-Storm state.

As I walked through the giant iron archway that spelled out *Sacré Cœur,* I remembered riding up the hill on the back of Émile's Vespa to the original *Sacré Cœur* in Paris. From up top, we had watched the sun set over the city. The view from the hilltop basilica had been worth the trip to Paris in itself. Despite the symbolic pair of hearts sculpted every few feet into the concrete base of the building, I had a feeling that this Sacred Heart wasn't going to be as romantic. One heart had a flame and a dagger piercing the center, the other was wrapped in a crown of thorns. I didn't know a whole lot about Catholicism, but it seemed kind of twisted.

Wandering into the main building, I tried not to gawk at the other students. The halls were full of the kind of beauty only money could buy:

glistening teeth, shiny coifs, sparkly jewelry on French-manicured fingers, and these were only the obvious details. Hair extensions, nose jobs, and even breast implants enhanced some of the more permanently modified minors.

The hallway buzzed with energy. I wondered if it had always been this lively or whether the recent integration of Holy Cross' all-boy student body had anything to do with it. I tried to muster enough courage to approach a group of students that looked my age, but chickened out as soon as they looked at me. *Pathetic.* Instead, I walked over to a lonely-looking tween whose nose was buried in a book.

"Excuse me, can you tell me where the administration office is?"

Her face lit up as she pointed me in the right direction, and then looked a little sad when I thanked her and walked away. *Please don't let that be me in a week.* I looked at my watch and hustled through the office door.

"Miss Le Moyne, I presume?" asked a white-haired lady.

"Yes. Hi, I'm Adele—"

"Here's your schedule. They're waiting for you inside."

I pocketed the small card and paused in front of the set of closed oak doors; I had never been inside a principal's office. She motioned for me to go in. I exhaled loudly – the doorknob began to turn on its own. I frantically grabbed it and looked back at the secretary to make sure she hadn't seen anything unusual. Luckily, she was hunched over, cleaning her glasses on her blouse.

PRINCIPAL CAMPBELL'S OFFICE WAS CLASSIC FEELING: navy-blue brocade drapes, walls of books and lots of framed accolades. A middle-aged woman in a red skirt-suit, reading glasses, and a tight ashy-blonde French twist stood behind a large oak desk. She looked more like a high-powered CEO than a high school principal. Across from her sat two other students: a boy with skin as dark as espresso beans and a close-shaved head, who looked even less excited to be there than me; and a short, buxom blonde with large ringlets cascading down her back, who appeared born ready for this meeting.

I felt a moment of relief when I realized I wasn't going to be alone in this endeavor. *Maybe the three of us could band together as newcomers? I might actually be able to survive this place in a group of three.*

All six eyes followed me from the entrance. I snuck a glance at the clock on the wall. I was still two minutes early, which at Sacred Heart apparently meant that I was late.

"Please take a seat, Miss Le Moyne."

I moved quickly to the empty chair next to the boy. He was rubbing his head as if he expected something more to be there. It must have been a new cut.

Three fat files sat on Principal Campbell's desk, one for each of us. I stared at the manila folder with my name on it. *What about my life could possibly fill a two-inch-thick file?*

"Dixie Hunter, Tyrelle Johnson, and Adele Le Moyne, you are the three *displaced* students who were carefully selected to join the junior class of the Academy of the Sacred Heart. Holy Cross, in your case, Tyrelle." There was something about the tone in her voice that said we were not actually welcome – like someone had forced her to invite us to her party. I think only two of us picked up on it: Dixie smiled cheek-to-cheek as if she had just won the lottery, while Tyrelle adjusted his tie and slouched to one side in his chair, despondent. I was pretty sure I could see a tattoo under the edge of his cuff. This was someone I could get along with.

"I hope you understand what a stupendous opportunity you have been given, as we almost *never* accept transfer students." She slowly took her seat. "Nearly all the student body has received their entire education within these walls, so you have a lot of catching up to do. The Academy of the Sacred Heart holds the utmost standards when it comes to both academic performance and grooming virtuous young adults, and it is imperative that this standard is upheld both on campus and off. You are now a part of this prestigious institution, and that privilege does not go away when you walk out of the door."

Do not fidget, I repeated in my head as she continued talking up the school. But I was completely uncomfortable, both physically and mentally. I had to concentrate just to sit up straight.

She only glanced my way once (at my messy bun, with total contempt) because she rarely took her eyes off Tyrelle. Her eyes kept dropping to his chest. I couldn't see him doing anything offensive from my vantage, but I was too scared to move my head to get a real look. She said something in Latin, and I made sure to nod as affirmation of my attention.

"You must maintain an above-average grade point average, or you will automatically slip into academic probation. You will be expected to participate in extracurricular activities and to perform community service to ensure that your Ivy League college applications are impeccable. The Academy of the Sacred Heart has a 98% acceptance rate into the Ivies, and I won't let anyone drag that record down. Do I make myself clear?"

We all nodded.

"Adele, we're thrilled to have you transfer from Notre Dame International."

I blinked my eyes repeatedly, trying to keep them from rolling at the pretentious mention of Notre Dame, where I had attended school for only two months, as opposed to NOSA, where I had been for over two years.

"We'll expect great things from such a worldly artist."

Worldly artist? These people really do choose to believe whatever they want. "Um, I'll try not to disappoint."

Dixie and Tyrelle both looked at me, equally unimpressed. I responded with an awkward smile.

"Well, I think I speak for the three of us," Dixie said in a heavy Texas twang, "when I say that we are honored to be here, and I can't wait to get involved with the Academy." She sounded like a perfectly rehearsed pageant contestant. There was a long pause as she looked over to me and Tyrelle, as if it was our turn to suck up. Neither of us obliged.

Principal Campbell handed us each a thick handbook of the school's policies and values, which we had to sign and date before she cut us loose into the sea of teenage *pirañas*.

WE STOOD OUTSIDE THE OFFICE, examining our schedules.

"Well, I'm the token kid from the hood. How'd the two of you end up here?"

Now I could see the outline of a large gold chain underneath Tyrelle's white button-down shirt and tie. I patted the hidden *gris-gris* against my chest.

"I have no idea how I ended up here," I said. "I don't even recognize my own life right now."

"There are no tokens at the Academy," Dixie enlightened us. "We all paid our way in, fair and square."

"What's fair and square about paying your way into something?" I asked.

She looked at me with total confusion, as if I had said something in Chinese, and then turned back to Tyrelle. "My family just moved here from Dallas. My father owns the third largest construction company in the South, and he says this place is a gold mine. Lots of things around here need reconstructing."

I was speechless. I certainly hadn't bought Dixie's sickly-sweet Southern-girl act in the principal's office, but I couldn't understand how *anyone* could be so crass about the city's fragile, post-Storm condition. Sadly, I suspected it wouldn't be my last encounter with carpetbaggers moving to New Orleans to exploit the current state of affairs.

Dixie got no response from either of us, so she turned her back with a swirl of her skirt and flounced down the hall.

"And then there were two," I said, watching her walk away with the misguided confidence of a teen beauty queen. I turned to Tyrelle. "What class do you have next?"

He looked me up and down for a few seconds, as if trying to figure out whether to trust me or not. I guess I didn't meet his criteria, because he plugged in his earbuds and walked off, shaking his head in disgust.

Zero for two. If I couldn't even befriend the two other *displaced* students, how would I ever win over the natives? The bell rang loudly.

Lockers slammed. The hands of couples tore apart, and cliques scattered like flocks of startled birds. I double-checked my schedule while the crowd thinned. I didn't even need to look up from the paper to know that heads were turning as they walked passed me. Like Principal Campbell had said, "They rarely accept transfer students."

Great. My first period was A.P. English, the senior-level class they had stuck me in since, coming from art school, I was ahead in humanities credits – as if I needed one more reason to stick out.

"Are you lost?" asked a tanned, dirty-blond guy with a polished voice. He stopped directly in front of me.

"Yeah, actually, could you tell me where to find classroom 317?"

He extended his hand, and I surrendered my schedule.

"It's in the east wing." He gestured for me to follow.

I became nervous. *Is this some kind of trick, or is someone really being nice to me?* He didn't stare at me like all the other people in the hallway had been. I adjusted the bag on my shoulder and prepared to hustle, but he seemed utterly unconcerned about getting to class on time. We strolled.

"If you just explain where it is, I'm sure I can find it... so you don't have to be late for class." I peered at my schedule like it was a hostage between his fingers.

"Thurston." He held out his other hand. "Thurston Gregory Van der Veer III."

"*Enchanté*. Adele Le Moyne, NOSA transfer student," I answered, with a firm shake. There was something about him that exuded elitism. Maybe it was his perfect diction, or maybe the way his perfectly straight back made him appear as if he'd had equestrian training since he was a toddler? Whatever it was, I felt like a total mismatch walking beside him.

The instant rubbernecking by the few students left in the hall only reinforced my feelings.

"So, when did they merge Holy Cross?" I asked, following him up two flights of stairs. Holy Cross was even closer to the levee breaches than NOSA.

"About two weeks ago."

"Sorry about your school."

"Luckily only a fraction of each school's student body has returned post-evacuation, so this campus is not too overcrowded, yet. But I'm ready to get out of here." He examined the rest of my schedule as we sauntered down the third-floor hall. "You're a junior? In A.P. English? Only the best at the Academy, eh?"

Did I sense a hint of sarcasm?

"Yeah, well, don't get too impressed. I'm also in the sophomore-level science class. So, I guess that means you're a senior?"

"*Oui,* we also have French III together. Wait a second, why do you only have four classes?"

Before I could answer, we arrived in front of the door marked 317.

"Well, thanks for showing—"

He opened the door and held it for me. "I apologize for our tardiness, Sister Cecilia. I found Miss Le Moyne wandering the hallways, lost."

I tried to whisper, "Wait, you're in this class, too?"

"How chivalrous of you, Thurston," she replied with annoyance. "Oh, yes, Le Moyne, the junior."

I felt my face turn red as all the ears in the class perked up at the mention of the lowly word.

"You can take the empty seat right here in the front row."

I scurried to the desk, while Thurston took his seat on the other side of the room.

"Who is that girl?" someone whispered behind me.

"I don't know, but I'm texting Annabelle."

I sank into my seat, already regretting walking in the room with Thurston Gregory Van der Veer III. The one advantage to sitting in the front row was that if I didn't turn my head, I couldn't see the gossiping, glares, or other snide gestures. Adversely, my back felt exposed for anyone to stab, which escalated my paranoia.

My back.

My back was sore where Niccolò had caught me. I could still feel the imprints where his fingers had held me – *they'd better not bruise.*

"Before his metamorphosis," said Sister Cecilia, "Gregor is alienated from his job, his family, his humanity, and even his own body. This is evident when he barely even notices his transformation..."

How could someone barely notice they had turned into a giant bug?

As hard as I tried to pay attention to the lecture on "Guilt and Sense of Duty," I couldn't stop thinking about Niccolò. I couldn't get the image of his bloody mouth out of my head. *More importantly, was I being followed before I bumped into him?* The thought made me shudder.

"WELCOME TO SACRED HEART. I've just arrived from Holy Cross – maybe we can figure out this place together?" Mrs. Burg joked when I entered Pre-Cal.

My classmates seemed unimpressed by my instant bond with our math teacher. I chose a seat in the middle, not wanting to insult her by going straight to the back row. I had arrived with plenty of time, but that wasn't going to make my assimilation any easier. Now I had to fill the awkward minutes before class started. I opened my notebook and began sketching out the *Sacré Cœur* symbol.

Five girls entered the classroom together.

A gorgeous girl with thick, auburn hair and perfect, creamy skin walked a beat ahead of the rest. I sensed all eyes follow her from the doorway across the room. Dixie Hunter walked directly behind her, talking excitedly. Jealousy plagued me – two and a half hours into the day and Dixie was already hobnobbing with the inner circle? *Had this chick arrived with some kind of popularity manual that I was not privy to?* Désirée trailed behind them, uninterested in whatever Dixie was babbling about.

I sat up straight. *Would Désirée actually acknowledge me in front of her friends?*

The redhead walked straight to my desk. The group followed suit, creating a cloud-like clique hovering over me. Dixie and I were the only ones who seemed surprised by their pit stop.

None of them said a word. They just looked me up and down, probably trying to figure out if they had prejudged me correctly. Désirée rolled her eyes in boredom.

I stood up so I'd feel less like I was being preyed upon.

"Nice bag," Dixie said in a sweet voice wrapped in bitchy sarcasm.

All eyes went to the black canvas tote hanging on the back of my seat. The girls standing around me were all carrying leather ranging from Vuitton to Hermès. I immediately regretted not unpacking the Chanel bag *ma grand-mère* had bought me in Paris.

No expensive bag is going to make you one of these princesses, Adele.

The redhead touched the canvas and examined the barely noticeable, hand-painted fleur-de-lis – the bag's only marking.

"It's from this season's *Mode à Paris*." She shot Dixie a look of disapproval, and for the second time that day I saw confusion sweep over Dixie's face.

"That's Fashion Week in Paris," Désirée translated for her.

"How'd you come across one?" asked the redhead.

"I went to the *Comme des Garçons* show," I replied as if it wasn't a big deal, even though it had been the most exciting twenty minutes of my life. I didn't feel the need to tell her I had actually PA'd the show, or that the stage manager had swiped the swag bag for me as a thank you for the abuse I had suffered during the twenty-two straight hours of manual labor I had contributed for free.

The redhead looked impressed, but the moment was fleeting; I could see her begin to mull over the question of whether or not I was a threat.

"She just got back from Paris a couple of weeks ago," Désirée said, throwing me a bone.

"Bienvenue au Sacré Cœur. Je m'appelle Annabelle Lee Drake." She smiled and went to her seat before I had a chance to respond.

Dixie was in a total state of shock at how quickly the tables had turned. I couldn't help myself and gave her a tiny *don't mess with me* look, which Désirée caught – she cracked a smile, which felt like a major score, considering the only other time I had seen Désirée smile was around Gabe. As they walked to their seats, she turned to me with a look that said: *don't say I didn't warn you about Annabelle Lee.*

"That's the girl who was hanging all over Thurston this morning," came a voice from behind.

I turned around to find the girl pointing at me. *Hanging all over Thurston? We'd barely exchanged fifty words!* My pen shot off my desk.

"Sorry!" I said to the pimple-faced boy who handed it back to me.

If they were purposefully whispering loud enough to get a rise out of me, it was definitely working. I closed my eyes, took a couple of deep breaths, and focused all of my attention on the logarithmic functions being drawn on the chalkboard.

17

downtown boys, pt. 1

AS SOON AS THE BELL RANG, I practically skipped off campus, elated to miss the terror that was the lunchtime cafeteria and go to my mentoring session, but I came to a halt when I got to the street – I hadn't thought about getting home from school without Désirée. The St. Charles Streetcar line wasn't close to operational. I contemplated calling my father, but I was curious about how the rest of this side of town had weathered the Storm and decided that three miles wouldn't kill me.

Walking in public wearing the Catholic school uniform made everything feel even more surreal; the fact that I had survived my first day at Sacred Heart only exacerbated the weirdness. The fact that it hadn't been *that* bad made me nervous, like the calm before the storm. I plugged in my headphones, floated my phone from my pocket, and searched for happy music. By the time I reached the desolate streets of the mostly abandoned Warehouse District, I had already forgotten about the catty girls.

It was easy to identify which houses had residents who had returned post-evacuation. The garbage-collection service hadn't started back up, so the occupied buildings had mounds of trash sitting outside them on the curb. Dismantled storm boards, fallen trees, uprooted shrubs, piles of ruined sheetrock, moldy furniture, and boxes and boxes of books, clothes, and toys beyond salvageable – all stacked up in hill-sized heaps twice my height. Even the pop music couldn't change the sullen atmosphere as I passed by one blighted building after another.

When I arrived at our house, I found that our own trash mountain had grown considerably since I had left that morning. Several jars of dried paint told me that my father must have been cleaning out his studio. I pulled a thick bundle of canvases from the pile and unrolled the top layer. It was a sketch of the Mardi Gras masked ballerina. She always had a certain sadness to her – like she was dancing a tragic scene – but now water had dripped down the canvas and the charcoal had dried in streaks, making her appear to be weeping.

It made my own eyes well. My father had always been so attached to this piece of work, seeing him let go of it into a giant pile of garbage was not something I could deal with. I rolled the canvases back up and ran up to my bedroom to stash them, not wanting him to argue with me about reclaiming them.

"DAD?" I YELLED as I bounced back down the stairs.

Music poured from his studio. I opened the door to find a shirtless guy, who was certainly not my father, ripping down the remaining plaster from the damaged wall. His ratty jeans were covered in splatters of dried paint, and his light-brown hair was just long enough to fit into a tiny ponytail.

I tried not to stare, but it wasn't often I came across a half-naked man in our house. He swung the sledgehammer into the wall a few times, and just as I became fixated on the way the muscles in his back moved with the motion, my father shouted my name from another room and caused the guy to turn around—

"What are *you* doing here?" I yelled, hearing the shock in my own voice.

The corners of Isaac's mouth immediately turned up, and I crossed my arms in an aggressive stance.

"What are *you* doing here?" he echoed.

"I live here!" I wasn't sure if I was more shocked at finding Isaac in my house or at the tone of his upper body. Either way, I was at a loss for words.

"Nice uniform. I didn't take you for the Catholic schoolgirl type." He laughed. "I can't believe you're Mac's daughter."

What the hell? Isaac is on a first-name basis with my father?

"You expect me to believe this is just a coincidence?"

He held up his hands in innocence, although he didn't really seem that surprised to see me. My father walked in from the hallway with two stools from the kitchen. "Isaac, keep your shirt on in front of my daughter, please."

"Sure thing, Mr. Le Moyne—"

"I told you, call me Mac."

Isaac grabbed a dirty, white T-shirt and stretched it over his shoulders. I snuck another glance of his chest as I grabbed my father's wrist and pulled him into a corner. "What is he doing here?" I asked in a hushed voice.

"Good news, I finally found someone to repair the wall. Name's Isaac Thompson. He's down from New York City with his pop, working with Habitat for Humanity to rebuild houses. You'll never believe it, but we're doing a barter. He's going to help me fix the wall in exchange for some art lessons."

"Wait, what?" I felt like I was on another planet. *Isaac has been rebuilding houses?*

"He wants art lessons. I figured since we are going to be working on your NOSA mentorship every day, it might be nice for you to have a partner in crime." He smiled. "What's wrong, sweetheart? Do you know this boy?"

"Apparently not," I answered, still trying to process this Dr. Jekyll side of him. Isaac put the measuring tape down and looked up at me. My stomach surprised me with a small flutter.

Insecurity erupted.

I ran upstairs to get changed, cursing the stupid school uniform on my way, and quickly came back down in jeans and an old concert tee. My father had cleared off his workbench to simulate a classroom, and Isaac was sweeping up wall crumbles. I took a seat on one of the kitchen stools and tried to hide my disbelief that I was about to start my apprenticeship with Isaac.

When he finished, he leaned on the table next to me and looked me straight in the eyes. "Do you want me to leave?" The vulnerability in his voice hit me unexpectedly.

"Whatever. This day couldn't possibly get any more random."

"Famous last words," he said and pulled the other stool next to me.

A smile twitched my lips. His usual smug attitude had been replaced with... something else. Even though I was glad my father could get the wall fixed, I wasn't buying Isaac's innocent act just yet.

My dad stood before us in full metalsmith safety gear: boots, rubber apron, giant gloves and helmet. I'd seen him dressed like this thousands of times, but now it seemed utterly ridiculous. I had to suppress giggles as he droned on for twenty minutes about the importance of safety when working with chemicals and fire.

"I can't believe you are willingly subjecting yourself to this," I whispered to Isaac, without moving my head to look at him.

"Whatever, Mac is so cool," he whispered back.

I rolled my eyes and smiled.

"All right, let's move on," my father instructed. He seemed a bit nervous. "Take out your sketch pads."

"What?" I asked. "Why? Aren't we going to work with metal?"

"We will. Later."

"Later? After all of that?"

His eyes pleaded to cut him some slack.

I dashed upstairs to get my supplies and, upon my return, found Isaac's sketchpad lying on the table. Recent café memories flooded back, and I had to sit on my hands to keep myself from throwing it across the room.

Breathe.

I'd never met anyone who stirred such polarizing feelings in me, besides maybe my mother. *Maybe his Dr. Jekyll/Mr. Hyde thing is rubbing off on me?*

My father put one of his sculptures on the table – a two-foot-tall prototype of the ballerina at NOSA.

"I'm going to give you twenty minutes to draw this figure." He set an egg timer. "I want you to think about proportion and depth perception. Try to draw it as close to scale as you can."

I gazed at the figure and then back down at the blank page, trying to figure out where to start. I had only drawn three lines before my father came over and changed the position of my pencil in my hand.

"It feels awkward now," he said, "but once you get used to it, you'll have more control over the amount of pressure you're applying."

He repositioned Isaac's pencil, too, and then sat down across from us with this own sketchpad.

When the timer buzzed, my father put down his pad, but neither Isaac nor I did. Out of the corner of my eye, I could see that my father had not only sketched the entire figure but had already moved on to shading it. Isaac seemed to have finished the outline of the dancer. I was stuck on the feet.

"Pencils down. Don't worry if you aren't finished. I probably should have given you a bowl of fruit, but, ya know, there isn't a piece of produce within fifty miles of this place." He stood behind me and looked over my shoulder. "Nice job for a first try, especially given the time constraint." My father was good at turning a critique into some kind of backhanded compliment. "You need to work on proportion. See how your dancer is elongated?"

"Commentary on the emaciated state of ballerinas?" Isaac joked.

I shot him a dirty look. Just because I let him stay did not mean I was interested in his critique.

My father moved on to Isaac's pad.

"Nice job with the form, especially the slight arch of the back. Capturing movement is one of the hardest parts of drawing."

I tried not to get into a competitive mindset, but I was definitely annoyed that Isaac was already head of the class. As I listened to my father give him advanced tips, my attention moved to the pile of drawing tools on the table. I could swear the pile was *moving*.

My nose inched closer – an X-Acto knife was vibrating, causing the pile of charcoal pencils to shake. I blinked a couple of times, and the knife bounced.

I quickly slapped the tool down on the table and reached for its safety cap, causing them both to look up at me. I smiled, and they went back to the critique.

The knife continued to vibrate on the table. Even capped, the little blade made me nervous. I rested a book on top of it.

"Are you okay, sweetheart?" my father asked with a quizzical look.

"Mm hmm."

It rolled out from under the book and onto the floor. *Out of sight, out of mind.*

"Okay, we're going to repeat the exercise." He turned the statue upside down and leaned it in between two stacks of books so she stood on her head. "But this time I want you to try to forget this is a ballerina. Forget you know she's a woman and that she's wearing a tutu. Forget she's wearing a mask. I want you to look at the object like a newborn baby would, and draw what you see. A series of lines and curves. Groups of shadows and highlights. Try to draw each line exactly as you see it, and replicate each area of negative space as it relates to the boundaries which create it."

"Why are we doing this, Dad?" I asked, genuinely interested in the process.

"Our minds are trained to call on experiences we already know. Since you know you are drawing a ballerina, your memory informs you what a ballerina should look like. Turning the statue upside down will help you to draw what you *see* instead of what you *know*. Fight your intuition; draw what feels instinctual."

After staring for a couple of minutes, my mind eventually let go of the image of the upside-down ballerina, and I began to draw lines and shadows as if it was natural. When the timer went off, we both put down our pencils and eagerly flipped our pads around. I expected to see a crazy tangle of graphite, but, to my surprise, a ballerina was staring back at me – feet and all.

"Whoa."

"This is crazy," said Isaac.

I looked over at his two sketches. The second was nearly perfect. "Nice job."

"You both did a nice job," my father said. "Sometimes, being an artist is about forgetting the constructs society has been instilling in you since birth."

"Oh my God, Dad, you sound like…"

"What?"

"You sound like an actual teacher."

He laughed. "Is that so shocking?"

"Well, yeah, kind of… it's just that teachers are old and bald, and you are… I don't know, not that."

"What are you saying? You think I'm cool?"

"Well, no, you are still my dad."

"On that note, I'm going to quit while I'm ahead. That's it for the day."

"Thanks, Mac. That was awesome."

Does he mean that, or is he just sucking up? My day around the student body of Sacred Heart had me questioning everyone's motives.

My dad turned the miniature statue upright and asked, "So, Isaac, how long have you been in town?"

"We arrived from New York about forty-eight hours after the Storm hit, since my father was consulting for the Feds on the initial damage assessment—"

"How exactly did you get in from New York that soon after the Storm hit?" I asked.

"We flew to Jackson, Mississippi, and then drove down to Stennis Space Center. The National Guard took us to the city limits in a giant Hummer, transferred us to a boat, and sent us downriver to the French Quarter. It was pretty surreal. We thought we'd be here for a couple of weeks, but you know how the story goes."

Isaac came down on a rescue mission? Seriously?

"So, how do you like New Orleans, despite everything?" my father asked.

"Well, to be honest, sir, I haven't really seen much of the city. I have to get up at four-thirty a.m. to be on site by five. Plus, the curfew."

"That's very admirable, son."

"Thanks. I would really like to see the city, though. It seems like a pretty special place."

I struggled not to snap my pencil in half. I could see where this was going.

"Well, I'm sure Adele wouldn't mind showing you around. Right, sweetheart?"

"Dad!"

"What? You know so much about the city from all of those books you read, and you can explain how everything is supposed to look. How it will be again, once everything is rebuilt—"

"I would love that," Isaac said, trying to look innocent.

Trickster, I thought, fuming.

"You want to see the town?" I asked sweetly. "Meet me in front of the Cathedral at seven."

"It's a date," he replied, with a look of concern over my sudden change in mood.

"It's not a date," my father corrected. "Don't make me change my mind."

"I mean, not a *date* date—"

"If she's not back by curfew, I can assure you, there will never be another nondate. Is that clear?"

"You've got room to talk," I muttered.

"What was that, sweetheart—?"

"Yes, sir," Isaac said. "You don't have to worry."

"I'm serious, Isaac. I get that you're from New York City, but crime's different here. If I hear that she leaves your sight, it will be the last time you hang out."

"Dad!"

"No problem, sir. I completely understand, Mr. Le Moyne— I mean, Mac."

"*I'll* make sure I'm back by curfew, not Isaac," I snapped. "Don't talk about me as if I am not here!" I began to yawn uncontrollably. I tried my best to fight it, but the sleepless night was catching up with me. "I need to take a nap if I am going to make it through our date tonight."

"It's not a date, Adele!" my father insisted as I left the table.

"Uh huh." I hoped it made him sweat. That was the least he deserved for inadvertently playing matchmaker.

"I'll see you at seven in front of the Cathedral," Isaac said. I turned back from the door – he was trying not to smile as he packed up his things.

"Don't be late or the deal's off."

18

downtown boys, pt. 2

I COULD HAVE EASILY SLEPT THROUGH THE NIGHT. Yawning, I cranked the Victrola, then forced myself out of bed and into sheer turquoise tights and a black sweater-dress from Paris. If I was late meeting Isaac, my grand plan wouldn't work out.

I quickly reapplied the day's makeup, stealing a few seconds to add a little smoky eyeliner – there was a decent chance we would run into my father down at the bar, and I hoped my appearance would make him think twice before putting me into this position again. Spritz of perfume. His behavior surprised me. Normally, he did anything he could to keep boys away. Especially boys with long hair and attitudes. Accessorized, I reknotted the loose bun on top of my head and skipped out the door just as "Ziggy Stardust" wound down.

THE SUN WAS SETTING; a breeze pricked my legs through the tights – the temperature had dropped since I'd last been out. I debated going back for a jacket, but didn't want to risk being late.

Jackson Square felt creepy without the fortunetellers, artists, and street performers that usually littered the pedestrian streets late into the night. I was surprised but happy to see a few other people standing around the old town square. Isaac was sitting on the steps of the gated park in front of the Cathedral. When the click of my ankle booties against the slate came within earshot, he looked up.

"Hey." The relief in his voice didn't escape me.

"Did you think I wasn't going to show?"

"No, but I guess I kind of deserve to be stood up."

"Yeah, don't ever pull anything like that again."

"Just say yes the next time I ask you out and I won't have to."

I immediately wanted to smack off his curt smile, but before I could fire back, he quickly added, "I'm sorry, I'm sorry. I don't want to fight on our first date."

"It's not a date, remember?"

"Call it whatever you want. I'm just glad I managed to get you here."

"It's not like I really had any say in the matter."

He ignored the comment. "So what are we doing here, anyway?"

"*Ma bébé!*" That was exactly the booming voice I wanted to hear. "To what do I owe this pleasure?"

I turned around, straight into a crushing hug. "Ren… ribs… can't breathe."

His eyes were fixed on Isaac before he even set me down. "Hmm, curious…"

"Ren, Isaac wants to learn about the great city of *La Nouvelle-Orléans*, so I thought, what better way to get to know the city than on your walking tour?"

"I see. *Oui, oui. Bienvenue.*" He looked Isaac up and down, as if assessing his heckler-likelihood.

Isaac leaned close to me and lowered his voice: "Nice one."

I tried my best to contain my extra-wide grin.

"*Laissez les bons temps rouler!*" Ren yelled, accepting the challenge.

Isaac looked to me. "Are you going to give me a clue?"

I laughed. "In Louisiana at least, it means, 'Let the good times roll.'"

"Gather around, everyone," Ren called out to the few people lingering in the square. "So glad you all decided to brave the nightfall. I'm sad to say this tour is going to be cut a little short thanks to the Parish-wide curfew, but don't worry, you'll still get all the tales because we won't be making any drinking pit stops. Unfortunately, everything is closed. Everything legal that is, er—" He cut himself off when he saw the inquisitive look on my face. "But please feel free to partake in your own libations if you brought them." He lifted his coat to reveal his flask. "It is perfectly legal to drink here on the streets of *La Nouvelle-Orléans.*"

The tour hadn't even begun and already people were enthralled by Ren. "I wonder if he dresses like that all the time?" one of them whispered. I chuckled. Ren was in full gear tonight, somewhere in between the gentleman pirate Jean Laffite and the vampire Lestat.

A quick round of introductions told us that five out of the eight other people on the tour were recovery workers from various organizations and one couple was visiting to help relatives clean out their house. The last person, a blonde woman, offered no real information about herself. Her hair, which flowed down her back in beautiful, wild waves, was so bright it glowed white, and despite the temperature she wore a skintight tank top and a gauzy pink skirt that blew when the breeze picked up. *How is she not freezing?*

I looked at Isaac, who was just in a white T-shirt. "Aren't you cold?"

"No, I'm a New Yorker, remember?"

"Right, how could I have forgotten?"

The woman looked at me, her lips puckering daringly. Chills swept up my spine. I looked away and crossed my arms.

"Oh, are you cold?" he asked.

"No, I'm fine." I dropped my arms to appear more convincing.

Ren went around the group, collecting money. When he got to us, Isaac pulled out two twenty-dollar bills.

"I can get my own ticket."

"No, I got it. You wouldn't even be here if it wasn't for me," he insisted, but I shook my head. I didn't want to owe Isaac anything.

"Like I'd ever take your money, *ma chérie*," Ren said to me. "But I'll gladly take yours." He plucked one of the bills from between Isaac's fingers.

"I promise, I'll be on my best behavior," he reassured Ren.

"Oh, honey, I love trouble. Don't change your ways on account of me."

"I'm not changing them on account of you," Isaac said and then glanced at me.

"Interesting...," Ren mumbled, looking back and forth between us, "very interesting."

My eyes dropped to the floor.

"Time to start, folks!" he yelled to the group and then beckoned us to follow him down Pirate's Alley just as the sun set.

The flames in the gas lamps became visible, creating the perfect ambiance for a ghost tour, and the bells in the steeple clanged as if they were a planned part of his act. He stopped halfway down the alley and, after an attention-commanding pause, proceeded to tell us the story of how the infamous alley got its name. As he spoke, he focused briefly on something behind us, and then the echoing sounds of heels on stone became louder. I turned to see the silhouette of a girl running down the alley towards us.

Is that Désirée Borges?

Isaac's back stiffened. "Do you know that girl?"

"Sort of."

"Sorry, I'm late," she grumbled, pulling cash from her wallet, but Ren shook his hand, motioning for her not to interrupt. She merged into the group next to me. I couldn't tell if she was annoyed or relieved to see someone she knew. Especially since that someone was me.

"What are you doing here?" I whispered.

"My dad forced me." She sounded annoyed. "You know, help boost tourism, support local businesses, blah, blah, blah."

"Hmm. I'm still surprised you came."

"I have a plan, and it doesn't involve staying." She pointed to a small camera in the pocket of her blazer.

"In that case…" Ren snapped the twenty from her hand. "*Bienvenue*." Even with the interruption, he didn't skip a beat. "Listen up, folks, there are two alleyways on either side of the St. Louis Cathedral: one is named after a pirate and the other for a priest. Scientists from all around the world flock to one of them, and claim that it has one of the highest records of concentrated paranormal activity on the planet. Can you guess which?"

Everyone laughed.

"Of course, we New Orleanians do not need gadgets and gizmos to record noises and auras in order to know when we're in a nexus of supernatural activity." He looked directly at the blonde woman as he carefully articulated the last sentence. Her back straightened, and her face lit up. She loved it.

"This way!" He walked us around the church, where an illuminated statue of Jesus cast a fifty-foot shadow on the back of the Cathedral. *I guess the Church thought Jesus deserved a generator?*

I tried to gauge Isaac's interest. Like everyone else, he was hanging onto Ren's every word. I had to force back a smile as I watched his fully engrossed profile.

"*Psst. Adele*, come take a picture of me in front of the statue, but wait until some other people are behind me so it proves I was on the tour."

"Come on, Désirée, it's rude. I don't want to distract Ren."

"Oh, please, that statue of Jesus could start twerkin' and Ren wouldn't break character."

She had a point. Plus, I wanted her to pick me up for school tomorrow. I sighed and grabbed the camera. "Get close to the light so I don't have to use the flash." I hurried to frame the shot as the group walked behind her.

She held her extra-fake grin as the shutter took the long exposure. I returned her camera and begrudgingly hopped back to Isaac, who was watching me like a hawk. Ren began describing the ghost of Julie, who haunted the Bottom of the Cup Tearoom.

"Only in New Orleans," I whispered to Isaac. He smiled.

Across the street from Café Orléans, Ren pointed out the luxurious Bourbon Orleans Hotel, explaining that it had once been an orphanage and was, to this day, haunted by children who had burned alive in a tragic fire. The possibility of little ghost children peeking through the curtains at us made me hurry Isaac along.

We walked another couple blocks and stopped on the corner of St. Ann and Royal Street. The moon shone over the corner building like a spotlight for us. The dark-green floor-to-ceiling shutters were latched closed, and wrought-iron balconies wrapped around the second and third floors of the maroon-colored, three-story residence.

"John and Wayne Carter were two brothers who seemed to be just your average men—"

The woman with the long, blonde hair let out a loud cackle and then quickly tried to calm herself. "*Pardon moi*," she said and squeaked out another giggle.

Désirée mouthed the word "nutcase" to me. I suppressed a laugh and turned back to Isaac, who was staring hard at the woman, and then became nervous that the naysayer might make an appearance. Luckily, Isaac fell behind with me as I dropped to the back of the group so others could gather close to Ren for the tale.

"By the way, you look really nice tonight," he whispered close to my ear. Feeling his breath on my skin made my shoulders tingle.

The compliment caught me off guard. "You look, uh, clean," I joked.

"Ha, ha. Some of us have to get our hands dirty while others go to fancy schools."

"That's not—"

Hands from behind wrapped around my eyes.

"*Piacere!* What's going on here? Did our invitations to the *festa* get lost in the mail?" There was no way Niccolò would say something so cheesy, which left only one *Italiano* to suspect.

"Your hands are cold, Gabriel," I guessed, spinning around to face him.

"How did you know it was me?" He kissed both of my cheeks and then moved out of the way so the younger Medici brother could do the same.

"*Ciao*," Niccolò said, looking almost bashful.

"The tour has already begun," said Ren.

Isaac smirked.

The blonde woman stared intensely at Niccolò. The way he stared back at her – it was like they were silently daring each other. *Was she the reason for Niccolò's early-morning stroll?*

Ugh. I tried to convince myself that what Niccolò Medici was doing at dawn was none of my business, but still… I wanted to know. Her stern expression faltered momentarily when Gabe smiled at her with a hint of glee. It was painfully obvious they all knew each other.

"Are you sure you can't take just two more?" Gabe asked, approaching Ren with a couple of crisp bills. "We're very generous tippers," he added, looking him straight in the eyes.

"I've always had a hard time saying no to a handsome foreigner. *D'accord*, the more, the merrier."

Out of the corner of my eye, I saw Isaac scowl.

Niccolò turned to me and, no longer bashful, touched my face. "Your wound is finally healing." He kept one eye on my cheek and the other on Isaac, as if he was some kind of abusive boyfriend – which wasn't fair and certainly didn't go unnoticed by Isaac.

"So little time, so much to see," Ren yelled, scooping his arm towards Bourbon Street. "This way people, *allons-y!*" Isaac grabbed my arm and pulled me along as the group began to move again.

"So, Dee, are you still leaving, or do you need more pictures?"

Désirée must have noticed the bizarre exchange between the brothers and the woman, too, because she looked straight at the blonde, as if rising to the challenge. "Oh, I'm definitely going to need more pictures." She wrapped her arm around Gabe and snapped a selfie. They looked like a pair of supermodels.

"I'm sure you all know that the *Vieux Carré*, or French Quarter, is the oldest neighborhood in New Orleans and was settled by Bienville in the year 1718. What you probably don't know is that most of the buildings around you are not actually French. Two great fires in the eighteenth century destroyed nearly everything in the Quarter.

"Spain occupied the city at the time when the old square was rebuilt, so most of the buildings standing before you were constructed by the Spanish. There are only four original French structures remaining" – he looked straight at me and Désirée – "a Voodoo shop, a Creole cottage on Burgundy Street, the Ursuline Convent, and this former brothel."

I had known our house was an original French cottage (there was even a plaque on the outside from the historic registry), but I had no idea it was one of only four.

"Wow, I can't believe I'm working on one of those places," Isaac whispered, nudging me.

"You might be thinking it's curious that these four buildings survived all of these years, through the fires and the storms. Was it a *coincidence*? After all, what do a convent, a brothel, a Creole cottage and a Voodoo shop have in common? Of course, it wouldn't have been a Voodoo shop back then…"

"Back then, that sort of thing wasn't legal," Désirée finished.

"That's correct, Mademoiselle Borges. In the early seventeen hundreds, so soon after the height of American witchcraft hysteria, any shop selling magic fixin's would've been illegal. It would've appeared to be just a cottage, except items may or may not have been sold out of a back room, and said items might have come with a little *lagniappe. Gratis.* But you would know more about that than li'l ole me."

Désirée rolled her eyes as his accent thickened for the tourists, and then he hurried us along towards the house of New Orleans's most famous murderess, Madame LaLaurie. I started to move forward with the group, but a tug at my sweater made me pause.

"Hey." Niccolò's hand lingered on my arm. "I just want to apologize for this morning." Just the sound of his soft voice brought me back to our tangled embrace.

"For what?"

"For acting so weird. The truth is, my brother and I were out drinking, and we got into a little scuffle with some guys who were being foolish. I didn't want you to think I was that kind of guy."

"What kind of guy?" I wrapped my arms around myself.

"Are you cold?"

"N—" Before I could answer, he stripped off his black leather jacket and swept it around my shoulders.

"*Grazie*. Someone hit you?"

"Oh, Adele, don't worry about Nicco," Gabe answered, joining the conversation out of nowhere. "You should have seen the other guy."

Niccolò rolled his eyes as Gabe tousled his hair.

"Why would someone hit you?" I asked. It was hard to imagine. Niccolò seemed like such the quiet guy in the corner. Gabe, on the other hand, I could totally see instigating a brawl.

"I could think of a couple reasons…." Isaac reappeared, Désirée in tow.

Niccolò's jaw tightened.

"Don't start, Isaac." I could see Mr. Hyde coming out to play.

"Save it for the fraternity house, boys," Désirée put her arm around me and walked us back towards the crowd. "Don't look back. Pretend you don't care."

"I *don't* care."

"Riiiiiight."

"She's beautiful *and* unforgiving," Gabe yelled. "My favorite combination."

I felt Désirée's entire body smile, not that it showed on her face. He ran after us, put one arm around each of our shoulders, and broke us apart. Together, the three of us hurried to catch up with the rest of the tour. Désirée let out a genuine giggle.

We had missed nearly the entire story on *le Comte de Saint-Germain.* Something to do with a residence on the corner of Royal and Ursuline.

"And the next two tales bring us to the end of the tour."

When I looked up from underneath Gabe's arm, we were standing directly behind the old Ursuline Convent. My heart began to knock. *Paranoid much?* Gabe looked down at me as if he could hear the pounding.

I moved from underneath his arm to the familiar gate.

This time when the chills rushed up my spine, I simultaneously broke out into a sweat. I tightened Niccolò's jacket around my torso and looked up at the convent attic – the window I had witnessed explode open was now completely bricked up, preventing even the moon's beams coming and going.

Ren leapt onto the hood of a previously drowned car and paused for dramatic effect as he prepared himself for *la grand finale.*

"New Orleans came to be thanks to the real *crème de la crème de la société Parisienne*. And by that I mean the thieves, crooks and murderers. That's right, folks, New Orleans started as a penal colony. These fine founding citizens were convicts from La Bastille who had been granted pardons by the King in exchange for building the grand capital of New France. So, early on, the city was a cesspool of scoundrels and scalawags, which means not much has changed since." He winked and then took an exaggerated sip from his flask.

"These unruly Frenchmen survived hurricanes, indigenous swamp creatures, and the cannibalistic ways of certain native tribes, but how could a population of only men evolve into the society meant for such a fine city? They demanded, pleaded, and begged the King to send over women! Being a reasonable man, the King emptied the female correction houses and raked the streets for ladies of the night, who were then shipped to New France like a platter of beignets, though not nearly as sweet.

"Now, King Louis XIV was on a mission for *La Nouvelle-Orléans* to be the Paris of the New World. Propaganda was launched across

France to arouse adventurous men to seek their fortunes in this new land of opportunity. In response, a new class of Frenchmen made the grueling journey across the Atlantic Ocean – only to find a giant swampland full of mosquitos, alligators, and serpents.

"Of course, it wasn't long before they, too, demanded the King send ladies! Having already ridden the French streets of extra undesirables, King Louis scavenged hundreds of virtuous young French women from convents and orphanages to send to these opportunity-seekers. He gave the girls a small dowry and sent them on their merry way to marry the colonists and propagate the burgeoning city. The small chests, or cassettes, given to the woman to hold their wedding dresses looked very similar to caskets and earned them each the title *la fille à la cassette,* or simply, the casquette girls, as the locals say."

"And what does the Ursuline Convent have to do with any of this?" asked a voice from the crowd.

"Excellent question! Now, for as much of this city's soul is built on Hoodoo traditions, Native American spirits, and everything in between, the Catholics also dutifully staked their claim into the soggy soil of *La Nouvelle-Orléans.* And there was no better example of that sense of duty than the sisters from the Order of the Saint Ursula.

"The Ursuline nuns came to New Orleans with the duty of opening *L'Hôpital des Pauvres de la Charité,* or Charity Hospital, which is the second-oldest running hospital in the country – or at least it was before the Storm. But the sisters were not content to simply run the city's only hospital, for their real mission was education. Before leaving France, they made a deal with the bishop: they would gladly make the perilous journey across the Atlantic to a bayou country full of savages and pirates, and tend to the sick, if – and only if – they were also allowed to open a school. And so they did on the property that stands before you, a school that served only girls – *all* girls, regardless of race, color or social class.

"It's said that it was the Ursuline sisters who took in the casquette girls when each shipload from France docked in the French Quarter. They stored the girls' cassettes in the convent attic for safekeeping, and then housed, educated, and chaperoned them until each was married off.

"As things go in New Orleans, scandal struck when the first marriage proposal was accepted, for when the sisters went to fetch the girl's cassette they discovered, to everyone's dismay, that it was empty. No dowry from the King. No wedding dress. Nothin' but cobwebs. Every cassette in their care had been emptied."

Ren switched to an unidentifiable Eastern European accent.

"Legend has it that the casquette girls had smuggled *strigoi* across the ocean in those casket boxes, and these vampires had been sleeping in the attic during the day and running amuck at night, feeding on anyone they fancied. New Orleans was the perfect cover. Between the crime and the disease, death rates were already astronomical. Who would bat an eye when another dead body turned up? Who was going to notice another missing ex-con or prostitute?"

I began to wrap and unwrap my chain around my fingers.

Blue eyes. Dead, blue eyes.

Ren looked around the silent crowd. "And that's the story of how the vampires came to New Orleans. To America."

"Riveting," said Gabe, looking at the blonde, who seemed oddly somber.

"So what's the deal with that attic window?" I blurted.

The group turned to see who had spoken.

"I'm so glad you asked, m'lady. If you walk around the French Quarter, you'll quickly find that every set of attic windows is permanently latched open. Can anybody guess why?"

"Because of the heat," Niccolò answered dryly.

"Exactly correct, my fair-faced friend! It gets hotter than Hell here in southern Louisiana, and in the early eighteenth century there was no central air. Since heat rises, the attics were the hottest rooms in these Creole cottages, and they were also where the children often slept. The shutters on the attic windows were kept permanently latched open out of fear they'd swing shut in the middle of the night, leaving the dreaming youngsters to cook to death.

"However, as you can see, the attic windows of the Ursuline Convent are all latched *shut*. Legend says that when the empty cassettes were found, the Ursulines contrived a plan in the name of the Lord and went to work. Nine thousand nails were sent from the papacy in Rome, after being blessed by the Pope himself, to secure the shutters of the attic windows. They closed up the attic completely to protect their convent and the citizens of New Orleans from the attic's deviant denizens."

The blonde's eyes lit with excitement. "Ha! Like za Catholic Church could imprison a clan of vampires!" she said with conviction.

Was her accent French?

Désirée slowly walked to the convent gate and peered through the iron posts. "I agree with blondie. It sounds like there was more going on here than the work of the Lord."

"Well, honey, you know that in the Big Easy, there's always more than meets the eye."

He gave us a minute to take it all in.

A history of strange or unusual happenstances flooded my head. My pulse began to race as I thought about every shadow, every creak, every unexplainable occurrence I had never given a second thought to before. Désirée also seemed to be processing something buried in her subconscious. *Maybe she was thinking the same thing?* After all, we were the only two who had been born in this town where the debate between fact and fiction is grayer than the newsprint it's read from.

"As you can see, a shutter is missing from one of the windows. I have it on good authority that it fell off only a week ago... and yet somehow, even in this time of chaos, the archdiocese managed to brick up the window right away. Whatever could cause such urgency when there are people to feed, houses to rebuild?" Ren slowly scanned the crowd. "I don't know the answers, I just tell the stories."

Violent chills spread throughout my entire body until my teeth began to chatter uncontrollably.

Breathe.

"Hey, are you okay?" asked Isaac. "You look even paler than usual."

I nodded, unable to move my eyes from the attic window.

"You're trembling." He put his arm around me.

On the verge of a claustrophobic fit, I quickly stepped away from him and followed Ren as he moved halfway down the block.

"Another version of the story claims that the vampires were able to move through the windows at night. Barely more than a decade ago, a college-aged couple came to town from California, with the brilliant plan to make a documentary on our extracurricular nightlife. A little home video. Capture footage of anyone who came or went from the attic windows at night. They set up their cameras and camped out in front of St. Mary's Church, which used to be the chapel of the Ursuline Convent. The next morning, their bodies were discovered… drained of eighty percent of their blood. On their tapes, nothing but static. There was no evidence of—"

"I heard it was a woman who killed zhat couple," said the blonde.

Niccolò moved to my side, and Ren hurried along with the story, speaking directly to her. "There were a few unreliable witnesses who claimed to have seen a young brunette bent over the bodies." His gaze moved to me. "But there was never enough evidence to hold even a single suspect for more than a long weekend."

He carried on with his story, but the memory of the methodical slaps of the shutter hitting the frame clogged my ears. It got louder and louder and faster and—

A sharp whistle brought me back to the present.

Everyone around me was clapping enthusiastically, cheering for Ren as he took deep bows. The tour was over. I put my hands together in appreciation and forced a smile. *It's only a stupid story, Adele, chill out.*

The blonde turned to Gabe with a smile that could only mean she was looking for trouble. "Surely zhere is something to get into tonight? It is still *La Nouvelle-Orléans,* after all. How much could it have really changed?"

Definitely a French accent. Definitely trouble.

Niccolò looked at her and then to me. "How are you getting home?"

"Uh, walking—"

"I'll walk you."

"That won't be necessary," Isaac said, stepping in between us.

Niccolò smirked, almost beckoning a challenge, which in turn made Gabe grin from ear to ear.

My eyes rolled at the ripple of testosterone. "Ren, will you walk me home?"

"At your service, *Mademoiselle*."

Isaac shot me an exasperated look, being unable to fulfill the promise he had made to my father about not letting me out of his sight.

Gabe offered his hand to Désirée, but Isaac walked in front of it. "I got it," he snapped, not giving her a chance to disagree, which I thought was kind of hilarious.

As Isaac pulled her hand forward, her head turned back to me. "See you at seven, Adele. And try not to be late tomorrow morning." She gave Niccolò an obnoxious look of approval, which everyone noticed. My cheeks burned like they were on fire.

"*Merci beaucoup,* and goodnight, folks!" Ren yelled with a giant grin. "*Au revoir,* boys. *À la prochaine!*" He spun me in the direction of my house, linking his arm through mine.

"*Ciao,*" I yelled over my shoulder to Niccolò, Gabe… and the blonde.

19

la fille à la cassette

"OH, TO BE YOUNG AGAIN and have so many gentleman callers fawning all over," Ren said with an exaggerated Southern accent. I laughed as he let out an exasperated sigh.

"No one is fawning over me. I have even less life post-Storm than I had pre-Storm, which I didn't think was possible."

"Oh, child, you are growing into quite the ingénue, aren't you?"

"Hmm… I'm not sure that's a good thing."

"Or maybe you are still too hung up on the Parisian *garçon* to see the hot young things right in front of your face?"

Ugh, Jeanne must have been running her mouth about Émile.

"Can I ask you something, Ren?" Nervousness flooded from my stomach all the way to my shoulders, making them tingle. "How much of that stuff do you believe?"

"There you go, changing the subject. That means you *are* sweet on one of them. Which one is it? I'm going to guess the Yankee. You two bicker too much to actually dislike each other."

"Ren!"

"So, it's the foreign fox?"

"Stop! I'm serious. It's important!"

"D'accord, d'accord. How much of *that stuff* do I believe?" He twisted the end of his moustache. "Well, I believe bits and pieces of all of it. Legends are legends for a reason; they don't just appear out of thin air. But over the years, they morph for different reasons. They evolve to serve a purpose of the time."

"But what about these stories? The Carter brothers, the casquette girls, the filmmakers…"

"You mean the vampire stories?"

"Yeah, I guess."

"In the words of the great Monsieur Baudelaire, 'The greatest trick the devil ever played was convincing the world he didn't exist.'"

My eyes moved to the lantern above his head, and I began to twist the ring around my finger.

"Why so serious, darlin'? What's the mat—?"

"I think I opened the attic window at the Ursuline Convent."

He looked at me blankly for a moment. "Why on earth would you think that, *bébé?"*

"It was right when we got back into town. I had just discovered a dead body in a car. I cut my hand on the broken window. I'd never seen a dead body before. His blue eyes were just staring at me and… I ran. When I stopped in front of the convent to catch my breath, the shutter just started flapping, only there was no wind…"

He put his hand on my shoulder and pulled me into a narrow alleyway. "Breathe, darlin'."

"I didn't mean to trespass. It was like the window pulled me in, and before I knew it, I was in the courtyard. I didn't touch anything, I swear— the shutter flapped itself until it came crashing down! The window shattered and…"

"And?"

The last words rushed out of my subconscious in a shrill whisper. *"And something flew out!"* I froze, admitting to myself for the first time what had happened that morning: something had come out of that window. I *knew* it. He looked at me with a serious but sympathetic expression.

"What flew out? Some kind of monster?"

"Well, no... maybe... I don't know! It was raining, and it all happened so fast, and my hand was bleeding all over the place— I didn't see anything, but I swear that I *heard* something, Ren. And I *felt* something."

The fear that flicked in his eyes made me immediately regret telling him. He drew me into a hug, but I quickly pulled away.

"You don't really think there were vampires trapped in the attic, do you?"

"Calm down, *bébé*. There is no way you opened that window. It's just some bizarre coincidence."

"I thought you didn't believe in coincidences?"

"Stop worrying your pretty little head." His acting skills were no longer as convincing, but I appreciated him not being patronizing. "I'm sorry if the story spooked you."

"How are you so certain I didn't open it?"

"Well, the story has more holes than a New Orleans' road. Besides nails from the Vatican, it's been said that magic was used to keep the vampires trapped inside the attic. Naturally, the church quickly quelled the rumor but, unless those nuns had some other miraculous gifts from God, that theory makes the most sense to me. The only thing I can tell you for certain is that there's no way you could have accidentally undone the spell of another. Only the original caster of a spell could undo it."

He smoothed my hair.

That seemed plausible to me. I didn't know anything about binding or unbinding spells, but I desperately wanted to grasp onto anything that proved I hadn't unleashed a drove of bloodsucking killers into the city I loved so much.

"Adele, you were traumatized: the city's a ruin, you had just discovered a corpse, and it was pouring rain. Plus, it looks like you have men lining up at the door to protect you." He winked, attempting to lighten the mood, but I was hardly paying attention – my mind was rewinding all of the weird things that had happened since the Storm.

"Can I ask you one more thing?"

"*Oui*, of course."

The two copper gas lanterns over our heads began to swing back and forth, creaking.

"Do you really believe in magic? Like, *really.*"

"*Oui, bébé.* Moving pictures and flying machines both seemed like magic at one time. It's not a huge leap to believe that what seems irrational or magical now will be commonplace in the future. I believe everyone has magical powers. However, only certain people – the ones who are open to it – can tap into the true capacity of the mind and push the current brink of human thought. Some are called geniuses, some are called prophets, others are called witches."

"So, if someone is not open to magic, they could prevent supernatural things from happening?"

He chuckled. "If only it were that easy, *bébé*. Sometimes magic finds us; we don't find it. And once it does, it's nearly impossible to close ourselves to it. It would be like trying to forget how to read or speak or walk. Usually people who unlock magic within themselves don't understand their importance in the world."

I frowned. *Hadn't I heard that before?*

"Just remember, everything happens for a reason. *D'accord?*"

"Okay."

"Anything else?"

I paused, debating whether I should tell him about my recent bout of telekinesis. Instinct pinched my lips and shook my head. Luckily, he let it rest and linked our arms back together.

"*Lâche pas la patate, bébé*," he said when we got to the front door. "That I can guarantee. Whatever it is, you'll figure it out." He kissed my cheek instead of giving me one of his bear hugs.

"Merci beaucoup."

"*Bonne nuit*. Sweet dreams." He waited for me to slip inside and lock the door.

Through the peephole, I watched him walk down the street. That's when I noticed the crow perched on top of the street sign, staring in my direction. I stumbled backwards into a small table and grasped the overhanging mirror as it slid on the wall.

"Dad?" I called out into the dark house.

No answer came. *He must be at the bar.* At least he wouldn't know that I had arrived ten minutes past curfew.

A MILLION THOUGHTS SPIRALED as I lay on my bed, arms crossed, staring at the lamp light. *You've got to relax, Adele.*

Like that's going to happen.

The Victrola suddenly cranked on, but the glam-rock beats just made me more restless. Without moving from my spot, I managed to move the needle off the vinyl, but I couldn't get the record to budge. I paused from my ceiling-staring, swapped in the Louis Armstrong album, and quickly flopped back down.

I didn't want to believe that I had released a bunch of monsters into the city… monsters who had been trapped in a convent attic for three hundred years and who were probably really pissed off about it. I *really* didn't want to believe that.

My fingers strummed my stomach, and my feet rocked nervously back and forth – then a loud crack exploded.

"Shit!" I sat up in the sudden darkness, clutching my chest.

The lamp bulb had combusted. *Breathe.*

As I sucked in air, all of a sudden a little flame slowly grew from a vanilla-scented candle on the fireplace mantel.

This is not happening.

This is not happening.

I stared at the fire, and a second flame ignited from a neighboring candle.

"This is happening."

I jumped up from the bed, flipped on the overhead light, and looked around the room, wishing there was a witness to tell me that I wasn't going crazy. When my gaze landed on the closet, the brass handle turned, and the door slowly creaked open a few inches.

I swallowed a lump in my throat. *At this rate, I'm going to have a heart attack before my seventeenth birthday.*

"*C'est parfait!*" I yelled like a lunatic, instead of giving into the fear. "A good cleaning project is exactly what I need!" I walked straight towards the little room and waved my hand through the air.

The door swung all the way open.

A yank on the rotting cord hanging from the ceiling bulb produced dim light in the claustrophobic room. I fought the urge to sneeze. Piece by piece, I brought everything into my bedroom: I stacked piles of books ranging from poetry to medicine along the wall, trashed piles of disintegrating linens, and moved a box of old vinyl to the Victrola. I consciously focused on each task, trying not to let the idea of vampires running around the city raid my thoughts.

An hour later, the last thing to go was a large, antique steamer trunk that had been decorated with stickers from all around the world. In theory it should have been easy to move because it stood upright on wheels, but it weighed a ton, and the wheels needed oil badly. I pulled the beast of a trunk with all of my strength. It moved an inch, and I slid down to the dirty floor, exhausted.

From the ground, I concentrated on the rusty metal wheels until they squeaked loudly and began to move. Slowly, the large chest wheeled itself into the bedroom.

After needing both my fingers and my mind to open the series of intricate locks, I was surprised but delighted to find it full of beautiful textiles, from pre-Victorian dresses to costumes clearly meant for the stage or maybe masquerade balls.

A lot of locks for a wardrobe, I thought, but could totally relate to someone cherishing the elaborate designs.

I hung each piece on a cloth hanger to air out, and then realized I had actually managed to distract myself for a half hour. Of course, once I made this realization, the vampires rushed my mind with a vengeance.

I grabbed the broom.

Once the wooden floor was swept, I aggressively repeated the process with the mop, only stopping when one of the strings snagged on a nail. I bent over to free it, but the nail refused to let go.

"Whatever." Yawning. I jerked the mop, ripping the string from its head, ready to be done with it.

When I reached up for the light, I felt my chain sliding off my neck. "No!" I yelped and tried to grab the medallion, but it clanked onto the floor.

I squatted down, worried that the chain had broken; luckily it had just come unfastened. I held my hand out to retrieve the sun charm and the medallion – they leaped into my hand, along with the nail that had snagged the mop string. It was a long, black, handmade carpenter's nail, like the ones I had picked up at the convent that morning.

I restrung the necklace, made sure the fastener was secure, and reached back for the light.

Again, I felt the slink of metal down my neck.

I slapped my chest, again, not fast enough. The necklace clanked back to the floor, as if it had suddenly become magnetized.

"What the...?"

For the second time, I reached out and for the second time gained another nail from the floorboard along with the medallion. I dropped the nail to the ground, but it leapt right back up.

"What the hell?"

All the nails in the two floorboards beneath me were vibrating. I quickly glanced around the room. The rest of the floor seemed normal – it was just this spot. My heart rattled in my chest as I knelt down over the shaking nails. Instinct led me to raise my hand over the boards.

Slowly, the nails wiggled themselves out and rose to the palm of my hand.

The wood was so degraded, I easily squeezed my fingers in between the planks and shook the boards until they loosened enough for me to pry free. I hastily cast the floorboards aside and peered into the dark hole, like a child about to discover a treasure – but I didn't find anything at all.

I slipped my hand into the small space and felt around. There was nothing but cool metal, like the inside of a safe.

The light bulb overhead flickered. My pulse climbed.

I hurried back to my room, grabbed the vanilla candle, and set it inside the hole to take another look.

Ugh. Nothing.

As I stared at the flame, frustrated, the candle shuddered, and the metal floor underneath it appeared warped. I held my hand over the surface, and the metal rippled. My whole body began to shudder as I held my hand in position. At first it was just a slight tingle in my shoulders, but then the energy traveled down my arms like a current, until my fingers burned and I cried out.

Just as I was about to rip my hand away, the metal parted like a wall of waves; I gasped as it revealed another compartment. The candle fell below, but before the flame extinguished, I saw something. Without thinking, I thrust my hand into the hole and grabbed the object of desire. As soon as I jerked my arm back out, the waves collapsed.

I pounded on the metal surface, dumbfounded. It was warm but solid. I raised an eyebrow at the leather-bound object in my hand and scurried back to my bed. *All that trouble for a book?*

But it wasn't just a book. It was a very old lock-n-key diary. The antique metal lock made the dense diary even heavier, and the hand-stitched leather binding and thick paper made me believe it must have been expensive in its time.

"How old is this thing?"

The edges of the pages were mismatched and browned, but the diary had been so perfectly preserved in the secret compartment, it was difficult to guess its age.

I imagined the metalwork unlocking – and the tiny latch snapped open.

An adrenaline I'd never felt before coursed through my veins as I carefully opened the cover of the unlocked treasure. A folded square of paper had been pressed in between the cover and the first page. Careful not to destroy the old stationary, I unfolded the paper and found a letter in handwritten French.

25th May 1728

Dearest Papa,

Today we finally set foot in the city of La Nouvelle-Orléans, *so this is my first opportunity to send a letter since leaving France those many months ago, for I did not trust the governor of Saint-Domingue with your location, nor did I consider one of the pirates we came across on the voyage to be a reliable postman. I will attempt to mail this letter today so you at least have news of our safe arrival. Although, I suspect you will be nowhere near the address you left me.*

I found the diary and letter you hid in my hatbox. As requested, I have documented my entire journey for you. At first I could not imagine why you would want such a boring account, but I did my best to fill the book each day nonetheless, and eventually, the days became more worthy of the ink.

However, I do not plan to send it. It will be here waiting for you in the capital of New France when you make the voyage yourself.

With all my love and affection,
A.S.G.

My fingers went to the medallion around my neck. *A.S.G.? This is A.S.G.'s diary?*

Excited, I fanned the pages. My heart fluttered as my eye caught a phrase amongst the motion.

I flipped the pages back, frantically scanning them for the words I knew I'd seen. And then, there they were, staring back at me.

> *You will never believe what the locals call the orphan girls. The townspeople have given them the funniest name,* "les filles aux la cassettes."

"A fille à la cassette?" I whispered. "The girl with the cassette... the casquette girls?"

> *Although, I shouldn't speak of them as if they are a group separate from myself. I may have boarded the ship under different circumstances, but after numerous events that have bound us together, I consider them to be my sisters.*

The ring around my finger suddenly felt warm. I rubbed my thumb over the silver disc with its spherical stone, when suddenly it began to rattle with such gusto that it dislodged itself from the ring's setting. As I examined the disk that held the milky stone, the medallion hanging from my chain floated into my hand, as if it had been magnetized once again.

With one silver disc in each palm, it was easy to see that they both had the exact same delicately engraved border. *How had I not noticed this before?* I pressed them back to back, and a golden flicker chased the edges, magically welding them together into one thick medallion. The design no longer looked incomplete – one side had the stone, and the other side had the imprint of the star and the initials.

I held the letter up next to the ornately engraved script on the medallion.

"Who were you, A.S.G.?"

According to my mother, the ring had belonged to my father's family. Which meant, in theory, A.S.G. was one of *my ancestors.*

Ren's voice boomed in my head. "Only the original caster of a spell could undo it."

part 2

adeline

"*Carriage, take me with you! Ship, steal me away from here!*
Take me far, far away. Here the mud is made of our tears!"

Charles Baudelaire

20

je t'aime paris

(translated from French)

3rd March 1728

SO, THE JOURNEY HAS BEGUN, PAPA. We have been aboard the S.S. *Gironde*, under the command of Captain Vauberci, for seven days now, although we have only completed three days' worth of our journey due to rough weather. Being trapped inside the private cabin makes me feel like a giant stuck inside a doll's house. I found this extraordinary diary that you gifted to me, and I am obliged to fulfill your wishes because you are my father, although I find the request odd. If your desire to be a part of this journey was so strong that you wish for the details of every passing moment to be recorded, then why didn't you accompany me instead of disappearing to the Orient three weeks ago? The mystery surrounding your actions has me ever-curious.

So, here I sit, with only paper and ink to keep me company. I believe the story begins the day before we left the dock in Paris…

From the moment you told me that you were sending me away, I began reading everything I could find about this new foreign land across the Atlantic. It is still so early in the King's exploration that there is not much information in circulation, so I spoke with as many people as I could, including some of the sailors down by the dock. (I kindly remind that it was you who forced me into this position.) There, I heard stories of all kinds, but no two were the same except for the tales of the hot and humid weather.

The day before my departure, I found myself in the tailor's shop, picking out fabric for a new cloak. I knew my traveling garments would serve well aboard the ship in the cold ocean winds, but what upon arrival? I had heard tales of men and women stripping off layers of clothing due to madness brought on by the sun! I confess, this idea made me even more excited to travel across the ocean.

The King's court advertises this New France as the pinnacle of modern society – all the luxuries of Paris but full of endless possibilities for people to make new lives, new investments, and new riches. It is said that a man can start over in New France, that his past can be erased, and that he can be whomever he wants to be. I wonder if this is the same for a woman? It is this prospect that keeps me from jumping over the ship's edge on this wretched journey.

Curiously, the tales of the seamen did not confirm the proclamations of the King. Some of the more inebriated sailors even went so far as to call the stories "lies" and the adverts "propaganda." Some of the sailors' news had allegedly even come from the church, from a group of nuns of the Order of Saint Ursula who are setting up a hospital in New France. The same Order that is traveling on this very ship with me! (Do not fret; I have not forgotten that you have taught me to never trust anyone on this journey, even those who walk in the eyes of the Lord.) The sailors also said that the land of *La Louisianne* is full of drifters, prostitutes and criminals – ex-convicts the King has pardoned in exchange for building the grand city of *La Nouvelle-Orléans.* (My apologies for this digression, but something tells me this is the true prologue of the story.)

Let us see. I was in the tailor's shop, getting a cloak made of a light silk. Louis draped the fabric over my shoulders and then pinned and snipped. This task took longer than necessary because of his insatiable need to gossip, but I didn't mind. I was going to miss not only his magical talent to transform even the ugliest duckling into a beautiful swan, but his friendship, and that was the reason I went down to the shop rather than sending for him. He asked me a hundred questions about my pending journey, and I was just telling him that he was welcome to take my place aboard the S.S. *Gironde* when in walked a very debonair man. Louis became excitable, which could only mean one thing: that the gentleman's purse was full.

The man waited patiently while Louis tended to me. To his credit, Louis did not leave my side (I am sure your position as count had something to do with it), despite seeming absolutely mesmerized by the man. And the man was indeed hypnotizing: his dark hair was held perfectly in place under a top hat, which matched his suit made of fine velvet, and he had the kind of green eyes that were impossible not to notice. It really is unfair when a man has the sort of eyes that sparkle. He had a smile like an innocent boy's, but a chill on my arms warned me that the innocence was deceptive.

Of course, I immediately longed to know more about this stranger. It would be false to say I was not excited when we began to converse. He said to me, "Mademoiselle Saint-Germain, what good fortune I have running into you." Our apparent acquaintance sent Louis into a head-spin.

To which I replied, "Dear sir, it is impossible that I could have forgotten your face, which means we have not met, and it is hardly fair that you know my name and I have not yet learned yours."

He paused and looked deeply into my eyes. "But we have met, Mademoiselle. I was a guest of Mademoiselle Jeanne-Françoise Quinault, at a masquerade ball at your father's estate last winter..."

Is that not ridiculous, father? As if there has been a person in our own home in my sixteen years whom I don't remember! The very idea is absurd. I can hardly explain it, but it was as if he was trying to will me into believing we had met before. I laughed, and the man appeared confused. I could tell he was becoming frustrated, so I pretended to play along.

"You will have to forgive me, sir, and tell me your name a second time."

He quickly composed himself, as if he realized he would have to deploy a different tactic to get what he desired. "Jean-Antoine Cartier, *enchanté*."

When he kissed my right hand, my left instinctively curled at my side.

There wasn't a part of me that believed for one second his name was actually Jean-Antoine Cartier. It's not that he seemed insincere. *Au contraire*, he had an extremely calm and inviting aura, but there was something about him that fired up all of my senses. He was a man who knew exactly what he was doing. In the spirit of the game, I asked him where he was from.

"Now, that is a very long story," he told me.

I warn you, Papa, you are not going to like the next part of this tale, but you are not exactly in the position to reprimand me, so I will speak openly about it, as we always do in the flesh. Despite our distance, it will comfort you to know that as I put these words on paper, I can feel you chastising me for my actions.

He said to me, "I realize it is forward of me to ask, with your father abroad, but would you care to accompany me this evening to the salon at the home of Mademoiselle Quinault?" I had wanted to go to that very gathering, but had given up on the idea without you to chaperone, Father.

His eyes were just as inviting as his words, but it was only when he said this that I really had to concentrate on keeping my brow straight: "I've been to New France three times already. Twice to the great city of *Montréal*, and once to the site of *La Nouvelle-Orléans.*"

He did not seem at all surprised that this information made my ears perk, and I didn't care why that was. This tease solidified my decision – his offer was the perfect invitation for mischief on my last night in Paris. Not that I needed more reason other than to simply quell my boredom, but a mysterious, handsome man, knowing the exact way to capture my attention, piqued my curiosity. I promise that I was not looking for a scandal, Papa, but really, how could I say no to someone who might satisfy my need for information on the land I would be traveling to in just one day's time? A land which not even you have yet been to. So, that evening, Monsieur Cartier's carriage picked me up.

When we arrived at the salon together, the look of surprise on the other guests' faces was alone worth the trip. Many of the women looked at me with contempt because I was on the arm of such a handsome man, but mostly they were all just desperately curious as to why the daughter of the *Comte de Saint-Germain* would be traveling to New France.

Do not worry, I did not tell them you were forcing me to go or that the reason was mysterious even to me – nor did I mention that doing so had seemed to cause you duress. I simply told them I was bored with Paris and that, if I couldn't explore the Orient because I was a woman, then I supposed I had to settle for New France. Of course, they drew their own conclusions. I overheard their little comments as we walked by.

"I heard the count is shipping her off to Tuscany..."

"Well, I heard he is locking her up in an insane asylum in London."

"Non, non, you both have it wrong. He is shipping her off to a Catholic nunnery in *La Nouvelle-Orléans* because she is so unwieldy."

"Oh, what I wouldn't pay to know who her mother is..."

"Either way, the count should have married. What else could he possibly have expected to happen? Raising a daughter on his own, letting her run completely wild?"

"I've heard that the count doesn't like women—"

"Well, I've heard that he just doesn't like sex—"

"I heard that he just didn't like you..."

As they laughed, I smiled and pretended to be so smitten by Monsieur Cartier's words that I couldn't possibly hear anything they were saying, as you taught me, so many years ago, to do in such situations.

When we made it through the parlor room of leeches, the lady of the house whisked me away from Jean-Antoine's arm and whispered in my ear, "Child, I am so glad you made it."

I greeted her with affection and apologized for not sending notice.

"Leave it to Mademoiselle Saint-Germain to show up with the most beautiful man in Paris when she couldn't show up with the craziest man in France."

Blood invaded my cheeks. "My holiday to New France was supposed to be a secret, but it appears all of Paris knows…"

"Well, my dear, you know secrets travel fast in Paris. It is not gossip that you must worry about, only the days when you are not worth gossiping about."

Her words made me smile, as did the boisterous call from one of your favorite, and rather drunk, budding playwrights.

"Adeline Saint-Germain! If I send a manuscript with you, can you make sure it is the first comedy performed in *La Nouvelle-Orléans*?"

To which I replied, "Of course, and perhaps I can convince François-Marie, I mean, Voltaire, to leave England and continue his exile in *La Nouvelle-Orléans*?"

Everyone laughed. I smiled, and before I could finish scanning the room, Monsieur Cartier was gently guiding me by the elbow through the crowd to a settee in a far corner.

"*Mademoiselle*," he said and offered me a glass of bubbling wine (it's becoming all the rage), which I gladly accepted after successfully navigating that female blockade of Parisian aristocracy.

He began telling me about his adventures, and not long after, I found myself clinging to his every word. This surprised me, since I have witnessed men telling their tales, shouting their dramas, or drunkenly sobbing their poems since the day of my birth, thanks to your constant need to entertain, Father. I tried not to fiddle with the medallion strung around my neck, but I couldn't keep my hands still and didn't want to have an unfortunate accident with an airborne utensil.

Time flew by, and the sparkling wine never stopped. He confirmed all the other stories I had heard: "The air is always wet, as if the clouds are about to burst." He spoke of the beautiful homes that the planters are building, and how *La Louisianne* is not like any of the puritan British regions of the New Colonies.

There was no arrogance to his tone, typical of Parisian intelligentsia, nor the abhorrent self-loathing of the artists they surround themselves with. He clearly knew I had been raised in the parlor rooms of some of the greatest salons in Paris, yet he was not intimidated in the slightest, and he seemed to take no notice of the other women in the room, who were all plotting their next moves to speak with him. He paid such close attention to my face that at times I couldn't help but feel like a caged canary and he a cat.

I had been utterly bored and lonely from the moment you left, and he was so charming – I soaked up his company. It all just felt too romantic, too perfect. His descriptions of the foreign land made it sound beautiful and exotic, and he confirmed that there are endless opportunities in New France for the right kind of people – people who are resourceful.

"And you, *Mademoiselle*," he said, "strike me as an extremely resourceful woman. You will love it there."

As the night went on, the more we drank and the more I prodded him for information, until the stories moved in a darker direction. He told me of serpents, and of rats the size of my arm, and of flying bugs that pinch all over your skin in the night. He warned that the streets were dangerous, and told me strange tales about the native people, and cannibals, and young virgins being kidnapped! He spoke of enslaved Africans casting curses on their owners. I was enthralled by his experiences, and jealous of his ability to live life as he so desired. His stories drew me closer and closer to him. At times I had to refrain from curling up into his lap.

He never once made me fight for his attention, nor did he stare at my bosom like most men, which made me question his intentions. Usually, the intentions of men are quite clear. I began to wonder if my corset was tight enough! I spent the entire night trying to figure out what he wanted. The more elusive one of us became, the deeper the other dug.

In a way that I found quite coy, he said, "You will find me to be a very patient man, Mademoiselle Saint-Germain."

"A quality not usually found in a man so young, Monsieur Cartier."

"I must confess that, despite my age, I feel I have lived many lives. I have had so many trips, so many adventures – and fortunately, because of my age, have so many yet to come." His eyes moved directly to mine, and I thought I might actually faint. This is the most peculiar part of the story, Papa, and I know I already confessed to drinking perhaps too deeply of the wine, but I can assure you I tell this next account exactly as it happened.

We left the salon in his carriage, and I asked him to tell me the darkest encounter he had ever witnessed in *La Nouvelle-Orléans.* Suddenly, he grabbed both of my arms with great excitement and begged me not to go. His reaction left me completely confounded.

"You don't understand," he insisted. "It is dangerous. It is not safe for someone like you."

"Someone like me?"

"Someone… so beautiful. Someone so pure."

"Dear Monsieur Cartier, I believe you have me mixed up with some other ingénue. I am certainly not as innocent as I look." I laughed.

"You mock me…"

"Of course I mock you. You are speaking nonsense!"

"I could travel with you – there will be pirates on the water, looking to plunder and pillage. You might not even make it across the ocean! It might sound like nonsense, but I am absolutely serious, I assure you."

"Serious? The ship sets sail tomorrow! How would you even get a ticket?"

"I don't need a ticket. You could sneak me onboard in your luggage." I stopped laughing when he grabbed my hands and held them tight. "I won't let anything happen to you; I give you my word."

His persona had seemed so demur all night – this behavior rendered me speechless. Now, I could feel his strength through his grip. His power surprised me, and his cool touch excited me. I thought he might attempt to break the silence by kissing me; instead, he looked intently into my eyes and said, "You will invite me to come with you, and you will allow me to stay inside your trunk, and you will tell no one we are traveling together."

Flabbergasted, I stared blankly at him with bated breath.

He didn't stir, nor did I.

I held still until I could no longer contain myself. Then I began to giggle uncontrollably, and again he huffed and puffed in frustration, as if he had thought he could will me into doing whatever he wanted. I laughed until I was gasping for air, and then leaned into his chest and took a deep breath.

His back stiffened, and he asked, "What are you doing, pray tell?"

I took another deep inhale of his coat. "Monsieur Cartier, I am trying to figure out if you smoked an opium pipe when I wasn't looking."

"Adeline, you know I didn't leave your sight all night."

"That is true, but I cannot think of anything else that would make you say something so absurd."

He gazed upon my smile, bewildered and a bit sullen, as the carriage approached *la maison*.

"Well, Monsieur Jean-Antoine Cartier, I do thank you for escorting me to the salon, and I do regret having only met you on my last night in Paris."

He helped me out of the carriage and bid me farewell before stepping back in. "It is not possible that we will not see each other again, Mademoiselle Saint-Germain, that I can promise you. I bid you *au revoir*, 'til we meet again in *La Nouvelle-Orléans*."

"I cannot believe this is my last night. I believe my heart will always be here. *Je t'aime, Paris.*"

He leaned out of the window curtain and kissed both of my cheeks. "And Paris loves you."

Absorbed by his words, I smiled and waved as his coachmen prepared to leave, but then he pulled my attention one last time:

"And, Adeline, do tell your father I called, *si'l vous plaît*."

His smile turned devilish as the carriage took off with a jolt, leaving behind only the echoes of hooves against the cobblestones.

21

knowledge, beauty, and metal

October 24th

OUR CITY HAD DROWNED two months and three weeks ago. Now, the world was moving on without us.

As fresher headlines popped up elsewhere, the media began to leave New Orleans, and slowly the world stopped paying attention. We were left to fend for ourselves on the eroding banks of the gulf, of the river, of time.

Time had always passed slowly in the South, but now it was like the Storm had hit the pause button, and Louisianians were frozen between frames. The pace of life went from slow to barely existent.

Progress stalled as local, state, and federal government agencies fought over control of funds and power. The longer things stalled, the more people blamed each other, and the more people blamed each other, the less rebuilding happened. We were quickly moving out of the we're-all-in-this-together phase into bitterness and resentment. Most people were still at the whim of the defunct electric grid. We were still living under the mandatory curfew. And we were still eating scrounged canned goods. Of course, my father and I were far better off than the hundreds of thousands who were still displaced and/or were now homeless. Not to mention those who hadn't survived. The dead. Smashed. Drowned.

Murdered.

Thoughts of death forced everything else to escape to the back of my mind, except the supernatural questions that had plagued me ever since the night of the tour. The longer the truth eluded me, the more torturous every hour of every day became, until eventually I was drifting along in an incessant dream state where nothing felt real. In this dream state I believed that vampires *could* exist.

Believing this fundamentally changed the way I looked at everything. It must be the way people felt when they found God – processing everything after that moment in a brand new way.

I had no proof of their existence, just this feeling, like the puzzle pieces of my brain had suddenly snapped into place. The only point of reference I had to compare it to was when I had made the Santa Claus discovery. I was only seven years old, but I can still remember that exact moment when it all suddenly made sense – the cookies, the presents, the reindeer – it was this very distinct moment of clarity. Upon this moment, I rushed to my father and demanded evidence as to how a fat man could come through our chimney! That, of course, sent him into crisis mode, stuck between the adult thing to do and the parental thing to do. When I threatened to drag the eleven-year-old future-scientists into the discussion, he caved and told me the truth.

We hadn't had any secrets since.

In retrospect, I think he was relieved not to have to keep up the fantasy any longer.

Even as a kid, I'd felt so silly knowing I'd believed the hoax when the truth had been so obvious.

I had needed proof then. And that's what I needed now.

Evidence that would weave this dream state in which vampires *could* exist with reality where I was taught that the idea was fiction. This time, I couldn't rely on my father or the twins to confirm my hypothesis. They'd think I was crazy. When I thought about it, I felt crazy.

Am I crazy?

When I asked myself too many questions, everything began to unravel. A little voice inside my head warned me to let it go, but that was no longer an option – it felt powerful to know something no one else knew. But with no idea of where to start, I felt like Alice chasing the white rabbit's shadow, fumbling around in the dark for the hole, for the fall, for the proof of its existence.

EVEN THOUGH IT HAD ONLY BEEN a few days since I discovered her, I had become obsessed with Adeline Saint-Germain. She was one more puzzle for me to figure out. Considering that my father's parents had died so soon after my mother left, family was not a topic I frequently broached with him – not that I really wanted to now – it's not like I could casually bring up a three-hundred-year-old relative without raising a few questions, which I certainly wasn't prepared to answer. That left me with Adeline's necklace and her diary, neither of which I ever left farther than arm's length.

My attachment to these artifacts was different from the love I usually had for all things vintage. I had an unexplainable, overwhelming need to protect them. Someone had obviously gone to extraordinary lengths to hide the diary, and knowing that they must have had the same kind of ability as me fueled my obsession.

Unfortunately, thanks to Franz Kafka and a mountain of other "so you can catch up with the other Sacred Heart students" homework, plus my mentorship, I was swamped. I fell asleep each night translating the pages, figuring that when I finished the entire thing, maybe I would show it to my father and ask him about it. The ornate handwriting, faded antique ink, and eighteenth-century French made the translation process drag, but I continued obsessively nonetheless, hanging on to every word, romanticizing her grand adventure.

I FELT MYSELF GRADUALLY BECOMING more and more withdrawn, which wasn't difficult given that no one at school spoke to me except for Thurston Van der Veer, (who turned out to be Annabelle Lee's boyfriend). This, of course, made me a massive target with Annabelle's clique. Having to avoid the one person in school who paid attention to me only further annoyed me. *Didn't he know other girls were not allowed to speak to Annabelle Lee Drake's boyfriend? Didn't he know that his attention was causing me to become the most hated girl at Sacred Heart?* Sometimes I just wanted to scream at him to GO AWAY.

The worst part was that although I could feel the hate emanating from Annabelle Lee (and so could everyone else), she was always sweet as pie to me, even though the fake tone in her voice sent a signal to all those within earshot that I was not to be welcomed, spoken to, assisted, or even looked at until she decided what to do with me. She was a shark, constantly circling, just waiting for the right time to attack. No one wanted to be near the shark bait. With good reason.

As far as I could tell, there were only three people who didn't bow down to her authority.

The first was her BFF, Désirée, who, don't get me wrong, was deeply woven into the social order threads of the student population but whose general attitude of disdain seemed to trump everything, including Annabelle's dictatorship. I guess that's what happens when you are born with everything, or when your father is the mayor. Or maybe it's just what happens when you are that beautiful – rules no longer apply to you.

The second was her little sister, Katherine Lee Drake, who was my chemistry lab partner. Knowing the only interaction I had to look forward to was the sophomore who was obligated to work with me made me feel extra pathetic, but I shouldn't complain because she was nice. Unlike

Dixie Hunter, who, every day, made it apparent how ready and willing she was to do whatever necessary to earn a permanent place in Annabelle's throng.

Ugh. Everything about high school seemed so trite now. I pretended not to care.

Then there was the only person who outright refused to bow down to any social hierarchy in the school: Tyrelle. I did everything I could to try to win him over – my next step was to cook up the dusty box of brownie mix in our pantry (with no milk or eggs, of course) and beg. The grapevine told me that he was the son of one of the most famous rappers to ever come out of New Orleans, or all the Dirty South. His father had been in more scuffles with the law than could be counted on two hands, and one of his brothers was currently serving time for an infraction involving a gun. So, everyone steered totally clear of him, as if he was suddenly going to pop a cap. Tyrelle seemed to like it that way, but I was pretty sure the only thing he was popping was the curve in our Pre-Cal class.

I tried to keep a low profile, but sometimes my parlor trick made that impossible. On multiple occasions, I hadn't been able to keep my locker from slamming open, and once it had nearly clocked the head of a burley lacrosse player whose locker was on my left; another time it nicked his hand. On that occasion, he had thought I was flirting and said something idiotic like, "So, you like it rough?"

Tyrelle, whose locker was on my right, had laughed (at the locker slamming the lacrosse player, not at the lacrosse player sexually harassing me). I wanted to punch them both, but I was so nervous wondering if Tyrelle had witnessed how my locker had flown open I just ran away.

The angrier I became at Annabelle Lee Drake, the more impossible it became to control my abilities – until today, that is. (Not that I found the logical explanation for why it was happening.)

I was at Café Orléans, technically working, but since customers hardly ever walked through the door, I was pulling double duty and having my French tutoring session with Jeanne. A week ago, I would have cherished getting to spend one of her rare moments away from the university laboratory, but instead it was agonizing. I just wanted to tell her everything and ask questions, but, with no evidence to support my claims, the scientist in her would have fretted over my lunatic hypothesis. Much more than her brother, Jeanne struggled to ever take off the lab coat and look at something without her soon-to-be doctoral title. Of course, I did have one piece of proof that something in my life was awry, but I wasn't willing to reveal that just yet.

I was returning from the bathroom, trying to fabricate an excuse so I could go home and curl up with Adeline's diary, when Jeanne looked up from the table with a perplexed brow.

"Why are you creating these lists?"

She was reading a page in my notebook – my documentation of everything I had successfully been able to move or not move telekinetically.

I grabbed for the notebook, but she quickly pulled it out of my reach. I coyly tried to turn the tables. "What do you think the lists are?"

"Ugh, a list of objects that contain metals and a list of… random junk."

I ripped the notebook from her hands and scoured the lists.

She was right. *I am an idiot,* I thought, but was too excited to be down on myself about the oversight. "How do you do that!"

"Do what?"

"Nothing. Never mind."

"What are the lists for?"

"Um…"

Maybe I should just tell her? Her giant brain might have just come up with the explanation I had been searching for. "It's just something for my chem lab."

"And what exactly are you studying in your chem lab?"

"Um, something about mineral properties… you know, melting points and freezing points, stuff like that."

"In a sophomore-level chemistry class? I thought that school was supposed to be the best? Sheesh, no wonder the sciences are going down the tubes."

My answer must have been spastic-enough sounding, because she bought it. At least, I think she did. We spent another forty-five minutes conjugating irregular French verbs, but I couldn't think about anything but metals. I was clawing at the walls to finish the lesson so I could get out and test her theory. Needless to say, apprenticing with my father in the metal shop was about to become a lot more interesting.

22

bon voyage

(translated from French)

10th March 1728

ONE WOULD THINK THAT, stuck aboard a ship with no one but nuns and orphans, I would be writing nonstop out of boredom, but alas, somehow the time has slipped by. The good news is I have finally gotten my sea legs, as the sailors say, so now it is easier to write without feeling dizzy from the constant push and pull of the ocean's grip. The weather has been tumultuous, with rain pounding down on our vessel both night and day, but now the sun is shining, and one of the sailors has secured my parasol to help shield against both the blazing rays and the spray of the ocean. The cool mists are refreshing, but they are good for neither paper nor ink.

As the sailors hustle around me, pushing the ship to her limits to make up for lost time, I sit in solitude, recording this adventure, wondering where in the world you are, and praying that writing will distract me from the ever-present cabin fever. Father, I do trust that you have a good reason for sending me to *La Nouvelle-Orléans*; however, I am angry about the way in which you sent me. I would have thought my nursemaid (of sixteen years!) would be a better choice of traveling companion than Monsieur and Madame DuFrense, who still seem like strangers to me, though we have had a few good conversations. I might as well be traveling alone, Papa, which is exactly what I told Monsieur Cartier that morning in Paris, when, to my surprise, he showed up at the dock to bid me *bon voyage.* It could have been quite a romantic parting, but he spoilt it by, again, rather adamantly insisting I sneak him onboard the ship in my luggage.

The gentleman has a funny sense of humor, Papa. He pretended to tease, but my intuition told me that if I had taken him seriously for even a second, his words would no longer have been a joke. I believe he *did* want to come aboard the ship in my trunk! Despite the strange request, I do admit to favoring him, and I do hope to see him again on the other side of the Atlantic. I feel like we could have many grand adventures together, just like you and me, Father.

Alas, keeping the spray of water from ruining the pages is becoming too difficult, so this story will have to continue at a later date.

11th March 1728

IT'S HARD TO IMAGINE BEING aboard this ship for months. Almost none of the other passengers will speak to me – everyone knows I am the daughter of a count. This leaves me with only the Monsieur and Madame DuFrense, Captain Vauberci, and the Reverend Mother Superior Marie Lorient. Apparently, the sisters of the Catholic faith have a strict hierarchy, which mirrors the rest of French society, and this is why three of the nuns do not speak to me at all. Thankfully, it wasn't because they thought I was a lady of ill repute. I hope that over time the usual societal hierarchies can be abandoned, even if only temporarily, while we are trapped aboard this ship, otherwise I might have to throw myself overboard to avoid dying of boredom. I will try not to harp on this now, and will instead give you the details you requested, no matter how banal I consider them.

The breakfast mostly consists of a little bread and hard cheese. The DuFrenses and I are also given a lump of sugar for our tea and some dried fruit, which riddles me with guilt as the orphans, who get none, sit near us at one long table. We eat breakfast with the captain at a small, round table.

If I have counted correctly, onboard there are twenty-six teenage girls, all being sent to *La Nouvelle-Orléans* at the request of the King, and six sisters of the Order of Saint Ursula, who are looking after them and who will, as I understand it, board and school them until they are all married off to French settlers in the new colony. All of the passengers are stacked in bunks of six to a room except for three orphans who for some reason were given their own cabin. Of course, I have my own *première classe* cabin, as do the DuFrenses.

I find the couple I am traveling with pleasant enough – Claude DuFrense plans to develop real estate in the city and has been telling me much about the layout of the town. His fervor for the endless investment opportunity is infectious; however, his wife is less than thrilled to be "ripped away from the heart of the world." Martine DuFrense is an opera singer, and she has made it abundantly clear that her life is over now, having left Paris. Claude promises to build her the grandest opera house in all the world and being reminded of this momentarily raises her spirits, but most of the time she stays locked up in their cabin, sinking further into depression.

I hope that once the weather permits a bit of socializing on the deck, we can be friends. As things stand now, I end up spending most of my time talking about our destination with the crewmen, who have no problem speaking out of social order – as long as the captain is out of earshot.

17th March 1728

I APOLOGIZE FOR NOT WRITING, but the task of reliving the boring days by writing them down is even worse than living them. My health has been good, but some of the orphans have suffered from seasickness. The poor things sometimes look so pale and can do nothing but lie in their cabins suffering from lightheadedness and fevered dreams. Other than a couple of screams in the middle of the night from these girls, there really has been nothing to report.

There is a strong sense of camaraderie amongst the orphans, despite the seasickness and only having the slightest amenities. Every day I grow more jealous of them because they have all become friends. The orphans have each other, the DuFrenses have each other, and the nuns have each other – even the crewmen have each other. I try not to wallow in my own misery because, as you know, being emotional makes it more difficult for me to control myself.

Captain Vauberci senses my loneliness and sometimes allows me to sit next to him while he uses foreign instruments to study the stars and keep us on track even as Mother Nature fights his efforts. He tells me stories as he drinks spirits in between shouting commands at the crew, always trying to make up for lost time. I often wonder if his kindness to me is just out of obligation because of the fame your name carries, Father? But I do not care either way; he is the only companion I have. If only the society ladies could see me now, sitting alone with the drunk, middle-aged captain. It would be enough gossip to keep them entertained all season.

23rd March 1728

AS MY LONELINESS CONTINUES TO GROW, there are three girls in particular whose relationship drives me mad with jealousy. They are sisters – triplets, in fact, with the exact same fair skin and blonde hair so bright it shimmers white like the moon. They don't get the same special treatment that my ticket affords me, but they are the ones I previously mentioned who have their own cabin to share, despite being with the "King's daughters" (as I have heard the orphans being called by the crew). These triplets have a sense of spirit that seems to transcend societal constraints, yet they still do not speak to me. I cannot understand why not, and this drives me mad.

I long to talk, to laugh, to sing, to dance, but more than anything, I long to know these sisters. And yet every time I approach them, they stop their excitable whispers. They don't look at the ground when I pass like the other girls do; they look at me with suspicion, as if trying to figure out whether or not to trust me – a feeling I am all too accustomed to from hobnobbing with the Parisian aristocracy. Sometimes at night, I pass a cabin and can hear them singing to entertain or comfort the other girls, and last night I caught them on deck, dancing under the light of the moon! They looked like goddesses, with their hair loose and wild, and their nightgowns fluttering in the nautical breeze. They danced and giggled, utterly unconcerned that their bare feet were exposed to the elements! I have never wanted anything more than to join them, but fear of rejection kept me in the shadows, alone in my misery.

Each day, I find myself becoming more and more withdrawn, Papa.

This is absurd! Let it be written that I am determined to befriend these girls. If I can survive sixteen years of the scandal and rumors that come with being the daughter of *le Comte de Saint-Germain,* then I can certainly win over three sisters aboard this ship. Tonight, I will devise a plan.

24th March 1728

AT BREAKFAST, I snuck my lump of sugar and dried fruit into a fold of my dress, along with a seashell given to me by a sailor, and left these small tokens, wrapped in a hair ribbon, on the pillow of the sister who I've heard called Cosette.

28th March 1728

AFTER THREE DAYS of leaving small treats to no avail, I returned to my cabin to find the hair ribbons tied to my doorknob. I hope this is a sign that things are progressing favorably.

29th March 1728

TODAY WAS THE MOST EVENTFUL EVENING I've had since you left me in Paris, Papa. I was feeling restless and could not sleep, after another day that had dragged on, and even though we are not supposed to leave our cabins after dark, I threw my cloak over my gown and slipped into the narrow path of light created by the beams of the crescent moon.

On deck, nightfall had unveiled a sky of a million stars.

The sounds of the crashing waves disturbed the silent night, and the cold spray enlivened my senses. The closer I got to the far end of the ship, the more I thought that I heard the beautiful sounds of song. I hurried to find the source.

At the end of the stern, I saw the backs of Cosette, Minette, and Lisette. They were sitting with their feet dangling, seemingly without fear of being washed overboard, singing "Au Clair de la Lune." The melody blended with the rippling waves in a delicate harmony, as if the ocean itself also knew this tune. The sailors sat perched like stone gargoyles at their night posts, so comforted by the lullaby that they allowed the girls to continue rather than sending them back to bed.

Careful not to disturb them, I sat next to Cosette, and after a breath I joined the verse: "*My candle is out, I have no more light.*"

They looked at me for a moment, and then we continued the lullaby together, looking back toward the hidden horizon. As I searched for the line where the real stars ended and their reflections on the black waves began, all thoughts emptied from my head. I closed my eyes and became lost in the motion of the boat.

Soaking wet, we continued to sing for another hour through our chattering teeth. At some point during the song, everything became as it should. We knew that our voices blended together were stronger than each was on its own. It was a feeling of kinship I had never felt before. A feeling of great power.

I had thought nothing could ruin that moment of perfect serenity, until a bloodcurdling scream suddenly tore through the S.S. *Gironde.*

Instantly the four of us, along with several of the lullaby-hazed seamen, took off running towards the screaming. By the time we reached the dormitory corridor, there were already half a dozen sailors with swords in hand, ready to battle any intruder who may have stowed away.

We found a nun cradling an orphan inside one of the cabins. Another nun was holding up a lantern to the girl's ghostly face, and a third began shooing the men out of the room. Sweat fell from the girl's shaking face and there was a smear of blood across her neck. Minette took her hand and called out her name, but, despite her chest rising and falling, nothing made her respond.

Cosette grabbed the hand of one of the other girls in the room and demanded an explanation. The girl told Cosette they had all been asleep in the pitch-black room and not seen a thing, and the other girls, all trembling, nodded in agreement.

As one of the nuns cleaned the wound, it was deduced that the sick girl must have suffered a terrible nightmare due to seasickness and scratched herself in her sleep. Nevertheless, the captain stationed a sailor to guard the door, and the novice stayed with her throughout the night in case she woke.

Alas, I just saw shadows pass through the faint light shining under my door. I must now extinguish my flame, as we are not allowed to use candles or lanterns in our rooms, not that I have either.

1st April 1728

THE INJURED GIRL, SOPHIE, keeps a temperature too high to wake from. Cosette sneaks into the girl's room in the middle of the night with a pulp made from herbs she brought onboard from Paris. She applies this to the girl's wound, which she seems to have developed a mild obsession with. I find this to be a tad gruesome.

Some of the girls continue to suffer from seasickness, especially in the mornings, but the symptoms usually dissipate by lunchtime. Nothing more out of the ordinary has happened. I spend my days either on my own or with the DuFrenses, and my nights with my three new companions.

7th April 1728

SOPHIE CONTINUES TO LIVE without waking. The nuns pray over her every morning and evening, but I am beginning to fear the worst.

Madame DuFrense does not approve of my spending so much time with the triplets, but their friendship keeps me from the brink of insanity whilst aboard this ship. We read to each other, play cards, or make up silly games to pass the time. Sometimes we gossip – we suspect one of the orphans is having an affair with a sailor! Lisette, or Lise (as she prefers to be called), claims to have seen the silhouette of a man sneaking into said orphan's room in the middle of the night…

I'm not sure who I would fear the most if they were to be caught – the captain or the Mother Superior, who has a kind face but whom I sometimes think is the one who truly rules the S.S. *Gironde.* I hate to laugh at the misfortunes of others, but at this point, the entertainment of it all would be grand.

It is a pity that we have aboard this ship a well-known opera singer and three sisters talented enough to have sung for the King of France, yet we spend the days and nights with no entertainment. It is my new mission to arrange a performance for everyone on the boat. I believe it will do wonders for the spirit of Martine DuFrense.

Allow me to explain my previous comment. Like me, the triplets are sixteen years of age, and they, too, lost their mother early on, but even worse, they also lost their father and were made wards of the state at the age of seven. At thirteen, they ran away from the orphanage to join a traveling theatre troupe, who eventually received an invitation to perform at the palace. The King loved the audition but especially loved the triplets, and so the whole troupe was invited to become a regular act in his court, and soon they were entertaining the French elite during *soirées* at the palace. Lise told me that Cosette is such a talented pianist the Queen herself arranged for private lessons, which caused quite a scandal with the more tenured court musicians.

Papa, for the first time in my life, I wish I had accepted more invitations to the palace— it's quite crazy to think that I could have possibly seen a performance! Never would I have guessed in a million years that I would meet girls aboard this ship who were able to trade stories about members of the King's court. These sisters know far more than any socialite, for they have witnessed so many events, so many parties, so many nights of debauchery.

"I don't understand," I told them late one afternoon while we were braiding each other's hair. "How did you end up on this ship? Why would you ever want to leave your troupe?"

Their heads shifted like dominos, as if to silently agree on how much information to share, and then Lise admitted with a sigh, "There was a scandal at the palace."

Minette clarified, "Well, not really a scandal, because nothing had actually happened."

"It was a *rumor*," said Cosette, but then Lise explained, "You see, many of the ladies at court envied Cosette. Everyone was jealous of her beauty and her talent."

Her words made Cosette blush deeply. "They were jealous of *all* of us. We are identical, remember?"

Her sisters giggled, and then without a twinge of jealousy, Lise said, "It's true that we look the same, but you are modest, sister, for it is you whom every man is drawn to."

Cosette peered out the tiny round window. "Yes, it was me who caused our demise..."

"Oh, don't be so theatrical," said Minette. "You know that is not what she meant."

I understood. All three look identical at first glance, but once you spend time around them, they begin to appear as different as the sun, moon, and stars, because their personalities are in such stark contrast. Lisette is cheery and optimistic, which makes her seem younger; Minette is bookish and shy, which makes her appear delicate; and Cosette is utterly fearless both with her actions and her tongue, yet somehow everything comes out of her mouth in flowery song. It is easy to see how any man would vow to follow her to the end of the Earth. I could imagine the ladies in court, whose riches make them bitter and plump, hating any girl with Cosette's magnetism, especially if she also had intelligence or talent, of which she has both.

"Well, it doesn't matter now," Cosette said. "Once a few of the ladies got it into their head that we were to be removed from court, it was only a matter of time."

"We're lucky we got out with our heads," said Lisette.

"What do you mean?" I asked, for that seemed a little extreme, even for the French.

Minette pulled me next to her on the bed. "Those women did everything they could to have us removed. They went to work digging up our past. You see, Adeline, we had been traveling with our troupe under the name of *Les Sœurs d'Or.*"

"Because of your golden hair?"

"Precisely. But when the women of court discovered our birth name was really Monvoisin, suddenly one of the servants turned up dead. When the doctor announced that the cause of death was poison, someone conveniently announced our relation to *La Voisin.* The women of the court demanded we be sent to the guillotine, but luckily for us the King's mistress understood what was going on and begged him to have mercy on us. The King consented, and so we found ourselves being smuggled out of the palace, each of us with a *cassette* containing a wedding dress and dowry, to join the girls being sent to marry the townsmen in *La Nouvelle-Orléans*."

"Lucky us," said Cosette.

Knowing the triplets were descendants of Catherine Deshayes Monvoisin, therefore connected by blood relation to *l'affaire des poisons*, only made me sympathize even more with their plight and feel closer to them. Living with the reputation of those who came before us is just one more thing in common that we shared.

10th April 1728

I KNEW DEEP WITHIN MY SOUL that it was bound to happen. Tonight was the night, Papa.

Despite the late hour, I was in the Monvoisin sisters' cabin. Minette was teaching me how to mend my skirt and Cosette was writing in her diary when Lise burst through the door.

"He's here! He's here!" she yelled, but then clammed up when she realized her sisters weren't alone.

She looked at Minette with duress, who asked, "Who is here?"

The question was not enough permission to get Lise to speak. Worried, Cosette wrapped an arm around her sister's shoulder and sat her on the bed next to me. Minette dropped to the floor in front of us, took her sister's hand, and asked in a hushed voice, "Are you trying to say what I think you—"

"*Oui*! He's here. The man from the dock is here, on this boat."

"What man from the dock?" I asked, trying not to become agitated by the sudden cryptic atmosphere.

"Shhhhhhh!" all three of them hissed at once.

"What man from the dock?" I whispered, my curiosity now fully piqued, but again, Lise looked to her sisters, unsure whether or not to divulge the answer.

The idea of having secrets between us broke my heart. I knew the possible implications of revealing myself to them – you have warned me of the consequences ever since I was a child, but as they continued to debate my trustworthiness in hushed voices, my shoulders burned. I sprang off the bed, yelling, "I cannot stand for there to be any secrets between us!" My words shook, knowing what I was about to do, although deep down inside, I trusted Cosette, Minette and Lisette completely.

As I raised my arm to a small iron candelabrum on the wall, my heart pounded so hard it felt like my chest might rip open. Without moving an inch, I tore the iron fixture from the wooden plank. The room became perfectly silent as the dusty, candleless piece of metal flew into my palm. I grasped it with my left hand and cupped the top of the metal with my right. Almost instantly, the light shining between the cracks of my fingers glowed so warm I had to move my hand and expose the flame to the wide-eyed girls.

I looked at each of them and then said, "You know my secret. Now, what man on the dock?"

I watched the reflection from the fire flicker in Cosette's golden-brown eyes. As her smile grew, I knew things would never be the same, nor would I ever again be alone with my secret.

23

a whirlwind romance

October 25th

"DON'T RUSH. PRECISION IS KEY. The more you learn to control your movements, the better you'll be able to control the outcome of the piece," said my father, a faint drone in the back of my head. Sitting in his studio, surrounded by tools used to work with fire, I couldn't stop thinking about Adeline. Two brass candlesticks he had made before the Storm, now hidden in a pile of metal awaiting polishing, kept grabbing my attention. I refused to let myself look at them, fearing a flame might suddenly ignite due to my own lack of control. *You're being ridiculous.*

"Ha. I thought *control* was for the scientists," Isaac joked.

"There is a fine line between art and science when it comes to working with metal. Blurring the two dates all the way back to the Bronze

Age… which is the perfect transition to today's lesson on casting. Take out your wax sculptures."

I peeked at Isaac's piece. Even in the cobalt-blue wax, the perfectly sculpted feather looked real – he must have spent hours scraping out each little hairline wisp. For someone with such an abrasive personality, he certainly had a delicate hand when it came to his art. It was going to look amazing once it was cast in silver: this lesson's metal of choice.

My fingers were still raw from accidentally scraping my skin with the metal files while carving my wax star. I'd become obsessive over the symmetry of the eight points, wanting the little lines to match up perfectly like patchwork. Next to his piece, it now looked basic, but I wanted to replace the missing star on Adeline Saint-Germain's necklace— on my necklace. *I'll do something more complicated next time,* I reassured myself, looking at the flames I had drawn in my sketchpad. My thumb rubbed over the rough impression the original star had left behind on the medallion. The little wax sculpture fit perfectly over it. I envisioned what the silver version would look like after I cast it, and then came to a realization that made my breath cut short.

"I am such an idiot," I whispered.

"What?" asked Isaac, looking up from his carving tools.

"Nothing," I snapped. I smiled to make up for the tone. "Just talking to myself."

"Right." He raised one eyebrow and then went back to his feather. My father was mixing plaster. I grabbed my phone and quickly banged out a text to Brooke, who still hadn't returned any of my messages since our call.

Adele	**3:30 p.m.**	Hi! I know this is going to sound really random, but do you still have the star charm I gave you a couple of years ago? Is it with you in L.A.?

A few years ago, I had found a star-shaped charm in an old cigar box, along with a bunch of other buttons, lose stones, and metal scraps that had been collected in my dad's studio over the decades. *An eight-pointed star charm,* if my memory served me correctly. I had fallen in love with it instantly. My father taught me how to polish it, and, afterwards, I didn't take it off for months. Not until freshman year, when Brooke was chosen to sing the "Star Spangled Banner" at the Superdome before a Saints game. It was the only time I'd ever seen her nervous before a performance. She was terrified. I took it off, wrapped it around her neck, and told her she was going to be a star one day. She killed it on stage and claimed the star as her good luck charm. Afterwards, my father surprised me with the sun charm currently hanging around my chain. I hadn't really taken it off since. Surely she had taken the star with her to Los Angeles? I texted her again:

Adele	**3:36 p.m.**	It's kind of important. Just want to know if it's here in the city. If not, maybe you could mail it back to me? I know you don't need luck anymore (not that you ever did).

What else could I say? *"I am looking for clues about the vampires I accidentally released from a convent,"* seemed slightly out of the question, although it may have elicited a quicker response.

A few minutes later, my phone buzzed.

Brooke	**3:46 p.m.**	Just b/c I've been busy, you want your necklace back? Why?
Adele	**3:47 p.m.**	Umm… it's kind of complicated. Do you have

		it? My dad is teaching me to cast, so I can make you a better one, completely made by moi!
Brooke	**3:48 p.m.**	Um… you want your charm back. Doesn't sound complicated to me.
Brooke	**3:48 p.m.**	And how can you say that I don't need luck anymore? Have you suddenly forgotten about everything that has happened to me in the last 3 months?
Brooke	**3:48 p.m.**	Whatever…
Adele	**3:49 p.m.**	Maybe it would sound more complicated if you ever returned my calls!? There is a lot of crazy shit going on down here! You aren't the only person going through a lot these days.
Brooke	**3:51 p.m.**	I'd know what's going on with you if you had moved to L.A.!!!!!!
Adele	**3:52 p.m.**	Thanks for understanding… can you just tell me if you have the charm?

Brooke	**3:53 p.m.**	I didn't bring it. Have fun digging around in what's left of our house. I'm sure one of your new friends at THE ACADEMY would love an old piece of tarnished silver.

I slammed my phone down.

"Are you sure you're okay?" Isaac asked again.

"Fine." I tried to contort my scowl into a convincing smile.

In the past, fighting with Brooke would have brought me to tears, but this was actually some semblance of good news: she hadn't taken the charm out west. I gave myself a reality check – the likelihood of being able to find something so small in her house was slim to none. But who knows? It was certainly worth a try. Plus, I needed time off from translating Adeline's diary – time to process the fact that one of my ancestors could apparently make fire appear from thin air.

"Dad, we're almost done for today, right? Brooke needs me to go over to her house and look for something."

"I have to go to work when we are done here."

"What does that have to do with it?"

"I can't take you."

"Take me?" Brooke's house was a fifteen-minute walk, tops, and an even quicker bike ride. I'd probably done it a thousand times. "Dad, I don't need you to come with me."

"Adele, I don't want you going out that far by yourself. It's going to be dark soon."

"Far? It's not far!"

"That's final. I don't want you going to the Tremé by yourself."

"What? That's ridic—"

"In fact, I don't want you leaving the French Quarter by yourself, Adele. The Jones's house might have structural damage."

"Dad…"

"I can take her," Isaac volunteered. "We won't go inside the house if the conditions are too bad."

"Don't *do* that!" I yelled at him.

"Do what?"

"Don't talk about me as if I am not here! It's *you*. I can take *you*." The carving tools on the table started to tremble. *Breathe*. Thank God both Isaac and my father were both too distracted by my outburst to notice.

"I'm sorry, Adele, I can escort you on your errand, if you'll allow me the privilege." He smiled at me in a way that was not meant to antagonize, so I tried not to take it that way.

Dead, blue eyes flashed in my mind.

"Merci beaucoup," I said through gritted teeth, knowing this was my only chance of charm-hunting today. I couldn't pass up an opportunity to find a missing puzzle piece.

"We'll be back before curfew, Mac—"

"Be back before sundown."

"Uh, okay, sir."

"Fine with me," I said with more bite than necessary. "There's no point in staying after dark given there is no electricity." *What was my father's obsession with getting the bar in order?* Nothing indicated that the curfew was going to be lifted any time in the near future.

"Here, take the car." My father tossed his keys to Isaac. "It will be quicker and safer."

Did that really just happen? My father is letting Isaac take his car out?

"Now I really feel like I am living on another planet," I said under my breath.

A huge grin spread over Isaac's face. "Thanks, Mac! You have nothing to worry about."

"You'll have my daughter and my car. I have everything to worry about."

Almost blushing, Isaac skirted out of the room to change into a cleaner set of clothes. My eyes rolled.

"I'm sorry, sweetheart, I know this isn't easy, but it's just the way it has to be right now. Things will go back to normal eventually." He kissed my cheek.

Normal? I thought, watching him hurry off to work. *What does that even mean anymore? Coexisting with a bunch of severely undernourished vampires?* Things were never going to be *normal* again.

As I waited for Isaac, I eyed his sketchpad on the table. Seizing the opportunity, I flipped it open, whispering, "This is a total invasion of privacy, Adele."

There was the sketch of his feather. I turned the page. More feathers of all shapes and sizes – some beautiful, others dark with severe lines and shading. I flipped through a few more pages and stopped, letting the book fall open on the table.

There I was, staring back at myself.

Or was it me? The girl in the portrait shared some of my facial features, but her hair was longer and swept up in an intricate style, and she wore a gown more likely to be found in Marie Antoinette's wardrobe than mine. On the next page – there she was again, and again, and again. I stopped when I landed on a sketch of the girl holding out a candlestick. There was no wax candle in the holder, and yet there was a bright flame, causing her face to glow. "What the hell, Isaac," I whispered.

"What the hell what?"

I slammed the book shut and spun around.

"Obsessed with feathers, much?" I squeaked.

He gave me a strange look and stuffed the sketchpad into his knapsack.

THE FAUBOURG TREMÉ BORDERED the northern perimeter of the Quarter, so the ride was quick, but nonetheless awkward. Surely Isaac knew I had been snooping, but he didn't seem angry. In fact, he seemed a bit sheepish, which was exactly how I felt. In a way, we were both guilty of the same thing: we had both been caught spying on the other.

To fill the silence, he gave me a progress report on the back wall. Apparently they'd have finished fixing it by now if supplies weren't so scarce. I listened over attentively as I directed him to the Jones's, but he stopped mid-sentence when we crossed North Rampart Street into the Tremé.

I mentally prepared myself as the conditions gradually got worse – I did *not* want to appear weak in front of Isaac. He was used to seeing this level of devastation every day.

We had no choice but to park three blocks away. Isaac looked nervous about leaving my father's baby out of sight with looters still running amuck, but I took off, giving him no choice other than to catch up.

Glass crunched underneath our feet, a sound I was getting used to, and even though the sun was still up, the street felt gloomy. We walked past a house that had been torn in half by a fallen oak tree, and another's whose façade had been smashed by a truck.

My nervous excitement about finding the charm fizzled as I walked up the porch steps of Brooke's house, which was painted a robin-egg color that used to make Tiffany's blue seem dull. Now the residence, like all the others on the block, looked as if it had been abandoned seventy years ago. The screen door was missing, and the porch was not much more than a pile of tinder. The water line cleared my head by several feet, and the now-familiar X had been spray-painted on the exterior in black and orange. Fortunately, it was filled with zeros.

I wrestled with the spare set of keys in the front door. My hands were already raw from filing away at my sculpture, but only when they nearly bled did I step aside and let Isaac bully the door open. Before we even entered, my hand jerked over my nose and I gagged on the overwhelming sour stench of rot.

I forced myself to walk inside.

Hundreds of thousands of tiny black specks of mold had spread up the walls, all the way up to the high ceilings, like an attacking virus. My entire body shuddered as I tried to keep my stomach muscles from jerking.

Isaac produced a square of fabric from his pocket. "Sorry it's not fresh. I used it this morning onsite, but it should help." He struggled not to cough as he tied the bandana loosely around my face like a bandit. I breathed slowly through the fabric, forcing myself to adjust to the disgusting, sticky air. The first two breaths into the cloth smelled like him, but that didn't last. Nothing would mask the smell of the Storm here in the Tremé. Not for a long time.

Tears welled as I looked around.

Every single thing the Joneses owned had been destroyed. All the furniture was scattered and upside down, chunks of sheetrock had vomited from the walls, and the fan was hanging dangerously low from the living-room ceiling. Nearly the entire ground level had been submerged. Only the attic's contents might still be dry, which was why so many people had died in attics during the Storm – they had sought refuge in the driest place in the house and become trapped.

I made a beeline to the back. Isaac trailed me, staying close.

When we got to Brooke's room, shock paralyzed me – I'd probably spent just as much time in this room as I had in my own bedroom in junior high.

It got harder to keep the welled tears from spilling; I quickly blinked them away.

Isaac's hand touched the small of my back as he moved around me. He picked up her desk and set it upright and then retrieved the chair from across the room and set it in place on its remaining three legs. It only stood up for a second before falling against the desk. It would all have to be thrown out, but I understood why he was doing it – it felt disrespectful *not* to.

He moved to her giant dresser, which had toppled to the ground. I ran to help him lift it.

Once we got it standing, I took a deep breath through my mouth to avoid the smell.

"Are you okay?" he asked.

I nodded, despite being utterly overwhelmed.

"I'm going to go and check the rest of the house. Just yell if you need me, okay?" My head continued to nod as he walked out the door.

I took another deep breath through the fabric, thankful for both the handkerchief and the privacy.

Focus, Adele.

I tried not to get emotional as I started scavenging, but every single thing I looked at brought me closer to a panic attack. It felt like my heart was shaking inside my chest. It took another moment to realize that the medallion was actually shaking underneath my shirt – it felt warm against my skin. Unnaturally warm. I pulled it out.

"I could really use some help right about now, Adeline."

The warmth crept through my hands and up my arms until a current of energy bolted through my shoulders, making me gasp.

"What the…?"

The medallion floated up on the chain and then moved to the right, pointing like a compass to a mountain of moldy fly-infested clothes.

I choked, trying not to gag on the bad air, as the medallion practically pulled me towards the pile, which appeared to be shaking. Beneath the pile, I saw the edge of a familiar black leather case poking out.

She left her box? She always brought it on evacuations.

I pulled the old trumpet case out and nearly threw up as her ruined clothes, which were damp with mildew, spilled onto me. I quickly swatted them off and moved the case back to the other side of the room. I knew it well: it had originally contained her father's very first trumpet, an instrument he'd once been forced to hock in his harder, younger years, and which he'd been able to buy back after his first gig at Tipitina's, where he had to perform with a borrowed horn.

The family had mounted the trumpet over the piano in the living room, but Brooke refused to allow the case to be thrown out. She used it to store her most precious things.

I opened the now-warped leather box and let out a delighted yelp. Its contents were dry.

Relieved for Brooke, I quickly rifled through her treasures: photos, her NOSA acceptance letter, notes from boys, several talent show ribbons – and there it was, threaded on a strand of black leather: the good-luck charm. Adeline's eight-pointed star.

My pulse began to race as I ripped it off the leather cord and placed it onto the impression left behind on the medallion. With a quick jerk, the star twisted itself so all eight points lined up with the setting. It fit perfectly. Another wisp of sparks traced the edges of the star, welding it into place.

I'm not sure what I had expected to happen next, but nothing else did. I flipped it over and over, trying to understand what I was missing. "Come on…"

I slammed the case closed. *Ugh.*

AS I STEPPED INTO THE DEN, looking for Isaac, I accidentally sent a piece of a clarinet rolling across the once-beautiful wooden floor, which was now warped like a roller coaster. It only stopped rolling when it smacked into a twisted tuba. The room contained enough musical instruments to supply a small orchestra, or at least a couple of Second Lines. I sucked in a big breath – the air in this room was much clearer than it had been in Brooke's – either that or I was just getting used to the Storm stench.

I put down the trumpet case and stood, frozen, staring at the graveyard of brass. It was heartbreaking. The golden records, awards, and other recording paraphernalia that had once decorated the walls were now wrecked, and thousands of sheets of music had been strewn about the room. Most had dried into crisp leaves while others had been pulped into giant lumps of papier-mâché. Most of the melodies and lyrics had washed away from the papers, but hopefully they were still stuck in the head of Alphonse Jones and not lost forever.

No wonder he had said there was nothing left for them here.

Guilt washed over me, and I struggled not to completely break down. *How could I have fought with Brooke? How could I have acted like such a brat?*

I suddenly realized Isaac was standing next to me. My throat clenched when I tried to talk, and the bandana slipped down to my neck. My muscles began to shake as I used every ounce of strength not to cry.

He looked me in the eyes, and for the first time I saw sympathy in his.

Even in all the chaos, the way he looked at me made my stomach flutter. *What the hell?* And that was all the emotion I could contain – my bottom lip started to quiver – but before the first tear could escape, he leaned in and kissed me.

My heart rate soared as he broke away just a couple of inches. "Breathe," he whispered, brushing away the hair that had slipped in front of my eyes.

I nodded and inhaled, my eyes barely able to meet his.

But then my hand moved to his face as if I no longer had control over it, and his arm snaked around my waist, pulling me closer. His touch made me forget about all the bad things that had been happening. My nose brushed his, and I paused, intimidated by my own behavior. He must have sensed the limit of my forward actions because he moved the last couple of inches to meet my lips.

My eyes closed. I couldn't think about anything else as he kissed me – as I kissed him back. I couldn't hear anything else, smell anything else. Only him.

For a moment, I felt like I was floating, like we were floating.

Like two joined feathers.

I pulled him closer, and a whimper escaped the back of my throat, followed by a pang of self-consciousness. He kissed me again, but this time a little voice in the back of my head screamed, *What are you doing!*

My body reflexively tensed.

It had only been for a fraction of a second, but it was enough for him to pull back. Suddenly we were back on solid ground, back to reality. I opened my eyes, a little terrified of having to face him.

I wanted to slap myself for giving in to him, and then I wanted to slap Isaac for taking advantage of such a vulnerable situation. And yet, I was desperate to pull him close and go back to that moment where I had felt nothing. That moment where all of the pain went away.

"I'm sorry," he said, flustered. "You just looked so sad. I didn't know what to do."

I couldn't keep my eyes from opening wider, nor could I get words to come out of my mouth. *What had I just done? I don't even like Isaac – not like that. Right? Why is it taking every ounce of my strength not to close the distance between us?*

I took a step backwards without thinking – a protective reflex I immediately regretted when I saw how the small move stung him.

My entire being ached for comfort. Right then, I wanted nothing more than to feel his strong arms around me again.

Do not cry.

Then I cracked.

Tears began to drip from my eyes. He moved towards me. I didn't have the will to take another step back, and I knew in that moment I might do something I'd regret later. A squeak of protest came out of my mouth, but he calmly shushed me, moving his bandana to wipe the tears from my cheeks.

My eyes nervously followed his mouth.

The second I prepared to give in to him, he pulled me into his chest and continued to whisper soothingly into my ear. With my face hidden, I couldn't stop crying. He wrapped his arms even tighter.

In his unlikely embrace, I cried even harder for Brooke, Klara and Alphonse Jones. I cried for their neighbors. I cried for all the displaced people of New Orleans. I cried for the man with the blue eyes and for all the others who had died. I cried for myself, because I had no idea what I was supposed to do about it. Pressed up against him, I could feel the pulse of his heart, and it made me feel safe.

And there we stood until I ran out of tears.

I began to feel lightheaded, again like I was floating.

A breeze brought my mind back to the present. *Breeze?* I blinked twice to remove the last of my tears and gasped.

Hundreds of pieces of paper were floating in the air around us, slowly spinning in a clockwise turn. It was as if we were standing in the middle of a slow-motion cyclone. Only… we weren't standing at all. We were levitating four feet from the ground, in the center of this whirlwind of faded music. My heart plummeted with vertigo, while my arms circled tightly around his neck—

"Oh, my God. What the… Am I doing this?"

His eyes opened. He looked down at me with a serene expression, and then up at the ruined leaves of paper dancing through the air around us in a symphony of rustles. He barely managed to whisper:

"No, I'm doing this."

"It's beautiful."

IN THE CAR, NEITHER OF US SPOKE another word about either incident. We were both in too much shock.

I felt him steal a glance. I looked away, out the window, and my stomach clenched into a knot.

My fingers touched my lips. It was just a desperate act of loneliness. *Right?*

I quickly removed them, but my eyes fell to his hand on the stick shift. I suddenly had this desire to crawl under his arm and tell him all of my secrets. I understood how Adeline must have felt with Cosette and the Monvoisin sisters. I wanted to show him these tricks I had no explanation for.

But I couldn't move.

We pulled up to the house, and before he could even cut the engine, I jumped out the passenger door and darted for the front gate.

He scurried around the hood of the car. "Adele, I am really sorry about before."

"Don't wo—" I started to say, but was cut off by another male voice.

"Always apologizing," Niccolò said, emerging from our neighbor's stoop across the street. "Tsk, tsk, tsk."

"Hey!" I was a too little overenthusiastic for the interruption – and maybe because it was Niccolò. "I was wondering when you would show up."

"Ciao, bella," he said quietly and kissed my cheeks, which were now burning.

I turned back to Isaac. "Thanks again for the ride and for making sure the roof didn't fall on my head. See you later."

I caught the stunned look on his face as my attention returned to Niccolò with an embarrassing quickness. "Hang on a minute. I'll be right back." As I leapt into the house, I felt guilty about the way Isaac and I were parting, but I really couldn't handle the two of them together.

When I returned a minute later with Niccolò's jacket, Isaac, of course, was still there, looking peeved – Dr. Jekyll was gone for the night.

"I'm so sorry," I said to Niccolò, passing him the soft leather jacket, which I may have worn on a couple of extra occasions. "I was so caught up in Ren's theatrics that night I completely forgot I was wearing it."

"*Nessun problema, bella.* It gave me an excuse to come see you."

Isaac made no effort to hide his contempt for the soft-spoken Italian while he placed my father's keys into my hand.

"Adele, how is the cut on your face?" Niccolò asked, carefully annunciating each word as he looked dead-on at Isaac. It was the second time he had mentioned the wound but directed the commentary at him. The night of the tour, I didn't understand why his question had sounded like a threat, but just as my thoughts started to accuse him of being a jerk, the absurdity all came crashing together. The cut on my face, the feathers, the wind, the levitating.

The crow.

24

stockholm syndrome

(translated from French)

11th April 1728

SECRETS ARE A PECULIAR THING, PAPA. Time after time, I have seen secrets tear people apart. Secrets cause scandal and distrust. But sharing this secret brought us together in such a way that I know I will never doubt our friendship. I trust Cosette, Minette and Lisette Monvoisin with my life.

After my little reveal, Lise told us she had seen a man going into sleeping cabin number seven. "But not just any man," she said. "The same man we met on our last night in Paris, who asked Cosette about her dowry *cassette* from the King… The same man who also showed up at the dock the morning of our departure."

My heart nearly stopped at the thought that my rendezvous with Monsieur Jean-Antoine Cartier had been merely one of many for him, and that perhaps he had visited all the girls readying for this voyage. But when I asked, Lise described him as garish, boisterous, and blond – quite the opposite of my salon escort. Regardless, the parts of their tale identical to mine were certainly enough to cause alarm.

According to their story, on their final night in Paris, immediately after the curtain had fallen to the stage floor, the three girls were whisked off to a brothel near the docks. The King's mistress had arranged their stay, knowing that no one would find them in such a place. Their voyage was supposed to have been of the utmost secrecy, since their safety depended on it, but somehow the blond man knew of their plans to travel to *La Nouvelle-Orléans*. He first inquired about purchasing the girls, to which they gave him a very firm *no*. Then he offered to accompany them and protect them from the dangers of the New World, which the sisters laughed off as absurd, just as I had when made a similar proposal.

Cosette said, "The strangest part of our conversation was not his question, but the way he looked at me when he asked if we would stow him aboard in my *cassette*. It was as if he was trying to play some kind of mind-trick. That is when Minette realized who he was—"

"Rather, *what* he was," corrected Minette.

"I do not understand," I said. "What was he?"

"A *strigoi*," said Minette.

"A child of the night," whispered Lise.

"*Un vampyre*," said Cosette.

Nervous laughter escaped my lips, but then their silent stares made my heart seize. Not at the notion of the existence of vampires, but at the notion of a *vampire* being aboard this ship with us, in the middle of the ocean, thousands and thousands of leagues from land, from an escape route, from safety.

12th April 1728

I CANNOT REALLY SAY the existence of vampires shocks me. How could it, Papa, knowing the secrets that our family keeps? However, this realization has heightened every moment on board the ship. Every creak, every shadow piques my curiosity. This can be extraordinarily unnerving given the constant bob of the ocean causes everything to shift all day and all nightlong. This morning I struggled not to fall asleep in my porridge.

From my table with the DuFrenses, I overheard Cosette asking about the empty chair at their table. When one of the girls casually mentioned the missing girl had woken with seasickness, Cosette sprang out the doorway. I went after her, ignoring Madame DuFrense's remarks about my disgraceful behavior.

In sleeping cabin number seven, we found the missing girl, pale as a ghost, shivering, and too nauseous to get out of bed. It was easy to see why her bunkmates had dismissed her symptoms as seasickness.

Cosette removed the scarf from around the girl's neck and found two perfectly round puncture wounds, already nearly healed. Although the girl claimed to have no recollection of how the wounds came to be, she nervously yanked the scarf back and tied it in place.

Cosette and I ran back to her sisters.

"It's as we suspected," she told them. "He's on board the ship and has been coming out to feed under the cover of darkness."

13th April 1728

THE ORPHAN GIRL SOPHIE HAS DIED. She never woke from her unconscious state and finally stopped breathing last night. We have had our first casualty, and thus can no longer just wait in a defensive position to be preyed upon like helpless animals. But what can we do to stop a hidden monster who leaves no evidence behind other than his victims?

14th April 1728

THIS MORNING, A CREWMAN WAS FOUND DEAD at his night post with no visible wounds. A rag was tied around his neck, but I found no reason to remove the fabric and spread panic. I am finding it difficult to sleep, for whenever I close my eyes, I see our monster.

15th April 1728

I AM AFRAID I ONLY HAVE MORE BAD NEWS. Monsieur DuFrense seems to have awoken with the seasickness symptoms. He only has a slight fever, so I hope that he will make a full recovery.

The monster is becoming more arrogant regarding when and where he feeds. He takes members of the crew from the deck, and girls even go missing for periods of time in the middle of the day. It is now more critical than ever for us to execute some sort of quiet retaliation. And, as if these two pieces of news weren't bad enough, a ship of corsairs was spotted. The crewmen are keeping a careful watch on the pirate ship, while the four of us girls are keeping a careful watch on our silent enemy.

16th April 1728

DARE I SAY THE NIGHT WAS AMAZING, PAPA? He was amazing! The monster ran across the deck in a matter of seconds and then straight up the sail like a spider. We kept to the shadows, getting closer and closer as he leapt across the masts, but then I stopped short and held the girls back— I realized he was very much aware of our presence and that we were chasing him directly to his next victim!

He leapt to the crow's nest with such delicate ease, the sailor on watch did not even notice: a sailor whose only duty was to be on the lookout for danger! The monster perched on the wooden bucket that held the poor seaman and simply looked down at us. Without saying anything, we understood his message: either we let him down without giving him away, or there would be another burial at sea. He was giving us the choice.

We slowly backed away until the sailor, his predator, and the crow's nest were all out of sight.

I can't say I wasn't tempted to shoot a flame at the monster, but the move would have been far too risky – it might have destroyed the vampire, but it would certainly have killed the watchman too. Was taking the life of one man to save the life of another something I could live with? To save the lives of many? I hope to never know the answer, but still the questions lurk in the back of my mind, and have caused me another sleepless night.

The tired seaman returned unharmed from his post this morning, and you can imagine his shock when I nearly knocked him over with affection.

17th April 1728

CLAUDE DUFRENSE'S CONDITION continues to worsen, but he tries to stay strong for his wife, who has become absolutely hysterical. Cosette gave me some herbs, which I brew and slip into Martine's tea to calm her down long enough to sleep.

The corsair ship has now been flanking our vessel for two days, and we can only surmise they are foe rather than friend. The captain is taking the necessary precautions in case there is an attack.

As they prepare the cannons, the sailors swap tales of pirates traveling the open sea in search of booty and a wild romp. The nuns spend the hours calming the other girls, but Cosette, Minette, Lisette, and I have all been too preoccupied with our dark passengers to worry about pirates.

Yes, *passengers.* Two other girls have awoken with the "seasickness symptoms," leading us to believe there is more than one vampire aboard the ship. Exactly how many we have no idea, but the number of victims climbs each night, meaning the monsters are growing stronger. Why they have the need to grow stronger with such haste keeps me up tonight, Papa. I can only hope that it is not because they sense our desire for retaliation.

Now, I must try to sleep, for the dawn will bring the confrontation with the pirates.

18th April 1728

BEFORE THE SUN HAD A CHANCE TO RISE, everyone on the ship made preparations for combat, by order of the captain. The crew armed themselves with steel, and the nuns armed themselves with rosary beads between their fingers. The captain did everything he could to create the illusion that we were a force to be reckoned with – all of the King's daughters were forced to dress as men to make it appear that our crew was larger than it was. I wonder what would have happened if the pirates had known from the start that the cargo he carried was just a few dozen virgin girls rather than a thousand barrels of wine or a hundred chests filled with emeralds? Would they have turned away, or would they have come faster?

If the captain was nervous as the mysterious ship inched closer to the S.S. *Gironde,* he revealed no signs to us. Neither did his first mate, nor the rest of the crew. Once the enemy closed most of the distance, I was ordered below deck with the DuFrenses. It was not long before I grew embittered, trapped inside with the hysterical Martine and the barely lucid Claude.

What happened next is a blur, Father. And now, it is difficult to keep my fingers from heating the quill as I try to record the story, but I will aim for accuracy:

We heard a loud bang, and then the boat shook. I jumped from the chair, realizing we had been hit by the enemy's shot. That was enough suspense for me—

I tore through the hallway as more shots were exchanged. Smoke was already filling the narrow passage, making it hard to see and difficult to breathe. I made it out onto the deck and discovered that we had raised the white flag in surrender, but, despite this, the pirates continued to attack. It was just a matter of time before they would invade the ship.

With their hair still hidden beneath borrowed sailor hats, the girls held each other, weeping, while the nuns continued to pray. But it was not God who was going to save us.

As the sun fell toward the horizon, the corsair lowered a small dory full of pirates. They rowed forward to investigate our ship, causing an undercurrent of terror to ripple through the S.S. *Gironde*. The uncertainty of our future made it difficult to contain my emotions, and every metal object quaked as I walked past.

The dory contained twelve men, if you could call them men. They clambered onto our ship, using hooks and ropes, and landed on the deck with hoots and snarls. Their long, wild hair was tangled with scraps of rag, and they wore mismatched ensembles of sailor's slops and threads that must once have been fine but were now tattered and salt-stained. I had never seen anything like them, and I think the sight of our group gave them an equal shock.

Mumbling in an undecipherable English dialect, one stepped forward from the pack with a curled lip that revealed only a few rotting teeth and hopped to Lise in a way which suggested he was drunk or insane. He got so close to her face their noses very nearly touched.

We watched in horror as he tore off her cap. "What've we got 'ere?" he asked.

She whimpered as her bright blonde locks fell loose.

A sickening smile spread over his face, and then he buried his nose into the crook of her neck, inhaling deeply, ready to lap her up like a starved dog. My shoulders burned like fire as growls of excitement came from his mates, making the other orphans recoil. Captain Vauberci drew his sword, but immediately found four blades touching his throat. I was so outraged that I shook violently, but Cosette managed to remain cool.

"Pardonnez-moi, Monsieur," she beckoned in a voice as soothing as Aphrodite's, coaxing the pirate away from her sister. Both relief and guilt washed over Lise's face as the pirate walked towards the hexing triplet with his pelvis thrust forward – his imminent death being the furthest thing from his mind as he scratched his crotch with great *élan.*

Getting people to oblige, this is Cosette's specialty. She can speak or sing or sometimes simply stare at someone, and that is all it takes for them to fall under her spell. When he reached her, the despicable pirate grabbed her bosom. In broad daylight! This appalling display brought our crew's hands to the hilts of their swords, but despite being assaulted by his fondling hands, Cosette calmed our men with one reassuring look, wanting to prevent a battle, not start one. Even as he ripped open her shirt, still no metal was drawn. The pirate stepped backwards as if to get a better view of his newfound treasure, but one more seductive smile from her gleaming lips and he suddenly became giddy. Her smile held, and his giddiness grew until his feet couldn't keep up with his fervor. He staggered to one side, dangerously close to the edge of the ship.

"Adieu, mon amour," she whispered as his seemingly own drunken stupor sent him overboard.

The pirate's own mates roared with laughter and called him a drunken buffoon. Lise ran to her sister.

"How do you do it? How do you control their minds?" she asked.

"You don't control their minds, *ma fifille*, you control their hearts," Cosette replied quietly as Minette hurried to restore her modesty.

The reunion was cut short when the scuffed boots of the enemy captain hit our deck with a loud thud, settling everyone into silence. The hideous-looking man had a wandering eye and a face like burnt leather. A large red bird rested on his shoulder – the beautiful creature a stark contrast to the villainous group. It broke the tense silence by chirping a song that on any other day would have sounded lovely but today sounded eerie and mocking. As he rounded the ship, examining his new loot, the wind blew open his ragged overcoat, and the startled bird fluttered into the air before gliding to a new perch on Cosette's shoulder.

His crew fidgeted with delight, eagerly awaiting instructions.

When the pirate captain finally stopped pacing, a smile spread under his untamed beard.

"Thanks be ta the King o' France!" he yelled in English, causing a roar from his constituency.

The crowd hushed as his eyes came to rest on me – I was the only lady still in a dress. He turned on his heel and slowly approached me with a walk of grandeur, almost a dance. A dance that I wanted no part of. Nevertheless, he stopped right in front of me and asked, "*Mademoiselle*, why don't ya cry like all the otha birds?"

I struggled to get the English words out and had to force myself to look at his face without wincing when I said, "Should you prefer me to cry?"

"I don't care what ya do, li'l lady, as long as ya do it lookin' like that." He gave me a slow wink with his good eye, and that's when I realized that his other eye wandered because it was not real. It was a stone: milky and iridescent like an opal.

His rank breath attacked me as he continued to yell ungentlemanly things. A burn raged through my shoulders, and I became extremely frightened, Papa. Not at the hideous captain, but at what I might do. My fist balled to hide the sparks trying to escape. I thought that I might explode if there was not some sort of release.

"Then you shan't care that I do this," I muttered and spat in his false eye.

His monstrous hand collided with the side of my face, spinning me to the floor. He let out a giant roar, like a true madman, and fell on top of me. "Yer a feisty one, aren't ya? All the better!"

My head throbbed, and a loud buzz rang in my ears. I dug my fingernails into the floorboards beneath me, struggling not to defend myself in ways that would cause alarm. I saw ten different things I could kill him with, but, remembering our audience, I let my head fall to the side in defeat.

When no more words came out of the captain's blistered lips, I looked back at him – his attention had moved from my face to my medallion, which had slipped out from beneath the fabric of my dress. Your gift, Papa.

He ripped the chain from my neck and became excited by what other riches might be aboard.

"Lock 'em below deck!"

The pirates chained all the passengers of the S.S. *Gironde* together, packed us into the dining hall, and bolted the door so they could raid the ship without distraction.

Whilst trapped, my thoughts spun. If I revealed my true nature, there was no guaranteeing I wouldn't be burned at the stake afterwards, even if everyone on the ship was saved as a result. It was the most dreadful night, Papa.

For hours, we wondered which would be crueler: to kill us immediately, or to leave us on the open ocean to starve and bake to death under the unyielding sun? Most of the girls prayed with the nuns, as did some of the crew. My thoughts were with poor Captain Vauberci, who the pirate captain had kept on deck.

Eventually, our crew began to sing songs and sip flasks of spirits. The more time passed, the drunker they became, and the sadder the songs sung. By the time the sun rose again, most had made peace with God and were ready to walk the plank, but I was wide awake and *not* content to rest eternally on the floor of the Atlantic.

And then the strangest thing happened, Papa.

Absolutely nothing.

No one came to get us. We heard no more noises. Another hour went by and still nothing happened. The others became restless, as the peace they had made with death faded. Something was clearly not right.

I made eyes with Cosette from across the room to tell her I was going to leave, and then focused on the shackles that bound my wrists until the metal expanded enough to slip my hands out. Everyone was so excited when they saw I was free, they did not even question how it had happened.

Breaking the lock on the door would have been an impossible task without being noticed, but then Cosette began to sing a lullaby. Minette joined a phrase later, and then Lise, until everyone was under the spell of the melody. The diversion made it easy for me to focus on the inner workings of the padlock until it popped open and fell to the ground on the other side of the door. I slipped out as they began the second verse.

With haste, I ran down the deserted hallway and climbed the stairs that led to the deck, but when I tried to push the hatch door open, it barely budged. Something was lying on top of it, trapping us below.

A little focus on the hinges, and they slowly pushed the heavy wood up. Sunlight infiltrated the crack, and a dark liquid dripped onto my face and shoulders. I wiped it away, and my hand came back smeared red. My heart pounded as the hatch opened, and the corpse that had been weighing it down slid to the deck.

My arms bent to shield my eyes from the blinding sun as I climbed out from below. When the scene before me came into full view, nothing could have prepared me for the sight. I ran to the edge of the ship as bile leapt up my throat.

The ocean breeze whipped my hair around, and the splashing waves glittered beautifully, as if the bloodbath behind me had not happened.

Despite knowing the answer, I wandered the deck to see if anyone was still alive. Bodies were strewn about as if it was the aftermath of a great battle, but there had been no battle; there had been a slaughter. Corpses draped from the blood-sprayed sails and hung from the railings like *des décorations de fête*. Every throat had been ripped out, and every pirate had died with a look of terror on his face. My fingers tingled; I knew exactly what had happened. Who… *what* had answered our prayers.

Do not mistake me. I had no sympathy for the pirates who had seemed so prepared to leave us locked up. *Au contraire*, a rush of excitement overwhelmed me, knowing we had not been defeated.

At the front of the ship, the pirate captain had been impaled with a large harpoon; the scent of blood choked me as I grabbed the drenched ring of keys from his belt.

I ran back down below to release the others.

The look of horror on my face must have begged for silence because no one pressed me for news. I led the way back to the deck, hearing the gasps behind me as one by one they took in the carnage. Tears escaped my eyes when I noticed the dead bodies of a few of our men, who had been caught between the two deadly factions.

"*Sacrebleu*!" whispered Minette.

"I don't understand," said Lise. "Are they protecting us?"

"They aren't protecting *us*—" I said.

"They are protecting their food source," Cosette finished.

Right then, the beautiful red bird squawked from the crow's nest and then swooped down to land on Cosette's shoulder, singing a few notes as if in agreement.

The rest of the hostages flooded onto the deck, each more stunned than the last. Screams fled the orphans. Some of the crew shed tears when they found the bodies of their brethren. The nuns seemed the most confounded of all. They fell to their knees in prayer, but knew not whether to thank God for our survival at such a cost of life.

As the crew raced around the ship, fearing irreparable damage, we found Captain Vauberci gagged, bound, and stuffed into a closet. He had only a few broken ribs and very little recollection of the previous night, although he twitched when asked about it. After many swigs from his flask, he became his old steadfast self and commanded preparation for the seamen's funeral.

Though it was apparent to all that something unnatural had occurred, Captain Vauberci announced that the few sailors who had perished on deck had defeated the pirates and died heroes. Of course, this was absolutely preposterous, but no one wanted to think about the alternatives. Songs and prayers were sung with haste, both because of seamen's superstition and fear of damage to our ship.

Shortly after the funeral, the captain made the announcement we all feared: "The S.S. *Gironde* is beyond repair. We have no choice but to abandon the ship.

Eager to flee the gory scene, every passenger, even Martine DuFrense, assisted in transporting our cargo onto the pirate ship. One of the crew assigned the rooms, and then once the orphans ensured their precious dowry *cassettes* were safely aboard the new ship, they began to scrub the cabins. But no amount of cleaning was going to remove the years of grime accumulated by the pirates.

While the captain and his top mates scurried around the ship, investigating the rigging, the triplets and I tackled the giant black rag on the flagpole and tossed it into the ocean. In its place, we hoisted the flag from the S.S. *Gironde,* and then Captain Vauberci claimed the ship for the King.

The night crew took their posts, and all the passengers retreated to their new cabins, while the Monvoisin sisters and I stole a few more minutes on deck. We watched the dark silhouette of the S.S. *Gironde* sinking under the full moon.

"Is it possible we will be done with these monsters after tonight?" Cosette asked.

The three of us knew it was not pirates to whom she was referring.

"We can hope," said Lise, as the distance between the ships became greater.

I nodded slowly, but hope wasn't enough for me. I grasped their hands and concentrated on our old ship one last time.

We were stronger together.

The girls began to sing, and soon enough a fifth voice joined us – the exotic red bird who was perched once again on Cosette's shoulder, looking perfectly in place next to the beautiful girl. When I turned back to the ocean, all I saw was a growing flame floating on the black water, bright against the black sky.

Smiles spread across our faces as the flames engulfed the ship, the pirate corpses, and anything else aboard the S.S. *Gironde*. We sang the last notes of the song and then retired for the night.

Both exhausted and enthralled, I entered the squalor of my new cabin. By what miracle of God could we have simultaneously survived a pirate attack *and* rid ourselves of our original predators?

I immediately flinched when I plopped down on the rough mattress of a now-dead pirate. I expected to find a rock underneath my back, but instead pulled out a smooth, round stone: it was milky and iridescent like a very large opal.

I sat up quickly, recognizing the stone as the glint from the pirate captain's eye socket. A trophy. Like a cat leaving a dead mouse as a gift for its owner.

I didn't know whether to feel grateful or threatened, but my intuition led me to the former. The fiery itch in my palms begged to differ.

My medallion was next to it – the chain broken but otherwise perfectly intact. I quickly mended the metal and slipped it back around my neck. The familiarity brought an immediate sense of relief. This, of course, didn't last for long—

I didn't know *who* had placed the treasures on my bed, but I knew *what* had. We may have defeated the pirates, but we had not escaped the monsters.

25

willkommen, bienvenue, welcome

October 27th

Isaac	**7:22 p.m.**	Hey, wanna hang out tonight? I know it's kinda difficult with the curfew, but maybe ur dad would let me come over?

I looked at the little brass alarm clock. 7:34 p.m. I'd been staring at the text message for twelve minutes. In that time I'd written at least six different responses and been unable to send one of them.

Determined, I typed in a dumb joke, but then quickly hit the back button until it vanished. My eyes flicked back to his message. *Like it's my dad's permission I'm worried about. He's never home anyway.* The thought of being here alone with Isaac made my stomach jerk. At the same time, the more I avoided Isaac, the more my stomach seemed to jerk. Although, I'm not sure if it counts as avoiding since he was at my house every afternoon… more like ignoring. I'd been counting the hours 'til the weekend to have some peace. This text message had popped up just when I stopped counting.

For the rest of the week after "the incident," we both continued to pretend like nothing had happened. Like we never kissed. Like he never demonstrated some kind of magical ability in front of me. But ever since that night it had been hard for me to focus on much else. *How am I supposed to think about Kafka when every bird I see reminds me of Isaac... and the memory of my face being ripped open, and... and that kiss?* The only time I could remotely distract myself was when I was translating Adeline's diary.

My fingertip traced the thin line on my cheek where the crow had attacked me.

"It's not possible, Adele."

Brooke's words echoed in the back of my mind: "*Oh my God! Can't you ever just let something good happen to you without sabotaging it*?"

Is Isaac a good thing trying to happen to me – and here I am convincing myself that he slashed my face open? What kind of twisted freak am I? Images of sketched feathers flashed in my mind. I clammed up. The thought passed.

"You're being ridiculous… Isaac is *not* the crow," I yelled. My gut told me otherwise.

I grabbed my phone, but before my thumbs could get a word out, it buzzed with a lengthy text message from an unsaved number.

unknown	**7:38 p.m.**	Hi, Adele. Little sis initiation starts this week and we thought it would be

nice to include u since u weren't here freshman year. Slumber party at my house 2night. We'll pick u up. Wear ur favorite pjs! xo Annabelle

xo Annabelle? My phone buzzed again.

Désirée	**7:39 p.m.**	Did you get an invite from Annabelle? I told her I'd pick you up. Be ready at 8:30.

I love that Désirée just assumed I would participate in these shenanigans.

Before I could overanalyze anything else, my thumbs flew over the screen, typed one little word, and hit send.

Adele	**7:40 p.m.**	Okay.

"Okay?" *Am I so determined to avoid Isaac that I would rather hang out with Annabelle's clique?* "Seriously pathetic, Adele. You deserve whatever you get from Annabelle."

From what I had gathered over the week, Sacred Heart had some kind of tradition to pair freshman (Little Sisters) up with juniors (Big Sisters). The Big Sisters were supposed to guide freshmen over the next two years and then pass on the Big Sister title when they graduated. I had the feeling that inclusion wasn't really what Annabelle had in mind for me tonight, but whatever stupid scheme she was cooking up seemed like marshmallows after reading about Adeline's and the triplets' problems.

Vampire problems.

Did I really just think that? And more importantly, do I have vampire problems?

As I texted my plans to my father, images of pedicures, underage drinking, and rounds of Truth or Dare flipped through my mind – all things I could handle. *What's the worst that could happen at a slumber party?*

At least I was already dressed for the occasion. And at least now I wasn't lying to Isaac when I told him I already had plans. For some reason, guilt still plagued me.

I don't know if it was Isaac, the anticipation of prep-school hazing, the pirate massacre, or the fact that the overhead light was now flickering on and off, but I was soon in a tizzy. I closed my eyes and sucked air in through my nose until the light bulb finally behaved.

"Two more bodies have been reported today," the DJ said as I turned on the radio. I sat at the vanity. A sound bite of the police chief was plugged: "We're not answering any questions. At the moment, all we can say is that the victims were missing a lot of blood."

I began aggressively separating my waves into two messy braids.

"As everyone knows, the city is operating with only one functioning hospital, and the morgue is completely overwhelmed, which means there is a queue for autopsies and we're losing more evidence while we wait." He sounded flustered. The poor man probably hadn't slept much since the Storm.

The radio host cut back in. "And we have Jack on the line, a pastry chef from the Warehouse District."

"Yes, hello, Jack Whitaker here. Rumor has it that the National Guard has set up shop in the old Brown's Milk Factory. Supposedly, they hooked up generators to the old refrigeration system so they can use it to store corpses yet to be processed."

"There you have it, folks. This city is so broken we don't even have the resources to deal with our dead, but this won't come as a shock to locals, who are still struggling to find food, gasoline, medical supplies, and, of course, their relatives. If these bodies weren't Storm related, then this message is going out to the killer. Just because the N.O.P.D. is backed up, doesn't mean the rest of us don't have our eyes on you. Citizens, be alert. This is the Wolfman, signing off."

Chills crawled up my arms.

Without moving, I twisted the dial and welcomed the familiar trills of Mr. Jones's trumpet. The nostalgia lasted for only a few bars before being interrupted by obnoxious honking from the street.

An unfamiliar grey Porsche SUV was parked in front of my house, engine running – not Désirée's white monstrosity. I strained to see the driver. *Ugh, Annabelle. I guess there was a change in plans.*

I grabbed my bag, snapped off the lights, and ran down the stairs, but as soon as I opened the front door, Désirée pushed her way inside, backing me into the hallway.

"Hey," I said as she shut the door behind her. "Are we—"

"Where is your room?"

"Up the stairs, why?"

Without waiting for an invitation, she ran up, dragging me behind.

"Take off your clothes."

"What?" I snickered.

She quickly began digging through my drawers, slamming each one shut until she got to my lingerie.

"What do you think you're doing?"

She spun around and stared me up and down with that look of disapproval I was getting used to. But I was unsure why my ankle-rolled sweatpants and thrifted Mickey Mouse T-shirt were unacceptable for a sleepover. *Sheesh.* She tossed me a cream-colored, satin camisole from the drawer and then started pulling my shirt off. I swatted her hands away.

"You are going to have to trust me on this one."

Coming from Désirée Borges, these were not words that made me comfortable, but the urgency in her voice made me obey. I ripped off my tee and slipped on the slinky cami I had taken from a box of my mother's abandoned things a couple years ago. It barely covered my stomach. I was tugging on it when a pair of tiny black spandex shorts hit my face.

"Shorts, now. Do not say anything to Annabelle about changing your clothes, and especially don't say I made you do it."

Her comment activated my defenses for the night as I realized she was breaking some kind of code. *Is Désirée actually doing me a solid?*

I slipped on the shorts, which had become far too short after I'd hit my final growth spurt, and she watched me untangle the *gris-gris* from my chain and tuck it into the slip. "Where did you get that necklace?" she asked.

"Umm, your grandmother gave it to me."

"No, not the *gris-gris.* The other one?"

"Oh, family heirloom."

"Hmm," she said as if contemplating, and then turned to dig through my closet. "Put on these." She tossed me a pair of plastic flats. I let them fall to the floor.

"I'm not wearing jellies. There's still glass everywhere—"

"Flip-flops?"

"Ugh, no! How does that help? I am wearing sneakers or my Docs." I was beginning to regret accepting this invitation. I stepped into my boots to show her I meant it. Her eyes went to the ceiling.

"Don't say I didn't warn you." She grabbed my arm and pulled me back down the stairs. Her behavior made no sense, especially since she was slumber-party-ready in an oversized cotton T-shirt and leggings.

I caught a glimpse in the hallway mirror as we went out the door. I looked completely ridiculous in the shiny shorts, nothing but cream-colored lace covering my cleavage, burgundy Docs, and two messily braided pigtails. I looked like a bumpkin teen prostitute.

"Who cares?" I whispered with a sigh. "It's just a sleepover with a bunch of snobby girls."

I pulled the gate closed and felt the mechanical pieces lock. Annabelle honked the horn again as I leapt down the stoop.

"Hey, sorry to keep you waiting," I said, squeezing myself into the back next to Dixie. "I couldn't find my phone."

Désirée shot me a look of approval from the front passenger seat.

Crammed into the row behind us were four freshman girls wearing a mix of boxer shorts and scrubs, and one timid-looking girl who had on some kind of unfortunate moo-moo. Dixie had obviously given careful consideration to her outfit: a purple, satin nightgown and a matching robe. As if that wasn't enough, she wore giant, purple, furry slippers that looked like tie-dyed sheep dogs.

The minions next to her were fellow classmen, Jaime, in a Tweety Bird nightie, and Bri, in a XL Saint's jersey with seemingly nothing on underneath. She caught me looking at her ankle boots and had to tighten her lips to contain giggles – the shoes were unusually fancy for such an occasion. Something was up.

Just as my suspicions were aroused, I saw Annabelle Lee looking over my attire from her rearview mirror. A slow smile spread across her face. Something was *definitely* up.

"All right, ladies, per Sacred Heart tradition, you each have to wear one of these blindfolds until we reach the secret location."

"Secret location?" peeped a small blonde from the back. "Aren't we going to your house, Annabelle?"

"Don't ask questions," Jaime said as she turned and tied the first blindfold on her.

I searched Dixie's face for any sign that she might know what the hell was going on. She didn't seem too concerned, which made me wonder if she was in the know.

"Dixie, you tie Adele, and I'll tie you," Bri ordered.

"My pleasure," Dixie said sweetly, securing the black cloth into a bow at the back of my head – just a little too tight, letting me know who was in control.

"Where are we going, Annabelle?" I asked. Suddenly the idea of being blindfolded by a bunch of girls who hated me didn't seem like the smartest idea in the world.

"It's not about where we're going. It's about how much fun we're going to have."

I could sense panic from the backseat, but I refused to ask another question or seem alarmed in any way. There's no way I was going to give Dixie or any of these princesses the satisfaction.

THE RIDE ONLY TOOK A FEW MINUTES, so I guessed we were still in the Quarter, or the Marigny, depending on how many stop signs she had blown through, although I couldn't really imagine the Queen of Uptown going past Esplanade Avenue.

My door opened, and Annabelle helped me step out of the car. "Be careful, we wouldn't want any mishaps before the party even starts."

The phrase "kill them with kindness" suddenly had a whole new meaning. I tried not to grow nervous as Annabelle linked her arm through mine and pulled me up the curb onto the sidewalk. Behind us, Dixie wasted her breath complimenting Désirée, and, as per usual, Désirée ignored her.

We walked about two blocks, and then Annabelle commanded, "Quiet until we arrive."

This would not be difficult for me; Dixie, on the other hand…

Feeling the stone under my feet, I deduced that we were still in the Quarter, and a few minutes later a loud creak gave away an iron gate. Then echoes of clacking high heels sounded like we were being shuffled down a narrow passage. *High heels?* I dragged my hand along the wall. Brick. *We're still outside… maybe heading into a courtyard.* A damp breeze kicked up a familiar smell. It was dull, but I would have recognized it anywhere: the mix of booze and bleach that only a barroom could produce. I used to wake up to that scent as a child – right after my mother left, my father had kept me with him at work until the wee hours, too scared to let me leave his sight.

Annabelle led me up a flight of wooden stairs and into a space that must have been incredibly dark because now there wasn't even the faintest bit of light coming through the blindfold. I was suddenly very aware that it must be close to 9 p.m. and we would soon be breaking curfew.

"All right, this is good. You can take off the blindfolds."

It took only a second for my eyes to adjust to the minuscule amount of light shed by the single gas lantern in the dank room, and only another second to realize that the juniors were no longer sporting pajamas. Each was decked out in a tight dress, ready for a night out on the town. Jaime must have been wearing the turquoise halter number underneath her Tweety Bird nightie. I yanked on my camisole, feeling seriously inadequate next to her. The girl could easily have been a swimsuit model.

Terror cracked through Dixie's pageant façade as she shed her robe.

"Flip-flops. Now!" she demanded from one of the freshmen, trading her ridiculous slippers. *I guess she hadn't been in the know after all.*

My jaw clenched as I watched the rest of the juniors pull accessories from their bags, but I was more terrified of what would happen at school on Monday if I bailed now than I was of proceeding. I peered down at myself. *Utterly ridiculous.* Annabelle Lee was looking at me too, laughing and saying something to Désirée, who gave me a look that wasn't exactly sympathy but seemed to say, "*I tried.*"

I guess my outfit was a serious improvement compared to the others being hazed. In a more risqué closet, my camisole could have been a top, and my shorts, hot pants. Just thinking the words "hot pants" was mortifying. The group of freshmen looked completely childlike in their pajamas. One girl seemed irate, and I could sense a revenge plot turning in her head, while the other three were on the verge of tears, anticipating the public humiliation that loomed ahead.

"Everyone ready?" Annabelle asked. "Follow my lead."

A strange sense of familiarity crept up as we walked a series of quick twists and turns. *Where the hell are we?* I searched for clues, but it was so dark I might as well have had the blindfold on.

"Who do we have here?" a deep male voice echoed as we turned into a long hallway.

Annabelle signaled to the freshmen to walk past him.

"I don't think so, sister. Let's see some ID."

He shined a flashlight, blinding us. His voice sounded familiar, but my eyes refused to peer into the bright light to get a look at him. Annabelle let out a hushed grunt in frustration, but then to my surprise she whipped a plastic rectangle over to the bouncer, who sighed but let her pass. Désirée, Bri, and Jaime each did the same and continued down the hallway.

Dixie stammered in her sweetest Texas-beauty-queen drawl, "Sir, it looks like I forgot my license. I can really be such a ditz sometimes."

Sometimes?

"No ID, no entrance."

As Dixie continued to try to flirt her way inside, I heard scuffles behind me and turned to find the freshmen scattering like mice. I didn't have a fake ID either; I relaxed a little and began to follow them out.

"Little Addie—"

I stopped in my tracks.

"Adele, is that you?"

I walked back to the bouncer, who turned the flashlight on himself. An awkward smile spread across my face as I tried to act casual.

"Hey, Troy."

The gruff man was a friend of Ren's and also a longtime employee of my father's. At least, he had been before the Storm. My smile turned genuine as I realized there probably wasn't a bar in the entire French Quarter I couldn't get into, for better or for worse. He gave me a hug and then pulled up my arm to better examine my outfit.

"That's quite a different look you got going on, girl."

Dixie watched us with her mouth gaping.

"Don't ask," I begged, making him laugh. "It's a costume I'm testing out for a school play." I was appalled at how easy the lie flew out of my mouth. Maybe I was more like the Sacred Heart girls than I thought.

"Shoulda figured it was something like that. You always up to something crazy." He gave me another hug and then passage. "Do me a favor and tell your Pa 'bout all these kids trying to get into this bar."

"Uh, okay," I answered, with zero plan to engage my father in any conversation that would place me somewhere one of his old bouncers was guarding.

I took one last look back and saw Dixie glaring at me with her arms crossed. The last thing I wanted to do was to walk into this weird place, but I couldn't pass up the opportunity to have something Dixie wanted and couldn't get – this would probably be my only chance. I gave her a little wave before I pivoted on my heel and flipped my hair, like I'd seen Désirée do so many times before. Only my version involved braided pigtails.

CANDLES HANGING ON BOTH SIDES illuminated a wooden door at the end of the corridor. The scent of cigarettes grew stronger as I approached it, and then muffled music and merriment on the other side drew my hand to the knob. *Here goes nothing,* I thought as I pushed it open.

It was some kind of old parlor room. I felt like I had walked into someone's house. Two men in suits sipped cocktails near a candle-lined fireplace. Others were huddled on couches engaged in deep conversation. A couple kissed in a dark corner. There was an odd sense of familiarity about the room. The billowing cigarette smoke made my eyes water; I hurried along.

As I walked past a series of windows, I pushed aside one of the heavy drapes – the tall windows still had their storm boards up but now, instead of keeping the weather out, they were keeping the flickers of candlelight and noise inside, obviously to hide from the curfew. Slipping from room to room in the darkness, I felt like I had unwittingly traveled to a night-gone-by.

The deeper I walked into the secret house, the more packed it became with folks from all walks of life. Young and old. Glitz and glam. Tattered and torn. I stopped when I entered a small ballroom, instantly taken aback by the scene, especially after the dullness of the last month. On a small, wooden, candle-lined stage, an androgynous female wearing a flapper shift, oodles of metallic-gold eye makeup, and a blunt bob belted out *"La Vie En Rose,"* while a pianist with a waxed mustache, bow tie, and bowler hat accompanied. People were draped over cabaret-style tables, soaking in the performance.

Suddenly paranoid about fitting into the hip scene, I approached the makeshift bar to get a drink; the bartender recognized me right away. By day, Liza was an architectural grad student, but now she better resembled Cleopatra. She glanced at Annabelle's group, shot me a look of sympathy, and slid me a glass tumbler full of clear liquid.

"You're gonna need it," she said with a wink of her ostentatious false eyelashes. "Oh, wait." She signaled for the drink back, reached under the bar, and then plopped something into my glass, making it fizz over. I licked the spillage from my hand and saw a limp, yellowish slice of lime sinking into the bubbles. *Whoa, fruit.* I raised the glass to her.

"Merci beaucoup."

She brought one finger over her lips to indicate silence, and then gave me a strange look when I tried to pay for the drink.

Prepared for the wretched taste of alcohol, I took a small sip from the iceless glass and turned to find the group. The gin assaulted my taste buds; I tried not to make a face as I took a bigger sip. *Don't drink it too fast, Adele.* I had a feeling I was going to need all of my wits to navigate this situation. I started to move in their direction.

The old house was falling apart – the paint was cracking, the wallpaper was peeling, and the furniture was a hodgepodge of hurricane-survived pieces someone had likely collected in a hurry for the secret club. Despite the physical conditions, it was energetic and alive, as if the scene itself had a pulse. The kind of pulse only illegal activity could illicit.

The sultry singer held the final note, and the crowd roared. But only for a moment, then they began to shush each other, whispering, "The curfew! The curfew!" The shushing only contributed more to the excitement. I felt like I had warped into a prohibition era – people were so ecstatic just to be out. *This place is so cool.* If it'd been open pre-Storm, I'd have known about it, surely. I'd have to ask my dad if he'd heard anything.

Dad.

I slowly turned a full circle. My heartbeat began to creep faster as I quickly turned two more. It was certainly unrecognizable, but I *had* been here before. The alleyway, the bouncer, the bartender. I was in *la garçonnière* of my *father's bar.*

"Shit."

"EXCUSEZ-MOI," I REPEATED CONTINUOUSLY as I pushed through people, wanting to get away from the bartender who knew me. I tried to not show any outward signs that I was frantically trying to compose myself on the inside as the evidence became more obvious – the door to the bathroom, the chandelier, a rug that used to be in our living room.

Ugh. How did I not recognize this place right away?

Originally, these small buildings at the back of properties (often mistaken for slave quarters) were private homes where French boys were sent from the main house to live when they turned fifteen. I'm not really sure why… to become men? This *garçonnière* had been rented out to the same old man most of my life. When he died five years ago, my father discovered termites in parts of the building; he had the house treated, but we didn't have enough money to renovate it, so it had sat vacant since.

Not only was the room looking familiar, I began recognizing faces among the mélange of college students and gutter punks: our neighbors; a group of brass musicians who played with Alphonse Jones; ol' Madame Villere, wearing pearls and white gloves, sipping a warm martini. Despite the volume in the room, Ren still managed to make himself noticeable. He and Theis were sitting around a center table with a few other goths. Whatever story he was narrating had the full attention of his group.

Totally paranoid, I waited until I was safely hidden by a gang of people near the left corner of the stage before I continued scanning the crowd, sucking limey gin-and-tonic through the tiny black straw.

My head did a double take when I saw Isaac's tiny ponytail sitting at the bar. Sadly, I could recognize the contour of his broad shoulders in his white T-shirt. When the wall repairs had to be put on hold because of supply scarcity, he started fixing anything around the house that needed fixing in exchange for his art lessons. Not that my father cared; he'd gladly give Isaac free art lessons for life just to have another male around the house. But Isaac wouldn't have it any other way – which, of course, made my father like him even more. Apparently so much so that he was letting him stay in the bar underage.

Wait, how does Isaac even know about this place?

My irritation compounded, knowing my father had told Isaac his big secret and not me. *We* did *not* have secrets. And to top it all off, Isaac hadn't told me either! *Ugh! Talk about secrets causing scandal and distrust. So much for him trying to get closer to me.* I imagined myself storming over to him and throwing the remainder of my drink in his face.

"*Mademoiselle*?" A tap on my shoulder interrupted my silent rage.

I turned and jumped an inch off the floor – a man with a clown-painted face was extending a tray of small drinks. *So. Random.*

"No, thank you." I shook my head, and the Marcel Marceau lookalike retreated with a bow.

Désirée was easy to spot across the room because of her height. Her trajectory led me to Gabe. *Shocker.* Annabelle did not look thrilled following Désirée, but I watched the queen bee's face go from annoyed to intrigued when Désirée stopped at the table of Adonises.

The elder Medici was at a corner table directly across the room from me, sitting with a few other equally runway-worthy people. A gorgeous woman with dark curls said something to the man next to her. *Were they the missing relatives?* They both sipped their drinks and stared severely at Ren, who was still entertaining his group with ardor. I assumed the back of the dark-haired guy across from them was Niccolò.

I took the last sip of my drink, and suddenly became hyperaware of my working-girl outfit. I tugged on the thin satin and slouched a bit, hoping to cover my exposed stomach. Annabelle laughed loudly at something Gabe said. Anger boiled inside me.

What the hell is going on? Gabe and Niccolò are my friends. They are French Quarter rats, like me... those snobs can't have them. The entire freaking world is upside down!

An angelic blonde draped herself on Niccolò's lap. I bit down on the lime slice, sending a squirt of sour down my throat. Face squirming, I set my empty glass down on a table out of fear I might crush it.

Ugh... Why do I care who sits on his lap?

The woman whispered into his ear. From my angle it was impossible to tell his reaction, but he certainly wasn't pushing her off. Without anything to occupy my hands, all I could do was stare in frustration.

Wait, I know that woman. From Ren's tour. Jealousy drew me closer, like a lame stalker.

The woman brushed her glowing locks from her face and laughed.

The singer bellowed out another jazzy number.

Another tap on my shoulder distracted me. The clown was back. This time I gladly accepted one of the drinks, just to have a prop. I slipped a few dollars into his flower-filled jacket pocket and turned back to the woman, whose arm had slid around Niccolò's shoulder. She drew the hood of her cloak forward to further conceal her whispers, and then her silhouette in the candlelight stirred my memory again.

Is she the woman who was following me?

I suddenly realized that everyone near was looking my way and smiling, as if waiting for me to do something. I turned my head: the clown had been miming a thank you for the tip, and I had been oblivious. I made a little curtsey, but it wasn't enough. He egged me on to play with him – the black paint on his stark white face amplified his silent emoting. I tried to shoo him away, but he wasn't having it. I quickly sucked down the drink, nearly choking on what I'd thought would be gin but definitely *wasn't*. I put it back on his tray, coughing, but he just spun it, offering me another.

I shook my head, fire coursing down my throat. *What the hell was that stuff? Rubbing alcohol?*

He set the tray down along with my glass and extended a gloved hand. Little by little, the room seemed to shut down and then even the pianist stopped playing. The entire room hushed in delight, giving the mime permission to pull me into his silent world.

As the clown began a slow-motion spin, there was a loud clunk of a bottle landing heavily on the bar. I was afraid to look, but something told me the sound was the shock of my father.

Mid-twirl, I saw Isaac jump from his barstool in surprise, and a glimpse of my father behind the bar, clutching a bottle of booze, looking distressed. It wasn't clear who was more busted: me for being dressed like a prostitute in an illegally operating bar after curfew, or him for operating said bar and lying to me about it.

The crowd began to clap slowly.

Clap.

Clap.

Beats synching, I felt like the slaps were pulling my heart from my chest.

The claps sped up, as did the twirls. He brought my arm over his head, forcing me to turn him. The crowd cheered wildly, and the piano started up again. He spun us faster and faster.

"Bravissima, bella!" Gabe yelled, standing with his glass raised. Niccolò turned to see the source of the commotion.

I planted my feet, jerking my partner to a stop.

All the sounds in the room seemed to fade away: Gabriel, the music, the whistling. I was only vaguely aware that the mime was now raising my hand for applause, or that Isaac was walking towards me. The only thing I could focus on was the boy holding the blonde girl – he wasn't Niccolò.

He was Émile.

I am losing my mind.

Am I drunk? Had he come to New Orleans to see me? This is not possible.

I blinked. But there he was, still staring straight at me. Smiling.

Behind him, Annabelle glared. I hated her for bringing me here. My father moved from behind the bar. This was all his fault. *How could he not tell me about this place?*

The mime took a bow while the crowd clapped with drunken glee. For the second bow, he bent my body downwards to join him. They whistled louder. As we came up, I let out an uncontrollable gasp – and every flame in the room extinguished.

The sudden blackout caused immediate pandemonium. Squeals came from every direction. *This is my chance to get the hell out.*

Focus, Adele. You know this place.

"Adele!" my father shouted over the crowd.

I pushed my way to the door. Tiny flickers of light appeared as people struck matches. *Faster.* With my eye on the handle, the door swung open long before I got to it, and then it slammed behind me.

The sounds of mayhem softening brought an immediate relief, but I didn't slow down. I yelled goodbye to Troy and bounced down the stairs and out of the courtyard. The sense of claustrophobia started to ease, but I didn't stop running.

On the post-curfew street, I realized my ears were ringing. I sucked in the fresh air and felt the alcohol coursing through my system – my fingers tingled like they were on fire.

Maybe it's the alcohol... I took the corner too sharp to see anyone coming from the other direction. *Or maybe it's just... me—*

"Dammit!" I yelled. My arm jerked in my shoulder socket as, once again, someone kept me from hitting the ground.

"We really should stop meeting like this, *bella*," Niccolò said, holding me steady and smiling at me with one eyebrow cocked. "Not that I mind it."

I was still too shocked by the evening's antics to engage in any kind of witty repartee.

"That's an interesting outfit," he joked as his eyes wandered, lingering in confusion.

I did not laugh. I did not even budge.

"What's wrong, Adele?"

I felt like I was going to implode. This was *not* how I had imagined our next encounter.

"Are you hurt?" His usual serious face was back. "Why were you running?" He rubbed my shaking shoulders – his hands were barely warmer than my arms, but the friction helped. I could smell alcohol on his breath, but that wasn't the reason he was trouble, and I knew it.

Hearing Isaac shout my name made me suddenly alert.

I flinched only for a millisecond, but that was all Niccolò needed. He grabbed my hand, and we started running. I didn't know where to, and I didn't care. Whether I was conscious of it or not, I knew exactly what I was doing. I knew exactly who he was, or rather *what* he was. And it was precisely that moment I decided I was okay with it.

For better or worse, I dove down the rabbit hole.

26

monster vs. myth

ISAAC'S SHOUTS FADED as we sped through the narrow streets. I had no idea where we were going, but I was overwhelmingly eager to be there with Niccolò.

To conceal our escape route, I began flicking out the gas lantern flames as we ran, hoping Nicco wouldn't notice – but his fingers locked tighter around mine. The gesture was tiny, but I could feel his excitement. And his strength.

I struggled to keep pace; he wasn't even breathing heavily.

Blue eyes flashed in my head. *Dead,* blue eyes.

Regardless, I didn't stop Niccolò from pulling me along. I pushed myself to run faster. I wanted to get far away from everyone. Everyone who was hiding things from me. Everyone who thought I was blind to everything going on.

We turned onto Pirate's Alley and ran into the courtyard of St. Anthony's Garden, through the gigantic shadow cast by the Jesus statue. The plastic popped against my bare skin as we ran straight through the yellow caution tape. My brain fired off warnings about breaking into the cathedral, but my heart unlocked the back door just before Niccolò touched the handle. He never let go of my hand.

That unmistakable church feeling crept over me as soon as we stepped inside – a mixture of guilt, as if I'd been busted doing bad things, and a total serenity: both wrapped into one. It kind of freaked me out.

Other than the moonlight shining through the stained-glass windows and a bright red emergency exit sign, the church was completely dark. This didn't seem to be a problem for Niccolò, who navigated quickly through the towers of melted candles and the basins of long-dried-up holy water.

We raced up the stairs, past the choir loft, and through the mezzanine that ran the length of the vast space. I had been inside the historical landmark countless times, but now all sense of familiarity was absorbed by the darkness. The emptiness. Now it was just us and our footsteps echoing back down from the domed ceilings that separated us from the stars.

I squeezed his hand as we entered a pitch-black hallway. All I could see was a trail of glow tape spiraling up the staircase. He pulled me in front of him, and I slowly made my way up the neon-taped steps, dragging my hand along the stone wall as we ascended.

Each board creaked in pain under my weight.

His hands brushed my waist. I began to take the steps faster, confident that he wouldn't let me fall. My leg muscles burned with exhaustion, but I refused to slow down in front of him.

I made the final turn and halted abruptly at a dead end: a small arched window shed a little moonlight on a small wooden door. It was sealed with a giant iron padlock.

My heart thumped as the metal tempted my fingers. *Don't do anything stupid, Adele. He would surely notice.*

Before I could think any more about it, he stepped around me, turning to face me from the tiny top stair and blocking my view of the door. Strain flashed across his face, and then there was a loud clank as the metal arch of the lock landed at his feet. I didn't have to see it to know that the base was in his hand. *Was he trying to hide his strength so he still had the element of surprise, or was he, like me, simply not ready to reveal himself?*

Ignoring the thought, I stepped past him through the little door into the bell tower. The slats in the eight long windows had been blown out, and the flooding moonlight seemed almost bright after the pitch-black staircase. Discreetly trying to catch my breath, I went straight to a window, collapsed against the stone wall, and looked out over the rooftops. This was certainly the highest point in the French Quarter.

I turned back to Niccolò. His eyes lit up with rapt attention as he watched me.

Other than the drop, there was only one way down, and Niccolò Medici was still standing in front of that exit, biting his lower lip.

"WHAT ARE WE DOING HERE?" the cross-breeze gave my voice a slight shake.

"You're upset about something. I have an idea to make you feel better," he said, circling behind me.

My thoughts spiraled back to what was possibly the worst night of my life. "Unlikely."

He gently nudged me to the center of the tower until we were underneath the enormous church bell. The giant brass dome dwarfed all the other bells it was intricately rigged to. The clapper itself was bigger than my head, making me feel miniature. Niccolò's chest brushed my shoulders, and I suddenly felt small next to him – not something I had paid much attention to until just then – the difference in our sizes. My pulse began to climb as my fingers warmed.

He swept both of my braids to the left side of my neck. "On the count of three, I want you to scream as loud as you can."

"What?"

As his mouth came closer to my ear, my brain no longer fired warning signs but "I told you sos."

"One…," he whispered, sending chills down my neck.

"Two…"

"Three!"

He jumped up and jerked the thick rope down.

Before I heard even the slightest noise, his hands swooped back around and cupped my ears. The clapper hit the brass rim right before the shriek left my lips. The gong easily masked the sound of my scream, and I miraculously couldn't hear anything under the protection of his hands.

Rather than the deafening sound of metal hitting metal, I heard a distant ping that didn't at all match the resonate vibrations beneath our feet. It was exhilarating, screaming at the top of my lungs, high above the silent city. My throat became raw, and my knees started to buckle. His hands never left my ears as he followed my slow slump to the ground.

By the time the chiming stopped, I was hunched into a ball on the cold floor, exhausted. It was hard to breathe with him cocooned over my back, but I liked the way his weight felt atop me.

For a few moments, he just let me be, and then he hooked my waist and drew me to my feet.

"Do you feel better?" he asked, still pressed against my back.

As I exhaled, a droplet slipped from my right eye.

"Yeah, actually," I whispered, turning around.

"Bene." He wiped the wet trail away with his knuckle.

The wind tingled against the light sweat brought on by the unexpected run, making my teeth chatter. He removed his jacket but, instead of handing it to me, dropped it to the floor and began unbuttoning his red flannel shirt.

"What… what are you doing?"

His expression contorted into a smirk. "Don't worry, your virtues are safe with me."

Blood flushed my cheeks as his black V-neck was revealed underneath.

"I can't take your jacket *and* your shirt. The wind is pretty fierce up here."

"Don't worry about me." He draped the flannel over my shoulders.

"Fine. I don't think lumberjack is really your thing, anyway."

"Oh, really? *Scusami, bella,* but you are in no position to be doling out fashion advice." A slight laugh slipped through his lips. "But you're right. It looks better on you."

I glanced down at my ensemble and became mortified all over again.

He gently lifted my chin so my gaze was back on him. "Stop worrying. It's very Seattle circa 1992." The statement was very matter-of-fact, as if he'd been BFFs with Kurt Cobain. Unconvinced my outfit had achieved Courtney Love status, I buttoned up the shirt for maximum coverage and turned to the nearest window.

Even in the darkness, the view was magnificent, high above the streets that held over three centuries of mysteries. I made room so we could both fit into the tight frame. Anxiety rushed through me. Despite not knowing his real intentions, despite not really knowing him, I didn't want to leave.

I slunk down under the window's stone ledge and wrapped his jacket around my bare legs. He slid down next to me, and we both just sat in silence in the cone-roofed tower.

The quiet was peaceful while my mind was empty, but little by little recent memories infiltrated my head, and I began to feel like a player in a game of Who's Going to Talk First. I wanted to play it cool, but more than that I wanted to know how many years of history he had seen unfold in this city.

"Niccolò—"

"You can call me Nicco. It sounds funny when you try to say my name."

"Oh." I blushed, repeating his name in my head, trying to figure out what was funny about the way I pronounced it.

"Nicco, have you found your family yet?"

Clearly not expecting the question, he hesitated, masterfully hiding his surprise, but the way his eyes examined my face for some kind of underlying hint gave him away. I gave him nothing.

"I have, actually."

"Oh, good."

"It has been a very disturbing process…"

"Oh, really, how so?"

"Well, I am sure you can imagine…" He seemed to choose his next words very carefully. "They are quite traumatized, having been trapped and abandoned in an attic for so long. They were very malnourished."

The slight smirk that followed led me to believe we were no longer talking about victims of the Storm, but we continued to speak obtusely, neither confirming nor denying my suspicions.

"So, does this mean you're all going back to Italy?"

"They are not well enough to travel, yet." He sounded sincerely concerned for them, but there was a slight fleck of excitement in his demeanor – he knew that I was inferring something else.

"But then?" I pushed, daring him to answer.

He looked straight in my eyes. "We'll see…" And then he relaxed back into the wall. "Like you mentioned the day we met, there is something very special about this city." His attention went back out the window to the stars, ending the conversation.

I tumbled deeper down the rabbit hole. And the next question that flew out of my mouth was the moment everything changed.

"Did Adeline ever tell her father you called?"

His jaw jolted, and a hushed snort forced out of his nose. I had his attention. I had no idea what to do next, but the standing hairs on my arms told me to proceed with caution.

"*What* did you say?" he asked, one hand strategically placed over his mouth.

I stood. His eyes lit up like an animal ready to pounce.

My words were sweet, careful not to come across as mocking. "Did Adeline ever tell her father that you called? *Monsieur Cartier?*"

Pain rippled through my shoulders and down my spine as my back made sudden contact with the stone floor. His head hung directly over mine, his breathing heavier with each inhale. I froze underneath him, as his cool green eyes assaulted me, terrified I had pushed him too far.

Despite beginning to tremble, I held out, waiting for an answer.

He kept his mouth clamped shut.

After another breath, he pushed himself up into a crouched position over my lap. Attempting to appear assertive, I sat up and looked him in the eye. Again, he nonchalantly moved his hand to his jaw as he asked, "Do you trust me, Adele?"

It was a perplexing question, but I knew he was serious because he had used my real name rather than the endearing Italian nickname. Every shred of my physical being burned like fire, urging me to scream *no*, but instead I whispered, "Yes."

"Never trust a vampire, Adele!" he yelled, slamming my shoulders back to the ground. A second surge of pain ripped down my torso, but my attention clung to his words. The one word I had been waiting to hear.

Vampire.

HIS BREATH WAS COOl on my burning face – breath that his existence probably didn't depend on. His mouth hung open somewhere in between a hiss and a growl, revealing the evidence that he, up until this point, had gone through such great lengths to hide.

Suddenly everything became very real. Too real.

His eyes pulsed with need, letting me know that one wrong move and everything would be over. Then they glazed over, and his nostrils flared as his face came even closer.

Trying to control the tremors rippling through my body only shook me harder. I was over the tears, the lies, the secrets. I thought about Adeline and Cosette.

Through the window behind him, I saw the silhouette of an iron cross against the moonlit clouds. Adrenaline raced through my veins like electricity, shocking me into action.

The cross broke off the neighboring steeple with a loud crack.

And in a quick whip, it flew through the window, bent around his cold, pale neck, and boomeranged back, slamming him against the wall. The tiny bell tower shuddered as the iron cross plunged into the rock, pinning him in place.

I jumped up and closed the gap between us, heart pounding.

"Do *not* mess with me," I spat. "I am *not* having a good night."

His fangs appeared to protrude even further as he reeled from the power reversal. "That's *it*, Adele!" he hissed. "Trust your instincts, *not* your intuition. Instincts exist for your survival. They will keep you alive. Intuition is muddled with emotion." He attempted to compose himself beneath the makeshift shackle. "Emotions will get you killed."

My instincts told me to run as he pulled the cross, but I easily held it in place. The tug-of-war only further charged him. With only a couple of spare inches, he slammed his neck into the iron with excited rage. The burst of emotion made me back away, but I kept my mind locked on the restraint. The more I focused, the warmer it became, until the iron nearly glowed and he had to stop or risk searing his neck.

And then we were back to silently staring at each other.

I HAD NO IDEA HOW MUCH TIME HAD PASSED. Ten minutes? Twenty? Thirty? The only thing I knew for certain was that I would never beat him at the silent stare-off. Niccolò Medici had the patience of a marble statue.

I loosened my grip.

As soon as my mind let go of the metal, he ripped it from the wall and was behind me in a flash – one crushing arm around my chest and the other around my head, forcing my neck to the side. With his lips against my nape he quietly asked, "Did you hear anything I said, *bella*?" His sharp points freely grazed my skin as he spoke, and he shook me in a violent rage as he asked the question again. *"Did you?"*

Blue eyes blazed in my mind. My upper arms were pinned to my sides, but my hands were free.

"*Si,*" I said. My fingers spidered outward, and with every ounce of momentum I could muster, I grabbed the tops of his legs.

When my hands made contact, he howled in pain and fell forward over me. I slipped out from underneath him and scurried to the wall, still confused at how I had gotten the upper hand.

"So, it's true," he mumbled under his breath.

A killer's instinct shone through his eyes, but the smile on his mouth said otherwise. I followed his gaze to my own palms and jumped back – only then feeling the heat. A small sphere of fire sat in each palm, miraculously not burning my skin. *What the hell?* My heart racing, I tried to hide my shock as we both slumped against the walls on our respective sides of the tower.

He winced as he carefully ripped the burned denim away from his thighs, and I watched in silent astonishment as his charred skin began to regenerate – my eyes flicking back and forth to the flames still hovering in my palms. Minutes later, there were two singed holes the size of my hands in his dark jeans, but they revealed nothing but his pale, China-doll skin. I sucked in air, still struggling not to panic.

Eventually my heartbeat calmed and my palms extinguished, bringing back the darkness. The burning sensation in my arms and the tingling in my fingers didn't go away as easily.

We defensively waited – watching, wondering if the other would make an aggressive move, but neither of us stirred. Finally, he spoke. "You fiddle with your necklace a lot… just as she did."

I looked down. My fingers were around the charms that hung on my chain. I hadn't even realized I was doing it. "So, I guess the whole 'church is a sanctuary from vampires' thing is not so much?" I said, looking back at him.

He laughed. My shoulders relaxed a little.

"No, not so much. That's just antiquated Christian propaganda. Recruitment strategy."

"Coffins?"

"Hmm… derived from a multitude of Eastern European superstitions, but you can mostly blame the nineteenth-century novel

Dracula." As he spoke, I tried not to stare at the two fangs he no longer attempted to hide, but my defenses wouldn't allow my gaze to wander too far from them. "Oh, and that atrocious German expressionist film *Nosferatu* in the twenties."

"House entrances?"

"There's no physical reaction when crossing a threshold without invitation, but philosophically most vampires believe that all creatures should be able to find asylum in their own homes."

"Holy water?"

"See 'church.' As with crucifixes, rosaries and exorcisms."

"Silver?"

"Most vampires do have a severe sensitivity to silver, but only in extreme cases would it have a grave effect like anaphylactic shock."

"Garlic? No, wait…" Ren's accent crept into my voice as I answered my own question. "Crypt keepers in New Orleans used to wear strands of garlic around their neck to help cover the stench of the corpses, not because they actually thought vampires would rise from the ground."

"*Molto brava.* And, centuries ago, people used to stuff cloves of garlic into the mouths of their beloved dead so they wouldn't return as vampires and hunt them… because the first thing on every newborn vampire's mind is to terrorize their previous family."

"Is that true?"

"The garlic? No. Terrorizing one's previous family? Not usually."

"Blood?"

"Sustenance."

"Mind-reading?"

"No. Mind-bending, yes."

"Mirrors?"

"Myth."

"Murder?"

"Inconsequential."

I looked away, trying to digest his blasé answer to my last question, but then forced myself to look back at him. I couldn't afford to be terrified if I wanted something from him.

"I have two more questions."

"Just two, *bella*? I have a sneaking suspicion there will be more, but please, go on."

"I thought vampires couldn't come out in the sunlight?"

"We don't need Vitamin D to survive. Our senses are heightened by the darkness and dulled by the daylight, so most vampire beings are nocturnal." He paused, smiling to himself.

"What?"

"All vampires are very susceptible to sunburn, but you won't find any who will spontaneously combust, if that's what you are wondering." He became serious again. "Humans think many things about vampires, almost none of which are true. Some think we are creatures spawned from Satan."

"Are you?" I felt foolish as the words slipped off my tongue.

"Do you believe that you descended from God?"

I stumbled over the question, picturing Jeanne and Sébastien sighing at me in the name of science. "Um, I don't know."

He smiled. Luckily, my answer was exactly the point he was trying to make.

"Well then, where *did* vampires come from?"

"Whoa, so existential. It's going to be one of those kinds of nights, then?" His long index finger stroked his well-defined chin. "The mythology is vast. Some vampires believe we descended from Cain and Lilith, some believe we are fallen angels, others believe we are alien life forms, et cetera. Most just believe the obvious – that we evolved from humans. Just the way humans evolved ages ago."

"It's not the same. Human beings evolved over an insanely long period of time, as a species, but you *used* to be a human, right?"

"Of course, I did. And no, it's not exactly the same. We have a far superior evolutionary process. I was just trying to make things as linear as possible to explain—"

"The point is, no one knows."

"Exactly. There are many theories for the genesis of man, vampires, and everything else on the planet."

We both gripped onto another moment of silence, contemplating the origin of the universe.

"What is your second question, *bella*?"

I didn't want to ruin the mood, so I ditched my original accusation and opted for triviality with a press-lipped smile. "Did you... ever meet Leonardo da Vinci?"

He let out a hearty laugh. "I'm not *that* old, *bella*," and then joked in a faux American accent, "Leo died, like, two hundred years before I was born."

The jest sounded strange coming from his lips. I smiled. His fangs retracted.

He may not have met da Vinci, but he had a million and one stories to share about the Italian Renaissance. My knowledge of Italian history was slim, so I asked a lot of questions, listened intently, and tried not to become too mesmerized when his eyes lit up as he zealously bopped from eighteenth-century Florence to Mussolini's Rome.

Hours escaped, and the city became even quieter – it felt like we were the only two people in it. Like we were the only two beings on the planet. Somewhere in the middle of the rise of Italian cinema, he moved beside me, causing my heart to pitter-patter and my brain to forget about the first half of the night.

"How is it possible that you've never seen *La Dolce Vita?* It's a cinematic masterpiece!" His accent became thicker the more passionate he became. "You have a lot of homework, *bella,*" he said without a trace of judgment. Trying not to swoon, I mentally filed away the name Federico Fellini.

I wanted to hide here forever. With him.

Before I could fall too deeply, a bloodcurdling scream shattered our night. We both bolted up and leaned out the back window of the tower just in time to see a dark figure dart through the humongous Jesus shadow in the garden below. The screams didn't stop after the one, and they sounded close. Very close.

"Emi..." he muttered under his breath.

"Huh?" I turned to ask. The rickety door was bouncing against the frame. I ran down the dizzying stairs after him, but catching up was a lost cause.

BLACK LINES OF MAKEUP STREAKED the traumatized face of a hysterical woman on her knees at the base of the statue. I fell beside her, squeezing my arms around her shoulders. She murmured words in Spanish, which must have been prayers because I kept hearing the word "Jesus" over and over.

"What happened? Are you hurt?" My head continued to flip in either direction, but I found no one else.

"Not me." She raised her head to the shadow. "Jesus."

The shadow seemed distorted. She pointed a shaking finger up at the statue. There were two extra appendages hanging around Jesus' neck. Two dead human arms. Trickles of blood had dripped down the slick marble to his knees. Vomit rose in my throat, and I gagged, forcing it back down. The body of a man was hanging on Jesus' back.

The ruffle of a large black bird in my peripheral vision distracted me. I whipped around, but it was too late – the bird became smaller as it flew towards the moon and disappeared into the distance.

The woman clutched my arm. I was clueless about what to do.

Breathe.

Through the fog, the muffled sounds of footsteps approached down Orleans Avenue. My grip on the poor woman's arm lessened when I saw Ren leading the way, flanked by Theis. It must have been part of the crowd from Le Chat Noir.

No sign of my father, thank God. Or Isaac. Or… Gabe's crew.

"*Bébé*!" Ren ran and scooped me into a bear hug.

"*Ça va bien, Ren.*"

He set me down, casually moving aside one of my braids to catch a glimpse of my neck. Theis looked at me with suspicion.

I suddenly remembered all the freshmen girls scattering away from the bouncer. Guilt attacked me. *Jesus. What had I been thinking? It was after curfew by then. I should have made sure they got home!*

I scanned the crowd.

Jaime and Bri were taking photos with their phones. Annabelle's face was buried into the pecs of some frat boy, crying, but she was obviously enlivened by the drama. I frantically scanned the rest of the crowd for the missing Big Sister.

There was no sign of her.

I hurried over to the girls, calling out, "Where's Désirée?"

"She went off with that ridiculously hot foreigner Gabriel," Annabelle said with an exaggerated tongue roll on the "r."

"What? Do you know where they went?"

She shook her head, utterly unconcerned. My cheeks flushed as she scanned the two additions to my grungy ensemble.

"Where did you get off to, by the way?" she asked. "That cute little ponytail ever catch up with you?"

I ignored her and checked my watch. 2 a.m. *Should I be worried about Désirée? Are Gabe and Nicco really even brothers?* Nicco's words echoed in the back of my mind.

Never trust a vampire.

Tires screeched to a halt. Lights flashed. Doors slammed. A voice on a megaphone told everyone to vacate the garden. Detective Matthews. *Dammit. This is way worse than being busted out past curfew. You didn't do anything else wrong,* I reminded myself. A plainclothes cop started shooing people away. I eagerly took the opportunity to exit with the crowd.

"Adele!" Detective Matthews accidentally said through the megaphone. Everyone looked at me as I stopped in my tracks. He hustled over. "Were you the first one to arrive at this scene?"

"Um… Not exactly."

"Oh my God! Look at his throat!" Annabelle shrieked as the cops lifted the corpse. The neck of the victim had been ripped open.

The crowd gasped. It was Wilson the Wolfman Washington, the DJ who, on that very evening, had warned the city to keep their eyes peeled. My back stiffened. *This could not be a coincidence. This was not a random act of violence.* Both of his eyes had been plucked out. Blood dripped from the empty sockets.

Detective Matthews began to interrogate me, going back and forth with his partner, asking me a hundred questions. All I could think about was Désirée. Warmth spread through my body, making me shake. Just as I was about to explode, an arm pulled me backwards.

"What the hell is going on here, Terry?" my father asked, pushing through a couple of forensics.

"I'm sorry, Mac," said the bleary-eyed detective. "I'm just following protocol."

"Well, my daughter is a minor, so all of your protocol can go through me from now on. Got it?" There was more aggression in his voice than I'd ever heard before.

"Of course, Mac, I think we've gotten everything we need. Why don't you take little Addie home?" He patted my shoulder and walked back to his team. My fingers twitched. One minute I was being grilled like a murder suspect, and the next being treated like a toddler.

"Adele, where the hell have you been? I have been calling and texting you for the last—"

"I'm sorry, Mac. She was with me." Isaac was staring straight at me, offering me an out. *How long had he been standing there?*

"Dammit, Isaac—"

"I know, sir. I'm sorry. We were just sitting by the river talking, and we lost track of time." Isaac looked at the leather jacket I was huddled into and the shirt hanging out below it. He knew exactly whom they had come from. He turned back to my dad, blinking away the sting.

"I expect more from you…," my father proceeded to yell.

Isaac quietly accepted the lashing.

When he finished, Isaac wouldn't even look my way. Another wave of guilt washed over me.

The body bag was zipped. My gut told me I was responsible.

And vampires.

My lungs pinched.

Where the hell is Désirée?

27

it's a bird

October 28th

"YOUR HAIR IS AMAZING, ADELE," said a girl with a faux tan and diamond-hooped earrings. "Did you do something different?"

"Ugh, thanks?" I replied, hoping she would turn back around and leave me alone. There was definitely nothing different about my hair, other than it being dirty and genuinely disheveled rather than purposefully styled into a messy bun.

I could have played hooky today, considering the circumstances, but I'd decided to escape to school rather than stay home with my father – we'd had a huge fight after our walk home last night (currently unresolved). Now that I needed pencils to hold open my eyelids, I regretted my choice, but I couldn't just blame my father. A multitude of other things had stolen my remaining few hours for sleep. For starters, the beady-eyed crow had perched on our neighbor's balcony all nightlong. Even after the curtains were drawn, it gave me an immense sense of paranoia. Then there was the fact that Désirée was still M.I.A. She hadn't returned any of my texts, nor had she picked me up for school. Lastly, and this was horrible given the circumstances, I couldn't stop thinking about Nicco. So, I knew that I looked terrible, and this girl's fake compliment made my foggy brain want to ooze out of my ears and flee.

Maybe I was just delirious, but out of all the bizarre things that had occurred over the last few weeks, today was the most confounding. A guy had helped pick up my spilled books, and a girl had complimented my necklace, which was hardly fashionable. At least half a dozen other upperclassmen had smiled, waved, or told me hello in the hallway. All before first period.

I waited for Mr. Anderson to turn his back, and then leaned close to my lab partner, the younger Drake sister, who was carefully pouring a clear liquid from a plastic bottle into a glass cylinder.

"What is going on today?" I whispered. "What is wrong with everyone?"

"What do you mean?"

"Why is everyone being *nice* to me?"

"Because you have something they want," she said without looking up. "Something that not even their parents' money can buy them."

"Huh? What?"

"Permanent entrance to the coolest underground club in town, duh."

"Ugh!" I yelped and suddenly the Bunsen burner ignited on its own. I didn't know what was worse – everyone in school knowing about Le Chat Noir's illegal operation, or that they were being nice to me because of it. Katherine looked at the Bunsen burner and back to me with confusion. There was nothing I could do to cover up the blatant magic except shoot back the exact same "What just happened?" face.

"What's wrong with you?" she asked, staring at the blur my pencil was making as I frantically tapped it.

"It's nothing." I wiped my clammy forehead with the back of my hand. The bell rang, and I leapt from my desk to avoid further questioning. "See ya later."

I ran to get my French book and was surprised to find the elder Drake sister waiting at my locker.

"Good morning, sunshine," she said. She seemed to radiate some kind of post-night-out glow, totally unfazed by the fact that we had witnessed a murder scene mere hours ago.

Next to her, Tyrelle shot me a look, denouncing my traitorous behavior. *Oh, now we're on the same side?* Lacking the energy to show restraint, I shot him a snarky look back, and my locker slammed shut on its own. Pain shot up my arm after I reflexively slapped it as a cover-up.

"Dammit!"

Tyrelle slowly shook his head as if I was the biggest spaz on the planet, and, luckily, Annabelle was too far off in lala land to notice the locker. I checked my phone for the umpteenth time as I rubbed my hand.

"Have you seen Désirée?" I asked, too concerned to process the fact that Annabelle Lee Drake and I were now walking down the hall together.

"No, but she can't ditch French because of our midterm. That wench didn't respond to any of my demands for details of her night with the hottie."

"Bonjour, Mesdemoiselles."

"Bonjour, Madame Wilson," we chimed in unison, as we walked into the classroom.

And there she was. Désirée. Giving her best deviant smile to the other minions.

I exhaled loudly as Bri shrieked, "You know you're gonna have to give us more details than that!"

I never imagined I'd be so elated to see Désirée Borges, but now that I knew she had a pulse, I became agitated. I dropped my stuff on my desk with a loud thud. They all looked over.

"What the hell? I've called you like fifty times. I thought you were dead!"

Bri's mouth hung open at my total disregard for social order.

"Yeah, Dee," Annabelle demanded. "Time to spill it."

I glared at Désirée. What she did or didn't *do* with Gabriel Medici was *not* what I wanted to know about, and I was pretty sure she knew that.

"Chill, Adele. Obviously, my father was alerted when the Wolfman's body was found, so he was waiting up for me when I got home. He freaked and took away my car and cell."

The bell rang, shrieking through my dehydrated head. *Ugh. I am never drinking again.*

"You could at least have found me this morning," I whispered. "Are you sure you're okay?" My eyes frantically scoured her neck. She seemed perfectly normal. In fact, she seemed better than normal. She seemed, dare I say, happy. It must have been the Gabe effect. "I'm sorry. I just really thought you were in trouble… or something."

She leaned over and said with absolute authority, "I do *not* have trouble with boys." Her eyes locked with mine. *Wait... Do we actually understand each other? Does Désirée know vampires are roaming the streets?* My fingers went to my necklace, as did Désirée's gaze. *Does she know about me?*

"Take your seats, and put everything but a pencil away," Madame Wilson instructed in French.

Everyone scrambled with varying groans. I threw my books underneath my chair, and when I looked back up, there was a note on my desk.

We need to talk. VP 6 p.m.

Désirée looked back at me for a moment, and I nodded in affirmation. The message momentarily calmed me – suddenly I didn't feel so alone. *She knows something,* I thought as I slipped the note in my pocket and resumed my pencil-tapping.

Dixie walked in late. "*Désolée, Madame Wilson.* I wasn't feeling very well this morning."

"*Ça va bien, Mademoiselle Hunter*, you look rather pale?"

"I'm fine. I mean, *très bien*." The French words sounded completely ridiculous with Dixie's thick drawl.

She clutched the chair as she lowered her body into the seat in front of mine, and then shot us all a smile before turning to her exam. She looked like she hadn't gotten much sleep, and her skin tone was more emo than her usual Malibu Barbie.

My pencil-tapping came to a complete halt when I noticed the Gucci neatly tied around her neck.

"Nice scarf," I whispered, leaning forward.

"Thanks. It was a gift." She smiled smugly.

Désirée's gaze moved from her test, to the scarf, and then to me.

"So Dixie," I whispered, trying to sound casual, "where'd you get off to last night?"

"Wouldn't you like to know!"

"*Je demande le silence!*" Madame Wilson threatened.

Was Dixie's hostility warranted? I had kind of left her hanging at the bar. A twinge of guilt pained my chest. I *could* have helped her past the bouncer.

I tried to concentrate on the test questions, but fear for the other freshmen distracted me. *Ugh, why do I even have to take this class?*

Focus, Adele.

I shut my eyes, took a deep breath, and pushed everything out of my mind.

IT WAS STRANGE WALKING DOWN THE SILENT HALLS. Even though I was only scheduled for half a day, my step quickened, as if I was going to get caught skipping.

Finally free from French, it took about ten seconds for my mind to wander back to Nicco. *How was it possible to reveal so much about myself to a stranger in one night?* I'd never felt so comfortable with someone in my life, and yet he had told me not to trust him. *What the hell—?* I opened the grand front door, and it nearly smacked a girl.

"Sorry!"

"Adele!" she returned with glee, although smiling appeared to be a struggle for her. It was one of the freshmen from last night... the one who'd worn the god-awful moo-moo. I felt bad that I didn't even know her name.

"Hey, are you just getting to school?"

"Yeah, I wasn't feeling so well when I woke up, but I'm okay now."

Her skin gleamed as if her fever had just broken, and her arms were wrapped tightly around her torso.

"So where did you ladies get off to last night?" I asked, loathing the fake pitch that rang from my own voice.

Her eyes lit up. "Are you my Big Sister?"

Guilt washed over me – great job I had done guiding the freshmen.

"Um... I don't think any decisions have been made yet, with all the commotion last night."

Her weight shifted, and I sensed uneasiness at the allusion to last night. She adjusted the pink silk scarf that was fashionably knotted around her neck. *What the...?* My hand automatically reached for it, but her eyes widened, and she hopped a quick step back.

"What did you all end up doing last night?" I demanded. "Were you out with Dixie?"

The poor girl suddenly looked like she was going to cry. "No. Bethany called her mom, and she picked us all up."

I knew she was lying, but I wasn't sure whether *she* knew it. I tried to soften my approach. "You didn't go anywhere before Bethany's mom came?"

She shook her head and mumbled something about getting to class. "I hope you're chosen as my Big Sis, Adele." And then, as if demonically possessed, my hand ripped her scarf off as she walked past. Her fingers flew to her neck, but it was too late: I saw the marks.

Her eyes glimmered, wet and horrified.

"I'm so sorry...," I whispered in disbelief at my own behavior.

In that moment, I knew she had no idea what had happened to her the night before. I tied the scarf back into a cutesy bow and grabbed my cell phone from my cardigan pocket as if I'd just received a text. "Hey, I just got a text from Annabelle. It turns out I am going to be your Big Sis. How awesome is that?" I forced a giant grin, trying to keep tears from welling. *This is all my fault.*

"This year is gonna rock!" I said, half-trying to convince myself.

She nodded and forced her own smile.

I BUTTONED MY SCHOOL-ISSUED BLAZER as I walked into the perfectly manicured garden. The sun shone, but the air was damp. When I thought about going home to my apprenticeship with my father and Isaac, a whole new wave of anxieties set in. They had both completely invaded my old routine. I missed my old life, back when I liked school and never worried about going home because the house was always empty. I missed Brooke. I missed sewing and my nerdy art-school friends and working with Jeanne and Sébastien. Central air and heat. Fresh produce. Sweet potato Hubig's Pies. Thanks to the Storm, nothing was sacred anymore. I ripped the bun from my head and let my unwashed waves ripple down my back, feeling an immediate release of tension.

At least I knew Désirée was alive.

I forced my shoulders to relax and skipped down the remaining stairs, but when I lifted my head to open the front gate, I saw him. Directly ahead of me, leaning against an oak tree, was Émile.

I quickly looked for an escape route, but he had already spotted me – he was waiting for me. With all the chaos, I had somehow managed to forget about him. I took a deep breath and walked straight over.

"*Bonjour, Adele, est-ce que je t'ai manqué?*"

Despite feeling his soft lips brush both of my cheeks as I greeted him, I was still stunned to see him here, in the flesh. I had practically convinced myself that he was a figment of my imagination brought on by trauma. *Proceed with caution,* my conscious warned.

"Did you miss me?" he repeated in English, as if my language skills were the problem in this scenario.

"What are you doing here?" I asked, the last word not much more than a gasp.

"I'm sorry for just showing up. I was so excited to see you last night, but zhen you disappeared before I could get to you. I didn't want to wait any longer. I miss you." He stepped closer, repeating the last touching words in French. When he took my hand in his, instead of making my heart race as it had in France, an electric shock zapped us.

"Static," I said, trying to pull my hand back, but he held on. I had fantasized about this moment ever since I'd left Paris, but now that it was here, it was nothing like I had dreamt. After all, I hadn't heard a peep from him since I crossed the pond.

"You didn't answer my question, Émile. Why are you *here*? In the States?"

He paused, and his usual confident expression turned puzzled. "Didn't she tell you? I waz invited to come to New Orleans to assist your mother on her new assignment."

"What?" I yanked my hand back.

"Adele, I am here with your mother – her grant from the government of France to restore some historic French exhibits damaged by za hurricane. Didn't you know?"

"Of course I knew!" I crossed my arms. "I just didn't know you were coming with her."

I wondered if he could tell I was lying. During our many bouts of espresso drinking, I had complained a lot about my mother. He had always listened attentively, but had *always* found a way to defend her. *"She has a very stressful career at za museum. It's just her artistic temperament. She's just French." Blah, blah, blah.* Sometimes I had wanted to slap him for knowing more about my mother than I did.

"Is zhere somewhere we can go and talk? We have so much to catch up on. A coffee maybe?"

I shook my head, feeling like I might cry if I opened my mouth. My mother was in town, and she hadn't even bothered to tell me.

"Can I at least walk you home?"

I couldn't manage to get a 'no' out, so when I started walking, he stepped beside me by default. I choked out a question about his flight. Luckily, he liked the sound of his own voice.

Whose life is this? Am I really turning away one boy and avoiding another? How could things change this quickly? It felt like a year since I had been in Paris, since Émile was the only person able to comfort me. It was typical Émile to just rock into town and slip in with the cool kids. The cracks in the cement became blurry as I blinked away tears. *Glad to know art could get my mother back to town.*

When we approached the last couple of blocks of the route, I stopped. My father would *not* like Émile – he'd remind him too much of his own wilder, younger years. Luckily, Émile took the hint. He kissed my cheeks and smiled his stupid smile.

"*Demain.* Same time, same place. See, it's just like Paris. *À bientôt.*"

Nothing was like it was before.

"ARE YOU GOING TO AVOID ME FOREVER?" Isaac asked.

Great. Two in a row.

He was sitting on my stoop, examining a thin silver object in his hands and obviously waiting for me. He looked exhausted.

"That doesn't really seem possible given you are at my house every afternoon…"

He stood to leave.

"No, I'm sorry. I'm just conf— it's just that…" I stopped and took a breath. "Do you ever just feel crazy?" I didn't even know what I meant by the question, but I found myself standing directly in front of him with my hand on his chest.

"These days? You have no idea." He looked at my hand, which I promptly removed.

The hurt in his eyes was evident. I asked myself how it would have felt if Nicco had turned his back on me after seeing flames rise from my hands, the way I had done to Isaac after he revealed so much of himself.

I would have been horrified. Humiliated.

Of course, Isaac hadn't revealed *everything*. My legs became wobbly.

I sat next to his feet; he sat back down. The knot in my stomach pulled so tight, I couldn't even sit up straight, so I rested my head on my knees, looking at him. A wave of brown hair fell over my face as the thoughts I'd been trying so desperately to ignore for the last few days infiltrated my head. I closed my eyes, and his sketchpad pages flashed through my mind.

Feathers.

Feathers.

Feathers.

He gently moved the hair from my face and tucked it behind my ear. "The cut is gone," he said, tracing the nearly invisible mark. Heat rushed to my cheeks as his fingers lingered. "It's hardly noticeable."

My lashes fluttered open.

The relief in his golden brown eyes over my lack of scarring gave me the answer, but I asked the question anyway.

"Did you do this to me?"

His gaze fell to the ground and then back to me.

"Yes."

I jumped up. He rose up next to me. My defenses skyrocketed even though he just stood there passively.

"I'm so sorry, Adele. I didn't know what I was doing. I still don't know what I'm doing. I didn't mean to…"

The whole world seemed to tilt as he spoke the words that proved he could turn himself into a bird.

"I think you should go now," I said, despite hearing the desperation in his voice.

His head bobbed. If I wasn't mistaken, there were tears in his eyes, but I couldn't be sure because I was fighting my own. *What the hell had he been doing in my house that night? Had anything between us ever been true?* My chest tightened.

"I'm really sorry, Adele. I never want any harm to come to you, especially not on my account."

My breathing became erratic. I looked at him one last time and slipped through the door, barely getting it shut before I collapsed on the other side in tears. Not just a few tears, chest-heaving, would-be-screaming-if-I-could-breathe tears.

"Isaac?" yelled my father from the back of the house. "Adele?"

The sound of my name sent me into a panic. I didn't want to talk to him, to see him. I didn't want to talk to anyone ever again. I couldn't even remember what it felt like to trust someone.

My father entered the hallway, and I nearly knocked him over as I sprang to the staircase.

"Adele, what's wrong?"

"Leave me alone!"

He ran up the stairs behind me, but I slammed my bedroom door, not caring whether he had seen the door fly closed by itself. I felt the bolt in the lock click as I flopped onto my bed.

"Adele, what happened? Come on, sweetheart, open the door," he pleaded, jiggling the handle.

My chest burned like something had clawed it raw. Like some*one* had clawed it raw.

"Please, Adele. Please let me in. Did something happen at school? Is this about last night?"

And then all of a sudden my tears stopped.

My dry eyes confused me. With the amount of emotion pummeling through my body, I expected them to continue like an endless river. *Even my emotions are betraying me now.*

The thought made me feel like a melodramatic child. I jerked myself from the bed and approached the door. I knew I was causing my father pain, but I didn't care.

I'd never felt so alone, so confused.

And to top it off, it felt like electricity was running through my bloodstream, and that I had to focus on not spontaneously combusting.

My forehead fell against the wooden door as I mumbled, "Did you know she was in town?"

"What, sweetheart? I can't hear you. Can you open the door, *s'il vous plaît?"* Resorting to French meant he was desperate.

"Did you know," I repeated louder, articulating each word, "that *she* was in town?"

"Honey, you are not making any sense. Did I know who was in town?"

My jaw was clinched so tightly I was barely able to get the words out: *"Brigitte Dupré."*

Silence.

Even through the thick wooden door, I knew my father was trying to compose himself. I felt as if I had put a knife through his heart. Knowing that my mother had arrived back in town for the first time in twelve years, without making so much as a peep, was possibly even more painful for him to swallow than for me. And the sick thing was that, in that moment, it made me feel a little better. Someone to share a little bit of my pain. My confusion.

"Your mother is in town? In *New Orleans*?" His voice cracked on the 'O.'

"That's the word on the street."

"According to who?"

I opened the door a couple of inches and saw him quickly wipe his eyes. "I ran into her assistant on the way home from school."

"What's she doing here?"

"Apparently something for work," I answered coldly. The words zapped a glimmer of hope from his eyes. "I'm going to take a nap, okay?"

He nodded. "I think I'll close the bar tonight and stay here with you."

"Don't bother, Dad. I'm taking a nap, then meeting up with Désirée to study for midterms. Probably 'til late."

"I don't want you on the streets at night, Adele."

"I know, Dad. We're meeting at Vodou Pourvoyeur, so it's just a couple blocks. She'll drive me home afterwards."

"All right," he said, defeated. "I love you, Adele."

"I love you too, Dad."

Guilt set in before I had the door shut. I'd never seen my father cry before. I didn't know what to make of it.

Counting on the distraction, I pulled out my copy of *The Metamorphosis* and tried to convince myself to start writing my English term paper, an essay on symbolism. I took one look at the cover and, for the first time, started to fathom how Gregor Samsa could have woken up one morning and not seen his own giant bug head in the mirror. I could hardly recognize myself anymore either.

28

voodoo queen dee

INCESSANT BEEPING from the alarm on my phone pulled my mind from the deep bowels of a REM cycle. Even as I became semiconscious, my eyelids remained swollen shut. Desperate for more sleep, they had encrusted themselves with a layer of gunk during my three-hour nap. I hobbled straight into the shower. While sleeping for eternity seemed like a great option, I was eager to meet Désirée at the Voodoo shop.

Black jeans. White cotton T-shirt. *Good enough for me.* The *gris-gris* was damp against my chest. I hadn't taken it or the medallion off in days.

I grabbed my Docs, but Désirée's disapproving disposition flashed in my head. *I really want this meeting to go well.* I dropped them and pulled out suede booties, and then layered on a houndstooth cashmere sweater – both courtesy of *ma grand-mère*.

A final glance in the mirror showed me that the steamy water hadn't done much for the giant circles under my eyes, but at least it had pulled me out of the zombielike state of mind. I tossed a couple of books into my bag in case we needed evidence that we were studying.

With five minutes to spare, I would be right on time.

The deadbolt on the front door clicked behind me as I hopped down the stoop. My bootie sent something skidding across the pavement, and, when I lifted my fingers, a small metal object leapt into my hand – it was the feather Isaac had made during our casting lesson. He must have dropped it during our fight. Beneath the autumn sunset, the silver version was stunning. Guilt sank my heart as I slipped it into my pocket.

I cannot feel bad for a boy who broke into our house, attacked me, and cut my face open. A boy who could turn into a crow! Did I really just think those words?

"What the hell was he doing in our house, anyway?"

And why am I plagued with guilt? He is the one who invaded my life. And more importantly, WHY is my stomach cartwheeling?

I never saw so much as a shadow or heard a second set of footsteps until it was too late. A hand slipped over my mouth, muffling my screams, and a strong arm hooked my waist, forcing me into an alleyway. Before I could react, my hands were crushed together by inhuman strength.

"*Shhh...*," a voice hushed into my ear.

My back arched, and I bucked all of my weight against the faceless person. My captor didn't so much as wobble but simply straightened to full height. My legs began to flail when my feet left the ground, but as soon as I thrashed about, a woman's voice whispered sweetly, "Don't bother, *ma fifille.* I can drain you dry and snap your neck in less than a minute if I like."

A woman? A woman with a very a thick French accent...

The more I struggled, the more riled up she became. Her fingers tightened around my hands, and I winced as my palms burned against each other. Her nose pressed into my neck, and her nostrils flared in ecstasy against my skin as she sucked in my scent, and then her cold, wet tongue slid from my collarbone to my ear.

Shuddering, my body went limp like a rag doll.

A second shudder rippled, and I became overwhelmed with fear when I realized it had come from her. A shudder of restraint.

"But I am not going to do zhat. Not yet. I am just 'ere to warn you, Adele, if you don't finish breaking zha curse, bad zhings are going to happen *dans le Vieux Carré*." Her hand slipped from my mouth to my forehead, holding my head tightly in place so I couldn't see her. "Very bad things."

"I can take care of myself, *merci beaucoup*," I grunted.

I could sense her lips spread into a smile, but she didn't mock me. "It's not you zhey will hurt, *ma fifille*, but every person you love. Zhey will show no mercy, for this is a very old grudge, and zhey play by very old rules. Zhey will destroy your *famille*, just as zhey destroyed mine."

"What grudge?"

"Whatever it is they want from your *famille*, you'd better give it to them, or you will regret it. *Je vous le promets*."

Then I was in a pile on the ground. Alone.

"Give what back to them?" I yelled down the alley.

My own voiced echoed in return, taunting me.

I dusted off my burning palms, cursing under my breath. *Finish breaking the curse or bad things are going to happen in the French Quarter?*

"Finish? What the hell?"

I picked up my bag and walked the rest of the way. *Is there really any point in running?* As I approached the shop door, another figure stepped from behind the shutter, nearly sending me into cardiac arrest.

"Jesus, Ren! I almost decked you!"

"Aw, *bébé, pardon moi.* My growling stomach caused me to rush." He was carrying too many packages to sweep me up into his signature hug, so he shuffled his bags until he could remove his top hat with a couple of free fingers.

"No tour tonight?"

"Er, it's supposed to rain later."

I looked up at the cloud-free sky, not that that really meant anything. It was New Orleans, after all; the weather was anything but predictable. "What are you doing here?"

"Oh, ya know, just makin' groceries."

"At Vodou Pourvoyeur?" I got the feeling he was being purposefully vague.

"And what are you doing here on this fine evening?" he deflected with a wink. "Love potion, perhaps?"

I tried not to scowl as I patted my bag – two could play at this game. "Studying for midterms with Désirée."

As he shifted the weight of the bags around, a strong botanical whiff blew my way. I peeked into one of his sacks – it was loaded with herbs. I sneezed.

"Jesus, Ren, did you leave anything in the shop? Whatcha got in there?"

"Oh, ya know, a little bit of this, a little bit of that: juniper berries, bay leaves, green cardamom, fennel, rosemary, coriander, lavender, and a pinch of black peppercorn for a little zing!"

"Please, don't tell me that y'all are so desperate for food that you've taken to eating herbs?"

"Oh, no, no. Theis unfortunately has a stockpile of canned fermented fish. His family sends it from Iceland. Tours are slow, so I'm tryin' to class up the ol' bathtub gin. People in New Orleans will drink just about anything, but, to quote your Pa, 'Why put hair on people's chests if we don't have to?'"

I nodded as if I knew what he was talking about. *So, Ren is making that god-awful liquor the clown was sampling at the bar?*

"Plus, if we can get the 'shine to taste more like the store-bought stuff, there's less chance of the law finding out, right?"

"Speaking of the law, has there been any news about the Wolfman's murder?"

"The wind in the willows says that more than eighty percent of his blood was gone."

"There wasn't *that* much blood at the crime scene."

"No, there wasn't, *bébé*," he paused, as if trying to subliminally lead me on. "I hate to say it, but it kind of reminds me of the story from my tour. The one where the two documentarians were found in front of the chapel at the Ursuline Convent with all of their blood missing."

I tried to recall the details of the double homicide. "When did that happen?"

"About twelve years ago."

"All of your other stories are so much older."

"*Oui*, centuries of unsolved crimes in this city."

"So they never found the person who killed those students?"

"No."

The first time we'd met, Nicco said they'd been to New Orleans before. *I wonder when—? Wait, did I really just consider him a suspect just because of missing blood? That's horrible, Adele.*

But the question lingered. *Would Nicco do something so barbaric? Even if he needed blood to survive?* I wanted to think *no—*

"All right, darlin', I need to get moving. Theis and I are cooking up a batch of hurricane gruel tonight."

"What's that?" I was scared to know.

"It's when you break out the biggest gumbo pot ya got, close your eyes, and dump in about a dozen random canned goods. *Laissez les bons temps rouler!*"

"Ew!" I choked out a giggle. As gross as it sounded, the very mention of food made me purr. The only thing that had entered my stomach today was anxiety.

"Eh, it all tastes the same after you add enough cayenne." He took a swig from his pocket flask and bent forward to kiss the top of my head. "Get some sleep, *bébé*, and go easy on your papa about the distillery. He was really torn up about hiding the hurricane hootchin' from ya."

"Distillery?" The question flew out so quickly I was unable to hide my surprise.

"Oh, er? I thought you... oh, don't listen to anything I say. You know it's all hogwash. *Bonne nuit, ma chérie!*"

He quickly walked away, cursing himself under his breath, "*Dammit, Ren, tuat t'en grosse bueche.*"

"*Non, merci beaucoup* for your big mouth, Ren." My voice faded into the night, and again I was alone.

INSIDE, THE SMELL OF WOOD, LILACS, AND CINNAMON permeated the air. *I can't believe I am here looking for answers,* I thought as I walked past the Voodoo dolls, tourist thrills, and alligator skulls. I found Désirée at the counter, doing what I assumed was homework. I would turn out to be wrong; at least, it wasn't homework in the traditional sense.

She nodded to acknowledge my presence and shut an oversized, leather-bound book with a loud thud. The atmosphere became awkward. It wasn't like we were really even friends, but something about the meeting felt natural, and that's what really felt weird.

"So…"

"I want to show you something. Wait right here," she said and disappeared behind a thick fuchsia curtain on the far wall.

Voices murmured, and then she returned with a rolled canvas. "Have you ever seen this painting before?" She leaned across the counter and slid it to me.

I rolled it open, and she secured the corners while I examined it.

"No. Never." Although… I felt like I had. I fell instantly in love with the picture of seven young women. "Is that the courtyard at the Ursuline Convent?" The garden was sparse, as if it had recently been planted, but the building was the same.

"Mm hmm."

It was hard to guess the year based on the style of clothing. Each woman's dress was so different looking from the other, it was almost like they were in costume. The color of their skin and the fanciness of their clothes varied, but it was obvious they were kindred spirits. Even through the stoic expressions, you could tell they were all close. Like they all shared a secret.

I did a double-take. Some of girls bore more than an uncanny resemblance. In fact, three of them looked exactly alike: stunning beauties with white-blonde hair that practically glowed.

"What the… could it be?"

"What?" Désirée asked.

The Ursulines. *La Nouvelle-Orléans*. Triplets. They had to be *Les Sœurs d'or*. Based on the description from Adeline's diary, I easily identified Cosette. Lisette had been right: the eldest triplet radiated a sexuality that shone through the painting even three hundred years later. Next, my eyes fixated on the brunette next to Cosette. My pulse began to race. This wasn't the first time I'd seen her face staring back at me – Isaac had captured her expression perfectly in his drawings. *But how could he…?*

"Have you ever hung out with Isaac Thompson?"

"Ugh, *no*," she answered with a quick lift of her eyebrow.

"How do you have this painting?"

She let a little excitement slip through her placid demeanor. "Who do you recognize?" My finger slid from Adeline to each of the Monvoisin sisters. "Four? That's three more than I was hoping."

"What do you mean? Who did you expect me to recognize?"

"Um, the woman wearing your necklace, duh."

My eyes flew back to the painting. It was small, but there was no denying that I was wearing the same medallion.

I took the heirloom off to show Désirée the bits of the engraving that weren't covered by the star. "Adeline Saint-Germain," I said, dropping it into her hand.

"This stone is so weird."

"It's kind of a long story, involving a pirate captain."

"And how would you know that?"

"How do you have a picture of my great-great-great-something-grand-something?"

"Because it's also a picture of my great-great-great-something-grandmother." She pointed to an exotic woman in a headdress similar to the one her grandmother had been wearing the day we met. "Marassa Makandal."

"What?" I lowered my voice. "This is so nuts!" I wasn't sure why I was whispering, but it definitely felt like we were on the verge of discovering something that had been hidden for a very long time.

"Can we go back to the pirate comment? And how did you find her necklace?"

"Um..."

Ritha Borges emerged from behind the curtain. "Sometimes when things need to be found, they find you."

The elderly woman came over to stand beside Désirée, and pointed to the canvas. "My ancestor, Marassa Makandal, was a remarkable woman. A very powerful woman."

"She was beautiful," I said.

They both nodded in agreement.

"So, how did you know about the triplets?" asked Désirée.

"Well, I've been translating Adeline's diary—"

"Wait, Adeline Saint-Germain had a diary? And you have it?"

"Yeah, her father asked her to record her journey from France to New Orleans." Excitement coursed through my veins. I was suddenly nervous, unsure of whether I should be confiding in the Borges, but it felt so good to uncork the bottle I could barely control what came out of my mouth. The mystery woman's threatening warning pounded inside me. I was out of time. I was going to have to start taking some risks.

"The things parents ask of their children often seem silly at the time, but rarely are," said Ritha.

"Yeah, it seemed he was adamant about it. Anyway, Adeline met Cosette, Minette, and Lisette Monvoisin on the S.S. *Gironde* – one of the ships that brought *les filles aux cassettes* from Paris to New Orleans."

"Adeline was a casquette girl?" asked Désirée.

"Not exactly, but she came over with a couple of other aristocrats on the same ship." I procured Adeline's diary from my bag and gently rested it on the counter. As a trade, Désirée pushed over the large, leather-bound book she had been reading when I walked in.

"What's this?"

"It's Marassa's *grimoire*."

"Come again?"

"It's where Marassa Makandal kept all of her most secret thoughts and experiments," Ritha explained. Pride resonated from her voice. "You can think of it as a Voodoo spell book that has been passed down for many generations. Most of the magic sold in this shop is still based off of things from that book."

Désirée seemed uneasy with all the talk of Voodoo and magic, but who could blame her?

I opened the book and carefully turned a few of the delicate, browned pages. Intricate sketches and diagrams were drawn between lengthy passages and lists that resembled recipes. I could only understand about one of every ten words, and those were in French.

"It's a Haitian *Kreyòl* dialect," Ritha said. "Very old."

"Looks old. What are all these notes on the sides?"

"The entire volume has been translated over the years by different witches from different generations of our family. The marginalia discuss discrepancies in translations. New interpretations."

Witches?

"Ugh, is this whole book in French?" asked Désirée, turning the pages of Adeline's diary. "*Ma français est pathétique.*"

"Don't beat yourself up too much. My French is okay, and it's still taking me forever to translate it. I'm just up to the part where some, er, stowaways helped them survive a pirate attack."

"How adventurous."

You have no idea.

We all got lost in the old texts for a moment.

I looked back at the painting. There were still two unidentified girls. One wore a simple dress with an apron. Her fiery red curls had won the battle with the bonnet she held in her hand. The other girl had long, black, pin-straight hair styled in braids. Her copper-toned skin and accessories indicated that she was likely from one of the indigenous tribes who predated French colonization.

Désirée placed her hand on the painting. "Was this Marassa's coven?" she asked her grandmother.

Coven? My brow furled.

A smile crossed Ritha's face. I got the feeling Désirée wasn't usually so interested in family affairs. "It certainly would have been unusual, as covens are usually formed by witches from the same variety of magic, but it's not entirely impossible. An extremely dangerous circumstance could have brought them together."

Then the question just vomited out of my mouth. "Would a clan of vampires running amuck and murdering people be a dangerous enough circumstance?"

Désirée and Ritha both raised their eyes from the picture to look at me. Then they looked at each other.

"Hypothetically," I quickly added.

Ritha smiled again. "Protecting life is always a good reason."

Encouraged by their lack of mockery, I continued. "Can I ask you something… about magic?"

"Sure, suga', what's on your mind?"

"What happens to a curse after the caster dies?"

"Unfortunately, there is no simple answer since all spells, and all witches, are different. In most cases, the spell is passed down to a descendant. If the witch dies without any progeny, then the spell usually breaks instantly."

I struggled to keep my face composed at her use of the W-word. "And if it was passed on, would said progeny be able to break the inherited spell?"

"Oh, yes, of course. Break it. Bend it. Enhance it. Once the spell is passed on, the new witch has complete control of the cast."

I could sense the medallion start to vibrate on the table. I quickly slipped it back on and hid it under my shirt. *What did you do to me, Adeline?*

I looked back at the painting of the girls. "And what if the spell was cast by a coven? How would you break it?"

"If the spell was cast by a coven instead of just one witch, each descendent would only be able to break the part of the spell that her ancestor was directly responsible for: the part she inherited. To completely break the old spell, you'd have to reform the coven with the complete new generation of witches who had inherited their ancestors' powers."

I looked at Désirée and then back at the painting. *Are we inheritors?*

No.

No.

No.

Did I…? Shit. No. Did I break Adeline's part of a curse by opening the attic window—

"Of course, there is one other way to break a coven's curse."

"How?" Désirée and I said at the same time.

"Just the same as for a single-caster spell. Break the spell line. If all the inheritors die without any progeny, then the original coven's spell will break piece by piece until the last inheritor is gone."

A breath escaped my tightly pressed lips.

"Death?"

Giant flames suddenly exploded into the fireplace, causing me to jump back. Désirée and I exchanged glances, but Ritha, as usual, didn't blink an eye.

"Mother Nature has a way of bringing people together in times of woe."

"That's very esoteric," I said.

"Welcome to my life," Désirée replied, cracking a smile.

At eight-thirty, I started gathering my things, shocked by how much time had passed. "I should go. Curfew and all." The idea of obeying a curfew seemed so insignificant now, but I was starving and wanted to get home in case my father had changed his mind about closing the bar.

"See you in the morning for carpool," said Désirée.

"What about your car?"

"I'm sure I'll figure out some way to coerce my father into giving it back. He can never really stay mad at me for more than a day."

I guess we had that in common. I waved to Ritha as I headed towards the entrance.

Désirée's mother was in the front of the shop, talking to a woman whose back was to me.

"Calm down, Ana Marie, you have much bigger problems on your hands than me being back in town."

I turned my head as I passed them; the woman looked me directly in the eyes. Horror stunned me. Without thinking, I rushed through the door without saying a word. The woman was my mother.

29

blood sucré

(translated from French)

1st June 1728

IT WILL TAKE ME SEVERAL DAYS to recount all that has happened since we docked in *La Nouvelle-Orléans* one week ago. So many reasons have inhibited me, I hardly know where to start.

On our first night aboard the pirate ship, I went to sleep with an odd feeling of gratitude towards them: our monsters. Despite their brutality, I could not deny the fact that they had saved us, even if their real motive was self-serving. Of course, this feeling disturbed me greatly. I wasn't so naïve to have forgotten it was they who were our original predators, leeching on us before the pirate attack. With only half of the voyage complete, I feared for the lives of the girls, especially after witnessing the murderous spree aboard the S.S. *Gironde.*

The conflicting feelings are maddening, Papa! I, for one, would rather be dead at the hands of a monster than a slave to one of those vile pirate men. This, of course, is easy for me to say because I was not the one being fed upon. Had it been me, or Cosette, or one of her sisters, there would be no sympathy. *Je promets.*

My gratitude changed one week later when I entered my cabin and found the ribbon I use as a bookmark in this diary left on a different page. My palms immediately inflamed as I scanned the small room. Nothing else seemed out of place, but still panic grew inside me.

It's hard to believe that any of the passengers would dare enter my cabin. It's unlikely that any of the orphan girls or any of the crew could even read, and even more unlikely that one of the nuns would pilfer, which left very few to suspect. My mind couldn't help but wander to our hidden passengers... but why would a vampire want to read the simple musings of a sixteen-year-old girl, Papa? Paranoia got the best of me when I thought about the unusual circumstances that had led to me being on this ship. Alone. You somewhere in the Orient. It had all happened so quickly – shutting down the estate as if neither of us would be back for a very long time.

Stealthily, I hid the diary in a place where only you or I would be able to retrieve it, and there it would remain, secure, until we abandoned the ship. And then I warmed my medallion in my hands. When it was glowing hot and pliant, I pressed the pirate captain's opalescent eyeball into the metal. From then on, not only would the medallion remind me of you, Papa, but also the massacre aboard the S.S. *Gironde* – just in case my feelings of sympathy ever resurfaced.

(cont.)

UNFORTUNATELY, THE HAPPINESS THAT AROSE from our victory over the pirates was soon superseded by sadness. It is with a heavy heart that I report the death of Monsieur Claude DuFrense. He never recovered from his "seasickness." Needless to say, poor Martine was completely distraught, for she had never wanted to be on the voyage to begin with. At times, she became completely hysterical and demanded the captain return her to Paris. Cosette was the only one who could calm her down – with her smiles and her lullabies and her herbs.

The next two weeks aboard the ship were relatively uneventful, but you won't have heard me complain of boredom. The orphans finally began to relax, the nuns continued to pray for our journey, and the crew was elated as much by the strong gales as by the endless barrels of sugary rum the pirates had hoarded.

Mother Nature finally took mercy on us as we entered a waterway called the Caribbean Sea. After weeks upon weeks of endless ocean, I did not think water could impress me, but the wild spectrum of greens and blues of this sea sparkled like a million jewels leading the way to adventures, romances, and happily-ever-afters. I hoped all of these would be our fate.

The best news was, no one came down with the seasickness. After all, our children of the night had just feasted like vampire kings. Regardless, each dusk, I couldn't help but wonder if we'd reached the night their thirst would unquench. How long would the pirates' blood hold them over?

Luckily, we made very quick progress; the captain was eager to be rid of the pirates' vessel, so he slept very little, pushing the crew to our next port of call. We were in high spirits when we entered *Port-au-Prince* in the French colony of *Saint-Domingue.* This common resting point for those en route to *La Nouvelle-Orléans* was nothing like the beaches of France: the small isle was like a page from M. Defoe's novel *Robinson Crusoe*, with trees that stretched towards the sun and bore fruits with hard shells and hair.

We were greeted with a grand welcome, and I, along with Martine, Captain Vauberci, and the top members of the Holy Order, was invited to dine at the governor's mansion, or plantation, as the *châteaux* are called here. At dinner, the governor told us that his plantation yielded enormous crops of sugar, coffee, sisal, and indigo.

"Very lucrative," he said.

"Lucrative but labor intensive," said the captain, gritting his teeth before excusing himself from the table.

When the dessert came, even though it was my favorite, *crème brûlée,* I politely excused myself and slipped out. I found the captain in a chair on the second-story balcony, which overlooked the expansive back of the property, smoking his pipe and taking swigs from his flask. It didn't take a mystic to sense he was upset.

"Lovely night," I said, breathing in the warm, moist air. He stayed silent. I took the chair next to him. "Everything seems so much more vibrant on this island, or maybe I am just used to the monochromatic palette of the ocean?"

"I prefer the sea," he said and then aggressively spat over the rail.

A moment later, he looked at me with the concerned expression of a father. "Adeline, now that you are out of Paris, there are many things you are going to learn about the French. About men."

Oh, if you only knew the irony in that statement, Monsieur, I thought, but held my tongue and looked at him with innocent eyes.

"This isle has become nothing more than a miserable hive of filth and depravity. It's a haven for pirates, bootleggers, and smuggled slaves. And it flourishes thanks to French involvement in triangular trade."

I asked him to elaborate. He nodded, but first unscrewed the top of his flask with a single flick, took a swig, and then offered it to me, a gesture he had never made before. It seemed impolite to refuse. I took too large a sip and immediately coughed as the fiery rum trickled down my throat.

"Easy, now," he said as I passed it back. He took another swallow and began again. "The triangle model refers to the route of the ships. In this most despicable example, French ships travel to Africa, exporting European goods in exchange for slaves. Then they sail to *Saint-Domingue,* sell the slaves en masse, and return to France with 'white gold' from the New World."

I gasped, thinking about the countless spoons of sugar that had passed between my lips in Paris, wondering if any of the delightful confections had come from this tropical isle. I hoped not.

"And that, *chérie*, is how this island has become the richest colony in the West Indies." He guzzled the remainder of the flask and leaned back in his chair.

"That is preposterous! How could the King allow this to carry on?"

"Gold, Adeline. Gold and power. Power and gold. The more a man has, the more he wants," he answered, but his mind was drifting far away. Without the familiarity of the waves, we rocked in our wooden chairs and lost our attention to the waxing moon.

Later that night, just as I was dressing myself for bed, there was a light knock at the door. I thought it would be one of the triplets looking to gossip, so I was surprised to find a pretty *Kreyòl* girl carrying a tray. "*Bonsoir*," I said and opened the door to let her pass. She put the tray of dishes on a small table.

"You left before dessert, and I saw how you was eyein' dem sweets. My mama makes the best *vani krèm* on dis island," she bragged with a smile as sweet as the *crème*.

And she was right, Papa. It was an amazing *crème brûlée.* But I was only able to take one bite out of politeness as she lingered. Once the girl left, I had a hard time even looking at the dessert, remembering what the captain had said about the sugar.

(cont.)

WE STAYED ON THE ISLAND OF *SAINT-DOMINGUE* for seven more nights while a new ship was prepared. On the eve of our departure, the governor threw a *soirée* in our honor, to which all of the orphans were invited, fortunately. Even the pirate captain's red bird, whom Cosette had practically adopted as a child, attended the party. We were having so much fun dancing and singing around the piano we almost forgot that we were not in Paris, for everything was prepared in such exquisite French style. After hours of socializing with the *crème de la crème* of island *société,* Cosette and I escaped to the balcony for some fresh air. We leaned over the railing and let our minds disconnect from the *fête* inside.

After a moment of silence, we could hear drumming in the near distance.

"What is that music?" Cosette asked and then pointed out into the darkness. "Is that a fire?"

The light was so faint and flickered so quickly, it was hard to be sure. With a mischievous grin, I answered, "There is only one way to find out."

We snuck down the stairs, letting the drum guide us. The beats were so round and full, they seemed to reverberate through the earth and pull us through the lavish flower beds and intricate patchworks of vegetable gardens. We passed fields of crops and finally came to a path that was dotted with several small wooden houses, one of which contained not only the drumming but several strange rhythmic sounds, foreign to my ears.

I never felt fear, only pangs of guilt for trespassing, but we were too far under the spell of curiosity to stop ourselves from taking a peek. Entranced, we perched our heads on the glassless window like children.

The house was nothing but a simple square room, crudely made of wood and leaves. An old man with the darkest skin I had ever seen sat in the corner with closed eyes, smacking his large hands against a drum made of animal hide. A woman, whose mind seemed to be in another world, danced in a way my body has never moved, as if her spine was possessed by a serpent. She carried a stick with an attached gourd, decorated with strings and feathers, that made a hissing noise when she shook it. Another man danced, holding a glass bottle with no regard to the liquid he was spilling onto the packed-earth floor. There was a table in the middle of the room with a centerpiece of unrecognizable wooden statues and bowls that must have contained liquid of some sort because flames floated in them like magic.

Three others were gathered around a *Kreyòl* girl at the head of the table. Her face was covered with a scarf, and her lips moved quickly under the fabric as if in song. A man drew a knife and carefully cut her upper left arm, chanting as he worked. I would have been screaming in horror, but the girl seemed to be in no pain. In fact, her mind seemed to be far away. It was one of the strangest events I have ever witnessed, Papa.

Before she lost much blood, the man packed the wound with a concoction of herbs and then dressed it with a tightly tied red scarf.

I was enthralled by the whole ceremony.

I knew not whether it was barbaric or divine, but the power in the room was undeniable. Lost in my own thoughts, I only noticed the fiery itch in my palms after rough hands were already over our mouths, dragging us away from the house.

"You are brave li'l girls to be out in da night spyin'!" said the man as he pulled us to a patch of tall green stalks that resembled bamboo. Even though he immediately let us go, two flames reflexively bolted from my hands, aimed straight at his chest. The balls of fire disintegrated into thin air just before they singed his bare skin. He did not even flinch – only stood smiling as if we were playing a game – and then looked at Cosette, who was smiling back at him without a flicker of fear in her eyes.

"Your witchy juju isn't gonna work on me either, *ma chérie*," he said in a strange French dialect, with a deep-throated chuckle. The *Kreyòl*, who couldn't have been but a few years older than us, also had a red scarf tied around his left upper arm, which was now dripping with blood.

The fiery feeling in my palms subsided, and my shoulders relaxed. I apologized and told him that we hadn't meant to intrude.

"Do not worry, *mesdemoiselles*. I bring no harm to you," he said. "It is quite da opposite. My name is Makandal, and I have a favor to ask of you."

Cosette and I exchanged glances, and I motioned for him to continue.

"I realize dat what I ask of you is as enormous as da moon herself, but it is a matter of life or death. You have been blessed by Mother Earth, and der is no one else whom I can trust with this favor." He came closer and bent one knee to the ground. "I will be forever in your debt if you oblige. I beg you. You must take my sister with you to *La Nouvelle-Orléans*. Dey will show her no mercy for my actions."

(cont.)

After only a short sleep, I met Cosette in the vegetable garden, and we ran hand in hand down the property until we came to the first field of sugarcane, where we had promised to meet Makandal. When we arrived at the rendezvous point, he was already waiting in the dark, hugging the girl we had promised to sneak onto the ship before everyone else boarded at dawn. I was shocked to see his sister was the same beautiful girl who had brought me the *crème brûlée.* She also wore a red scarf around her upper left arm.

"Je vous présente ma sœur, Marassa Makandal," he said to us.

"*Enchanté,*" we both whispered and then retreated back into the sugarcane to give them a moment of privacy and allow them to say their goodbyes. We all knew it would be their final exchange, although none of us dared say so aloud.

From a few feet away, partially hidden among the stalks, we waited patiently in silence.

"I promise dat I will be right behind you to live our new lives together," Makandal told the teary-eyed girl as he embraced her.

The girl cried and spoke words to her brother that we couldn't understand, making giant tears roll from his determined eyes. In that moment it somehow became obvious that the boy was a born martyr – he loved his sister, but was willing to let her go to serve a greater cause. Any doubts I might have had about our decision to help them were now feelings of the past. But our plans were about to become a lot more… complex.

"What have we here?" a voice bellowed, and suddenly a large white man was standing right behind them, outrage visible in his eyes.

Fear flooded Marassa's face, and we shrank back, hoping he hadn't seen us in the sugarcane.

"Surely, the makin's of marooning," the foreman yelled. "Just wait until the governor hears about this!"

With one solid shove, Makandal pushed his sister into the stalks toward us and yelled to the foreman. "This is no concern of yours."

The white man's lumbering fist pounded onto Makandal's face, and blood gushed from his split nose. Cosette's hand went around Marassa's mouth to muffle her screams.

"Take her now!" I whispered. "I will be right behind you. Be safe!"

The disgusting man continued to assault Makandal, who did nothing to retaliate.

My senses were drawn to a rusty blade that had been left lying on the ground in the stalks – a tool used by the slaves to hack down sugarcane. Blood sugar. Anger rose inside me like a growing fire. *Could I really kill a man?* I could not let Makandal die in a sugar field helping his sister.

There was no more time for thinking, only for action.

I focused on the machete, and it slowly rose from the ground. Up and up it floated until it was high above the crops. Then, with a flick of my wrist, I sent it plunging down over the man.

I watched in astonishment as the blade pierced the earth, missing the foreman – and yet he still landed on the ground with a bone-crushing thud. A flash of teeth gleamed before they sank into the flesh of his neck, spraying crimson across the tall stalks.

The sun began to rise, throwing a million shades of pink across the sky as the blond head bobbed up and down, feeding, feasting, finishing off the foreman. Goosebumps tore through my flesh. I told myself to run, but my legs seemed paralyzed. I hardly want to admit it, but I was oddly exhilarated by the display of sheer power.

"What have I done?" whispered Makandal, barely conscious but gazing at the creature with horror.

I rushed to him, promising that his sister would be safe with me. "Please don't be frightened," I begged, but my fingers trembled as I squeezed his hand.

The blond looked at us with rabid eyes as crystalline as the Caribbean Sea. He remained in a crouched position and edged our way, squinting in the dawn light.

Protectively, I hovered over Makandal, but the monster pushed me aside with one sudden movement. I protested, but my words tapered when I saw he wasn't looking for a second course. Instead, the vampire looked kindly into Makandal's dark brown eyes and said in a soothing hum, "Everything went as planned. You succeeded in your mission to get your sister off the island. She is going to be fine. You are free to do great things."

An aura of triumph washed over Makandal's face, and his breathing slowed.

The monster drew his own wrist to his mouth, bit down deeply, and then held the bleeding punctures over the boy's mouth. He waited patiently as the blood dripped over his lips and seeped down his throat. I found myself inching closer in amazement as the boy's ribs began to snap back into place and his wounds began to heal.

My senses were wildly confused as the vampire rose and I finally saw his face in the light. He looked so much like a man, and not at all like the hideous creature I had dreamt about all of those nights at sea. The burning in my hands pulsed as if unsure what to do.

He looked at the foreman's corpse and then back to me and said in perfect French, "Every species has their monsters."

I nodded and stood. "Are you the man— do I call you a man?"

"Well, I'm certainly not a woman," he answered and taunted me with a devilish smile.

"Are you the man who met the triplets on our last night in Paris?"

"*Si, signorina.* Stubborn, those three." He smirked and licked the foreman's spilled blood from his own hand. "Mmmm… sweet… tropical."

He focused on the task for another moment before raising his head back to me. "Luckily for me, I found someone else willing to oblige.

Unfortunately, my brother wasn't as lucky." He searched my eyes for acknowledgment, of which I gave him none. "But don't fret; I'm sure he found a willing passenger on the next boat out from Paris. My brother can be very… persuasive." He walked closer and reached for my hand. "But apparently, so can you. Gabriel Medici. *Enchanté*." He gently kissed it.

"Adeline Saint-Germain," I whispered. The brush of his cool lips sent a shiver up my arm, clashing with the fiery defenses wanting to leap from my fingers.

"Of course," he said. "We all know who you are, *bella*."

"Medici?" I stuttered, not understanding why a vampire would know who I was. "That's quite a famous name."

"*Si.* But not nearly as infamous as yours." He took another step closer, his leg brushing my skirts.

"You know, I had everything under control here." I tried to assert myself, but my voice cracked at an unfortunate moment.

"*Si, si.* I didn't kill that man because you were in over your head, *signorina Saint-Germain*. I killed that man so you wouldn't have to."

He licked the rest of the blood from his teeth, and my heart pounded so deep I felt like I was standing on top of a Kongo drum. His fangs slowly retracted, making him appear even more like a normal man. He came one step closer, causing me to step back. My shoulders knocked against the tall sugarcane stalks, but closer still he leaned until it was more than my skirts that he touched.

"I am sure one day you will have to kill a man, but there is no need for that day to be today."

"*Merci beaucoup*," I whispered, trying not to choke on my own breath.

A loud whistle grabbed my attention. "The boat is boarding!"

When I looked back to Gabriel, all I saw were the sticky stalks of sugarcane bending in the breeze.

I lowered down to Makandal and kissed the top of his head.

"*Vive la révolution*," he whispered beneath the tremors of a breaking fever. He brushed my cheek, and his eyes rolled back as he began to chant words over me.

"We will be like sisters," I promised, giving his hand one final squeeze before I took off running.

My lungs stung, pushing the humid air in and out as I raced to the ship. Frantic, I told myself Captain Vauberci would never set sail without me.

When I arrived at the dock, everyone was waiting for me. The governor and captain were talking by the boarding ramp – both looked relieved when I approached. I apologized for being late and told them I had decided to take one last stroll in the beautiful garden and lost track of time. The captain glanced at the state of my dress and raised an eyebrow, but said nothing. The governor accepted my excuse with good cheer and took me aside to present a gift he had loaded onto the boat for you, Father, as a gesture of goodwill. Six giant barrels of sugar, along with the message that you are welcome in the Caribbean any time. Papa, the vastitude of your reputation never ceases to amaze me.

When the crew weighed anchor, I hoped that, by some miracle, our stowaways had seen this tropical oasis and decided to stay on the island, but the chills that rippled up my arms as the boat set sail told me otherwise. As horrible as it sounds, I hoped that at least they had left the boat to feed. We still had five hundred leagues to go. At one time I would have celebrated this, but now that we had been forced back into the role of caged prey, every league might as well have been a lifetime.

That night when I dreamt, our monster's face was no longer horrid. His face was Gabriel Medici's.

(cont.)

FOR FOUR WEEKS WE HID MARASSA in my private cabin with little effort. That was until one morning when the vessel jerked to a halt and flung us both from my bed.

I lifted myself up, and she rolled from underneath me. "*Désolée*," I apologized. "I should have strapped myself with the rope."

I quickly threw on my cloak and boots and ran out to see what had caused the jolt.

Half the crew, including the captain, were leaning over one side of the ship, while others flooded up from below deck.

"Captain, looks like we hit a sand bar," said one of the men. "Good thing the winds are calm. No speed. No damage."

Our vessel might not have incurred any damage, but we were indeed stuck.

Hours went by as the crew attempted to maneuver the ship without getting it to so much as budge. Finally, the captain ordered the men to start tossing things overboard to lighten the ship's load and float us off the sand.

First, he ordered the thirty-seven barrels of pirate rum to be thrown over. Watching the crew lament the spirits, you would have thought they were throwing over their own mothers. Sadly, it was done in vain. Next went forty-two barrels of wine. When this didn't change our fate, the captain ordered the cannons overboard. I stayed on the deck and focused on each of the iron weapons, lifting them up just enough to take some of the burden off the tired crew. Two more stagnant hours went by. People grew restless knowing we had abandoned our weapons, also in vain.

"*Mesdames et Messieurs*," said the captain. "I was hoping we could avoid it, but it appears the time has come when we have no choice but to throw the passenger luggage overboard if we are to stand a chance at survival."

"Isn't there something we can do?" I whispered to the triplets.

"Unfortunately, I can only persuade the hearts of men, not sand," Cosette responded, looking at me with hopeful eyes. "Can you not?"

"I don't see how a fire is going to help get us out of this one."

Being ladies of God and not attached to their material possessions, the nuns volunteered their luggage first. The orphans wept, realizing their *cassettes* would be next. The long boxes containing their gifts from the King were the only security they had going into the New World.

After the nuns' luggage was tossed and the ship still didn't move, the captain ordered the *cassettes* to the deck. The girls tried to hold back their emotions, as they knew our survival was more important than their dowries.

"But what kind of life are we surviving for?" one of them cried and burst into tears.

The men emerged from below, carrying the first wooden box as if they were casket-bearers. The mood was somber as they passed the mourners on the deck.

That is when everything suddenly made absolute sense, Papa.

I don't know how I didn't see it before. On our last night in Paris, *Monsieur Cartier*, or Medici, or whatever his real name is, had asked if I would hide him in my luggage. The blonde man, Gabriel Medici, had asked Cosette if he could stow away in her *cassette*. How many other vampires had visited how many of the other orphans and tricked them into giving them passage – and meals?

I recalled the crew moving the *cassettes* from the S.S. *Gironde* to the pirate ship and then to our current vessel. These vampires had made it so far, and now they were about to inadvertently walk the plank. We would finally be rid of the monsters for good!

My head spun with images of Sophie and Claude dying, and the bloody massacre on the S.S. *Gironde* – but also the compassion Gabriel had shown Makandal that night in the sugarcane field. Was it even possible for such a creature to have compassion?

"Wait!" I suddenly found myself yelling. "*Attendez!* Stop!"

All eyes on deck turned to me.

"*Oui, Mademoiselle Saint-Germain?*" asked the captain.

"*Le sucré! Le sucré!*" I gasped, running to help the men keep the first box from tipping overboard. "The sugar! Throw over the sugar! You have to at least try before we toss their dowries." My heart pounded, knowing that Gabriel might be inside *la cassette*.

A flitter of relief rippled through the orphans, and a smile spread across the captain's face. "You heard the lady: bring up the sugar!"

The men finished dumping the governor's golden gift overboard, and all the passengers ran to one side of the boat to redistribute the weight. We anxiously waited as the rudder fought, but it wasn't enough. Another half hour went by, and we were no freer than before.

I could feel the hearts of each passenger begin to sink when, all of a sudden, a wave rocked the boat, and then another. They grew in strength, and the boat lurched, knocking everyone to the floor.

I gripped a thick net and hoisted myself up. It was difficult to see through the wind and splashing water, and at the time I could hardly believe it: the sand was taking on the shape of the waves and parting, allowing the ship's release.

"A miracle," one of the nuns rejoiced, crossing her chest. Another jolt knocked me back on to the deck, and that's when I saw her. In the crow's nest, with her arms held out to the sand bar, head rolled back: it was Marassa, speaking into the wind with the red bird singing loudly from her shoulder.

My confounded gaze brought everyone's attention to the *Kreyòl* girl.

"Who is that?" yelled one of the orphans.

"Stowaway!" shouted one of the crew.

"What is she doing?"

"Who smuggled the contraband!"

"Witch!"

The crowd gasped.

"Witch!"

"Come down here, girl!" yelled the captain. "We won't hurt you."

The nuns pulled out their beads and began to pray. Panic spread throughout my body as Marassa slowly came down the pole. Her feet hit the floor, and she took off running; the first mate raced behind her as she fled below deck. The captain yelled for order, but I flew past him with the triplets in tow; we chased them into the first-class cabin marked "DuFrense."

I burst into Martine's room, yelling, "Get off of her!" as he grabbed the back of Marassa's neck. The captain and Mother Superior entered the cabin, as his first mate yelled back at me, "Did you steal this contraband from the island?"

"I didn't *steal* her," I hissed. "You can't *steal* a person. She's not a *possession*." My heart pounded, Papa. After all of the trouble – after weeks of hiding – we were finally exposed.

But then a voice of superiority rang loud and clear. "What do you think you are doing? Take your hands off my property at once!"

A small hiccup prevented Martine from any more speech, but she grabbed Marassa's arm and pulled the girl to her side. Everyone looked on in shock, including me and Cosette.

"Pardon, Madame DuFrense," said the first mate. "This girl belongs to you?"

"What do you think I spent all of those hours shopping for on the island? Sugar? Do you think I have ever baked a tart in my life?" She stood in front of the frightened girl in a protective stance.

"Our apologies, Madame Martine. You should have let us know, to ensure that she was properly added to the passenger manifest," the captain halfheartedly scolded her, but his eyes never left me.

I made a face to declare my innocence, and I knew he had to concentrate lest he betray a smile.

"Well, add her to your documents!" Martine said. "Now, don't you have a ship to navigate? Get out of my cabin, all of you!"

As soon as everyone but the triplets and I had cleared the room, Martine fell onto the chaise and let out another hiccup. The four of us fell to our knees beside her, showering her with thanks.

Marassa stood frozen in bewilderment.

"Don't fret, *ma chérie*," Martine told her as she poured rum into a glass and quickly swallowed the drink. "I would no sooner own a child than I would birth one on my own accord."

30

plastic cheese

THE SUREST WAY TO PUSH ME back into my father's arms was certainly the sight of my mother. After the bizarre encounter at Vodou Pourvoyeur, I ran (literally) straight for Le Chat Noir. This time it made way more sense when Troy the bouncer asked me to give my father a message.

There weren't nearly as many people in the *garçonnière* as the previous night, but it wasn't even nine o'clock, yet, and in pre-Storm New Orleans, that would have meant the night hadn't even begun. I headed straight for the bar, but stopped short when I overheard Detective Matthews' voice. He was sitting at the bar, leaning over a glass of clear-colored spirits, talking to my father, who was drying tumblers with a rag.

"... I'm just saying, it's a little strange that she reported one of the victim's bodies and then was first on site to another crime scene."

Are they talking about me? I slipped beside an armoire and strained my ears to listen.

"You better not be insinuating what I think you are, Terry." If I wasn't mistaken, there was a bit of threat in my father's tone.

"I'm not trying to cause trouble here, Mac. It's my job to look at all the facts. Don't you think it's a little peculiar that most of this picked up right after she arrived back from France?"

Did the detective actually consider me a suspect? Of murder?

"The way the Wolfman was drained and hung over the statue reminded me an awful lot of the deaths of those two filmmaker kids."

This time, my father wasn't so quick to defend. He dried two more glasses before looking up. "I can't believe I'm about to say this…"

"What is it, Mac?" The disheveled detective leaned closer to my father.

"Well, I've gotten wind Brigitte is back in town."

"Your ex-wife?"

"Wife."

"What?"

"Well, technically we never got a divorce. After she skipped town, there was never a real need to," he paused, "and I guess I always hoped she would come back."

"I'm sorry, Mac, but this is just too much of a coincidence. Do you know when she got back in town? Where she is staying?"

"Nope. Haven't heard from her, so I'm guessing she's not here to see me." He tried not to let the disappointment clog his throat.

Whatever animosity I'd been harboring towards my father totally dissipated. He was the only person who'd always been there for me. While I didn't appreciate him *hiding* things, the world was too crazy right now to hold a grudge. I sheepishly stepped out of the shadows.

"Hey, Dad."

"Sweetheart!"

"Addie," chimed the detective, "what a pleasant surprise."

"Hi, Detective." I greeted him through gritted teeth. "How's the case coming?"

"Slowly but surely. Just got a new lead, actually. I need to run. You can have my seat."

Is he referring to my mother as a new lead? What the hell is going on here?

After a quick cough, the detective drained the booze and shook my dad's hand. "Mac."

"Adele, I hear your mom's back in town. You seen her?"

Concerned, my father set down his glass, waiting for my reaction.

"No," I lied. Well, I hadn't talked to her, anyway.

"Do you know where she is sta—"

"Terry. Minor. Out!"

The detective gave my dad an apologetic look and headed for the exit. My gaze stayed with him until the door closed.

My father treaded with caution. "Did you get some studying done with Désirée?"

"Yeah, it was far more educational than I ever could have guessed."

"Good."

"I'm sorry, Dad. About last night. About everything. It's just that everything is so different now... I feel like I'm on another planet sometimes."

"I know, honey. And I'm sorry for keeping the bar hidden from you. I didn't want to implicate you in any way. After all, it *is* illegal...." He paused and then changed the subject with a softer voice. "She'll turn up eventually, Adele."

"That's not very comforting, Dad. Why do you think she's here?"

"I don't know, honey, but I am sure it's got something to do with you. She probably couldn't stay away after having you for two months."

I gave him my best "get real" look. *Does he not remember that she shipped me off to boarding school the second she had the chance to be with me?* "Is it okay if I just sit here and study for a while?"

"Sure, but don't tell Terry I let you stay out after curfew." He winked.

"Me being out after curfew is the least of Detective Matthews' problems."

"Ain't that the truth." He plunged the cork from a bottle of Cabernet and poured a heavy glass for a bar patron. "Only two more bottles... soon we'll have nothing left."

"Hmm." I looked at the empty bottles lining the floor behind the bar: various wines, rums, bourbons, vodkas, Sazerac, Pimms, but on the shelf – a dozen bottles of gin, all full.

I shook my head and kept my mouth shut, as I took out Adeline's diary and my notebook and began translating.

6th June 1728

I spent the rest of the journey in agony, Papa. Always anticipating the worst. We went nearly two weeks without any evidence of the vampires, but, just as my nerves began to settle, two orphans woke with symptoms. The guilt began to consume me, being the one who had saved the monsters from drowning. I tormented myself with regret, thinking I should have let them all sink to the bottom of the ocean.

Every morning I prayed with the nuns for good weather and strong winds to expedite the journey. After a few days, only one of the girls had woken. I spent night and day with the remaining unconscious girl, until one morning her chest no longer moved up and down. I became hysterical. Cosette did her best to calm me, and the captain assured me we would reach La Nouvelle-Orléans *in two days' time.*

Thank heavens he was correct. Two days later I stepped onto the dock of the port de La Nouvelle-Orléans *with a heavy mix of emotions. I was elated that the passengers I had come to know so well were no longer trapped at sea with the deadliest of predators, but I could not celebrate this victory knowing that the vampires would soon be unleashed upon the unsuspecting citizens of this new land.*

I never told the triplets of my theory regarding the cassettes. Knowing innocent people had been bitten after I saved the monsters was too shameful. Despite my heavy mood, the girls made me celebrate our arrival by attending a parade commencing that very afternoon, honoring the completion of the new Ursuline Convent on Rue de Chartres.

Women led the way, tossing flower petals into the newly stoned streets, while the men beat drums and blew horns. Children twirled strips of fabric tied to sticks, and an elderly man rode a mule, waving the King's flag. The parade did raise my spirits, mostly because I couldn't help but marvel at the procession of people. There were rich and poor. Men of the Holy Cloth and women of the very unholy cloth. White. Black. Dark. Light. Young girls with tanned skin and shiny black hair tied into intricate braids adorned with feathers and beads held hands and walked side by side with the Sisters. I overheard a local Frenchman nearby call them "savages" as they passed.

Most of the colonists are French, but I occasionally hear words of Spanish, English, German, and others I do not recognize. The mixture makes La Nouvelle-Orléans *seem so progressive, so scandalous! Of course, I immediately fell in love with this land. Maybe it really is true that a person could start over here...*

"SWEETHEART, YOU SHOULD REALLY GET HOME," my father said. "It's a school night, and you have midterms. I'll ask Troy to walk you."

"I can escort her home," came a voice from behind me. "If that's okay with you, Adele."

I turned around, but I already knew from his accent that it was Nicco.

"And who are you? I've seen you around here with that blond guy. Quite the ladies' man, that one."

"Niccolò Medici, sir. And I can assure you, my brother Gabriel is harmless. He's just been cooped up for a long time."

My father raised an eyebrow.

"In the library," Nicco quickly added. "Cooped up in the library. He just finished writing his dissertation."

You'd think someone who'd been around for so long would be a better liar. The idea of Gabriel Medici sitting in the library writing a dissertation was absurd.

"Dad, Nicco and Gabe came to town looking for missing relatives, and they've stayed on to help with the recovery efforts. They were staying with the Palermos for a while, helping Mr. Felix clean out the shop." I think that was all actually true.

"Well, welcome to New Orleans, son. I hope everything is all right with your family." He poured a stiff drink and slid it across the bar to Nicco, who caught it right before it went over the edge. A little spilled over, which I was sure he did on purpose. He brought the drink to his mouth, and I could tell that he was trying not to make a face as the scent hit. He glanced at my father and then back at me, set the glass down, and slid it back to my father. "I'd better not."

"Correct answer."

"So this city can't get a real food or petrol supply, but you can get shipments of liquor?"

"No, no, no. That which you just turned down is the finest Hurricane Hootch your lips will ever taste. And by the finest, I mean the only Hurricane Hootch in existence."

"And who distills this magical moonshine?" asked Nicco.

"Yeah, Dad, who distills this magical moonshine?"

He looked at me, knowing full well that he was busted. "Er, an old family friend."

I shot him a "no more secrets" look. He returned a look of concession that also begged to drop the subject. I smiled, satisfied with our exchange, and he stepped away to help a customer.

Nicco turned to me. "You know, at one point in time it would have been insulting *not* to accept that drink. It's strange the way humans have evolved."

"You know, at one point in time, the general populous believed in vampires?"

"Like I said, it's strange the way humans have evolved."

"Touché." I tried not to sound smitten. "Where did you come from, by the way? I didn't even realize you were here."

"I've been sitting in the corner, waiting for an opportune time to approach you."

"What do you mean?"

"Well," a small smile flashed, "it's a little intimidating."

I laughed. "What could possibly be intimidating?"

"I mean, with your father and all…"

I looked at my dad, who was slinging moonshine but still watching us, and then back at Nicco. I didn't know what to make of a vampire being intimidated by my father.

"Three-hundred-plus years later and you're still intimidated by the fathers of girls?"

"Not the father of just *any* girl."

The task of inhaling air suddenly felt very difficult. "Then let's get out of here," I barely squeaked, gathering my things. When we were nearly at the door, I yelled goodbye to my father, not giving him a chance to stop me.

"Be careful, and go straight home!"

ONCE WE WERE OUT OF TROY'S VIEW, Nicco extended his elbow. "So, *bella,* which way?"

As I curled my palm around his arm, last night's memories fluttered. *I mean, I'm not in danger of being drained by a malnourished child of the night if I'm out with a nourished one, right?*

Never trust a vampire.

I pushed Nicco's words away and racked my brain for a post-curfew place to go. It was too cold (and too illegal) to just wander about. *I can't invite Nicco back home – surely he'd get the wrong idea...*

"Can I make a suggestion?" he said, interrupting my internal freak out.

"Sure." Where could he know about that I didn't? Two blocks later, he led me to the Clover Grill and pushed the door. Surprisingly, it was unlocked.

"I noticed it late last night," he said, holding open the door. "Have you been here before?"

"Uh, yeah, it's only an institution."

The twenty-four-hour diner was known for its omelets, flamboyant staff, and hangover-curing patty melts. There was usually a line outside. I had never seen the place empty, but tonight it was just us, and the feeling that we were getting away with something.

Inside the old eatery, the temperature was barely warmer than outside, but the counter was lit by a row of tea lights, music was playing, and the smell of recently heated grease hung in the air. As soon as the glass door shut behind us, we were greeted with a menacing growl, and a pit bull appeared from the shadows. Nicco stepped ahead of me, but I looped in front of him and knelt down to greet the chocolate-colored canine, who in turn ran her drool-covered tongue over the line on my cheek.

"Stella, gross!" I wiped my face with my sleeve.

"Addie! Little Addie, is that you?" shrieked a voice from behind the grill. "You come over here right now and give Blanche some love!"

I scurried to the other side of the counter to embrace Blanche, who was kind of a downtown celebrity, famous for both his mammoth omelets at the Clover Grill and his drag performances a few blocks over at Lucky Cheng's. Tonight he sported a white-ribbed tank, baggy jeans, and a hair net. False eyelashes accentuated with glitter-swept eyelids.

"Well, you look fabulous," I said.

"Of course I look fabulous. You think imma let some little thang like a hurricane keep me from lookin' fabulous? I don't think so, honey!" He snapped his finger and did a full twirl. Blanche talked faster than anyone I knew, and he rivaled Ren in Oscarworthy performances.

"Wait. Stella and Blanche?" Nicco asked. "As in Blanche DuBois?"

"As in Blanche Du-whoever-I-felt-like-when-I-woke-up-this-morning, thank you very much." He rolled his head to me. "He's quick."

"Nicco, this is Blanche." I held back giggles. "Blanche, this is Nicco."

"En-shan-tay, baby." Blanche grabbed Nicco's hand and raised it to his lips. "You a quick one, and you pretty too."

Nicco's cold blood ambushed his otherwise pale cheeks, making him look more human. My imprisoned giggles burst from their holding tanks.

"Take any seat ya like. As you can see, folks ain't exactly beatin' down the do'."

I slipped into one of the red leather booths, and Nicco grabbed a candle from the counter before sliding across from me. It was almost, dare I say, romantic. Not a word I ever dreamed I'd use in reference to the Clover Grill.

"What are you doing open?" I asked Blanche as he came to take our order. "What about the curfew? Not that I'm complaining."

"Honey, if they want me to close, they gonna haf to come down here and drag me to the O.P.P. in cuffs. And I know that's not gonna happen 'cause there ain't a single pair of cuffs ta spare. They ain't got no room in that Orleans Parish Prison to arrest a girl for makin' omelets." He waved a spatula in a tizzy. "But you know after that curfew hits, ain't no one gonna come in here for the rest of the night. You know the only ones who comin' up in here are?"

"Hmm?"

"The po-pos! So I end up jus' fryin' eggs for half the parish precinct. But that's okay, honey" – his voice dropped an octave – "'cause I love a man in uniform."

Nicco seemed a little taken aback, which made me smile, considering how much he must have seen over the last three centuries.

"Whatchou want, baby? I got omelets, and I got omelets. My egg-guy seems ta be my only guy back in bidness. Well, not my *only* guy, if ya catch ma drift." He hooted and slapped his knees. "Wahoo! It's good ta see ya home, Addie Le Moyne. And how is your mighty hot daddy?"

"He's fine," I responded, cringing when I realized the word I had chosen. This time it was Nicco who couldn't refrain from laughing. "Welcome back to New Orleans," I said to him through blushing cheeks.

"How 'bout I jus' bring y'all the Hurricane Special?"

"The Hurricane Special sounds perfect," I said.

Blanche's hip cocked as he turned to Nicco.

"When in Rome…"

"Alrighty, baby." Blanche went back behind the counter, fired up the grill, and cranked up an old boom-box, blasting a classic Mariah Carey album. Stella came to our booth with a rumbling growl and rested on the floor. She quieted down when I petted her head, but she never took her eyes off Nicco.

"Tennessee Williams, such a tragic fellow." Nicco's hand brushed mine as he picked up the plastic menu on the table. My heart thumped as he looked at me. "You know he used to live not too far from here, on Toulouse Street?"

"Everyone knows that, son!" Blanche yelled from the grill without turning around.

I raised my head to peek at the boom-box and turned the volume up just enough to mask our conversation.

My attention came back to the table just in time to see Nicco finishing a silent exchange with someone on the other side of the window. She rushed off, her mane of bright blonde hair swinging behind her, luminous in the night. It was ultraquick, but I swear she'd given him a threatening look, which he had returned with an equally hostile expression. His demeanor changed as his eyes dropped from the window.

"What was that all about?"

"It's nothing."

"Who is she? The blonde?" I tried my best not to sound like a jealous lunatic. "She keeps showing up – the night of the tour, last night at the bar, and she was the one who walked past us that morning, right? Following me when I ran into you, after you had... gotten into the fight?" I paused, but then continued before he had the chance to answer. "Is she the one biting my classmates?" Anger edged through my tone. "The one killing people?"

Our eyes locked. I focused on keeping my mouth shut so he could speak.

"*Si,* she was the one following you. I'm not sure if she is the one killing people, but it's likely. She's volatile on a good day, but, in her defense, self-control would be difficult for any vampire who'd just spent three hundred years trapped in an attic." His voice had a bit of an edge. "Being a newborn, it's a wonder she even made it out alive. Some sort of *magic* surely aided her survival..." His voice trailed off, and I became immediately nervous by the mention of magic. "As for whether she's the one biting your friends, who knows? All vampires bite people, Adele."

"All...? Even you?"

"What would happen to you if you stopped eating?"

"Sorry, stupid question. It's just so hard to fathom that humans aren't at the top of the food chain."

"That's because humans are arrogant."

"And vampires aren't?"

"*Touché*." He smiled.

Blanche finished belting out the popular chorus, and I slowly began to lay my cards out on the table. "Earlier tonight, someone attacked me—"

"What?" he asked, leaning in. "Who? Were you hurt?" His eyes flickered.

"No, I'm fine. To be fair, it wasn't really an attack." I paused. "She jerked me unwillingly into an alleyway and demanded that I break a curse."

His jaw tightened ever so slightly.

"She?"

"Yes, her face was hidden, but it was definitely a she. She was taller than me, and inhumanly strong. *Elle est française,* or at least she had a heavy French accent."

"What *exactly* did *she* tell you?"

"She said if I didn't break the curse that very bad things are going to happen in the *Vieux Carré.*"

He touched my fingers, trying to comfort me so I would continue.

"She said they would hurt every person I love… destroy my family." My heart raced as he looked at me in silence. He was not happy. I had every intention of stopping there, but my tongue ran away from me. "Meaning that *your* family would destroy *my* family."

His long pause warned me not to push it any further.

"That's all she said?"

"Yes."

He remained completely calm, but I could see that multiple scenarios were spinning through his mind.

"Do you think it was your blonde friend?"

His silence answered for him, which had a dizzying effect on me.

"Who is she? Is she dangerous?"

Silence.

It was as if he was trying to decide how much information to reveal, which only further frustrated me. He waited through another Mariah verse, but I refused to allow my eyes to wander. Then I saw the exact moment he gave in.

"Her name is… Liz. And all vampires are dangerous, Adele. *All.*"

My heart thumps ricocheted against my chest. "Even you?"

"Especially me."

"Why especially?" I intertwined my fingers with his. The small gesture was bold for me.

"That's why." He yanked his hands away and dragged them through his hair, causing my self-esteem to plummet.

"I'm sorry—" we both said at the same time.

The awkwardness that followed made my stomach knot come back tenfold. I desperately wanted to get back to the place we had been last night, in the bell tower. I wanted to jump into his side of the booth and wrap myself underneath his arm. Instead, I twisted a napkin until it morphed into a ropelike shape. I wanted answers more.

"Did I break Adeline's curse? Is that how the v—your, er, family escaped the convent attic?"

His eyes flickered again. "What do you know about Adeline *Saint-Germain*?" He nearly spat out her surname.

A wave of energy rushed through my limbs, collecting at the tips of my outer extremities, and the chain around my neck gently rippled against my skin. Suddenly I remembered the woman in the alley saying that she was warning me and not threatening me.

"Nothing really," I lied. "When I found Adeline's necklace, there was also a letter she had written to her father but never sent. It described the night she met Monsieur Jean-Antoine Cartier. The night she met you." Lying to him hurt me more than I could have imagined, but something deep inside pushed the words out.

I quickly glanced at Blanche, who was using the spatula as a mic and riffing trills. "Why do they expect me to break the rest of the curse? I don't know anything about spells!"

"Well, if Adeline's dead, then it's your curse now—"

"I don't want any of this!" I whispered loudly, leaning across the table.

He jerked forward in his seat, his nose suddenly brushing mine. "Do you think I did?"

Despite keeping my gaze fully locked on the green eyes, only inches away from mine, I knew his fangs were extended because my fingers ached. The song ended, leaving a moment of silence.

And then the soft sounds of air pushing in and out of his nostrils sent a shiver down my spine.

His mouth stayed shut, but I saw his fangs retract. We both sank back to our leather cushions. I sat on top of my hands for a minute.

His words about murder being inconsequential rang in my head. Given that the only *other* way to break the curse was death, telling him that I *couldn't* actually break it on my own didn't seem so smart.

"You'll figure it out, *bella.* When you woke up yesterday, you didn't know that you could throw fire to defend yourself from a vampire—"

"So, you also want me to break the curse?"

"I usually let my brethren clean up their own messes, but I'm not fond of my family members being cursed."

"Gabe," I whispered. *Had he been one of the vampires trapped in the attic?* Of course. He had been on the ship with the casquette girls. "Shit."

"There's *no* more time, Adele. I cannot control what will happen – not that I haven't been trying. People *will* die in retaliation if you don't break the curse."

The look on my face must have made him pause. His words became softer.

"Don't be too hard on yourself, *bella.* You didn't even know you were breaking the curse – not that I am upset about it breaking – but I'm sure you had help, unbeknownst to you. I may not be a witch, but I have lived long enough to know that sometimes unexplainable things happen, especially when Mother Nature is involved."

"The Storm."

"Si."

His foot knocked into mine. I was surprised when he didn't immediately pull it back. Over the next few moments, our legs slowly crept into each other's and locked together. The bend was awkward but somehow still felt perfect. I knew that he could feel my pulse speed up – a small smile hid under his serious disposition.

His eyes dragged from the table to mine. "I won't let anything happen to you, Adele."

"One Hurricane Es-pec-i-al," Blanche said, dropping a single plate with a mound of eggs dripping in gooey cheese, and a mysterious, powdered-sugar-dusted log. "*Bon appetite.*" He placed a fork next to each of us, not knowing we only needed one.

"Wow, Blanche, you really outdid yourself."

"This really is… special," said Nicco.

"Always, baby."

"What is this?" I poked the long lump of fried dough. "A Twinkie?"

Blanche opened his mouth—

"No Twinkie jokes!" I yelled.

He mimed zipping his lips. "Yeah, baby, that's a fried Twinkie. You know that shit'll survive the apocalypse."

Gross. I waited for Blanche to return to the grill before I pushed the sponge of fried preservatives to the side and tried to separate some of the egg from the cheese.

"This is something you have to explain to me," Nicco said, suddenly serious. He straightened up quickly, and our still-intertwined legs pulled me down the leather seat until my ribs hit the table. Had the tabletop not been there, I would have slid right on top of him. I wished it hadn't been there.

"What?" I was fully intrigued by something *I* could explain to *him.*

"This stuff you Americans eat. This American cheese. Is it good? It looks like—"

"Plastic," we both said simultaneously.

As the last syllable came out of my mouth, a series of latent memories buried deep in my subconscious between "jet lag" and "too much to drink" pounded through my mind like a flashing camera bulb:

Plastic cheese.

Half-James Dean, half-Italian Vogue.

Leather jacket.

Innocent smile... deceptively innocent.

Fork. Clank. The waitress yelling, "Don't worry, honey, I'll bring ya a new one." Coffee mug on top of a ten-dollar bill.

The room began to spin.

"Adele?"

"Adele?"

"Addie? He-llo! Girlfriend, you in outer space right now. Here ya go." Blanche handed me a fork.

When I looked down, I realized mine was missing.

"Try not to take my eye out with this one, m'kay?"

Clutching the fork, I nodded, and he walked back to the grill.

Breathe.

I looked back at Nicco.

"I've said something to offend you?" He sounded genuinely concerned. "Are you okay?"

Was Nicco at the Waffle House? In Alabama? I stared at him for another moment – he absolutely was that guy. My body tensed. *Dammit*! *I knew he looked familiar. What the hell?*

"Adele, what's wrong?"

Ren's words about no such thing as a coincidence repeated over and over in my head. *Is Nicco stalking me?* Suddenly uneasy, I tried my best not to recoil so he wouldn't think I was on to something. *If I am on to something.*

"Are you okay?" he repeated.

"No. I mean, yes, I'm okay. No, you didn't say something to offend me."

"You're lying. I can hear your heart racing."

I tried my best to mimic one of Désirée's sultry smiles. "My heart's racing for a lot of different reasons right now."

"Oh, really?" He leaned closer over the table, pushing my tease.

Never trust a vampire.

I fell back into the booth. "American cheese, it's kind of an acquired taste."

His brow crinkled. He knew I was still lying – and he seemed to be upset by it.

"Are you sure you're okay? Or is there something else on your mind?"

And that's the first time I had the thought: *What if the curse wasn't meant to be broken?* I poked the eggs, trying to think of something to cover for my sudden nervousness. "I do have a question."

"Go on," he said with confidence and leaned even further across the table.

"The Carter brothers, John and Wayne… the story Ren told on the tour." I looked up at Blanche to make sure he was still preoccupied. "John Carter? *Monsieur Jean-Antoine Cartier?*" As the words left my mouth, a gigantic flame shot up from the grill, causing a high-pitched yelp from Blanche.

My eyes fluttered to the grill, but Nicco's absorbed gaze never left me.

"*Si.* My brother and I," he said quietly. "It was the depression. Everyone rationed."

I had to consciously keep my mouth from gaping at his flippant response.

"Those weren't really my best years," he added.

Is he really comparing saving half a potato to stringing people up and slowly bleeding them to death? I barely heard the words come out of my mouth as I asked him something trivial about life in the French Quarter during the prohibition. I swallowed a few bites of egg and slowly drank my coffee, trying not to rouse suspicion.

"People always want what they can't have," he said, a bit lost in his own thoughts.

"Nicco?"

"Si, bella?"

"If Gabe spent the last three hundred years locked in the Ursuline Convent, then how was he rationing people with you during the Depression?"

"It wasn't Gabriel roaring through the nineteen-twenties with me." He sighed. "It was my other brother, Emilio."

I wheezed as I swallowed my last sip of coffee incorrectly. "You have another brother?"

"Si, although, we're a bit estranged now. That's also why I am eager to get Gabriel back."

I felt like I had been bitten by a snake and the venom was slowly coursing through my veins, taking over the function of each organ. At the bar last night, Émile had been sitting at the table with Gabe's crew. *Is he really Emilio Medici? My Émile? My mother's assistant Émile?* I suddenly felt very tiny, like a pawn in a life-size game of chess where the stakes were real. *How many wrong moves had I made, unaware that I was even a player?*

Player.

I had been played.

How could I have been so stupid? Energy streamed through my system like fire, burning out all the venom. All the fear.

The worry that he'd lost me now shone in Nicco's eyes. He didn't know how or why, but he knew everything had changed. Why did he care? *Did* he care? *Maybe he just needed something from me? What had he needed Adeline for all those years ago? Was it really only passage and a meal ticket aboard a ship?*

There had been nothing coincidental about their happenstance meeting. It had all been so perfectly romantic. So calculated.

"And Adeline, do tell your father I called, si'l vous plaît..."

When had Adeline realize she was just a pawn?

Suddenly the idea of trapping the players in the attic made the corner of my lips gently twitch. My palms burned.

Then I looked back up at Nicco and just wanted it all to go away. It was so easy to get lost in his stories, in his smiles, in his leather...

When I told him I had to go home, the disappointed look on his face seemed genuine.

INSIDE OUR EMPTY HOUSE, I ran from room to room engulfed in paranoia, locking the windows and doors. Not that it really offered much protection, but it made me feel better.

"Philosophically, most vampires believe any creature should be able to find asylum in its own home..." Asylum? Maybe... Solace? No.

For weeks I had felt like I was being watched – now I knew I had been. By Émile. By the blonde woman. By Niccolò. And by the crow, who had followed us from the bar, to the diner, and then to my home, and who had patiently waited in the shadows while I flirted with a monster.

When I peeked through the kitchen door curtain, I saw the crow perched on the fence, just like he had been last night. I remembered how tired Isaac had looked before our fight. He must have gotten even less sleep than me. Part of me wanted to invite him in.

I closed the curtain and made coffee instead.

I've already broken Adeline's spell-line. Isn't that enough? Breaking the rest of the curse is not my problem. I couldn't even if I wanted to… not without a coven.

"The only other way to break it would be if all the inheritors died," I whispered.

"People will die in retaliation if you don't break the curse—"

"UGH! This cannot be happening!"

Exhausted, I gulped the cup of black coffee and reluctantly pulled out both my journal and Adeline's diary to search for answers. I uncapped a pen. A yawn so strong overtook me, my eyes watered, and I thought about my bed. The front burner on the stove exploded with flames.

"Well, help me, then!" I yelled, jumping up from my seat. "If you don't want your stupid curse broken, then help me, Adeline!"

I blew out the fire, but the flames just popped right back up. I blew out the burner again, opened the stove, blew out the pilot light, and turned back to my chair.

But instantly I felt the glow beckoning from behind me.

When I turned to give it my attention, rings of fire began to light around the other three burners until all four were ablaze. My fingers burned, but the warmth was comforting.

"It's your curse now," Nicco had said.

Focused on the fire, I took deep breaths, trying to calm myself. The flames slowly simmered into nothing.

I sat back down, turned the page, and began to think in French.

"ADELE, WAKE UP," my father said, frantically shaking my shoulder.

"What?" I carefully peeled my face from Adeline's diary.

"I don't know how to tell you this."

I twisted my back in pain, realizing I had fallen asleep sitting at the kitchen table. He squatted down so he was eye level with me and took both of my hands.

"Dad, what's wrong?" The look on his face made my eyes well.

"There's no easy way to tell you this, darling. Something horrible has happened to the Michels."

My heart leapt out of my chest.

"Jeanne and Sébastien?"

"No, honey, the kids are fine."

"Then…"

"It's Bertrand and Sabine."

"Has there been an accident?" I choked out. Tears began to pour down my face as Nicco's comment about retaliation echoed in my head.

"It wasn't an accident, sweetheart." He squeezed my hand.

I began to hyperventilate.

He didn't have to say anything else. I knew they were dead.

part 3
brigitte

"I can't go back to yesterday because
I was a different person then."
Lewis Carroll

October 30th

BLUE. WHITE. RED.

"Adele?"

Red. White. Blue.

"Adele?"

Blue. White. Red.

I stared directly into the flashes of light, and the colors began to blur together. Everything faded into bright white, and then went black. A spectrum of spots began dancing in front of my eyes until dizziness filled my head like a balloon. I wanted to float away.

"Adele, can you please answer the question?"

I blinked a few times, and the detective came back into focus. My nose was cold, as were my ears. He continued to say my name. My cheeks were warm from two steady streams of tears. I watched my breath vaporize in the chilly, dark air, as I wrapped my hands around Jeanne's freezing fingers. Her head was buried in my lap, whimpering.

"Adele, where were you last night from the hours of nine o'clock to midnight?"

"Back off, Detective," someone said, almost as if he were pulling the words from my mind. "You heard what Mac said." It was Sébastien's voice – he was sitting next to me on the cold bench. I'd never heard him say my father's first name before. It sounded strange. His arm tightened around my shoulder.

"I know this is difficult, Sébastien—"

"Back off!" he yelled, standing up so he was eye level with the detective. "She's in shock, and she's a minor."

Sébastien *never* raised his voice. It made Jeanne cry harder, but Detective Matthews got the message and walked away to consult with his team.

"*Merci beaucoup*," I whispered as he resumed his position next to me.

I had no clue how long the three of us had been sitting on the bench in front of Café Orléans, but the sun still wasn't showing signs of rising and my back was numb from the cold bench. My father wouldn't let us inside, and we didn't dare look behind us through the window, where the two bodies were being catalogued and prepped for autopsy.

A man with a portable crime-scene lab walked passed us, yawning, and entered the café. "Did you guys really have to wake me for this one? I've worked three shifts in a row. I don't even see any blood spatter."

"That's just it," answered one of the crime scene investigators. "There's no blood on site. No blood at all."

My stomach lurched, causing Jeanne to lift her head from my lap and sit up. I pinned my lips shut and bolted as vomit rose in my throat. I made it just far enough to turn the corner of the café before the contents of my stomach spewed into the gutter. It didn't take long before my system was totally void of plastic cheese, but I couldn't stop gagging, and soon, I was staring into a puddle of neon-colored bile. The stomach acid burned my throat, but all I could think was that I deserved it.

This is all your fault.

In between my wheezing and coughing, someone scooped back my hair. I continued to dry heave, and a strong but delicate hand rubbed my back.

"Breathe, *mon cœur*," a woman whispered.

I whipped around, and my mother steadied me as I barely avoided a tumble into my own vomit. I quickly regained my balance and jerked away from her. "What are you doing here?"

"I am so sorry, Adele." Her voice was as solid as her touch. "I wish I could take away your pain."

"Ha!" my raw throat croaked. "All you've ever done is cause pain!"

"I know. This is all my fault. I never should have left you. You were so young. I don't expect you to forgive me, nor to understand."

"Understand?" I shouted. "Do not patronize me."

"That wasn't my intention. I simply meant, things are complicated… more complicated than anyone should have to deal with. Especially a sixteen-year-old girl as sweet as you."

Her words induced another wave of nausea, but there was nothing left in my stomach but pain. Somewhere deep down inside me was a little girl who wanted the comfort of her mother, who wanted to cry into her sweater and confide everything, but I had no recollection of what a mother's comfort was. There was nothing my mother could do to help. The horror would continue unless I took care of it myself.

"I can't do this," I mumbled and walked down the foggy street, wiping tears and snot onto the back of my hand.

It was my turn to make a move, but I didn't know the play.

I MANAGED THREE BLOCKS ALONE before I saw Isaac coming towards me in his work boots and barely-there ponytail. Yesterday I would have crossed the street to avoid him, but my issues with Isaac didn't matter anymore. All of my energy had been used up hating myself.

He stopped when I got close.

"Not now, Isaac," I said, defeated.

"Your dad just texted me. I know I'm the last person you want to see, but I just want you to know that I'm here for you. Okay?" He pushed the loose hair from his face, revealing concern. I was already tired of getting that look from people. I didn't deserve sympathy – if they only knew what I'd done.

"Okay."

"He's looking for you. Mac. Check your phone."

I nodded and hurried away, hoping the dense morning fog would quickly hide me from the worried gaze I could feel on my back.

THE SHRILL OF DÉSIRÉE'S CAR ALARM being activated made me wince. I squinted at the watch on my trembling hand. It was light out… I hadn't even noticed the sun rising. I'd only been sitting on the stoop at Vodou Pourvoyeur for twenty-three minutes, but I hardly remembered calling her. The entire morning felt like a dream. A bad dream.

"Jesus Christ, Adele! You're shaking," Désirée said, crouching down in front of me. "Why didn't you ring the bell? Gran would have let you in."

I tried to think of an answer, but the question felt overly complex, and I just ended up staring at her blankly. She helped me up from the cold cement step and ushered me inside.

When she reached out to lock the deadbolt behind us, the metal snapped shut before her hand touched it. She raised an eyebrow but didn't ask questions. Instead, she motioned for me to follow her to the back room.

I collapsed next to the fireplace and concentrated on taking shallow breaths while she bent to light the hearth. Again, I beat her to it.

She looked at me as the bright orange flames leapt higher. "You really need to try to calm down, okay?"

I nodded and shut my eyes. The memory of begging my father – forcing him to return us to town – suddenly became very vivid. This could all have been avoided had I just stayed in Paris. At boarding school. With my mother. With Émile.

Émile. Emilio?

My stomach twisted. *Had all of this really started in Paris, just like it had for Adeline?* My memories spun. Sneaking around Paris with Émile. His promise to see me soon, when I left France. The Waffle House. The crow attack. The convent. The rain of metal as the nails dropped to the ground. The shutter flapping, drawing me closer and closer. Controlling me. Crashing. The whoosh of energy as the monsters whipped past me.

Me.

So stupid. So *naïve*.

Only now was I starting to recognize that sensation of supernatural energy.

Désirée waved her hand in front of my face, and a sharp scent filled my nostrils, followed by sweet notes. Citrus.

"What is that?"

"It's just oil: sandalwood, blood orange and sage. It should help you calm down." She sat down on the floor across from me, and I closed my eyes as her warm fingers rubbed the oil into my temples.

Breathe.

The fire crackled. The warmth from the flames made my face tingle. It felt like it was defrosting.

"She warned me," I said, still shaking. "She warned me last night, on my way here, but I didn't know they would act so fast. I should have listened... done something, but I didn't know what to do." My voice cracked. "Even Nicco told me they were going to retaliate, but I was so tired. I fell asleep when I got home."

"Who warned you?"

My throat croaked, fighting the tears.

"It doesn't matter now, Adele. There was nothing you could have done." Her arms circled around my shoulders. "This is not your fault."

She rested her forehead against mine and held my head up with hers as I cried out the remaining tears from my system.

The pungent aroma soaked in, making me feel a little high; I straightened my back, wiped my eyes, and inhaled deeper. She took both of my hands and whispered unfamiliar words under her breath, almost like a chant. My mind began to drift.

Suddenly her grip tightened, and her big, almond-shaped eyes popped open as she gasped.

"What just happened?" I asked. "I feel really light."

"Nothing, I just transferred some of your energy."

I didn't know what that meant, but I thanked her anyway. I didn't exactly feel chipper, but the physical pain had numbed, like someone had given me a jumbo dose of morphine.

"We have to break the curse," I said.

"Either that or we have to kill all the vampires."

My heart nearly stopped. *I knew that she knew.*

32
the brothers three

MY NOSE NUZZLED INTO A SOFT, WARM FABRIC. I felt safe, and for a few seconds I was awake without remembering the nightmare that had become my reality. Then, as I sat up from the cocoon of brightly colored blankets and pillows, it all rushed back like a boulder to the chest.

Where the hell am I?

My stirring caused a head to peek through a fuchsia velvet curtain. "Finally, you're awake," Désirée said, dropping to her knees next to me.

I focused on my watch. "Holy shit! It's 6 p.m.? How did I sleep that long? Did you drug me?"

"No. Yes. No. Well, kind of. I went digging through Marassa's grimoire and found this herbal tea concoction. I'd like to take credit, but I think in your case it was mostly extreme exhaustion. The tea just helped ease your mind so your body could rest."

I rubbed my eyes.

"I think the original recipe came from Cosette Monvoisin. Pretty sweet, eh?"

"Yeah, I kinda feel like I know those girls."

"Well, not *all* of them. Two are still total mysteries. While you were sleeping, I tried to read Adeline's diary. Epic fail. So I jacked your journal to read the translation in English."

"That's fine," I said, surprised by my lack of sensitivity towards Désirée Borges, of all people, invading my privacy. I still kind of felt like I was in outer space.

She exited through the curtain and returned a few minutes later with a cup of coffee and a bottle of mouthwash, which she threw at me. "Pretty sure you were puking earlier."

"Thanks."

I forced my stiff body to stand up, lifted the shroud, and reentered the land of the living (well, mostly living).

Only after washing my face did I feel brave enough to look at myself in the bathroom mirror. My eyes were red and swollen, and my hair resembled that of a 1980s monster ballader. I looked only half-alive, and my stomach was back in its semi-permanent knot, but the sleep had done wonders for my mind. As the lingering effects of the tea wore off, I felt alert, focused, ready for the battlefield.

But as soon as my mind became more active, misery flooded back in. I thought of Bertrand and Sabine Michel. *How could something so horrible happen to the sweetest, most wonderful people I knew?* My gut wrenched, recalling the warnings I'd received, but I forced myself to push all my emotions to a deep, dark place so I could concentrate on protecting the people who were still alive. I shuddered thinking about Jeanne or Sébastien getting hurt – they were the closest thing I had to siblings. I couldn't even think about something happening to my father.

I pulled out my phone as I reentered the tiny altar space behind the curtain – eighteen text messages and way more missed calls. *How had I slept through that?*

Sébastien	**5:37 a.m.**	Adele, you disappeared. Are you okay?

Sébastien	**5:51 a.m.**	The detective is gone; you can come back now.
Dad	**6:00 a.m.**	Adele, where are you?
Jeanne	**6:12 a.m.**	*Où es-tu?* You're scaring me.
Dad	**6:15 a.m.**	Come home now, sweetheart. The streets aren't safe.
Dad	**6:25 a.m.**	Adele, where are you? Please tell me so I can come and get you.
Dad	**6:40 a.m.**	Please call me.
Sébastien	**6:53 a.m.**	You don't have to return, just let me know that you are okay. I'm about to call the detective back.
Isaac	**7:00 a.m.**	Your dad is freaking out. I'm coming to look for u. Don't be pissed if I find u.
Isaac	**7:01 a.m.**	This is Isaac, btw.
unknown	**9:17 a.m.**	I had no idea this was going to happen last night. It doesn't change things, but I need you to know, bella. *Sentite condoglianze.* ~Niccolò

Émile	**11:26 a.m.**	Your mother sent me out to find you. *Où es-tu, ma chérie?* You can't hide forever.
Isaac	**3:42 p.m.**	You've been sleeping all day. Starting to think D put some kind of Voodoo spell on u.
Isaac	**3:43 p.m.**	That was a joke, btw.
Jeanne	**4:07 p.m.**	Isaac found you asleep at Vodou Pourvoyeur???? I feel like I'm in *The Twilight Zone*.
Dad	**4:21 p.m.**	Call me when you wake up if I am not at the Borges'. I love you.
Brigitte	**4:49 p.m.**	Adele, I'd really like it if we could talk. There are things you need to know. *Bisous.*

I plopped back down on the pallet next to Désirée, whose nose was buried in my journal. "My dad is freakin'."

"My mom talked to him," she said without breaking focus from the book. "Oh, and Niccolò came by at least three times. There's a good chance he's still perched outside like a hawk, which I have to admit is something I sooner expected from that Isaac guy than him."

A halfhearted chortle slipped out.

"What?"

"Nothing, I'll explain some other time."

"Whatever."

I touched the crow's mark on my face and felt horrible remembering our recent interactions. Isaac had clearly been trying to make amends.

"I'll be right back. Gonna make a quick call."

Wrapped in a blanket, I stepped out into the setting sun to get better reception. My nerves fluttered as I tapped the callback button, knowing I'd have to apologize.

I paced down the sidewalk, but before I even heard the second ring, a figure whipped down the street. Startled by his speed, I dropped my phone into the gutter. The blanket fell from my shoulders, and my feet glided on air as Nicco abruptly pinned me against the wall of a neighboring house. The rough stucco scraped my back through the thin T-shirt.

"Are you okay?" he asked, jerking my head to the side.

"I was unt—"

He pushed my head again, closely examining the other side of my neck.

"That hurts, Nicco!" I still had bruises from our night in the bell tower.

"I'm sorry." His grip loosened. "I didn't mean to hurt you. Sometimes I forget how fragile you are."

"That's bullshit! I can carry an egg without cracking it. Or a rabbit without killing it. Or a bird—"

His mouth twitched at the mention of a bird.

"You're right. I'll try to be more careful with you."

"I'm not asking you to try. I am telling you to stop!" My fists slammed into his chest. He grabbed both of my wrists and gently lowered my arms to my sides. My arm muscles shook, trying to fight him.

"Don't, *bella*, you'll just hurt yourself."

He was so close I could smell him. Leather and soap, just like... his brother. I couldn't bring myself to look at him after what had happened this morning.

"I don't understand," I choked out, losing the battle with my tears. "Why don't you all just leave?"

His calmness was a stark contrast to my emotional wreckage.

"Do you want me to leave?"

A sharp pain tugged in my chest. I wanted this all to go away. I wanted Nicco to be normal. *I* wanted to be normal. A part of me wanted to destroy him for everything he'd done, whatever his role… For following me. For not telling me everything. For letting me fall for him. I hated myself for wanting to cause harm to someone else. I wanted him to be stronger, to change, to want the same things as me. I wanted him.

"Yes, I want you to leave," I whispered.

My eyes looked past him.

"I don't believe you, *bella*."

My pulse raced as his stare burned into my face. I forced myself to look directly into those perfect green eyes. My vision became blurry and wet. Not being able to see him clearly gave me the courage to repeat myself.

"I want you to leave."

I lost all ability to contain myself, to retain any sense of maturity. I didn't want to think or reason. "Leave," I yelled, attempting to push him away, but only ended up shoving myself backwards into the stucco wall. He barely wavered. "Leave!"

"It's not that simple, Adele." His tone was much sharper. "We can't just leave."

"Of course you can! Surely you're all *strong* enough to travel by now. You've all certainly had enough sustenance." My voice lowered on the last word.

"Do you really think you are *that* powerful?" he shouted.

I shrank back. The raised voice of the otherwise demure Italian was far more distressing than his physical strength. He quickly quieted, but I could tell he was barely restraining himself.

"Do you really think you are *so* powerful that you *accidentally* broke a curse *so* strong it contained a group of vampires for more than three hundred years, and now they can just walk away?" He snorted. "You may have somehow opened the window, but don't forget that parts of the curse still remain. So here they will remain, confined to the city limits of *La Nouvelle-Orléans*. And not even the entire city, just the part that existed in 1728, when the spell was bound." He bit down on his lip.

"So, you are telling me that not only did I let a group of vampires escape, but now they are confined to the French Quarter?"

He rested his left elbow against the wall next to my face, and bowed his head just above mine. "*Si, bella.*"

"But you weren't cursed. You weren't trapped in the attic."

"*No. Grazie a Adeline*, I didn't make it on the ship with Gabriel and my cousins, so I wasn't trapped in the attic with them. I can leave whenever I want." He leaned so close it felt like we were touching.

And then we were.

His fingers brushed my face, and I let my head move slightly so that his cool hand cupped my cheek. Every part of my being tingled. Maybe out of excitement? Maybe as a warning to stop flirting with the enemy? My lashes batted shut as his face came closer to mine, and my heart pounded deep like a base drum— but then Nicco swung around.

Behind us, Émile was slowly clapping his hands. "So, this is why I'm getting the cold shoulder, *ma chérie?*"

In the silence that followed, I heard the faint sound of my name being shouted over and over again. "Adele! Are you okay?" All eyes went to the sidewalk, to my phone. *Dammit. The call must have been connected this whole time.*

Before I could reach it, Émile scooped the phone off the ground. "I'm sorry, but Miss Le Moyne is preoccupied at the moment. Can I take a message?" His French accent was totally gone, and he now sounded just like Nicco, but more bitter and slightly insane.

He moved the phone from his ear as Isaac yelled on the other end: "Go to hell, bloodsucker!"

Ugh. Isaac... Wait, did he just say bloodsucker? What the hell?

"How sweet," Émile teased, hanging up the call and handing the phone back to me. "A love triangle." There was no anger in his voice; he was just taunting us. Smiling. "*Fratello*, please don't tell me that you're really competing with a bird for the affection of a human?"

Embarrassment boiled over inside me, and then anger, but I focused on controlling myself. One of the only things I had going for me in this nightmare was the element of surprise, so there was no point in flying off the handle and giving myself away – that is, if Nicco hadn't already told his brothers about my abilities.

"Go back inside, Adele," Nicco muttered, pushing me behind him so forcefully I nearly fell to the ground.

"I can take care of myself," I said, trying to keep my balance.

He ignored me and yelled something in Italian to his brother, which only made Emilio scoff. "Of course I would get to her first, brother. Please…"

Get to me first?

"This really is adorable," he continued, hanging a lanky but intimidating arm around each of us. An arm I used to love having wrapped around me when we rode his Vespa together. *Ugh.*

"*Je ne comprends pas, Émile*," I said.

"Well then, let me make it perfectly comprehensible for you, since my little bro is probably being vague – it's his specialty." Emilio dropped the arm from Nicco and walked me away. He rested his forehead against the side of my head when he spoke, but looked straight at his brother. "As you already know, I am very direct."

Nicco's fangs snapped out.

I stepped away, nauseated by my own naïvety.

"Do not listen to anything he says, Adele."

"What? Why?" I yelled at Nicco, totally sick of being in the dark. "Don't tell me what to do without telling me why—"

"That's my girl!" Emilio yelled. "Don't listen to his over-romanticized, always-the-dark-knight bullshit, Adele."

"Shut up, Emilio." Nicco turned to me. "Because he is my brother and you are just going to have to trust me on this one."

"Ha!" I yelled. "Never trust a vampire."

Emilio sneered in delight, practically dancing around me.

"Leave her alone…." Nicco's voice neared a growl. "She doesn't know anything."

"What the hell?" I yelled.

Nicco's face pleaded with me to stop, so I whipped around to Emilio. "What don't I know?" I just wanted answers. I didn't care who they came from.

"Oh, Niccolò, wasn't it your *inexorable* gullibility that got us into this predicament in the first place? Haven't you learned anything in three and a half centuries, brother?"

Nicco moved quickly to meet him face to face. "I am hardly the reason—"

"You and Gabriel are pathetic!" he said, pushing Nicco backwards. "He's been free for weeks. Father is probably rolling over in his mausoleum at the two of you."

When Nicco didn't push him back, Emilio walked over to me and put his hand on my face, just as he had done so many times in Paris. But this time, I swatted it away. The aggression only made him smile. *"Ma chérie,* this is quite simple. The curse will be broken one way or another—"

"This is about more than a curse, Emilio!" Nicco yelled.

Emilio ignored him and continued. "You have until *tomorrow night* to do it your way, or I'm going to rip her throat out," he said, pointing to Vodou Pourvoyeur. "Then I'll pluck every feather from your little bird friend, and then tear that hot redhe—"

A flash of flowing chiffon rushed past me and knocked him into the street with a bone-cracking thud. "Over my dead body, Emilio!" my blonde stalker growled, her exposed fangs just a couple of inches from his face.

"It appears my brother already beat me to your dead body—"

She hissed.

"Mm. Mm. Mmm. Aren't you spunky? Three hundred years old, but still with the unpredictability of a newborn."

"Do not test me," she said, glaring at him.

"Gabriel," Emilio said, "can you please control your progeny?"

"Lizzie, please remove yourself from my brother," Gabe said, stepping out of the shadows.

Jesus. They're everywhere. How long had he been standing there?

She hissed one last time before she retracted her fangs and stepped off.

Laughing, Emilio popped his arm back into place, rolled over and propped his head on his hand. “And then I will drain you and break the curse myself, the old-fashioned way.”

Nicco grabbed Emilio by the collar, forcing him to stand up. “And what good will that do? Killing the only link we have to him?”

Gabriel intervened, pulling his brothers apart. “Well, I will have my freedom back, for starters.”

“Gabe!” I screamed.

“I’m sorry, Adele, but this feud has gone on for entirely too long. I’ve grown weary of it.”

TRYING TO KEEP MY FINGERS from frying themselves off, I stormed back into the shop, leaving the Medicis to their fraternal spat. *Why were they being so secretive if they were only after the antidote to a three-hundred-year-old curse? What the hell were they really after? What feud?*

I threw open the fuchsia curtain to find Désirée nestled in a blanket, drinking a cup of tea. All the candles on the altar were lit, and she was surrounded by an assortment of artifacts, including Adeline’s diary, Marassa’s grimoire, and the painting of the casquette girls.

“Who are you? And what have you done with Désirée Borges?”

“I’m not as stupid as I look.”

“I don’t think you look stupid. I just didn’t think you cared about… well, anything.”

“Ouch. I guess I deserved that,” she said dryly and looked up from the grimoire. “Actually, I kind of have a confession.”

I settled in next to her. “This should be good.”

“A few weeks ago…” – she let out an exasperated sigh – “I-kind-of-might-have-broken-Marassa’s-part-of-the-spell.”

“What? You know about the curse!”

"Adele, where are you right now? Please. Nearly every spell cast in this city has come through these doors in some way, shape, or form. Ingredients, advice, blessings, dolls, *gris-gris*."

I touched my necklace through my shirt, and she pulled out a similar one from underneath hers. "My grandmother forced mine around my neck the morning you first came in the shop. The morning of the incident."

"What incident?"

"The incident at the convent."

"Excusez-moi?"

"I was in a bad mood when you came into the shop, 'cause Gran and I had been fighting. Ever since my sweet sixteen, she's been on my back about preparing for this ritual."

"Ritual?"

"Yeah, to join this coven—"

"You're part of a coven?"

"Ugh, *no.* I didn't want any part of all of this hocus-pocus, especially not some coven prearranged by my gran. I mean, what year is this, 1650?"

"Er?"

"She was refusing to eat, like she's Gandhi or something, so I was in a foul mood. I ditched first period, parked my car out of sight on Esplanade, and walked around the Quarter for a while. Nothing was open, so it was pretty boring. I felt guilty about the fight with Gran, so I began practicing some simple spells – and that's when it happened."

"That's when what happened?"

"First, I accidentally turned this bird into a cat. I tried to bail, but the cat was freaking out. Like, really freaking out. It followed me for like four blocks. We were right in front of the Ursuline Convent when…"

"Uh huh…"

"I felt bad for the cat, so I started casting every reversal spell I knew to try to turn it back to a bird."

"And?"

"And, I think I may have overshot it."

"What do you mean?"

"The cat turned back into a bird, but then my hair got really frizzy."

"Huh?"

"The straightening spell I had performed last year vanished, duh, along with every other spell I had ever cast. It was like I accidentally hit the reset button. The entire side of the block where the convent is warbled like there was a glitch in the Matrix or something. Then there was this really loud noise, like a cartoon rooster waking up."

"Then what happened?"

"Then I left."

"You left?"

"Yeah, my hair was crazy, and I needed to redo the spell."

"Riiight," I said in disbelief. "And here we are."

"And here we are. Oh, and F.Y.I., just because I care about my hair, doesn't mean I don't care about anything else. If one of those fangsters touches my gran, there's going to be hell to pay."

My eyes immediately welled. She paused.

"I'm sorry about Bertrand and Sabine, Adele."

I nodded and quickly wiped my tears away.

She hastily changed the subject. "I *really* wish I had paid better attention during all of those lessons."

"What class could possibly prepare you to battle vampires?"

"No, I mean my gran's Saturday night circle. When I was eight, I was playing with my cousin in the shop and accidentally turned his hand green. Gran was furious: she made me practice reversal spells until I could turn his hand back to normal – it took me days – and after that she forced me to attend her Saturday night circle every single week without fail."

"Ha. I feel you. When I was six, I burned off a pigtail playing in my dad's metalwork shop and have been getting lectures ever since on the hazards of playing with fire." As soon as the words came out of my mouth, the flames on the candles grew.

She looked back at me and smiled. "A new coven comprised of the new generation of witches."

I nervously returned the smile.

"I wonder what the vamps did to get locked up in the attic for what would have been eternity?" she asked.

"What?" I reached for Adeline's diary. "That never came up during your night with Gabriel?"

We both laughed.

"I knew that prima donna was just trying to get some kind of quick fix from me," Désirée said, turning her attention back to the grimoire. "He told me that whenever he tried to leave the Quarter, a giant gust of wind would push him back in."

"Wind?"

"That's what he said."

"Dee, one more question."

"What?"

"What kind of bird was it, that you turned into a cat?"

"Um, a freakishly giant black crow," she said without looking up.

death of a diva

(translated from French)

17th June 1728

LA NOUVELLE-ORLÉANS REALLY IS UNLIKE ANYTHING I have ever experienced, Papa. There are no words to describe the sticky heat. (It is absolutely impossible to maintain Parisian fashion. I find myself wearing less and less clothing each day, so I fear for what will be left when August comes!)

Although it's not an island, there is water everywhere – a great river, a great lake, and many bayous. Even the land is wet, making the air always thick and damp. The heavy atmosphere holds the scent of cream-colored blossoms as large as my face, and vines of honeysuckle flowers wrap themselves around anything that obstructs their path, marking their territory with a lingering perfume. The tree branches, which are covered in a hairy moss, droop to the ground as if Mother Nature herself is weeping.

To call this place a miniature version of Paris would be preposterous. In truth, it is quite the opposite. While Paris feels like the epicenter of the world, *La Nouvelle-Orléans* feels like the fringe. It's as if we could sink into the marshy glades and no one would ever know. I may still curse you every night for not taking me with you to the Orient, but coming to this foreign land on my own has given me an understanding of your sense of adventure and your longing for independence above everything. The people here seem to share this sensibility, making the city a very lively place to be. Even on the streets, there is always talk of what's to come rather than of past traditions, which dominates the conversations of the French aristocracy.

As previously mentioned, we docked in *La Nouvelle-Orléans* on the 25th of May. Martine, Marassa, and I stayed with the Ursulines for one week while the DuFrense estate was prepared. The religious property is simple but large, with a small labyrinth of shrubs, a vegetable garden on either side, and a special building for the orphans to live in while the nuns mold them into ladies fit for society. I never thought I would be happy to stay in a nunnery, but after such a perilous journey, it was like heaven.

Unsurprisingly, the DuFrense estate is even more grand then their original in Paris, just as Claude had promised Martine it would be. It's not very far from the convent. Of course, nothing is far from the convent since the town is still so small. This makes it easy for me and Marassa to see the triplets and even to attend a religious class on Sundays. I confess that I only go to this catechism so as not to miss this chance to see my confidantes, and because Marassa is allowed to attend. It's a fascinating afternoon, for this is the day the nuns welcome all the girls from the community to attend class, including slaves and those from the indigenous tribes.

Naturally, Martine is still distraught over the loss of Claude, and being stuck in this new land without him is testing her health. Marassa continues to live under the cover of Martine's slave, residing in a private house across the back courtyard of the property. The opera star's tongue has become sharp to anyone who crosses her path, mostly because she is drunk for more hours of the day than not.

Much to Martine's dismay, I have taken a liking to a large wolf-dog, who seems to be as independent as you, Father. He refuses to come into the house at night but is always waiting at the door in the morning to escort me on my daily errands. It has become a joke around town that Adeline Saint-Germain no longer requires a chaperone. Others whisper behind my back, "The daughter of *le Comte de Saint-Germain* has turned her chaperone into a wolf!"

I ignore the whispers, but it does make me fear that I will be alone forever. What man would want to court a girl who might turn him into a wolf? I try to tell myself that just because I am without you, I am far from alone. Cosette and I, along with my furry friend – who I have named Louis after my good friend the tailor – often escape for late-night strolls along the river, of which I have heard the local people call this word: '*Miss-i-ssi-ppi,*' which is horrendous to say the first dozen times until the tongue is trained. As we walk, Cosette often mourns the absence of her red bird, whom we haven't seen since we docked, or, when she is in a lighter mood, she might joke about her own flight from French court. Sometimes I feel that perhaps I was fleeing Paris as well, unbeknownst to me at the time. But I suppose I won't know for sure until I receive a letter from you regarding our next rendezvous. I long for that day, Father.

As far as our dark-natured friends, I know they are still here.

The streets have been paved with new stones, and the buildings are freshly painted, and yet sometimes when I am out walking, I can sense things far older hiding in the shadows. I pray that their plan is to move on to some land far away from this one. Although… I confess that sometimes when I am alone, late at night, I can't help but wonder about Gabriel Medici, and why he was aboard that ship, and how he knew my name. On two separate occasions I have even risen in the middle of the night and hurriedly dressed with the intention of seeking him out. But do not be alarmed; both times I came to my senses before I opened the front door. My intuition always wins out over the often overwhelming curiosity I feel towards this man.

22nd June 1728

I THOUGHT OUR SECRET CIRCLE WAS COMPLETE when we discovered Marassa's talents onboard the ship, but that all changed when I encountered Susannah Bowen at the convent. She was the maid who served tea while I was trying to persuade the Mother Superior to host a ball so that the orphans might have the chance to mingle with the town's bachelors. I am desperate for the girls to be married off rather than be left cooped up together, unprotected, like animals waiting in the slaughterhouse. I have no idea how to rid the town of the monsters, but I've been doing everything in my power to try to protect the girls who had survived that journey from Paris. It has become my obsession.

Susannah's bonnet was no match for her fiery red curls, which spilled out and hid her face, but even underneath her locks I could see those icy blue eyes noting my every move. I returned her gaze with equal suspicion as she poured my tea. I was surprised, however, when a jolt of energy swept through me so quickly that I couldn't keep the silver spoon from stirring itself in the bergamot-flavored tea. I quickly placed my fingers on the utensil and finished mixing in the crème, while stifling my smile.

I tried my best to remain calm, but I became overwhelmed by the sudden surge of possibilities a sixth member would bring to our circle. When, during our talk, the Mother Superior paused at the window to contemplate my suggestion, I glanced at the wall sconce above the servant girl's head, spun it out of the wall, and let it drop. In retrospect, my behavior was brash and risky, but, as I suspected, her natural reflex wasn't to move out of the way as the sconce fell. Instead, she sent a burst of wind upwards, and the iron fixture bobbled in the air like a marionette. Her eyes darted to me, and a taut smile spread across her face as the sconce gently floated into her freckle-dusted hands. She quickly hid the piece of iron behind her back just as the Mother Superior turned to face us.

Mark my words – it will only be a matter of time before Susannah is folded into our group.

26th June 1728

FOR THE LAST TWO SUNDAYS after the Catholic service in the chapel, I have invited the girls back to the DuFrense home, where we sing around the piano, paint, or share French lessons with Marassa and the new girl, Susannah. I've yet to extract her entire story because her French is poor, as is my English, but I have gathered she is of English descent by way of the isle of Bermuda. Speaking a common language would make it so much easier to communicate, but I believe this barrier has brought us together in a strange, intimate way. In lieu of mindless gossip, we share our secrets by teaching each other things passed down by those before us: Susannah and Marassa spend hours exchanging notes and diagrams on the healing properties of herbs and flowers; Cosette teaches Lisette the ways to a person's heart by showing her first how to speak to animals; and I have found an unsuspecting partner in Minette, who has quite an aptitude for the sciences. Her curiosity about the origins of material sometimes reminds me of you, Father.

It's such a strange relationship, Papa, having grown up without siblings and with no close friends among France's *crème de la crème*. I never learned to trust anyone until now. Other than you, I'd never met anyone like myself. You've always told me that people are brought together for a reason, and I keep that wisdom close to my heart.

4th July 1728

I WORRY MORE ABOUT MARTINE EVERY DAY. At night, she can sleep only if Cosette slips an herb solution into her brandy, which she consumes as if she is looking for death, and death, I'm afraid, is far too easy to come across in this town. Conditions are poor for most people – the streets are filthy, and disease runs rampant. What people do not know of is the real epidemic that was unleashed when our ship docked in the *port de La Nouvelle-Orléans* – the true reason bodies are scattering across the city.

Each night more of the population disappears, but no alarm bells are rung when they go missing: a faceless prostitute, a nameless pirate deckhand, an orphan girl sent by the King.

But I notice, Papa. And I am overridden with guilt.

After so many months coexisting with these predators, developing this strange bond through the shadows, I have become complacent. I constantly have to remind myself that the relationship could turn lethal if there is any disruption to the current arrangement – such as me exposing their bloody secrets.

5th July 1728

I AM BEGINNING TO SUSPECT that they want more from me than just silence, and yet my intuition tells me it's not my blood they are after. At night, I can feel them following me. Watching, waiting for me to waver. What they expect from me I have no idea, but the simple fact that they have never tried to harm me leads me to believe that whatever they want is *very* important to them. There is something about the way they said my name – Jean-Antoine, just before his carriage took off, and Gabriel that night in the fields – that makes me wonder if it has something to do with you, Father. I lie in bed at night wondering what they are after. Unless it is simply you they want?

19th July 1728

I FEEL LIKE I AM GOING MAD, PAPA. Marassa made me a necklace she calls a *gris-gris*. She fears I need protection, and says that this little satchel strung on a ribbon will help repel evil. The girls are all beginning to suspect that I need protection. I don't know how to explain it, but I have this looming feeling that darker days are coming. Perhaps this is because Louis, the dog, has gone missing. I haven't seen my furry companion in days, which saddens me. I always felt safer with him near – he seemed to have a sixth sense for knowing when danger was lurking.

In more disturbing news, a boy from one of the local tribes – the only son of the chief – has gone missing. His family suspects foul play, and they are causing quite a stir here in town, trying to find the culprit. His sister, a stunning girl named Morning Star, who attends the religious class on Sundays, has taken to questioning me on the street. I don't know why she thinks I know something about her brother's disappearance, but her interrogations bring me to tears. I can only guess what, or rather who, has caused her brother's sudden disappearance, and I can't help but feel responsible. If it wasn't for me, the monsters would be at the bottom of the ocean instead of terrorizing the population of *La Nouvelle-Orléans.*

I know something needs to be done, but I am not strong enough on my own, and I don't know if I can jeopardize the lives of the five girls I hold so dear. I don't know what to do, Papa.

Your silence is making me fear the worst. You should have arrived by now. I tell myself I should be used to your unpredictability… I never gave a second thought to your erratic behavior in Paris, but here, where everything is unknown to me, it's unsettling.

I pray you are well. You always are.

1st August 1728

THE DAY I FEARED WOULD COME has finally arrived. Lisette received a marriage proposal from one of the local townsmen. I wanted so much to share in her joy, but my heart ached, knowing the sparkle in her eyes would fade when she realized her dowry was missing.

Fearing for their lives, I followed the nuns to the attic to retrieve her *cassette*. With each step, I couldn't help but remember walking up the stairs to the deck of the S.S. *Gironde,* the first witness to the pirate massacre. My heart pounded like death knocking, and the temperature rose so high that by the time we got to the last room of the attic, I swear we had left the Earth and entered Hell. The Mother Superior opened Lisette's chest from the King.

At once, all of the holy sisters gasped.

But nothing happened.

Nothing was awoken.

Nothing sprang forth.

They must have been out feeding. I breathed a sigh of relief. How horrible is that, Father? I was thankful they were out feeding on other humans! What kind of monster have I become?

The sisters scattered like a flock of geese, pecking at each box to examine the contents. "We've been robbed," said one of the novices after each box produced only air.

The local nuns panicked, but the postulants who had traveled on the S.S. *Gironde* did not. I watched misplaced guilt flush each of their cheeks. Though none of them dared say the words aloud, I could see suspicions in their eyes about why the boxes might be empty. No matter how strong their faith, they could not deny the supernatural events that had occurred on our voyage from Paris. Mother Superior said something in Latin and fell to her knees, with her hands clenched together, and the others quickly followed suit.

I fled to find Lisette.

7th August 1728

TODAY HAS BEEN ONE OF MELANCHOLY, PAPA. I so wish you were here. When I got home tonight, I found the front door ajar and, while nothing inside seemed to be awry, there was a disturbance in the air. I wanted to yell for Martine, but the surge of energy tearing through my body, threatening to bolt from my fingers kept me silent. I dropped my bundle of flowers and ran through the silent house.

A strange sense of déjà vu dizzied me as I entered the parlor and found her. And *him.*

The vampire Gabriel.

He was bent over Martine, who was splayed on the floor. Even my presence in the room did not distract him from his meal. I yelled repeatedly for him to stop, but he barely moved – his eyes shifted to look up at me, but his lips remained locked on her neck.

"Remove yourself!" I screamed, running to them. I grabbed his shoulder and attempted to pull him off, but my touch only scorched his clothing before his shove sent me sliding across the slick wooden floor. Keeping the flames from rising from my hands caused me great pain, but I couldn't risk it. He was too close to her. Not to mention the possibility of setting fire to the entire town. For a moment, I just stood, terrified at the perverse sight.

He finally unlatched his teeth from her throat and then staggered as he tried to stand, nearly falling backwards. "*Madonna mia,* how much does this woman drink?" he slurred. "Opium too. There are more toxins in her blood than in a Parisian sewer."

"You monster!" I screamed, which didn't seem to faze him in the slightest. My eyes welled as guilt clutched my throat – it was obvious that she was dead.

"Oh, my sweet, don't be angry with me," he said as if the offense he had committed had been eating the last *macaron.* "She begged me for it. You should thank me for putting her out of her misery."

"You are the reason for her misery! You killed her husband!" I reminded him with fury.

"Well, that was actually my cousin Renzo, but I see your point." He stumbled back to her body and bit his own wrist, just as he had with the island boy, then looked back to me and said in a very serious tone, "Adeline, you should leave now."

I refused, telling him that I was a guest of this house and it was he who should leave. He paid no attention but simply focused ceremoniously on his task. Instead of allowing only a few drops to drip into her mouth, like he had for Makandal, he drizzled the blood until her tongue moved, lapping up the sticky red liquid.

"What are you doing?" I stuttered in disbelief.

Before he could reply, she screamed as if in great pain. Her torso thrust upward, and with an indescribable desperation, her jaw clamped around Gabriel's wrist. Dumbfounded, I screamed her name, unable to turn away from the vulgar act. She sucked on his wrist faster, harder, with the glee of an infant attached to its mother's teat. And then her eyes rolled back in her head, as if she were possessed.

I continued to call her name until I sounded hysterical, but she was lost. Nothing was going to distract her from drinking. I looked to Gabriel. "What is she doing? What did you do to her?"

"Adeline," he said to me, "you should really leave now. You are worth more to me alive than dead."

I shuddered violently as Martine slumped to the ground; my voice warbled with fear as I yelled to him, "I'm not leaving her!"

If you can believe it, Papa, the absurdity only increased from there. Just thinking about it gives me the urge to loosen my corset so I can breathe easier.

"Fine, don't say I didn't warn you," the vampire said as he licked his own wounds, which miraculously healed before my eyes.

Luckily, I had no idea what he was talking about when Gabriel then asked, "Where is it, Adeline?" He looked at me with such a savage tenderness it would have been impossible not to give him what he desired.

"Where is *what*?" I asked him with genuine curiosity.

"Oh, don't play coy with me, *bella*." He slowly licked his lips. "I promise, you will not like where it leads you... but I will like it very much."

Before any more threats could be spat, Martine's eyes flew open – red and insane like a rabid animal's – and Gabriel yelled with a hunter's smile, "Adeline, *run*. Now!"

Every shred of my instinct told me to obey him.

Martine still seemed disoriented, giving me a few more seconds to dash for the nearest exit. When I glanced back, she was gone. Startled, I reached for the door, and there she was, standing in front of me, blocking my escape. I was barely able to stop myself from hurling into her.

From behind me, Gabriel said in a teasing voice, "You could have had a head start, had you listened to me. But listening isn't a strong suit of the Saint-Germains, now is it?"

Martine grabbed my throat with her cold, dead fingers and lifted my entire body with the strength of just one arm. My fingers clawed at hers, and my legs flailed in the air as she walked me back into the room.

"Marti—" I choked out. Just as I began to question whether I could fight my friend, I saw her fangs: pointed and lethal as a snake's. My sympathy drained as I gasped for air. On the verge of consciousness, I cursed myself and, for the first time, truly regretted not allowing the captain to toss the *strigoi* overboard.

The house became cold and dark – I thought it was death coming to take me. A howling wind entered the room, blowing out the hearth along with every candle and lamp.

Disoriented by the loud whistles that filled our ears, Martine dropped me to the floor. My hair whipped around my face, and the layers of my petticoats blew around me as I tried to stand.

The gusts became so strong I could barely open my eyes, but it was enough to see the sudden squall launch Martine into the air and through the glass window. It shattered into thousands of tiny shards, and she fell three stories to the street.

I whipped my hand around the room to reignite the candles.

A fire exploded into the hearth, and I found Gabriel sneering at a girl standing in the rear doorway. It was Susannah. She brought her arms down slowly, and the strong gale tapered to a slight breeze, until we were left with nothing but the soggy, summer air.

I hurried to the broken window.

Instantly, Gabriel was by my side. I leaned over the sharp glass fragments jutting from the frame to look down. Nothing could have prepared me for the sight. "*Sacrebleu!*" I whispered as Gabriel leaned over me to see for himself.

Martine had landed on her back with such impact the bones in her legs were protruding from her skin. A circle of blood was slowly pooling in the street around her. And then – I swear to you, Papa – despite her splintered limbs, Martine slowly began to stand up.

Above my head, Gabriel cursed, "*Maledetto*! Now I have to go and fetch her before she causes a scene." He pulled me away from the broken glass and exited the room in a flash.

Susannah stared at the spot where he had touched my arm.

Still in shock, I approached her, already feeling disappointed in my own failure to take control of the situation.

"I'm sorry, Adeline!" she said before I had the chance to speak.

Still in a deep daze, I looked up at the red-haired girl and whispered, "That was incredible."

"We can no longer stand idly by," she said. I nodded in agreement as she continued vehemently. "We must take action against the vampires."

"You knew about them?" I asked.

"Of course I know. We all know, Adeline. It is no longer just your burden."

34

carpe noctum

"WHOA," I SAID OUT LOUD as I translated the last line.

"What?" Désirée asked. "Did you find a clue about the other two casquette girls?"

For hours we'd been scouring the grimoire, the half-translated diary, and even the painting for clues that would reveal the identities of the other two members of the casquette girls' coven or their present-day descendants.

"I think so… but that's only the half of it. Gabe *killed* Martine DuFrense and turned her into a vampire."

"Shut up."

"I swear… well, at least according to Adeline's diary. They witnessed it – Adeline and Susannah."

"Susannah?"

I flipped back through the pages. "Susannah Bowen, from Bermuda. She was a servant in the convent, likes plants, used magic right in front of Adeline, and they let her into the coven. After Martine DuFrense turned,

Susannah saved Adeline's life by throwing the newborn through a third-story window. That's all I've really gotten so far." I handed her my journal. "Here, double-check it. My eyes are starting to cross."

She scanned the first few pages. "Do you think Gabe and Adeline had a thing?"

"Really? Out of everything happening in those pages, *that's* what you're taking away?"

"It's a totally valid question," she mumbled and went back to reading.

When the pages in my journal became blank, she sighed in frustration, pushed it aside, and flipped to a bookmark in Marassa's grimoire. "I want to test out some of these protection spells, considering Emilio's ultimatum. If I'm reading between the lines correctly, I think these are the same spells the casquette girls coven used when they started feeling threatened."

As if the death of my surrogate grandparents wasn't enough, reading the account of Martine DuFrense's death at the hand of Gabriel Medici sent me over the edge. I couldn't stop wondering if I was going to *die* tomorrow night. The feeling was unsettling to say the least. I found myself looking back to my phone more than once, flicking open the text message from my mother, of all people. My fingers refused to respond to her plea to talk, but I did decide there were issues that needed to be pressed elsewhere.

"Cool," I said, "I'm going for a walk. I think there might be some clues out there in the real world." I picked up the painting of our relatives. "Can I borrow this?"

"Sure… don't lose it. Gran will kill me."

And so we split up. Désirée stayed back, brewing up potions, while I went out into the night to beat the street. I wasn't sure whether I had the right questions, but there were three people whom I was determined to get answers from.

My first stop was Ren's house in the *Faubourg Marigny*, which meant I had to leave the *Vieux Carré*. He lived even closer than Brooke, but my father's rule about not leaving the neighborhood still argued with my steps. Little did he know how much more dangerous the streets within the borders of the Quarter were – the inside of the bullring.

When I crossed Esplanade and felt the slight warble, I wondered whether the Storm's destruction was worse on the other side of this oak-lined avenue solely because of topography, or because the girls' antique protection spells had played a part in saving the French Quarter. Images of large gusts of wind flinging back vampires who tried to cross the street brought a strange smile to my lips.

It vanished as the sound of breaking glass cracked the night air. *It's probably just looters,* I told myself, wondering if Isaac was lurking in a nearby tree. Previously, I'd found him tailing me to be annoying, but I'd grown accustomed to the crow's constant presence. I wouldn't have admitted it out loud, but knowing he was there might have had something to do with my ballsiness as of late.

Five blocks later, I arrived at Frenchmen Street, where I knew Ren's house to be – next to the Spotted Cat. The street was famous for its jazz clubs, but tonight it was a strange sight to behold. Laundry lines were strung everywhere, with sheets rippling in the cold night air, as if everyone had decided to wash their linens at the same time. Despite the cold weather, people were on their porches with BBQ pits fired up to cook dinner, while others stood around open flames burning in old tin garbage cans. My guilt sunk deeper because we had working fireplaces, a gas oven, *and* a generator.

"Miss Adele?" Ren called out from his porch. "To what do I owe this pleasure?" He set his book and reading candle down at the base of the rickety rocking chair.

"*Bonsoir!*" I yelled, hopping the steps, and then kissed him on the cheek.

"Please tell me you need advice on fabric swatches for a school project?"

"Not even close." The severe stare I gave him squashed any further joking.

"Well, shoot. *Kommon in, bébé.*" He looked both ways down the street before shutting the door behind us.

I'D NEVER BEEN INSIDE Ren and Theis' house before. To say it was a reflection of their personalities was an understatement. A large oil painting of their white Persian cat and a particularly gothic-looking M.C. Escher print of a skull and eyeball hung on the dark-purple living-room wall. Dozens of candles had dripped wax onto the windowsills, and a large, black pot hung over a low flame in the fireplace, filling the air with peppery notes that meshed with the smoky scent I now knew to be sage. Theis was stretched out on a red velvet couch. He looked like he was sleeping, except a harsh cacophony of sounds billowed from his headphones, and he was gently petting Fluffy, who was lounging on his flat stomach.

Ren hurried into the kitchen; I watched through the doorway as he threw a plastic tarp over a strange metal apparatus that connected to different barrels by a mess of copper coiling. It looked like some kind of homemade chem lab. Various dried herbs, flower petals, and berries were separated into loose piles on the counter.

"Ren, the cat's out of the bag," I said loudly, sinking into a paisley armchair across from Theis. "No need to try to cover up Operation Bathtub Gin."

"Your pa is going to kill me," he mumbled from the other room.

Theis' eyelids slid open. "Want to see my new tattoo?"

"Uh, sure." I think it was the first time he'd ever acknowledged my existence.

Fluffy jumped down as Theis lifted up his tight black tee to reveal simple black symbols inked across his bony ribs.

"Cool. Nordic runes?" I guessed.

"Yeah, it means protection during battle in Old Icelandic."

"Cool," I repeated. My mind immediately spiraled, thinking about whether or not I was going to need more protection for this battle, or feud… whatever it was?

"Leftover hurricane gruel?" he offered, pointing to the pot.

"No, thanks."

Ren sat in the chair next to me and snuck a quick sip from his flask. Theis put his headphones on, settled back into his previous position with his eyes shut, and appeared instantly consumed by his music.

"I want to know about *ma mère*," I blurted out.

"Your mother?" He took a larger swig. "Isn't this a conversation better suited for your daddy, *bébé*?"

"I'm not a child anymore, Ren. *You* know something, and I am not leaving until you tell me. I can't ask my dad… a little piece of him dies every time I mention my mother's name."

I said nothing else and just waited.

"*D'accord, d'accord.* What do you want to know?"

"I want to know everything. What happened when she left? No one ever talks about it, but there has to be more to the story than her simply waking up one morning so consumed by her love for Paris that she just bailed on me and my father."

He stroked his mustache. "I don't know everything. I'm not sure anyone does. Certainly not your father. Anyway, I've already told you part of the story."

"*Quoi?* Not possible. Like I could have forgotten that."

"Oh, I did. The night of the tour. Those two students who had the bright idea of capturing our urban legends on tape? Back then, locals used to spook tourists by telling them vampires lived in the attic and came out at night to feed. Both you and I know good and well that no one's passed through those shutters for the last three centuries."

Not until a couple of weeks ago, I thought, looking at Theis.

"Don't worry about him. He can't hear anything through that racket. Anyway, as you know, those kids didn't make it through the night; they were found in front of the church, drained of most of their blood—"

"Ren, what does any of this have to do with my mother?"

"Are you sure you're ready to hear this?"

"*Oui!*"

He scooped up Fluffy to use as a buffer, and the chains around my stomach tightened.

"Their cameras were still rolling when they were attacked. A friend at the precinct told me that the tapes showed an unidentifiable Caucasian woman with long, brown hair approaching the victims. But that's pretty much it. There were screams, and the camera crashed to the ground. Blood splattered across the lens, and then the screen went black… after that, nothing but static.

"An elderly couple who lived across the street told the police they'd seen your mother talking to the documentarians. Then a group of college kids also identified your mother from a lineup. They claimed they'd seen her leaving the crime scene – covered in blood."

"What?"

He slowly smoothed the cat's fur. "Brigitte Dupré Le Moyne was the only suspect the police ever had. It was the most heartbreaking thing I've ever seen. She adamantly denied the charges, but she had no alibi, and when they came for her arrest, she simply went along with them – she was in such a state of trauma that she almost seemed indifferent to it all. Needless to say, your father was outraged. The entire French Quarter was."

"*Ma mère* went to jail? Madame Perfect?"

"*Oui.* Well, she wasn't incarcerated for very long. I don't know all the details, but the story I heard was that after they rounded up the witnesses to build the case for the bail hearing, every one of them suddenly retracted their statements. It was as if every single witness suddenly had amnesia."

"Sounds so Mafioso."

"I suspect there might have been Italians involved, but members of organized crime, I think not."

My mind reeled as I read between the lines.

"But perhaps the strangest thing of all was when the cops went to release your mother, she wasn't there. Her cell was empty. At least, that was the word on the street. The police were never going to publicly admit that a murder suspect had escaped from jail, and since she'd been cleared anyway, they just swept it under the rug. She was never seen again. Her friends were told she went back to Paris, too disgraced by the scandal. It was a plausible explanation, so no one dug too deep – except, of course, your father. The file was dumped into the bin of unsolved cases, and people turned back to the drama of their own lives. It's New Orleans, after all, so it wasn't too long before the next scandal took center stage. *C'est la vie*."

"*C'est la vie,*" I whispered. *What the hell? My mother deserted me and my father twelve years ago because she was a suspect in a double homicide? I mean, I am bitter towards my mother, but do I think she's capable of murder?*

"Adele, your ma was the sweetest, most charismatic lady I've ever met. The whole scandal nearly killed your pa. He was never the same, understandably so."

"He went after her." A latent memory started to make more sense. "I was only four. He said he was going on vacation with Mommy, and that she wanted me to stay with Jeanne and Sébastien and speak only French until they got back. Then he left me with the Michels. I was young, but I knew something bad had happened. He came back alone and told me she had gone to live with *ma grand-mère,* because *grand-mère* was sick. I hated my grandmother for taking her away from us. Of course, when I got older and realized she had just been the cover, my misplaced anger moved to my mother for abandoning us. Over time, I nearly forgot what she looked like… at one point she seemed like just a figment of my imagination, buried with my earliest memories."

"*Mo chagren, bébé.* I'm so, so sorry."

My head spun.

Does that make Brigitte a fugitive? What could be so important that she risked coming back to New Orleans? And what the hell is Emilio doing with her? I always thought she had such a dominating way with her assistant, but is she actually the one under his spell? Did he kill those students and just let her take the fall? Is he the reason I grew up without a mother? Why I grew up hating her?

A wave of guilt washed over me. Then anger. Tingles carried through my shoulders as I imagined myself engulfing Emilio Medici in flames. My thoughts darkened, and the sensation intensified like fire across my back. I winced. Fluffy sprang away.

"I knew it would be too much… your pa is gonna kill me."

"Ça va, Ren. Merci beaucoup."

"ONE STOP DOWN, TWO TO GO," I said to myself as I crossed Esplanade Avenue back into the French Quarter, not skipping a step when I felt the warble.

A couple weeks ago, Nicco had told me they moved into their own place. I hadn't asked where, but I had only one guess. With my cold hands stuffed into my jacket pockets, I quickly retraced the path of Ren's tour to the corner of Royal and St. Ann – the home of the infamous Carter brothers.

I took a moment in front of the three-story brick building to give myself a pep talk. My senses sharpened, and my fingers burned, telling me I was close to something, although I wasn't sure what. *Danger? Nicco? The ghosts of the poor souls he and Emilio tortured?* I tried not to picture the gruesome events of decades ago, but also reminded myself not to forget them.

Despite his admission of guilt, I still had a hard time believing Nicco would do something so vile. *And why was he at the Waffle House that night? Ugh.* Some stupid part of me was holding out for a reasonable explanation. With a wave of my hand, the gate swung open; I moved quickly to the old wooden door and cupped the heavy knob until I felt the lock release.

I am seriously beginning to doubt my ability to make good choices, I thought as I shoved open the door and stepped inside the pitch-black entrance. The door swung shut behind me, hinges squeaking in agony.

There I stood, frozen.

The silence invited fear.

Then a small flame sprang out of my palm.

Breathe, I told myself and tried not to look at the small ball of fire. I focused instead on the shadows it cast on the black-and-white marble floor. The once-splendid foyer was now smothered in dust so thick I left footprints behind.

Intuition guided me to a wide staircase that curved up to the second floor, over which hung a chandelier quilted so thick in cobwebs that it looked more like a giant paper lantern.

The first stair creaked loudly as I placed my weight onto it, as did every step after. Just as I was cursing myself for watching all of those eighties slasher movies where any girl who went up a dark staircase never came back down, a step gave way beneath my weight.

"Shit!" I fell forward, banging my knee and wrists. My blood pressure skyrocketed, but at least I had avoided a face-plant.

I pulled my leg from the rotting floorboard, now cursing the termites who had long since moved on, and then carefully edged up the stairs without further mishap.

On the second story, I crept from room to room, holding out my lit palm. Each room was different, but all had the same heavy brocade drapes covering the long windows, cutting off the outside world and the current year. It was easy to imagine lines of corset-clad ladies dancing with wigged gentlemen in the ballroom, or the ghosts of flappers in fringed dresses dancing the Charleston around the piano in the old parlor.

A warm glow shone from a door left ajar further down the hallway. My pulse thumped as I extinguished my light source and quietly approached.

Flames blazed in an opulent marble fireplace, and on a sofa, soaking in the warmth, was the back of a bright blonde head.

"Your boyfriend iz not here," she said without moving.

"He's not my boyfriend," I stammered, my cheeks flushing. I instantly recognized the voice of the woman who had accosted me in the alleyway. The girl Nicco had called Liz. "Besides, I'm not here to see him. I'm here to see you."

Her head turned, and she nodded permissively to admit me. As I approached her, my rational inner voice screamed, *Abort!* so loud I was worried she could hear it as I sat nervously next to her on the tufted couch.

"Je m'applle Adele."

"Je suis Lise."

"Enchanté, Lise." As soon as her name rolled off my tongue with a French accent, I realized who she was. "Lise? You are Lisette Monvoisin?"

A smile spread across her pale lips.

"Finally, someone who can pronounce my name correctly."

Dumbfounded, I tried to comprehend the fact that I was talking to someone from the early eighteenth century. I knew Nicco was even older, but this somehow felt different. Meeting a figure I'd come to know so well from Adeline's diary was like meeting a character from a fairytale.

Lisette rose from the couch and walked to an antique cart. "Would you like somezing to drink? We have bourbon or bl— or I could make you some tea."

"Thé, s'il vous plaît."

She removed a small kettle from a hook on the fireplace, not seeming to care when the iron handle singed her skin as she poured the water over the tea strainer. I tried not to gawk as she splashed a generous amount of dark liquid into a brandy snifter for herself. Just as I heard the sugar cubes click against the saucer, she was back on the couch next to me, placing the dainty cup into my shaky hands. I blew the water as the tea steeped, and then, with no patience, took a small sip, welcoming the warmth.

"You're just like her," she said flatly. "Adeline was never able to eat a lump of sugar after zhat stopover in *Saint-Domingue.*"

I desperately wanted to hear more about Adeline, but my attention was fixed on the snifter she was swirling under her nose. The thick, sticky liquid coated the inside of the glass red as she swished it, enjoying the rising notes. My stomach churned.

"Could you not drink that in front of me?"

"Would you prefer for me to drink *from* you?" she purred and rose slightly from the sofa cushion.

"Where are the boys?" I asked, remembering what Nicco had said about her being volatile on a good day.

"Out."

"Out where?"

"Don't ask a question if you don't really want za answer." She smiled.

I pulled the rolled canvas from my bag. Lisette didn't look exactly the same. On one hand, she was somehow more beautiful, more perfect than in the picture, but the sparkle was gone from her golden eyes. I don't know if it was her innocence, or her pulse, or her soul, but she looked different now. She had an edge. She seemed consumed by bitterness. Pain.

"Shouldn't you be… dead?"

"Someone has explained za whole vampire zhing to you, right?"

"I mean—"

"I did die zhat night."

"What night?"

"The night the coven cursed the convent attic—"

"What?"

"So did my sister. Zhen I evolved and went to sleep for a very long time, and she went to sleep forever."

I pulled the rolled canvas from my bag and handed it to Lise.

She had to set the glass down while she studied the image. "I thought I'd never see them again." Her finger lingered next to Minette. "It waz all my fault." She paused and closed her eyes for a minute to compose herself before she began again in French, forcing my brain into overdrive to understand her old dialect.

"The plan was going perfectly. Minette and I had just finished bewitching the attic door when Cosette ran through with Gabriel, Lorenzo, Giovanna, and Martine chasing behind her like puppies. Minette dashed out the exit, and I was right behind her. I can still remember my sigh of elation when I stepped through the doorway.

"But Gabriel must have heard it, too. That's when he screamed, 'Cosette!'

"I hesitated for a second. A lethal second. I knew Cosette wasn't still in the attic – she was supposed to have jumped straight out of the window before Adeline slammed it shut – but then again it was exactly the sort of thing she would have done: stayed in the attic to martyr herself for our sakes. I realized immediately he had tricked me and that I would die for my hesitation. That little fraction of time was enough for Gabriel to grab me."

Lisette's eyes dropped to the ground. I wanted to hold her hand, but my own survival instinct drove me to take another sip of tea and wait patiently instead.

"It all happened so fast." She drained her glass. "I screamed. When Minette turned around, I begged for help instead of telling her to run. I was weak. She leapt back for me, and the door slammed shut. We had cast the spell perfectly, but had ended up on the wrong side of the door."

It was strange: when I heard the word "we," I realized I was suddenly thinking of her as one of *us* instead of one of *them*. She was no longer the unpredictable blonde stalker, but Lisette Monvoisin.

"Minette pulled me down to the ground, wrapped both of her arms around me, and screamed incantations at them. But it was Cosette who had always possessed our real strength. She was the only one of us who could really control people.

"Gabriel jerked me away, snapping my arm as he pulled me directly to his mouth. His fangs plunged into my neck without hesitation. With each suck, I could feel his fury grow. Blood spurted from the bites faster than he could drink in his fit of rage. It drove Martine DuFrense so mad, Lorenzo had to hold her back. My pulse slowed. I knew my life was ending. In a state of destructive ecstasy, Gabriel pulled his fangs from my vein, and with his long fingers still wrapped around my throat, whispered against my ear, 'do you want to die? '

"When I pathetically whimpered *no,* he growled, 'That's what I thought,' and bit into his own wrist like a madman.

"I didn't think about the consequences of that one little word, like Minette or Cosette would have.

"Gabriel forced my head back and rammed his wrist against my pinched lips. Soon, my sister's screams became faint, everything became bright, and I gave into the numbness brought on by the venom coursing through my veins. I can remember that first drip as if it was yesterday…."

At a loss for words, I continued to sip my tea, trying to imagine Gabe doing something so barbaric.

"When the first drop of maker-blood melts onto your tongue, it tastes repulsive, like some kind of noxious rust. It courses through your system, mixing with your human essence, suffocating and mutating your old blood. Then, as you drink, each drop becomes sweeter, like candy. You want more. The evolutionary process is immediate, as is the addiction. The craving flips from desire to dire – the blood no longer like candy but like opium. Your existence depends on it. Your new life. A life that feels stronger, sexier, superior to anything you have ever known.

"The venom seduces you until you are totally unable to make decisions with logic and reason, as you once could. Lingering in this demonic purgatory – no longer a human but not yet a vampire – your body defaults into survival mode, and your instincts take over. Of course, the only way to complete the transition is to drink. Drink the blood of another human." Lisette paused and became so still that it was difficult to tell if she was even alive until she began to speak again.

"I clawed at the door, but I was trapped inside my own spell, my own curse. I knew there was no chance of escaping. I was dying, and not just my human death: the clock was ticking on my evolution. Every hour after that, my hunger became more excruciating.

"Gabriel wouldn't let anyone near my sister. He was saving her… I wanted to bite her. Taste her. I wanted to rip my own triplet limb from limb and feed. I wanted to kill her. And he was saving her… for me.

"Afterward… knowing I had caused my sister's death, I only wanted to die. Ironic, the way things turn out. Now I will have to live with it forever."

"What?" I asked, understanding as soon as the question came out.

"Minette was cowering in the corner, watching me in horror. Gabriel asked her if she still wanted to save me. Without fear, she stood and said, '*Oui,*' then reached for a jagged nail on the floor. When I realized what she was going to do, I screamed out for her to stop, but I was so weak. Dying. She sliced open her own wrists—"

A gasp squeezed through my lips, but Lisette continued, looking straight ahead.

"'Drink,' Minette said. Tears streamed down her face, but she told me to drink. It was the sweetest voice I have ever heard, like an angel from heaven coming to save me.

"She sacrificed her human life for my immortal life." Her eyes dropped to the floor, and she switched back to English. "But zhat's not the worst part."

"What could be worse than that?"

"I love him."

"Who?"

"The one who made me. It is impossible to explain the Maker relationship to a human. Gabriel is like my father, my brother, my best friend. I would do anything for him." Her eyes narrowed, and she turned directly to me. "Do you understand zhat? *Anything.*"

My back straightened. "I'll try not to put you in any position where you'd have to kill me… and I ask you to do the same," I quickly added.

She shrugged off the threat and looked at me tenderly. *"Oui, ma fifille."*

I laughed uncomfortably, drank my last sip of tea, and saw the Lisette Monvoisin I knew from Adeline's diary. The girl who had been so excited about her engagement, the one Cosette had saved from a pirate, the one who would have followed her sisters to the end of the Earth. Just as I mustered the courage to ask her about the coven's curse, I registered the sounds of clunky footsteps and voices of merriment approaching.

There was a blur of motion, and Lise's fingers were suddenly wrapped around my throat. The teacup flew from my hand as she pushed me to the floor. Her eyes were apologetic, but her fingers squeezed with no mercy. Over her shoulder I saw Gabe and Emilio enter the room arm in arm, singing in drunken glee. I gasped for air, feet kicking.

Just my luck, I began to think, but then to my surprise Emilio whipped over, knocked Lisette off, and sent her flying across the room into a tall grandfather clock.

"*Maledetto, Emilio!*" Gabe yelled, rushing to Lisette.

Her fangs were out, but she didn't retaliate.

Nicco had trailed in behind them, looking sullen as ever. I coughed, wondering why he hadn't come to my rescue. His eyes were focused on one spot: my neck. He glanced at Lise and then back to me – he was onto our charade. He was the only one who knew I could have defended myself.

"Why are you helping me?" I choked to Emilio, rubbing my neck.

"Adele, I said you have until tomorrow night." He pulled me up from the floor and onto the couch with him. Too close – as if we were still in France. "I am not completely unreasonable."

I rolled my eyes and pushed myself off of him.

"Don't take everything so personally, *ma chérie.* I really did cherish our time together *à Paris*," he rambled on in French, but all I could think about when I heard the word "Paris" was my mother.

"You disgust me...."

His ear lowered closer to my mouth. *"Répéter?"*

"You're a monster!" I yelled. "You killed the Michels. And the Wolfman. And those two filmmaker students twelve years ago." My entire body was shaking.

Everyone in the room stopped and stared in silence, waiting for Emilio's reaction.

He stood, towering above me. *"Oui... Oui."* He took a dramatic pause and then bent over until our noses were even. *"Et, non.* I might have killed the old French couple and the disc jockey." He wagged his finger in my face. "But it wasn't me who killed those students."

"Stop it, Emilio," Nicco warned from the corner.

Oh, now he is interested?

"But you *do* know the killer," Emilio continued. His eyes wandered to his younger brother. "In fact, I think the two of you are quite close."

"*Stai zitto!*" Nicco flew across the room and knocked his brother to the floor again, demanding silence.

Instead of getting up and fighting, Emilio just rolled over and started laughing. "Oh, brother, you have got it bad. What's the big deal? She's going to find out eventually."

"It's not your story to tell," Nicco spat and moved back to the couch. "We're done here." He grabbed my arm, lifting me from the sofa, and dragged me out of the room.

"NICCO. ARM!" I YELLED, but he didn't loosen his grip until we were down the stairs and out the front door.

I yanked my limb back.

"I'm sorry, Adele."

I was about to yell at him again, but then I realized he wasn't apologizing about my arm. His eyes were filled with pain. My chest tightened.

"No... *No.*"

"Adele—"

"No, don't tell me!" I shouted, shaking my head. "Don't tell me you kil—" His hand quickly muffled my voice, and I yelled the rest of the sentence into his hand.

Nicco *could not* be the killer who ruined my mother. My family.

After a moment, he dragged his fingers from my lips and rested them at the back of my neck. My voice rushed out in a desperate whisper. "You are the one who killed those students?"

His face twisted as his hands dropped to my shoulders. "No, it—" He stopped as my eyes welled.

"Did you… kill… those students?"

His lips remained pressed as he watched my big teardrops threatening to bubble over. The silence was torture.

"Did you do it?" I screamed and pushed him in the chest.

He didn't move; I teetered. He reached for my elbow.

Once I was steady, the words slipped from his mouth. "I did it. I killed those people."

I jerked away, stumbling a few steps backwards. Despite near-hyperventilation, I pulled my coat tighter around my chest.

Hearing someone is a killer never gets easier.

Despite his confession, I still didn't want to believe him. *Why would he lie about this when he's already confided so much in me? Adele! Stop rationalizing his repulsive actions. Actions that destroyed your own mother.*

I looked coldly at his stoic face.

"I told you to never trust a vampire," he said.

I turned on my heels and walked away before the tears could fall. I wished I could be more like him, less emotional.

"Adele, wait!"

When he didn't follow me, it felt as if my heart was physically ripping in two – that's when I realized Nicco somehow had a hold of it.

My heart.

I didn't look back.

35

birds of a feather

MY PACE QUICKENED until I had to consciously keep myself from breaking out into a run. *How could I have been so wrong about someone?* My lungs burned, and, just as two pathetically loud sniffles escaped me, everything became blurry.

"No… No. No. No," I whispered angrily. "Pull it together, Adele. No crying."

We only had about twenty-four hours until Emilio's "sympathy" expired. *There's no time to worry about boys.* I took a deep breath, stowed my feelings, and hoped they would stay that way for the duration of my third stop: the one I had saved for last because I knew I'd have to apologize to Isaac and inevitably admit I was wrong. Just thinking about him made my threatening tears turn into huffs as I stormed down the street.

When I arrived at Jackson Square, I realized I didn't even know where Isaac and his father were staying. It's not like there were any hotels open. I'd never had to find him before… he'd always just been around. I crossed the front of the Cathedral and hopped up the three stairs to the Place d'Armes, the small park in the center of the square. The surrounding iron fence had been closed since the Storm, but at this point the lock was child's play.

I stopped in the middle of the formerly manicured garden, which now better resembled an overgrown swamp, and just waited.

"Brilliant idea, Adele," I said to myself with a sigh. I started to whistle, as if I knew some kind of magical bird call. Nothing. I stomped on a Coke can and sent it skidding.

Exasperated, my arms flung up in defeat. "Hello? I know you're there!"

Sure enough, Isaac walked through the gate. Even though it was the result I desired, and even though he himself had admitted this insane ability – the proof still made me struggle for words.

"Hi," I said meekly.

"Jesus, Adele! What the hell do you see in that guy?"

I gritted my teeth as anger flooded me. "Ugh! Why do you have to do that? I came to apologize!"

"You did?"

"Why do you always have to ruin everything?"

"I don't know!" he yelled back. "Probably because I'm barely eighteen and not four hundred years old?"

I paused for a moment, biting my lip, but couldn't help it: giggles burst out of me. "I bet that's not something you ever thought'd come out of your mouth?"

"That's for sure." He cracked a smile. "But I never thought I'd pull feathers from my hair when I wake up in the morning either." He brushed a small black tuft from his shoulder, and we both watched it float away.

"About that...," I said. "We have a lot to talk about."

"Yeah, and you don't have to apologize. I'm the one who slashed your face. I'm so sorry, Adele."

"You already apologized."

"I know, but it doesn't make it okay. I still feel horrible."

"It was an accident. Apology accepted. We have a lot to get done and very little time."

"We do? Does it involve exterminating vampires?"

"You're doing it again."

"I'm joking! But does it?"

"Possibly."

My own words sliced my heart, not to mention my morals. *Could I kill something? Someone?* "Either way, let's stop apologizing and move forward. Agreed?"

"Done." He stood taller, as if a massive weight had been lifted from his shoulders.

"But that doesn't mean I don't have like eight thousand questions," I added and started walking out of the park towards the river. He followed.

"Yeah, I figured."

As we exited onto the street, he dipped his hand into the water that filled one of the long cement boxes in the sidewalk. "What are these things?"

"Troughs."

"Troughs? For what?"

"For the horses to drink out of."

"Horses?"

"Normally there are horse-drawn carriages lining this block."

"Really?"

"Really."

"That's so weird."

"Yeah, I guess it is." I laughed as we crossed Decatur Street to the concrete amphitheater. Side by side, we jogged halfway up the stadiumlike seats and then sat down on one of the cold rows. Even though it was still quite a distance behind us, we could hear the river thanks to the curfew-imposed silence. There were no trains, no barges, no music to muffle the sloshing tide.

Isaac leaned back on his elbows, seeming perfectly at ease. I leaned back too.

We stared at the empty stage.

When I was a kid, my father would bring me here and give me dollar bills to tip the street performers, all of whom I knew by name. It felt like a lifetime ago.

"I don't even know where to start," I finally said.

"What do you want to know the most?"

"Why were you in my house the night we returned home? How do you turn into a bird? Why do you have so many drawings of my ancestor Adeline Saint-Germain—?"

"Whoa." He laughed. "I am completely content spending the entire night with you, but you're the one who said we're on a time constraint."

I blushed.

"You're right. Give me the abridged version, *s'il vous plaît*."

"Okay." He paused for a moment to think. "I suppose it started before we came down to New Orleans. Before the Storm. The dreams started… just after my great-grandmother died."

"I'm sorry."

"Thanks." He smiled, taking a moment. "My dad and I were upstate, helping my grandpa take care of her affairs—"

"Wait, Upstate? I thought you were from New York *City*."

"I am. I mean, I was born upstate, but we moved to the city when I was five because my mom was an actress."

"Was?"

"Yeah, before she died."

"Jesus, I'm so sorry, Isaac." My hand went to his leg as I racked my brain, trying to recall if I had ever said anything horrible about my own mother in front of him.

"Thanks." His gaze flicked to my hand, which I promptly removed. "We were clearing out my great-grandmother's estate, which wasn't worth much, but she grew up during the Depression, and never threw anything away, so there was a lot of stuff." He took a breath and looked at me.

"And?"

"And that's where I found this." He pulled out a large leather-bound sketchbook from his knapsack and handed it to me. It wasn't the one I had previously wanted to beat him with; this one was old. *Very old.* My hands instantly felt alive, holding it.

"Open it."

The delicate pages were filled with perfectly depicted scenes from a tropical island: cliffs over water, sunrises, fields of dandelions, exotic birds, and sketch after sketch of the same suntanned teenage boy. Then the images gradually became darker. Billows of smoke. Large plumes of feathers. Flames. Waves. A woman swimming underwater— no, drowning. The page margins were full of gibberish.

"This is amazing, Isaac. Your great-grandmother was an artist?"

"No, that book's way older than my great-grandmother. It must have belonged to one of her ancestors."

I carefully turned the pages: a decrepit ship, a voyage, scene after scene of *La Nouvelle-Orleans,* a convent, nuns. If Adeline's diary was the novel, then these were the illustrations.

A page with a familiar-looking girl made me stop.

Her curls were whipping wildly in the wind, and underneath the sketch were the words:

Self-Portrait, June 1727

It was Susannah Bowen, the red-haired girl from Désirée's painting – the Bermudian coven member – staring back at me. My pulse raced as I looked at Isaac.

"For a couple of weeks up until she died, I had been having these crazy dreams about flying," he said. "It's hard to explain, but when I found the book, it was like I couldn't put it down. It felt almost painful to leave it." His hand brushed mine as he gently closed the book to show me the cover. A small bird had been carved into the lower right corner of the leather. "My grandpa knew I was applying to art schools, so he let me keep it—"

"You were applying to art schools? Wait, you're in high school?"

"I was a senior this year, but my dad let me drop out so I could come with him to New Orleans to help rebuild. Getting my G.E.D. was part of the deal, but since nothing's running here, I haven't been able to do it yet. I'm supposed to be studying when I'm at the café."

Good lord, how much do I not know about this boy?

"Anyway, after we got back to the city, my dreams changed. They were no longer about flying, or feathers, or birds. They were about fire. And there was always this girl in a long dress, always surrounded by flames. Then the Storm happened, everything got crazy, and suddenly my father and I ended up here.

"One night, I was walking to a recovery site – at that point, missions were still around the clock – and I saw your house. I mean, I didn't know it was *your* house at the time, but seeing it nearly gave me a heart attack." He flipped the book open to a page marked with a ribbon.

"Whoa." It was a sketch of my house – the iron gate, the long shutters, the attic windows; the Creole cottage looked exactly the same, only there weren't houses on either side of it yet, just trees.

"Yeah. It couldn't have been a coincidence, right? I was standing there, kinda tripping out, when I heard a noise inside. I could tell from the looks of things that the residents hadn't returned, so I grabbed a broken piece of fence and walked around back to investigate. Everyone was really on edge back then, and I had already gotten into a couple of scuffles with looters.

"The kitchen door was broken, and then… it's hard to explain, but something pulled me inside. Sorr—"

"Don't apologize." I remembered the magnetizing feeling the shutter had had on me.

"You're going to think I'm crazy…."

"No, I won't. *Trust* me."

"I didn't find anyone, at first. Or rather, I didn't see anyone. It was pitch black. But I could *feel* someone else there. It was like they were whipping behind my back every time I turned around."

"When I couldn't find anyone inside, I pulled out the sketchbook to see if anything else looked familiar. No more clues popped up, but here's where it gets weird. I started having these pains in my shoulders and arms. My body felt like it was going to explode. Like it was warning me something bad was going to happen. When I tried to shut the book to get the hell out, a burst of wind came through the door and held the book open. I kept trying to shut it, but it wouldn't close. If I changed the page, it kept blowing back open to the same one. This one."

I looked down at the page he was pointing to. A black crow was painted across the centerfold, and verses in curly script filled what little white space was left.

"I started reading some of the words. I sounded ridiculous, like I was reciting poetry in Old English, and then before I knew it, I was flapping around, squawking. And that's when I saw my first blood-binger."

"What?"

"Yeah, it was crazy. I'd never seen anything like him. I mean, I made all-state in track, but this guy was nuts, whipping around your house at warp speed. My eyes could barely follow him. He wasn't destroying anything, and, as far as I could tell, he didn't leave with anything either. I guess he didn't find whatever he was looking for."

My brain raced. The spell hadn't been broken at that point, so it couldn't have been any of the vampires from the attic. That left only two possible suspects. "Who was it? Was it Émile—? I mean Emilio—"

"Wait a second, don't tell me the latest douchebag in town is the same guy you were all hung up on when you got back from Paris? The one Jeanne and Ren were always teasing you about?"

My face burned with embarrassment, both because it was true and because he knew about my unfortunate past life.

"So much for your headphones being on all those days in the café," I snapped.

He jumped up in front of me, laughing. "No wonder you don't like me. You have the worst taste in men *ever*!"

My shoulders burned. I told myself to breathe, but no amount of air to my lungs was going to help.

"*Ever!*" he taunted, bouncing backwards down the stairs.

That was it.

I sprang up. My arm flung upwards like I was pitching a softball, and then a perfectly round ball of fire flew from my palm and whizzed right past his ear. Stunned, he whipped around and watched it sail another hundred feet. It landed in one of the troughs with a satisfying sizzle.

My pulse raced.

"What the eff?" he yelled, twisting back around. "How did…? You just… That was AWESOME!"

A rush of relief passed through me.

"Do it again!"

"You want me to throw fire at you again?"

"Uh, if it's coming out of your *hands*, then yes."

"Okay, don't say I didn't warn you." I lobbed another flame, but this time I aimed it directly into the horses' drinking station. He ran back to me, unable to contain himself.

"You're like Super Mario!"

"You really know how to make a girl feel special."

"You're like Super Mario, but a hot girl." He blushed a little when he realized the compliment had slipped out.

My eyes immediately dropped to the ground. I didn't deserve any compliments after the events of the last few days. I tried to look back up at him; my cheeks burned, remembering our kiss that night in the *Tremé*.

"Hey," he said gently, taking my hand. My heart skipped, and for a second I worried we were back there. But when I looked up, he smiled, quickly let go, and started jogging backwards down the rows to center stage.

"Hit me!"

"No, Isaac, I don't want to burn you."

"You aren't going to burn me," he scoffed. "Just do it."

Without answering, I launched a fireball at him.

"Again, again, again!"

I launched another. Then a third. Just before the first flame hit his face, he raised his hand, and a small gust of wind redirected it thirty feet upwards. He yelled for more. I threw a forth. Fifth. Sixth. Gravity pulled the first fireball down, but right before it fell into his hand, he popped it back up. A smile spread across his face.

Isaac was juggling my flames, and it was the most amazing thing I'd ever seen.

I walked down the steps, totally mesmerized by the coolest street performance in history. When I got near, he moved the trajectory of the flames, causing me to jump closer. I landed on his foot as the flames circled us, but he didn't waver. With my back turned to his chest, I craned my neck to watch the flames swirl around us. I even shot a few more into the gentle twister.

His arms came down, but the flames continued to dance around us, warming the wind. For the first time, my power seemed beautiful. Isaac had this way of making everything he touched beautiful.

He lowered his head so it was level with mine. "You see, we are better together."

A smile that I hoped he couldn't see came from somewhere deep inside. I slowly inhaled and fought the urge to relax into his chest. "You're right."

"I am?" A fireball fell, squelching into a puddle.

I turned around to face him. "We are better together. Stronger. The three of us."

"Three?"

"You, me… and Désirée," I said with a Cheshire Cat-sized grin and jogged backwards. The flames rained down around us as he chased me with his mouth gaping.

"You mean like a threeso—"

I chucked another fireball towards his head. He easily flung it out of the way.

"You better watch out," he scolded me, catching up. "This city has already burned down to the ground, twice. Right?" He looked at me for confirmation.

"Someone give the boy a beignet. Every building except the Ursuline Convent, Vodou Pourvoyeur, and my house, apparently."

"There was one other building."

"Huh?"

"Weren't you paying attention at all on our first date?" He winked. "There was one other original French building that survived the fires, but now I can't remember where."

"There was?" The wheels in my head started turning. "There's no such thing as a coincidence."

"What?"

"Isaac, we have to figure out which other building survived!"

"I thought we had to stake some vampires?"

"Don't you see? Adeline must have lived in my house on Burgundy Street. Marassa at the Voodoo shop. Your ancestor, Susannah, lived at the convent. What if that house belonged to one of the other casquette girls? What if her descendant still lives there?"

"What are you talking about?"

I grabbed his wrist and took off running. "Now *I* have a lot to tell *you*."

"THEY SHOULD REALLY LOCK THEIR DOORS this late at night," Isaac said as we burst into Vodou Pourvoyeur.

"No one here has to worry about burglars."

"I hope you found some answers," Désirée yelled from the back of the shop.

"I did way better than that," I shouted, dragging a suddenly incredibly uneasy Isaac through the long shop. "I found our third."

"Your what?" he asked.

Désirée looked up from the cauldron she was meddling with. The room was a mess. Books were scattered about. Discarded, crumpled sheets of paper. Herbs, oils, powders. A scattering of bones and other fragments that I'd rather remain clueless about.

"You've got to be kidding me." Her eyes scanned Isaac up and down. And then she extinguished the fire in the hearth so whatever she was brewing wouldn't burn.

"You two are starting to freak me out," Isaac said. "Can someone tell me what is going on here?"

"Isaac, show Désirée what you can do."

"What?" His eyes widened, and he said my name under his breath.

"Show her. You can trust Dee. I promise."

He looked at Désirée with caution.

She crossed her arms. "This better be good."

His eyes rolled to her, and then suddenly he was gone.

"Shit! Where'd he go?"

My gaze rose to the wall behind her, where he was perched perfectly still on the top shelf in between an enormous animal skull and two taxidermy bats.

Désirée craned her neck backwards, and suddenly he launched down towards us.

"Jesus!" She jumped, grabbing my arm as he swooped over our heads to the shelf behind me.

I spun around. My eyes didn't move from him. Unlike our first encounter, the bird wasn't scary – his shiny, jet-black feathers, his wingspan, his animal grace all left me momentarily breathless.

He transformed back to his human form, cracking up with laughter. "Désirée, you should have seen the look on your face."

"Anthropomorphic spell. Big whoop."

"Anthro-what?" he asked. "Oh yeah, it was a real big whoop for you that day you accidentally turned me into a cat and couldn't turn me back!"

"OMG, that was you?" She laughed. "Serves you right for creepin' me."

"I was not *creeping* you! You were being followed by a vampire!"

"Oh."

"Show Désirée your sketchpad," I interrupted, trying not to laugh.

"Not until you tell me what the hell is going on."

"That's what I am trying to do!" I pulled the painting of the casquette girls from my bag along with Adeline's diary. Désirée pulled out Marassa's grimoire, and we put everything on the wooden counter and looked at him. He didn't take his wary eyes off of Désirée, but conceded and placed the old book of art on the counter. I flipped it open to Susannah's self-portrait, and moved it next to the painting.

"What the hell?" Isaac asked, looking back and forth between the two.

"Goddess help us," Désirée said. "You are legit."

"That's not all. Go on, Isaac."

He looked at me one last time before he raised his hand. A slight wind began to blow back our hair, and soon the scattered mess Désirée had made all over the floor was gently arranged into neat stacks of papers and orderly piles of herbs.

"Thanks, but that mess meant something to me." Désirée raised her hand, and the floor's pattern of wooden planks began to shift like a *Rubik's Cube* until all the objects were back to their seemingly chaotic state.

"Whoa…"

"Mother Earth," she said and then pointed to him. "Wind."

"Fire," we both finished as she pointed to me.

"So… the next question is, who the hell is empowered with water?" Désirée asked. "Who are the other descendants that are supposed to be in our coven?"

"Excuse me," Isaac said. "Our *what*—?"

"Oh," I yelped. "That reminds me!"

I quickly explained my theory about the residences of the old coven being the only French buildings to have survived the great fires of the eighteenth century. "But what was the fourth property?" I asked Désirée.

"The brothel."

We all took off running.

I DON'T KNOW IF IT WAS THE TOTAL DARKNESS or the fact that my pulse climbed with every pound my feet made to the pavement, but the block where the brothel was felt particularly creepy. We slowed to a walk.

Isaac shone his weaponlike flashlight on the mystery residence.

The brothel was a massive, pink Creole plantation-style house . The kind that you would imagine on acres of land in the middle of nowhere, rather than a few feet from the sidewalk in the middle of a city block. The pink paint was peeling; some of the windows were broken, while others, along with the door, were boarded up – not in a protection-from-the-Storm kind of way, in a decrepit haunted-house-on-the-hill kind of way.

The first floor sat high on top of a raised basement, which hid the staircase that led to the front door.

"Do you guys feel that?" Désirée asked as I unlocked the basement door.

"Yes," we both replied, although I had no idea what she actually meant.

Even though the bricked basement was above ground, it was still cold and damp. We hurried up the staircase that led back outside to the sprawling porch. The closer I got to the front door, the warmer I felt, both metaphorically *and* physically.

Isaac flicked his flashlight on the dormant gas lamps. After a little mental focus, flames shone through the mucky glass boxes and the smell of burning grime wafted over us.

Désirée held her hand over the crooked boards on a window, and they popped themselves off one at a time into her hands. She gently placed the wood on the ground, and we peered through the impossibly opaque glass. It was obvious that the building had been abandoned long before the Storm.

"Look at this," said Isaac, shining the flashlight on some kind of plaque next to the front door.

"No!" I moaned, running over. There was an emblem of the Louisiana State Department. "It's property of the state?" There was also a list of the board of directors, along with the Museum Director. "Ugh, the building is a museum now?"

"Maybe once upon a time," Isaac said. "I don't think it's been anything for a while."

"I know there has to be a clue here somewhere!" I shook the front door handle frantically, too overwhelmed with disappointment to focus on the metal.

"Adele!" Désirée pulled me away from the door.

"We're so close! I can feel it. We have to find out who the previous owner was!"

"Even if we do," she aggressively whispered, chasing me back down the stairs, "it's not like we'd be able to locate them tonight and then convince them they're a witch who must join our coven to break a three-hundred-year-old curse before some maniac-middle-child vampire kills us all!"

I sank to the curb, my arms cradling my head.

The gas lamp exploded behind me.

"Chill!" she yelled.

Breathe.

Without opening my eyes, I knew that Isaac had sat next to me.

"Hey," he whispered, his hand lightly touching my back, "whoever the descendant is, they're probably not even in town because of the Storm, okay?"

When I didn't freak out on him, he moved his hand up and down my back until my breathing normalized and I nodded in affirmation. "Y'all are right. We're on our own for this one. Let's go back to the shop. We need a plan."

Désirée helped me up from the curb and looked over my shoulder at the mess of glass. "Let's not go back to the shop just yet."

IT'S HARD TO EXPLAIN HOW OR WHY, but *everything* just changed being around them. It was instantly apparent that we were meant to be together. We decided that the banks of the Mississippi would be the safest place to continue our show-and-tell, because my flames and Isaac's wind together quickly became unwieldy – the river water was a natural fire extinguisher.

We hurried down the Moonwalk until we were technically out of the Quarter. Hidden among the few trees that had survived the Storm, we could practice more freely. Every spell we tried became a spectacle, and at one point Isaac produced a gust of wind so strong he accidentally launched Désirée into the river.

"Stay back!" she screamed when we ran to the water to pull her from the dangerous Mississippi.

A drooping tree branch suddenly twisted past my head, growing longer and longer until it plunged into the murky water. I just stood gobsmacked while the enchanted vine pulled her from the current.

I thought she would kill him for it, but instead, she danced around us, reeling from the coven's surge of power. For the rest of the night, however, Isaac couldn't walk past any fauna without getting his butt smacked by banana tree leaves or, even better, tickled by Spanish moss – which amused me greatly. He took the beatings with grace, but yelled to me through the tickles, "Is this funny to you?"

"*Oui*," I replied with an innocent smile, and he swore he'd get me back for laughing at his misfortunes.

Any tension among the three of us eased. Brought together under extraordinary circumstances created an immediate bond, but the quickness with which it formed made it feel surreal.

The secret, fantastical nature of it all made casting magic feel extremely personal. It was still hard for me to trust the magic so *completely*… to let people in on something I was still jostling with believing myself felt strange. But being around Désirée and Isaac calmed me down in a way that I'd never felt around friends before. These contradicting conditions of the coven somehow made me simultaneously anxious and completely at ease at the same time.

Sometime in between Désirée's river-dunk and sunrise, we ended up back at the shop, settled into the mound of pillows behind the fuchsia curtain. Désirée made Isaac a *gris-gris* while I gave him the *Cliff Notes* version of Adeline's diary and picked little feathers out of his hair.

As I finished the story of the pirate massacre, he picked up the medallion resting against my chest and rubbed the captain's eye.

I filled him in as much as I could, but when I got to the Emilio part of the story, I couldn't get the death threat out. It was hard enough grappling with the idea of my own mortality, but handing someone else their potential death sentence was too much. Désirée finished for me.

"I knew there was a reason I hated that douchebag!" he yelled after she broke the news.

Désirée shrugged and said with the same light tone as if heading off to whip up a batch of brownies, "I want to work on this elixir I found in Marassa's grimoire… The original coven had seven members. We're going to need all the help we can get."

She went out into the shop with her eighteenth-century ingredient list, and I watched through a crack in the curtain as she began to pull an assortment of jars and boxes from the shelves. Isaac was on the floor, glancing at Susannah's book while he sketched in his own. It had taken him all of thirty seconds to get over the shock.

He must have felt me looking at him.

"It helps me think," he said. "I swear I'm not just doodling."

"I know." I settled under a blanket in the cushions next to him, uncapped a pen, and began translating, but, just like in the dad's studio, my eyes kept flicking to his artwork. He was sketching my medallion. He swept the pencil across the page, scripting out the letters A.S.G. As he began to layer over the star that covered the monogram, I couldn't help think about my dad and my mom, and *Adeline et le Comte de Saint Germain*, and wonder how deep the crazy in my family history went.

36 circle of seven

10th August 1728

IT HAS BEEN THREE DAYS, but I still can't believe that Martine is dead. Although, dead doesn't seem like the appropriate word, considering I saw her walking—no, *dancing* in the street last night. I tried to speak with her. I long to know that she is okay. At least, that is what I tell myself, but my true desire, now that she is one of them, is for her to convince them to go back to Paris, or wherever they came from.

13th August 1728

MY ATTEMPTS TO COMMUNICATE with Martine have been fruitless. She will not even look at me. Gabriel says this is common with newborn vampires –

they often reject their former human families, as part of their transition. And I was the closest thing that Martine DuFrense had to family.

14th August 1728

THE GUILT OVER THE DUFRENSES' DEATHS consumes me. The guilt lies twice as heavy now, Papa, knowing that not only could I have killed the vampires on our journey across the ocean but also that their presence here seems to have something to do with me. With us.

I lie awake at night, thinking about the words Gabriel Medici spoke the night he killed Martine. His demands and his threats. He doesn't believe me when I say I don't know your location. So this is why you were so secretive about your journey, Papa? It brings me great sadness that you thought I could not carry this burden with you.

I haven't told the other girls about his threats, for I feel this is a matter of family affairs.

15th August 1728

SOMETIMES I THINK GABRIEL BELIEVES I am teasing him by not telling him the information he desires. Sometimes I think he is drawn to this game of cat and mouse. And sometimes I think his assumption that I have information he wants makes it safe for me to be around him. At other times, I wonder if he just leads me to believe I have the upper hand.

16th August 1728

GABRIEL SAID THE MOST PECULIAR THING TONIGHT. As usual, the hour was late, and he appeared to have drunk quite a lot, so I also attributed his chatty mood to the anise-flavored wine he is so fond of. As gentle as a man could be, he asked me if I like *La Nouvelle-Orléans.*

When I told him that I liked the city very much, he grabbed me with force and told me I had better start saying my goodbyes, and that if I haven't revealed your hiding place by the time his brothers arrive, then I would be going away with them – that he would make me a Medici. The misplaced comfort I feel around him made me smile and ask him whether that was his twisted way of asking for my hand in marriage.

To which he smirked and replied, "Well, that would require me asking your father's permission first, wouldn't it? No, I have a much more permanent idea in mind."

17th August 1728

I JUST DON'T KNOW WHAT TO THINK about anything anymore. The world has gone mad. My head is too foggy and my hand shakes too violently to pen the events of this evening.

19th August 1728

THE LAST DAYS HAVE BEEN A BLURRY HAZE. Susannah fed me strong medicinal concoctions for the injuries to my neck. They reeked of fennel and left me fading in and out of sleep in a near hallucinogenic state. The pain was excruciating, and soon I began to feel infection setting in. In my state of semiconsciousness, I could hear the girls fluttering around me. There was a fierce debate amongst the circle – they seemed to be split on my course of treatment. In the end, Cosette said strongly, "Her temperature is *too* high. I am going to get him! He is the only one who can save her now."

"We're not letting you go alone," her sisters yelled out the door, running behind her.

Before the triplets made it back, Gabriel was in my room, hovering over my head. "How did this happen?" he growled.

"Why don't you ask your cousin Lorenzo!" Susannah spat back.

I will never forget the look in his eyes. The fear... mixed with a strange glimmer of hope. With angered huffs, he wiped my fevered brow. The chill of his hand sent waves of shudders down my chest.

"You bedda not do anything but help her, *Monsieur*," Marassa said with threat.

He hissed at her and then cupped my face with his hands. Although I shook violently, his touch began to bring down my body temperature immediately.

I think every girl in the room was holding her breath as he removed the bandages, exposing the infected puncture wounds.

Susannah frantically asked him questions in English, which I couldn't understand. He replied in her native tongue and then bit the fingernail on his right index finger so that it cracked at a sharp angle.

My eyes widened as he held my neck steady.

"Wha—" I stuttered.

"This is going to hurt, Adeline, but I will be quick," he said, looking into my eyes.

Before I could even nod, he slit open the puncture wounds on my neck with one quick swipe.

I screamed in pain as his lips suctioned onto my neck. His left hand held me down as he attempted to extract the venom.

He released me for a moment, quickly spat into the basin of water next to the bed, and in a flash was reattached to my neck, and I was screaming again. I felt my eyes roll back in my head as he spat and sucked and spat.

"It's not enough!" he yelled. "The venom is coursing too deep in her bloodstream. Why didn't you call for me sooner?

No one said anything for a moment, and then Susannah screamed,

"No!"

My eyes flipped back open to see Gabriel lowering his wrist to my mouth.

I clamped my lips shut just before his blood could enter.

"It's the only way!" Gabriel said and then looked grimly at Susannah. "If she dies," he said softly, "it will be on your hands."

My head fell sideways, and the blood smeared across my face. All I could think was, if all that has happened had something to do with our family, Papa, then I deserved to die, not the others. Not Sophie, or Claude, or Martine, or Morning Star's brother, and none of the nameless souls in *La Nouvelle-Orléans*.

Marassa rubbed my shoulder and said gently, "You gots ta do it, Addie."

And then Cosette was by her side, squeezing my hand. "You have to drink it, Adeline! It will only be a few drops." She shot a look at Gabriel. "Just enough to save your life, *ma fifille.*"

Tears fell from my eyes.

Gabriel distracted me by wiping the blood from my cheeks with one hand while parting my lips with his other. When his open wrist dripped blood onto my tongue, I immediately choked on the vile metallic taste. Cosette squeezed my jaw like a babe so I couldn't shut my lips.

The blood slipped down my throat, and then suddenly, with animalistic impulse, I found myself pushing Cosette out of the way and clutching Gabriel's wrist, pining for him. For his blood.

But no sooner had I started drinking, was he forcefully detaching himself from my mouth. "No more, *cara mia.*"

Panting, I looked back to him with begging eyes. He slipped underneath the blanket next to me and pulled me into his chest.

"Go to sleep, little lamb," he said gently, scooping me so close my entire body pressed tightly against his.

"What do you think you're doing?" cried Cosette. "Get away from her! Get out of the bed."

"Precautionary measure," he told the girls, his sturdy arms wrapping me into his chill. "You are going to want me around if she drank too much." His voice was solid, but I could sense his worry. "Not that I really care if she rips off all of your heads, if that's what she wants, but I'd rather avoid an encore of Martine's performance. I'm here for the night, just in case."

"Just in case?" Cosette yelled, fuming.

"When it comes to death," he said, "just as in life, there are no guarantees."

"I knew this was a bad idea," Susannah said, pulling the blanket away.

In a flash, Gabriel rolled over me and grabbed her tiny waist. "If you think a blanket is going to keep me from taking *anything* I desire tonight, then you are an even sillier little girl than I thought."

"Remove your hands from her," I heard Cosette say from behind me.

And, just like every other man, Gabriel did as Cosette commanded.

But then Gabriel had the final word: "You have two options. "Leave… or settle in with us." I could tell by the inflection on his last word that he was smiling.

Cosette then picked up the blanket, pulled it over us, and crawled in next to me. "You're going to be okay, *ma fifille,* you will always be one of us," she said, burrowing against my back.

Her close proximity to the vampire made her sisters gasp, but then they, too, lay down at our feet. Marassa settled onto the sofa at the edge of the bed, and Susannah curled into a chair in the corner, keeping a sharp eye on Gabriel.

"Well, I'm no stranger to the *ménage à trois,"* Gabriel said, "but I can honestly say that seven is a record for me."

In her goddess-disguised, *femme fatale* voice, Cosette replied sweetly, "Don't make me sew your mouth shut for the night. It would bring me great pleasure."

He stroked my hair. Even through the numbness of the vampire venom and medicinal concoctions, I could feel his blood coursing through my veins, fighting the infection.

"Go to sleep, Adeline, and don't even think about trying to get seconds. If you bite me again, you'll end up stuck with me for the rest of your immortal life."

His words made me shudder.

Pressed up against him, barely lucid, everything about Gabriel Medici made me shudder.

(cont.)

WHEN I AWOKE THE NEXT MORNING, atop his chest, I hesitated before opening my eyes, allowing myself a brief moment to be held in his arms. He knew I was awake; his heart had flickered the moment my consciousness returned. I remained still for just a few more seconds, lingering in his scent.

Just a single stolen moment before I appropriately I screamed for him to get out of my bed. To which he replied, "Are you sure you don't want to lie with me a little longer?" His gaze burned straight through my thin gown.

"Get out!" I yelled once again, pushing him up.

The other girls woke, and quickly they were making a fuss over the status of my health. Sitting on the edge of the bed, Gabriel pulled on his boots and stretched his arms into his jacket, shielding his eyes from the sunlight that pierced the cracks in the drapery.

He stood and took my hand as if to kiss it goodbye, but instead pulled me to my knees, just long enough to whisper in my ear, "This doesn't change anything, *mademoiselle.* I am still going to drain your father." He discreetly kissed the lobe of my ear and was gone.

Cosette pulled me back down to the bed. I barely got the words out: "I despise him…" But I meant them. I despised the way he made me feel about him.

She unwrapped the bandages and examined my neck. "It's perfect," she said and kissed it.

"He is an ass," Susannah said with a clenched jaw. "Their time is near."

Lisette giggled. "He is an ass who saved Adeline's life."

"Gabriel Medici did not save me… Louis saved me."

"Louis, the dog?" asked Lisette. "Adeline, Louis has been missing for weeks. You must still be feeling the effects of the tea Susannah made you last night."

"No, it was Louis! I swear to it! He attacked Lorenzo; that is how I escaped."

I explained to them that I had gone out for a stroll to shop for new ribbons, when someone whipped past me, not at all trying to hide his supernatural speed despite being out in broad daylight. Lorenzo Medici made no threats, no demands; he simply pulled me into an alleyway and snarled, "I want to leave this hellhole!" And then he attacked my neck like an demonic animal. I tried to fight back, but he was drinking so quickly, it was like the magic was draining from my body with my blood.

Then a giant dog sprang from nowhere and attacked him.

"That's all I remember," I said.

Cosette took my hand and gently explained how they had found me, near death, on the curb two blocks away from the estate.

"There was no one else in sight. Animal or otherwise," she said.

I sprang from the bed. "We have to find Louis; he might have been hurt saving me!" My boots were not even laced as I ran down the stairs to the front door.

"Adeline, come back! You are not well!" Marassa yelled.

But she was wrong. I was never better. Footsteps rattled as the five girls filed behind me. They could hardly keep up with me, for I now had Medici blood coursing through my veins. I didn't stop running until I was back in the alley where Lorenzo had dragged me.

"Louis!" I called over and over again. The other girls began to peek through the rubbish.

"*Sacrebleu*!" cried Lisette.

"He's badly hurt!" said Minette.

To my surprise, Lisette had been right: the animal we found wasn't Louis, the furry friend who had been following me for weeks. This wolf-dog was a shiny gray color, unlike my black-haired companion. There was a silver star tied to a piece of leather around its neck. When I slid the ornament around to show the others, Susannah shouted, "We must bring her back to the house at once!"

I asked Susannah what was wrong, but all she did was repeat herself and use wind to lift the animal and support its weight. The five of us huddled around the giant beast regardless, pretending to lug her so as not to arouse suspicion. When a gruff man offered to help, all six of us yelled, "*No!*" at once.

"On the bed!" Susannah yelled when we burst through the door of my bedroom.

"Why is the bed necessary?" I asked as I closed the door behind us, thinking only of the garbage heap the animal had been lying in. Simultaneous gasps answered for me. When I rushed back to the bed, there was no more wolf but a young native woman.

"*Rougarou*!" gasped Marassa.

"*Loup-garou*!" yelled Lisette.

"Because she's not a dog, Adeline. She's a lycanthrope," Susannah said. "A wolf-charmer."

I had not the slightest idea what they were talking about, but when I pushed the girl's hair from her face, I knew exactly who she was: Morning Star, the daughter of the chief and sister to the boy who had vanished without a trace. And that's when I made the connection over my missing dog and the chief's missing son.

Morning Star had been badly beaten but did not appear to have been bitten. Marassa, Minette, and Cosette quickly went to work healing her injuries.

"How did you know, Susannah?" asked Lisette.

The girl on the bed answered for her, in broken French: "Because she has the power of wind beneath her wings."

We all looked back at Susannah, but she wasn't there. In her place was a magnificent red bird. And not just any red bird – the pirate captain's red bird.

Cosette yelped in glee. "You were with us! You've been with us all along!"

"It's about time you showed your true self," said Marassa.

But then the daughter of the chief interrupted the strange moment of truth with the question I fear the most.

"Why are they after you?" she asked, staring straight at me. "They stalk you every night. That's why my brother always stayed close to you. He feared for your life. What do they want with you?"

I stammered, put on the spot for the first time. "I don't know. Something to do with my family."

"We are your family, Adeline," all three triplets said at the same time.

"And this madness must end once and for all," I said and watched the smiles spread across all of their faces. "We are six, and they are three. We can beat them."

"No, they are four," said Morning Star. "The one who killed my brother is a woman called Giovanna. She is the sister of the one who attacked you. They are four, but we are seven."

And just like that, our circle gained a native.

28th August 1728

THERE WAS NO TIME TO WASTE. Not only because of the chronic threat of death the monsters plagued the city with, but also because I was afraid of myself. That if I waited too long, I would lose my strength. After all, I had already passed the chance to rid the world of them at sea.

Mother Superior had taken action the day we set foot in *La Nouvelle-Orléans,* demanding nine thousand nails be sent from the Holy Pope himself, all the way from the Vatican in Rome. I admired the immediate action taken by the Ursuline sister, but I knew that not even a million nails from the papacy would contain this group of undead.

Our coven was complete. Our circle was cast. And together, a plan was devised. It was hurried and risky, but it made good use of each girl's unique skills. We outnumbered them, but they were physically superior and more experienced in the art of deception. We could only hope that they would dismiss us – a group of silly girls, barely able to communicate with each other. What they didn't know was that we each had a story, a destiny, a *raison d'être*.

I wish I could say our plan was perfect and the execution was flawless, but nothing is ever so sweet.

On the night of our attack, I sat perched in a tree under the full moon, the perfect vantage point to see through the attic windows. My heart raced, knowing the lives of others would soon be in my hands. A lullaby attracted my attention; it meant Cosette was close to luring them into the convent, and soon it would be my turn to act.

Moments later, I watched the vampires file into the attic behind her. By the way they moved, I could tell their senses had been dulled, thanks to Susannah's herbs. It all happened within seconds, but it was exhilarating.

I launched a stake into the air, and the first set of shutters snapped closed, secured forever by the bewitched metal stake. The second set also closed without notice.

The slam of the third set made Martine DuFrense turn her head.

Then the Medici boys perked up as well – their heads turned towards me – realizing it was a trap. I sent another stake sailing, and the fourth set of shutters snapped closed.

As they rushed the window, Lisette and Minette ran to shut the attic door, and then the vampires lunged back towards them.

My heart pounded, and a preemptive smile spread across my face when, just as we planned, Cosette jumped out the last window. She landed on the roof, and I threw the last stake into the air, but then… I saw the horrors unfolding inside. I screamed and tried to pull the stake back. Its speed slowed, but it was too late to stop it. There was just enough time for a woman to jump out of the window before it snapped the shutters closed, muffling Minette's bloodcurdling scream and veiling the image of Gabriel's fangs ripping into Lisette's throat – an image that will forever be branded in my memory.

There was no time to react, because Cosette was hanging from the roof with a blonde woman attached to her waist, screaming in Italian. I could only assume this was the vampire, Giovanna, whom Morning Star had spoken of. They dangled in thc moonlight, and then the vampire began to swing their bodies back and forth. Cosette clung to the ledge. If they both fell, I was sure that only one might survive.

I yelled for Susannah and Marassa, but it was Morning Star's deep-throated growl that answered first. Without hesitation, she leapt through the air, and her jaws tore into the waist of the living corpse. The dangling vampire was an easy target for her animal form.

Both vampire and wolf tumbled to the ground with a roll.

Overwhelmed with the thought of losing another one of our sisters, I jumped down from the tree. Pain shot from my ankle up my leg, and a surge of energy charged from my toes to the tips of my fingers, but it was my human strength that I became consumed by.

My memory is so blurred it hardly even seems real now, Papa. I snapped a branch from the tree – it was sturdy, but thin enough for my hand to fit around – and charged. Morning Star was on top of the Italian girl, but she was struggling to hold the flailing vampire down. Giovanna bared her teeth dangerously close to the wolf's neck. But just as she was able to bite down, I plunged the splintered wood into her heart.

Blood trickled from the corners of Giovanna's lips, who still looked oddly beautiful in the slashed-up gown. Her gaze never left mine. Even as her heart pumped its last beat, the sparkle never left her dead green eyes.

I don't regret my action for even a breath, but that image will haunt me forever.

Morning Star clamped her jaws around the dead girl's neck and dragged her body down to the river, where we would later ensure that she would never resurrect again.

Marassa and Susannah came running from around the convent, and I realized Cosette was still dangling from the ledge. Marassa began shouting words I didn't understand but was never more grateful to hear, for suddenly the branches of the tree I had been perched in began to grow longer, until one of them was underneath Cosette's frantic feet.

She ran along the branch fearlessly.

Even before her shoes touched the ground, she was asking in between gasps for air, "Where are my sisters?"

It was the most horrible news I have ever delivered.

She ran away before I could even finish the sentence. We chased her through the garden, into the convent, up the stairs and to the attic door… the enchanted door that held the monsters, and the two Monvoisin sisters.

Susannah and Marassa pulled the hysterical triplet away as she tried to beat down the cursed door. We attempted to break the enchantment, but we could not, as it was Lisette and Minette who had bound the door. However, the fact that the curse hadn't broken itself gave us a strange sense of hope that they might still be alive.

Before the sun rose, I raised my hand, and all nine thousand nails rose from the crate and went pounding into the shutters. Instead of setting fire to the attic as we had originally planned before this tragic turn of events, we cast a sleeping spell, sending all of its inhabitants into a life-preserving coma and buying us time to figure out a way to get the girls out safely.

At least, that is what we told each other. But we all knew the lives of Minette and Lisette Monvoisin had ended that night.

37

artemisia absinthium

I QUICKLY READ MY TRANSLATION OUT LOUD to Désirée and Isaac. I didn't intend to skip parts, but my eyes naturally flew past the words when I got to the lines about the Saint-Germain's family affairs. *My family's affairs.*

"What was that chick's name?" Désirée grabbed Adeline's diary from me and began scouring the pages. I became nervous that she might notice the parts I had left out. "There she is: Morning Star… the seventh coven member."

I breathed a sigh of relief. The French words had kept our family secrets.

"How the *hell* are we supposed to find the descendant of someone named Morning Star?" she asked. "Why do I have a feeling she is not going to be in some kind of eighteenth-century phone book?"

"Probably because there were no eighteenth-century phone books," Isaac said.

Desiree rolled her eyes. "You know what I meant."

"Listen to this," I said and began to translate the next two entries out loud.

(cont.)

The feeling is indescribable, Papa. The whole world feels like it is slightly off balance, like I have drunk too deep of the bubbly wine...

I did not think, nor did I hesitate, before I killed that woman, whom, before last night, I had never even laid eyes on, although... something tells me she had laid eyes on me.

So, I now know the answer to the dilemma I posed to myself that night on the S.S. Gironde, *when I first saw Gabriel Medici running across the masts to the crow's nest. Was I capable of taking one life to save the lives of others?*

I would kill one hundred more of them if it meant I could bring back Lisette and Minette Monvoisin. It should not have been those two who found eternal slumber.

After we cremated the corpse and disposed of the remains in the river, we sat at the water's edge, watching the sunrise and basking in the glory of that big ball of fire. We mourned the lives of our fallen sisters, and brothers, and all of the others who had died by the fangs of the monsters.

You are the only one who will ever know, Papa, as I sat there, holding Cosette, stoically staring at the rising sun, I was secretly glad we hadn't torched the attic. That we hadn't killed Gabriel.

28th Nov 1728

Months have gone by, the season has changed, and I am afraid this is the final chapter for our little circle of casquette girls. Morning Star is moving further out with her tribe, as the strife between the French and the Indians worsens. As a parting gift, she gave me a silver, eight-pointed charm and said that "as long as we live under the same blanket of stars, we will be sisters."

Susannah received a marriage proposal from a merchant. I suspect they met prior to La Nouvelle-Orléans, *for I have never seen two people so happy to have found each other. They plan to leave tomorrow for the port of New York. I wish for their happiness, but Susannah's absence will make my heart heavy. I've learned so much from these two women in such a short period of time. I will carry their spirits with me every day, and I do hope we can all meet again in the future.*

As for the rest of les filles aux cassettes, *I turned lead into gold to replace their dowries. I know I am only supposed to do this under grave circumstances, Father, but this is the only chance these girls have to be married. If it wasn't for me, the vampires wouldn't have used their royally-bestowed cassettes as coffins to rest in. Everyone in the town knows of your wealth, so there was not one eyebrow raised when the gold was suddenly procured.*

Martine's affairs were all left in perfect order, which leads me to believe that she really did beg Gabriel to turn her into a vampire. She named me as her sole beneficiary and left the proper paperwork to declare Marassa a free woman.

Every day, Marassa and I stroll to the port to see if the arriving ships are carrying you or her brother. They never are.

But we worry most about Cosette. She hasn't been the same since that night. She wanders the streets after dark, lamenting her sisters and blaming herself for their deaths. Every night she ends her wandering by seeking solace in the arms of another man.

She lures them in with her looks and her lullabies. It's as if she is trying to use up all of her powers so she can forget who she is. Her behavior eventually got her banned from the convent, after which she refused to stay with me, so as not to tarnish my reputation. Marassa and I watch over her silently from afar. I tell myself she just needs time. I know she will end up on top; after all, she is the granddaughter of La Voisin Magnifique, *one of the greatest, most scandalous sorceresses in the history of Paris.*

I CLOSED ADELINE'S DIARY. "Hmm... Cosette Monvoisin got banned from the convent for—"

"Stop thinking about the brothel, Adele. There's nothing behind those doors other than antique perfume bottles, opium pipes, and STD-filled air—"

"Gross!" I said, but smiled. *Opium...* "Did you read how Martine was so messed up when she died, it made Gabriel loaded when he drank from her?"

Désirée looked up from her stirring her pot. "Unless you want to get loaded so we can use you as bait to weaken them, come and help me with this spell."

"Hmm," I murmured.

"Don't even think about it," Isaac quickly said.

"Hmm."

"Adele! There will be *no* martyrs tomorrow night." He looked at each of us.

"You don't have to tell me that," said Désirée. "And, technically, you mean tonight. It's past midnight." Navy-blue smoke began to rise from her pot, swirling around in perfect loops as she moved her fingers.

"What is that?" I asked.

"It's a Heightening Elixir, but it's not going to be ready until tonight. I figured that since none of us can control their minds like Cosette Monvoisin could, we're going to need all the strength we can get."

"She controlled their hearts, not their minds," I corrected.

"Okay, well, not *all* of us can control vampire hearts." Désirée smirked, wagging her eyebrows.

I immediately blushed. "I can't control—" I couldn't even get the rest of the sentence out with the way Isaac was looking at me – with that overwhelming disappointment he was so good at. I pretended to focus on Susannah's sketchbook, which was open in his lap.

"Too bad we can't dose them with some kind of reversal elixir," he said. "Even out the playing field a little more."

"That would require getting them to ingest something… just like you are going to have to do."

As she went on about how she created the elixir, I focused on the sketchpad. The two open pages were covered in drawings of three plants labeled *Green Anise, Sweet Fennel,* and *Artemisia Absinthium.* In the upper-right corner was a tunic-wearing goddess, under which was a banner that said, "*Artemis, Goddess of the Hunt.*"

"Ha! This reminds me of my Halloween costume."

"You're dressing up as a Greek Goddess?" Isaac asked.

"No, not Artemis; the plant."

"You're dressing up as a flower?"

"Not exactly..." My voice trailed off as an idea danced into my head. "We can't control their minds..." I looked up with excitement. "But what if they couldn't control their minds either?"

"You're doing that thing where you don't make sense."

I pointed to the page. "This isn't just *any* recipe for absinthe. It's instructions for how to enchant the herbs!"

"Let me see that," said Désirée.

Isaac passed her the sketchbook. We both scurried behind and peered at the pages over her shoulder. "Fennel and anise we could get, maybe," he said, "but where would we get *Artemisia Absinthium,* whatever the hell that is?"

"Pfft," Desiree said, and we both followed her out through the curtain. She walked straight to the wall of herbs and tossed a jar to Isaac. "Wormwood. As it's known on the streets."

"So," I asked her, "can you do it?"

"I can brew it, but there's still one problem. It's still a Percolation Potion."

"Meaning?"

"It still needs to be ingested—"

"Can you make it undetectable?"

"My gran could, easily... but me... on the first try? Probably not."

"So we'd have to spike something they'd want to drink."

"Something with a really strong flavor – taste and smell."

"You make the potion and leave the rest to me—"

"Like hell—" Isaac interrupted.

"Isaac!" I yelled. "I'm not going to dose myself into human bait! Contrary to what you might think, I do not *want* to be eaten by a vampire." I wasn't sure whether my words were more for his sake or mine – Isaac and Désirée must have been wondering the same thing because they both stared at me in shock. "The moonshine," I said in a quiet voice. "We're going to lace the Hurricane Hootch."

Désirée started laughing. "That's kind of brilliant."

"Then why are you laughing?" I asked.

"Because the only way we can guarantee it will hit their lips is if we spike the entire batch."

I started giggling too.

"I don't get it," Isaac said.

"All those curfew-breakers drinking at illegal little Le Chat Noir are going to be extra loaded tonight," I answered.

"Ha. That's sounds pretty par for the course, from what I hear."

"Yeah," said Désirée, pulling more jars from the shelves, "I don't think the locals are going to mind one little bit." She handed us each a jar of herbs and two large rocks. "Don't stop grinding until you're left with powder."

A couple of hours later, I put the last stopper in the last little bottle and massaged my aching fingers. My nerves were starting to fry. The bottles looked like little perfume samplers, but the clear contents were nothing so innocent.

A COPY OF *LA DOLCE VITA* was waiting on my doorstep when I arrived home at dawn with Isaac, who had insisted on walking me. Luckily, the alleged "cinematic masterpiece" meant nothing to him, so I was spared any further lectures on my choices in men.

He stood in front of my stoop with confidence, but his fingers were anxiously turning the little vial around and around in the front pocket of his jeans.

"Are you sure you don't want me to come with you to the bar?" I asked.

"No, it will appear too suspicious if someone sees you out this late. It's too risky. I can just fly in and out."

"*D'accord.* But no perching tonight, okay? Go straight home after, and get some sleep. We'll need all our strength tomorrow."

"All right," he said, but didn't move. "It's so weird."

"What?"

"That you know all of my secrets now."

"I know. It's weird that you know mine, too. But it's kinda nice. I hate secrets."

"Me too. I just wish I'd told you sooner."

"You tried… but I wouldn't listen."

"Well, I don't want you to listen to guys who break into you house and attack you… even if it *is* an accident," he tried to joke." I'm sorry for keeping things from you, Adele. I promise I won't anymore."

As my pulse picked up, I grasped the little plastic DVD box, quickly kissed him on the cheek and slipped inside.

My jacket hit the bedroom floor next to my unlaced boots; I didn't even bother undressing before I flopped onto my bed and slipped under the covers. The film, still clutched in my right hand, taunted me. I contemplated watching it. Then I contemplated leaving to find Nicco so I could hand it back to him while saying something cutting about his family's fascist behavior.

I shoved it under my pillow, unopened.

Do not think about him, Adele.

The plan was set. There was nothing left to do with my nervous energy other than try to relax. Désirée had given me a thermos with the instructions to drink before bed. I took a giant swig and sank back into the mattress.

My body ached from the excessive magic, but it was the kind of pain that felt good. Like after going to the gym.

I took an extra-deep breath through my nose, letting my lungs fill up until the air moved into my diaphragm, just like our drama teacher had taught us to do. As the air slowly began to leak out of my mouth, I felt big droplets roll down my cheeks to the pillow.

Finally alone.

I thought about death. The plan was either going to work or it wasn't; there were no other possible outcomes. Tomorrow someone was going down. The vampires or the witches. The Medicis or the Saint-Germains.

Me… or Nicco.

38

toil and trouble

October 31st

SHAKING.

"Adele, sweetheart, wake up."

"Hmm… what?" I mumbled, barely able to understand the presence of another person. In the next split second, I sprang up, nearly smacking heads with my father. "What happened? He said I had until tonight!"

"Shhhh. Nothing happened." My father squeezed my hand. "Nothing bad happened, sweetheart. You must have been dreaming. I'm sorry; I shouldn't have woken you up like that after the other night."

"No one died?" I stammered.

"No, baby. No one died."

A very tired Mac Le Moyne was sitting on the edge of my bed, holding a white paper bag.

"Did you just get off work?" I looked at the clock; it was nearly nine in the morning.

"Yeah, it was a late one with so many people pre-gaming for Halloween. Some of your friends, the European ones, closed the place. Apparently one of them works for your mother, " he quickly added, "but she wasn't there."

"Was Niccolò there?" I asked, not wanting to care.

He hesitated before saying yes. I could tell he wished it had been otherwise. "Although, he was brooding, while the others seemed to be celebrating something."

"He was upset?" My eyes must have lit up too much because he frowned.

"I guess so. He wasn't taking part in the libations nearly as much as the others, but I couldn't understand anything they were saying. Hardly any of them were speaking English." He chuckled. "At one point, I thought they were going to get into a fight with Ren's band of misfits. Can you imagine?"

My back tensed. Only then did I realize what I had done – I had made my unsuspecting father the poisoner. I tried not to look panicked.

The little brass alarm clock dove off my nightstand.

He picked it up off the floor and examined it. "Weird. Must be broken." His face twisted into a yawn.

"Dad, you have bartenders, you know?"

"Not many since the Storm. Anyway, if the place gets raided, I need to be there to take the heat."

"Like you are going to get raided," I grumbled, rubbing my eyes. Désirée's sleeping tea definitely hadn't worn off yet. "Did you say Halloween?"

"All day. Your favorite day of the year, and boy, do I have a surprise for you."

"Surprise?"

"Please accept this token as a modification of our tradition." The heavenly combination of sugar and fry wafted out as he extended the white bag.

"What?" I uncrumpled the paper. "Oh my God!"

"Café du Monde is officially back in business – well, at least for two days a week until they can get regular deliveries of ingredients. Who knows when that'll be."

I shoved one of the warm beignets into my mouth and took a large bite, blowing confectioner's sugar all over my bed.

"I know they aren't sugar cookies in the shapes of ghosts, but—"

"This is way better than sugar cookies, Dad!" I mumbled through a stuffed mouth, inadvertently blowing more powdered sugar on him. He laughed.

My mother used to bake sugar cookies every Halloween. It was a task my father had taken over after she left because Halloween has always been my favorite holiday. With all the chaos, I hadn't even realized the day had arrived, and I certainly wouldn't have expected to uphold our traditional baking session. I looked over at the costume I had cherished not so long ago, but had collected dust ever since I arrived home from Paris.

"Thanks, Dad. Thank God something's finally reopened." Soon, all of my attention was consumed by strategically pressing the beignet so that it absorbed as much powdered sugar as possible.

"My pleasure. All right, I'm gonna try to sleep all day. Tonight is sure to be crazy. The buzz is that people have been flooding back into town the last couple of days to be home for the festivities. What are your plans for tonight?"

"Um… I'm gonna hang out with Désirée." *Although our plans hardly involve trick-or-treating.*

"You've been hanging out with her a lot lately," he said with a little trepidation.

"Well, she's the only person at Sacred Heart with any kind of tolerance for downtown. And," I added, "we invited Isaac."

"Oh, good. What about that boy from the bar?"

The vague reference to Nicco felt like a squeeze to my heart. "Um, probably not."

"Costume?" he asked, changing the subject, but I caught the look of relief.

"You know it's a surprise, Dad!"

"Okay, okay. Stop by Le Chat Noir on your way to the parade—"

"The parade is still happening?"

"Oh, yeah. In full force. It's what people are coming back for."

"Awesome. *Merci beaucoup pour les beignets,* Dad."

"Anything for you, baby-doll." He kissed my forehead.

I took advantage of his close proximity and wrapped my arms around his neck. The moment he began to shift away, I hugged tighter. He pulled me in with a gentle rock until I was ready to let go.

"Everything's going to get better, Adele."

"I know it is, Dad." *Especially if everything goes according to plan.*

He kissed my head again, snagged a beignet for himself, and closed the door on his way out.

I squirmed under the covers, eager to get back to sleep. A hard-edge protruding from under my pillow poked my arm. The DVD. I pulled it out and then aggressively stuffed another beignet into my mouth.

Don't open it, Adele.

I popped open the plastic case, and a piece of paper, folded thrice, landed on my chest. For a minute I just stared at it, trying to convince myself that everyone would be better off if I set the note on fire. But then I conceded to curiosity and ripped it open.

In otherworldly handwriting was a long Italian quote, presumably from the film. I grabbed my phone and prayed to the network gods for a strong enough signal to run my translator app. The circle on the screen began to spin. I shook my phone, as if that would give me more bandwidth. The spinning icon had a hypnotic effect, and for a moment I didn't even realize that I was staring down at the English words.

> *"Sometimes at night the darkness and silence weigh upon me... We need to live in a state of suspended animation like a work of art, in a state of enchantment. We have to succeed in loving so greatly that we live outside of time, detached."*

I read the quote three more times. Then suddenly had the urge to spring out of bed, run for the nearest DVD player, and indulge in the narrative that these words, so *à propos,* had been plucked from. Instead, I chucked the DVD across the room to prevent myself from any such romantic downward spiral. I fell back into the bed and slammed my still-damp pillow over my face.

What kind of twisted trick is this? Love? Is this his ploy to rattle me on D-Day?

If it was…

It was working.

I AWOKE A FEW HOURS LATER with the energy usually summoned by my favorite holiday. But soon enough even the smallest thoughts made my nerves nip. *Should I even bother making my bed?*

Yes. If today was my last day on Earth, then people would inevitably come into my room after I was dead, so I wanted it to be clean.

I flipped on the radio and nervously hummed along as I picked up dirty laundry, imagining my father tomorrow morning, sitting on my bed, crying. *Would my mother cry? Would she even care?* I had bitten the bullet late last night and texted her back, but hadn't gotten a response.

I grabbed my phone to double-check, but all I saw were my own words staring back at me.

Adele **11:47 p.m.** What do you need to talk to me about?

"Whatever."

I threw the phone back on the bed. My expectations of my mother were so low, a stupid text message, or lack thereof, was nothing to get disappointed over.

Last night's memories flooded my mind. *Me, Désirée, and Isaac. Who'd have thunk it?* This power – magic, whatever it was – had made me feel electric in the past, but practicing my abilities with those two was far more ecstasy-like.

Fourteen hours later, I was still basking in the euphoric high.

Poor Isaac. At least Désirée and I got to ease into the whole cursed-attic thing. He got a crash course. Thank God I hadn't had to drop the whole "vampires exist" bomb on him as well. Then again, being able to turn yourself into a bird would probably make it easier to believe in the unlikely natures of others. I, however, was still living in a perpetual state of semi-shock.

Isaac could always just fly away if the situation got too out of control. Although, my gut told me that if things got messy, Isaac would never bail. Dee, on the other hand… well, I hoped not.

"Ugh! Don't think like that." I kicked shoes into the closet, tossed in an armful of clothes, and slammed the door. "Désirée is *not* going to bail."

Our plan was mediocre at best, but if we wanted any chance of pulling it off, absolute trust in each other was essential. And trust wasn't something we had had a lot of time to build, especially as a coven. *Does three even count as a coven?* I couldn't shake the feeling that I was responsible for this whole mess. Or at least, my family was. *Am I unnecessarily putting Désirée's and Isaac's lives at risk?* I mean, Minette and Lisette *died* getting these vampires into the attic. *Why did Lisette demand I give them what they wanted? If there is more to what they want than just breaking the curse, why the hell aren't any of them willing to just come out and ask me for it?*

"Totally shady," I grumbled, snatching up a fresh towel and walking towards the bathroom.

Eighteenth-century grudges?

Feuds?

Curses.

UGH!

With a loud pop, the light bulb in the floor lamp spontaneously combusted, spraying shards of glass all over the floor.

"Dammit, Adele, *chill out*!"

MY PHONE BUZZED as I walked out of the steaming bathroom.

Annabelle	**3:40 p.m.**	D + A, where have u bitches been hiding? Everyone's going downtown tonight to this Halloween homecoming parade. Guess I'll see u there, since it's ur stomping ground.

Oh, joy.

There were also a couple of group texts from Désirée and Isaac.

Désirée	**3:32 p.m.**	I "mended" the attic shutter u destroyed. Isaac is going to rehang it at the convent.
Isaac	**3:34 p.m.**	I already hung it, but one of the stakes for the hinge is missing, so it's not very secure. Going to the salvage yard to try to find a replacement. Fingers crossed they have something.

My fingers flew over the digital buttons as I hurried my reply.

Adele	**3:51 p.m.**	Thanks, Dee. Isaac, don't bother, I have

		the missing stake. I'll bring it tonight. Meet y'all at Le Chat. 6pm?
Isaac	**3:52 p.m.**	Word.
Désirée	**3:53 p.m.**	Don't be late.

I typed something snarky, but before I could press send, caught sight of a paper airplane lying on my bed. *That definitely hadn't been there pre-shower.* I tightened the towel around my chest, as my eyes darted around the room.

Nothing.

Regardless, I hurried to the window and slammed it shut before returning to the homemade toy. I could see the pencil lines peeking through before I slowly unfolded the plane – it had been made from a page ripped from a sketchpad. Even though the sharp lines made it seem like the artist had been in a hurry, there was enough detail to capture my expression perfectly. The words "last night's dreams" were beneath my portrait. Isaac. In the picture, the attic window was behind me, shutters closed. The rest of the page was filled with flames, feathers, and vines. Not an inch of the paper had been left uncovered.

Smiling, I rested the drawing on top of Nicco's note, and sat down at the vanity. I soon found myself wondering if he had also made one for Désirée.

I LINGERED UNDER THE WARMTH of the blow-dryer, slowly twisting my waves. There was something ceremonial about getting ready, as if I was getting into character. With the anticipation of tonight's events setting in, I went to the garment rack to retrieve my costume for the final act. My *magnum opus*.

The base structure of the dress was a vintage burlesque costume I'd found at an antique shop in *Le Marais,* near *ma grand-mère's* house in Paris. The shop owner had told me the costume once belonged to some famous vaudeville dancer. I had no idea if that was true, but I felt no remorse handing him my grandmother's credit card. She had instructed me to buy dresses, but never specified what kind. Every weekend thereafter, Emilio (then Émile) drove me to the *atelier*, where I took a Master Class on couture beading. I didn't even want to know how many hours I had spent hand-stitching the thousands of beads and sequins that now adorned the corset. Émile had constantly teased me about wanting to view my masterpiece – never in my wildest dreams did I think he would actually get to see me wear it.

I slipped into the bodice. It took a yogalike contortion for me to tie the laces up my back, but it fit perfectly. The weight from the beads made it feel a bit like armor. The short skirt of dangling bead strands and ostrich feathers fit high on my waist and showed off my legs, over which I pulled on a pair of shimmery nude tights. My feet tapped to the drums as the DJ played "Iko," and all of the candles in the room lit up as I sang along.

For inspiration, I opened my father's art history book and flipped the pages until I found the painting *Absinthe Drinker* by Viktor Oliva.

I swept a large makeup brush over my face, leaving a trail of sparkles down my chest, shoulders and arms until my skin reflected light like a disco ball. Black mascara. Shiny peach lip-gloss. Finally, I piled my waves on top of my head, secured them with strategically placed bobby pins, and inserted a large green plume into the crown of twists. I couldn't help think of Isaac as I gave the silky feather a quick stroke.

Now, for the *pièce de résistance*.

The wings were simple cuts of iridescent chiffon that attached to a choker around my neck and hung down my back like a shimmering cape. The ends attached to my wrists so they blew open when I raised my arms.

I stood in front of the mirror and blinked a few times, barely recognizing myself. I felt beautiful. My heart thumped, realizing I was about to play the most dangerous role of my life.

I hoped the lavish costume wasn't my death shroud.

The clear plastic, Barbie-esque shoes I had bought in Paris certainly weren't going to work for tonight, so I wriggled on my worn high-tops, laughing.

"Désirée is not going to approve," I said to my reflection. "*C'est la vie.*"

I tucked the *gris-gris* and Adeline's necklace into my cleavage and blew out the candles, ready to leave.

"The stake!" I yelped, running to my nightstand. A surge of strength traveled through my arms to my shoulders as soon as I retrieved the metal object from the drawer.

Again, its weight felt powerful in my hand, but this time I recognized something else. A familiarity.

The enchantment.

Adeline.

With nowhere else to put it, I tucked the metal through the laces of my corset, and then made sure I could easily grab it through my wings.

For what might be the last time, my keys flew into my hand. I paused and then set them back into the bowl. I didn't need them anymore.

INSTEAD OF GOING STRAIGHT THROUGH THE GATE to the courtyard, I waved my hand over the front door to unlock it and walked through the old bar my grandfather had opened so many moons ago. So many of my childhood memories were set in this bar: an eight-year-old me doing my French lessons with my legs dangling from a bar stool; ol' Madame Villere telling me about the birds and the bees when I was nine (and my father subsequently freaking out on the crazy bat); listening to Cajun plantation tales from Ren; hearing about the healing powers of crystals from Wiccans; Caulfield Mooney sneaking me sips of Scotch to cure my junior high coughs. *Could tonight really be my last night at Le Chat Noir?* I suddenly felt all grown up.

I made my way to the back door, pushed through the overgrown banana-tree leaves, and crossed the courtyard to the stairs of the *garçonnière*. In the third-floor ballroom, I found my father standing behind the makeshift bar and transferring clear liquid from plastic jugs into empty gin bottles.

"I'm not even going to ask," I said as I approached, pretending I didn't know what he was doing.

"It's really best you don't." He smiled and shook his head without looking up.

I suppose it had been unfair to hold my father to telling me everything when I was keeping so much from him – but I was just trying to protect him. I guess he was just trying to protect me too. He secured the large jug to a funnel and finally turned to me. His eyes bulged like a cartoon's.

"What are you wearing?"

"*La Fée Verte.* My costume!" I whirled around. "I'm the Green Faery!"

"I know what you are; I'm a bar owner, for Christ's sake!" He held his head. "My sixteen-year-old daughter is dressed up as a hallucinogenic."

I took that as a compliment and twirled around a few more times with exaggerated glee. "Well, you did raise me in a bar and ship me off to Paris at sixteen." I was finally getting my payback.

"Why does it have to be so short? You look twenty-five!"

"Stop, Dad! You are going to make me self-conscious."

"Good, then maybe you will put some pants on."

"Dad!"

Before he could protest further, the door opened, and Désirée walked in with an even shorter plaid skirt, braided pigtails, and a white button-down shirt tied at her waist, cropping her stomach.

"Oh, lord," my father said with a slap to the head. "I know your father didn't let you leave the house in that."

Before she could answer, our third wailed through the door. "Macalister!" Isaac carried a tangle of black curls.

"I don't envy you tonight, son," my father said, shaking his head. "You are going to have your hands full."

"You have no idea," I murmured under my breath.

Isaac didn't say anything.

"Pick your jaw up off the floor, Isaac," my father said sternly.

"Sorry, Mac." With rosy cheeks, he turned and greeted me and Désirée.

"Is the bathroom locked?" Désirée asked, patting a tiny backpack. "I need to do finishing touches."

"I'll show you the one downstairs," my father answered. "The one up here is officially hazardous, thanks to termites." They walked off, my father pleading with her to unroll her skirt, and I was left alone with Isaac. My stomach jerked.

I would never have admitted it to him, but he looked hot in his simple get-up: black leather pants with a matching vest over a fitted white V-neck. A few strands of hair fell to his chin from his usual nub of a ponytail. We looked at each other awkwardly, but neither of us said anything.

He pulled a long red silk scarf from his pocket and hung it around his neck. I opened my mouth to guess who he was, but he held up his hand. "Wait." He bent over, flipped the wig onto his head, and tied back the long, synthetic curls with the scarf.

"Oh my God, you're REN!"

"Yeah." He tried to say something Cajun, but he couldn't stop laughing.

"It's amazing!" I yelped, throwing my arms around his neck, catching us both off guard.

"No, you're amazing..." the words came out with the utmost sincerity as he lifted me off the ground.

I loosened my grip around his shoulders, but he didn't move his arms from around my waist, and I dangled against his chest for a moment. "You look beautiful," he whispered before letting me slowly slide down.

"*Merci beaucoup.*" I felt every inch blush from my neck up. "I made it while I was in Paris."

"You're obviously really talented."

"Too talented." My father cleared his throat as he walked back into the room.

We jumped apart.

"Dad, Isaac is Ren!"

"I spent all morning trying to find the wig, so I didn't have time to hunt down a ruffly shirt."

"Where did you get leather pants?" I asked, casually trying to create a little more distance between us by leaning on the bar.

"They're mine!" my dad said, laughing as he walked behind the counter.

I groaned. "You have leather pants? This is something I could have lived without knowing."

"What do you think I wore to all of those Bowie concerts back in the day?"

"Who are you supposed to be?" Isaac asked, leaning on the bar next to me. "Tinkerbell?"

"Not exactly."

My father reluctantly grabbed a bottle of green liquid from his secret hiding place and slid it across the bar to Isaac.

"Whoa, absinthe. Is this the real stuff?" he asked my dad and shot a smile at me, now understanding my comment from last night.

My father leaned over and grabbed it back. "Don't even think about it." He looked at the both of us.

"You do realize that no one is going to get your costume?" Désirée said to me, walking back into the room with a compact mirror in front of her face.

"You need to spend a little more time downtown, Dee," I said.

"Everyone in the Quarter is going to get it," my father agreed.

"Besides, that's the least of my concerns at this point," I mumbled, my nerves starting to fire up.

"Who are you supposed to be, Dee?" asked Isaac. "Catholic schoolgirl? Very original."

The look of death she shot him was way scarier than her normal ones. She must have just put in red contact lenses. "*Sexy* Catholic schoolgirl." She slowly opened her mouth into a sly smile, revealing two enlarged, pointy canines.

She lunged at him, hissing.

"Isaac!" I screamed as they crashed to the floor. Désirée landed on top of him and buried her face in his neck. I grabbed her shoulders, trying to pull her off, and she burst out laughing. I fell back to the floor as she spit the two fake teeth into her palm.

"Désirée Borges, cracking a joke," I said in between deep breaths. "Maybe today really is the day of reckoning."

"I am *so* gonna get you back for that, witch," Isaac warned as he took a deep breath of his own and gently pushed Désirée up to her feet.

"I'd like to see you try." She smoothed out her costume and carefully reinserted her fangs. "I hope you are more ready than that tonight, feather boy."

My father shook his head at us, trying not to laugh at Isaac, who was now adjusting his wig.

"Please be careful tonight, honey. All the loons will be out with a vengeance."

"*Oui*... We're counting on it."

"Isaac, I'm holding you responsible. I'm tempted to give you a baseball bat so you can keep the boys away from these two."

"DAD!"

"I'm serious. Be safe." He kissed my forehead, grabbed the empty jugs, and walked out of the room with a glittered mouth.

I led the way out through the corridor. "Y'all ready for this?" I asked over my shoulder as we began to descend the stairs.

"Can we get some food first?" Isaac answered.

I turned to him. "How could you possibly eat before… you know?"

"How could you *not* eat at a time like this?"

"You're such a guy."

"Actually, food is probably not a bad idea." Désirée patted her potion-clanking bag with a fangy grin as we stepped into the courtyard. "These are going to be pretty strong."

"*Bonsoir, Adele.*"

The three of us whipped forward to find Sébastien and Jeanne standing near the old dormant fountain. Our anxiety-ridden laughs quickly faded.

"*Bonsoir*!" I said, surprised. They were the last people I'd expected to see tonight. I ran over and kissed both of Sébastien's cheeks. When I moved towards Jeanne, she wouldn't even look me in the eyes.

"You look *magnifique*," he said, overcompensating for his sister's silence. "*Tu est envoûtante.*"

"Watch out. She's leaving a trail of glitter behind." Isaac raised his sparkling arm.

"We're here to see your father," Jeanne said in a way that sliced right through me.

"Oh… *d'accord.*"

"He's helping us organize the funeral arrangements," Sébastien explained.

Jeanne looked at my two new friends and then back to me, apparently confused by the kindred vibe. "Double, double toil and trouble." Only Jeanne Michel could insult someone by quoting Shakespeare.

"Fire burn, and caldron bubble," I finished with a meek smile, not knowing a better way to comfort her.

"Maybe the three of you can go as Macbeth's witches next year?" she said sharply. "Where have you been, Adele? Too busy making Halloween costumes?"

"*S'il te plaît sois gentille,*" Sébastien pleaded with her.

And then I witnessed something I had never seen before – Jeanne started to cry. Even though her expression remained cold, fast streams of tears suddenly poured down her cheeks and rolled off her chin.

"*Désolée!*" I whispered as my eyes welled.

She pushed past me and ran up the stairs. Before I could go after her, Sébastien grabbed my arm and whispered in French, "Don't listen to her. She's still in shock—"

"*Elle a raison,*" I said. "You have no idea how right she is."

"What do you mean?"

"Nothing. *De rien.*"

He looked to Isaac and Désirée and back to me. Sébastien might not have been the beat-someone-up, big-brother type, but he was way too intelligent *not* to know something was up. Jeanne was too distraught to be thinking rationally; otherwise she, too, would have realized something was awry.

"Have fun at the parade," Sébastien said to the three of us.

"You should come out later tonight," I said. "Maybe it will take your mind off things for a little while." Those were the words I said, but what I meant was, "Can you please stay in a very public, very crowded place for the rest of the night?"

39

fight or flight

We headed over to Bourbon Street and only had to wait in line for ten minutes before snagging the corner booth at the candlelit Clover Grill. I never thought I'd be happy to wait in line for a table, but it was a sign of life coming back to the city.

A waiter I hadn't seen since before the Storm greeted us loudly as Isaac and I slid in into the booth across from Désirée. It was always a letdown to miss Blanche's shift, but this guy had that happy-to-no-longer-be-displaced glow. For tonight's festivities, he wore a teased beehive wig with a fake, bloodied nutria rat nestled into it.

"Is Blanche off?" I asked.

"She's gettin' into character, baby. You'll find her on the royal float tonight. Queen of this Hallow's Eve."

"Rat's nest." Isaac laughed. "Nice one."

Our waiter posed for a second, with the *je ne sais quoi* that occurs in New Orleans when someone *gets* your costume. This moment could happen on Halloween, Mardi Gras, any of the other two dozen holidays that require masquerading, or really, just any Saturday night in the French Quarter.

"And what can I get the Green Faery?"

I didn't miss the opportunity to shoot Désirée a gloating smile.

"I'm not really hungry," I told him. Giant crawfish pinchers seemed to have taken hold of my stomach.

Désirée took a small vial from her bag and waved it around, reminding me that I'd shortly have to consume something nasty. Our waiter gave us a *those-crazy-kids-and-their-drugs* headshake.

"It's part of the costume," I explained, grabbing the vial. The last thing I needed was for gossip about me taking drugs to get back to my father. Gossip that would falsely explain my erratic behavior as of late and get me grounded for life.

"Mm… hmm," he hummed. "Addie, you aren't gonna wanna take a pass today. We got two boxes of frozen patties this morning."

"What? Actual meat!"

"You can beat our prices, but you can't beat our meat!"

"I'll take the lot!" I yelled. Everyone laughed. "Okay, you twisted my arm. I'll take a patty melt."

"We don't got all that. How 'bout patty, with egg on toast?"

"We'll take three," Désirée said, eager to get on with it.

"Four," corrected Isaac.

We all looked at him.

"What? I said I was hungry."

Once our waiter was back behind the counter, performing with the spatula (it was a common theme here), Dee said, "Drink that now. I have no idea how long it will take to kick in."

"What is it?" I asked, examining the small bottle of midnight-blue liquid. Little flecks of silver dotted the viscous substance, creating the effect of a star-swept sky.

"*That* is the Heightening Elixir," she replied, as if no further explanation was necessary.

"It's going to make her grow?" asked Isaac with sarcasm.

She rolled her eyes. "No. It's going to heighten all of her senses. And ours." She slid a duplicate bottle to Isaac, and turned back to me. "Please be careful, Adele. I'm hesitant to dose you because you're already *so* emotional."

"What do you mean, heighten our senses?" I asked, ignoring the dig.

"The spell is going to increase all of your natural abilities – your strength, your speed, and whatever else it is you do. But it will also increase the strength of your emotions. Happiness, hate, whatever – you'll be extra susceptible to it all. So, ya know, just watch it." Her eyes bopped between me and Isaac. "I don't know how long it's going to last, but this is a super-concentrated batch, so at least until midnight. You'll probably feel some kind of lingering effect until tomorrow morning. Maybe longer."

"So, that's how you knocked me to the floor earlier," Isaac said.

"Ha, you wish." She smirked and pulled a third serving out for herself. "Bottoms up!" she cheersed as our tiny bottles clanked together.

I tilted the little glass back and waited for the contents to slowly seep out and coat the back of my throat. My hand slapped my mouth as I forced myself to gulp the bitterness.

"Gross," Isaac said, shaking his head like he had just done a shot of tequila.

Other than the acidic taste lingering on my tongue, I didn't feel any different. "So, that's it?" I asked. "We just hope that the symmetry of this plan holds up and that the elixir will heighten our senses right as the wormwood potion disrupts theirs?"

"Pretty much," Désirée answered. "But a symmetric balance would be a dream scenario. Don't get overconfident because of the elixir. It's going to give you a boost, but you won't have anywhere near the strength of a vampire – not even with the wormwood."

"So no arm-wrestling contests?" Isaac joked.

Désirée looked at him blankly.

My mind lingered on the problem of their strength.

"The *Artemisia Absinthium* is totally unpredictable. Assuming they *all* drink the moonshine, the spell will affect each of them differently, depending on how much they drank and how susceptible they are. At a minimum, they'll start hallucinating and find their strength and speed muted because the connection between their minds and bodies has been compromised. In the best-case scenario, the ones that drank the most will experience a kind of berserk effect on their nervous and immune systems."

"I wonder how long it's been since any of those bloodsuckers have felt pain?" Isaac said with a little glee. "I don't mind taking a hit or two if it means I get to see the shock on their faces when I hit back."

I hesitated before asking the next question. "But… the potion's not going to *hurt* them, right?"

They both gave me a funny look.

"I'm… I'm just worried about my dad. Since he's inadvertently become the potion dealer."

"It won't hurt them," Désirée said. "It'll just give them the trip of a lifetime."

"Don't stress," said Isaac. "Mac's going to be fine. I'll have them in the attic long before they even make the connection between their hallucinations and the moonshine."

I didn't even like hearing the words "Mac's going to be fine" because that meant there *was* a possibility that he might not be.

Désirée pulled four candles out of her bag. This might have seemed weird anywhere else, but carrying candles in your purse was a normal thing 'round these parts post-Storm. "Don't light them," she instructed me as she unscrewed the cap on the saltshaker. She circled her arm around her head, allowing the salt to pour out behind the booth, and then handed Isaac the shaker.

I shrugged when he looked to me, and then he mimicked Désirée's motion, and I completed the circle, emptying out the remaining grains.

Next, Désirée placed a full glass of water in front of the empty seat next to her, put a large crystal next to the candles, and strung a long vine of ivy around her neck

"What else ya got in there, Mary Poppins?" I joked nervously.

Isaac tried not to snicker.

Désirée ignored us and grabbed Isaac's hand.

My pulse picked up. *Is this really the most appropriate place to be doing this?* I looked around – the old diner was dimly lit with candles, patrons were yelling over the blaring music, and everyone in the place looked like freaks in costume. There was less of a chance being noticed here than in Vodou Pourvoyeur.

"What are we doing?" Isaac asked.

"Casting a circle for protection. To pool our magic and activate the elixir. And more importantly, to bind us. We'll be stronger together." Désirée took my left hand. "Hang onto your horses, kids; we're about to be a legit coven."

Isaac conceded and took my right hand.

"Close your eyes and concentrate, just like we practiced last night." She took a deep breath and began to murmur indecipherable words. Through one cracked eyelid, I watched the candles spark until all the wicks burned bright.

"Repeat after me: Let all who enter the circle of the casquette girls and all of our lineage under your guidance do so in perfect love and perfect trust, Mother Earth, we invoke you."

Warmth began to swell from their hands to mine. We repeated the verse with her again and again, until her words turned back into gibberish. Energy radiated through my veins, causing the beads on my costume to ripple as the warmth spread to my chest and neck and then to the back of my head.

Static broke up the radio waves. Isaac squeezed my hand.

I felt all the candle flames in the room flicker as we repeated the last lines of the incantation faster and faster. The coffee mugs on top of the espresso machine rattled. The booth trembled. I tried to contain myself, but a small gasp escaped my lips as I absorbed the supernatural essence. My eyes popped open.

"Wahoo! I love bein' home!" came a cry from the grill, which in turn got a receptive roar from the room of patrons.

Around us, everything looked as normal as normal gets on Bourbon Street.

And so the casquette girls coven was re-awoken at the Clover Grill on All Hallow's Eve, the year of the Storm. The three of us exchanged smiles, and my nerves slowly began to subside. *I can do this. We can do this together.*

Or maybe it's just the elixir talking?

"Don't remove your *gris-grises,*" Désirée continued, as if we hadn't just caused something totally freaky to happen. "My gran might look old and quiet, but she's, like, as high up as high priestesses go – so those protective amulets are as good as it gets in this town."

My hand rested on my chest where the little satchel lay beneath the glitz of sequins.

"Four patties," said Rat's Nest as he dropped the plates onto the table.

The glorious smell of grill-marked beef encased us, and I was immediately grateful Désirée had changed my mind about ordering. The very first swallow of previously frozen protein felt like a sponge absorbing the tidal wave of anxiety crashing in my stomach. I eagerly took a second mouthful. Dee spit out her fangs and munched her sandwich with the small, controlled bites of a supermodel, smiling with verve, and Isaac grabbed his second patty before he had finished his first, making us both laugh. Then for a few minutes, the only sounds coming from our table were the rustles of napkins wiping grease-dripped chins.

But, as the last bits of crust disappeared, the vibe became heavier, and I knew the same question weighed on all of our minds: *Is this our last supper?*

"*Merci beaucoup,* Dee, for everything," the words flew out of my mouth in a garble.

"I don't think you need any more stimulants." She pushed my coffee cup away. I grabbed one more sip of my *café au lait* before relinquishing my mug to her.

"You ready?" she asked me.

"*Laissez les bon temps rouler.*"

THE DOOR DINGED as we exited onto a sunset-pink-hued Bourbon Street.

Despite the confrontation to come, I couldn't help but feel happiness at the sight of people lollygagging. The post-Storm haze was enlivened by the brewing energy coming from folks in brightly colored costumes.

"I wonder if they're going to try to enforce the curfew tonight?" Isaac asked.

Désirée and I laughed in response. He raised one eyebrow.

"You've never been to a parade in New Orleans," I explained. "The cops are going to have many a thing to enforce tonight before they get around to the curfew. Plus, if everything goes according to plan, they can count on *extra* mayhem tonight."

Désirée smiled in agreement.

"All right, everyone's dosed. We bound our circle. Time for me to head back to the shop so I can start casting those protection spells Marassa and Susannah used three centuries ago."

My pulse began to race, and my chest tightened as Désirée continued, "I'll hold off as long as possible activating the *Artemisia Absinthium* so they don't suspect anything too soon."

I turned to Isaac. He had the hardest job… provoking the vampires to chase him into the attic. "Are you sure you're okay with this, Isaac? It's so dangerous."

"Maybe the leather pants were a bad idea?" he joked, pretending to stretch his leg.

An image of Gabriel ripping into Lisette's throat flashed through my mind.

"Hey," he said, looking at me. "Me pissing off the Medici clan enough to get them to chase me is the only part of this plan that's guaranteed to work."

Désirée scoffed, but then said, "True. You do have that effect on people."

"All right, I'll be waiting on the convent roof," I said. "You better fly out of that window fast."

I tried to give him a smile so he couldn't tell how nervous I was to have his life in my hands.

Breathe.

Isaac cracked his knuckles.

Désirée strapped on her miniature backpack of witchy goodies. "I'll see you at the rendezvous point when it's done," she said, just as sure about our victory as she was that the entire senior class wanted to take her to the homecoming dance. "And Adele, if you see Gabriel tonight, kick him in the balls for me."

"Will do."

Isaac cringed. With a cock of her hip, Désirée took off before we could have any kind of coven-bonding moment.

"How does she do it?" I asked. "She looks like such a badass."

"She does look like she was born to slay vampires."

I tensed up. He noticed.

An awkward silence crept over us as we realized we had been left alone. Possibly for the last time.

"Oh, I have something for you!" I pulled the chain from my bodice and started to unlatch the silver feather. "I think you dropped it on our steps that day we were figh—"

He wrapped his fingers around my hand. "No need."

"Why?"

"Because I made it for you."

"You did? Why?"

"Adele, are you kidding me? You are the girl of my dreams. *Literally.* I almost had a heart attack the first time I saw you through the window of Café Orléans. Watching you make coffee all those days… I thought I had entered some kind of alternate universe in New Orleans."

My cheeks burned, but my eyes didn't move from his. "I think you kind of did."

"I think you're right."

"Um, can I get that on record, please?"

"Plus, I like seeing you donned in feathers." He dragged his fingers across my ostrich skirt, sending shivers up my spine. Only then did I realize how many feathers I was wearing. "Even if it's just for tonight," he quickly added.

The plume atop my head swayed as I nodded, unable to get even a thank you out.

He gently brushed the glitter on my cheek. "You ready?"

I nodded again. "I'll see you when it's over," I said, beginning to get nervous. "Promise me you won't do anything too stupid?"

He slowly nodded, and we both turned in opposite directions into the thin crowd.

I got four steps away when my arm was jerked back.

Isaac pulled me into his chest, wrapping his arms around me.

His forehead gently knocked into mine. I took a deep inhale of his musky scent and committed his warmth to memory. My heart pounded wildly, reminding me what it meant to be alive.

"I really, really want to kiss you, Miss Adele Le Moyne. One of those epic just-in-case-it's-our-last-chance kisses."

"But that would be like sealing our fate."

"Exactly."

"So, then let's get out of this alive, okay?"

"I promise we will."

Blood rushed to my cheeks, remembering the magic of our first kiss – something I hadn't allowed myself to think about because of a certain *Italiano*. Isaac tilted my head and kissed my temple. The touch of his lips nearly made sparks fly from my fingers. *Is it the effect of the elixir?* We parted a second time, both wearing my glitter.

A surge of confusion hit me as I feverishly walked towards my post. *Am I really going to die tonight? As a sixteen-year-old virgin with only one passport stamp and no driver's license?* My breathing picked up, and I was shocked to find myself wishing I had kissed Isaac. *What if that really had been our last chance?* I spun around. There was still time. He couldn't have gotten that far. My neck craned as I rushed back through the thickening crowd to find him. But I slowed when he came into my sightline. He was shaking hands with a dark-haired guy, and he didn't seem happy about their agreement, whatever it was.

The guy turned to leave, and I abruptly halted.

Niccolò.

"What the hell?"

My feet flipped back around, and I quickly walked away. *They hate each other!* My wings whipped behind me as I gained speed. *What could they possibly have been agreeing on? And tonight of all nights?*

All morning, I had wanted nothing more than to hunt Nicco down so we could watch his stupid art-house film, limbs intertwined. *If I had to restrain myself from fraternizing with the enemy, then what was Isaac doing with him?*

When I got to my turn, I just kept walking straight, all the way down Bourbon to Esplanade, and then continued straight out of the French Quarter. I felt an immediate sense of relief when I crossed the neutral ground of the avenue I knew *they* couldn't cross.

I didn't stop until I got to NOSA. No progress had been made on the campus since the last time I had been there, but the familiarity brought a slight sense of calm. It was too difficult to sit in my costume, so I lay on a patch of grass underneath the ballerina.

Deep breaths went through my nose and gushed out of my mouth. After a few more tries, I felt more in control. *How the hell did I get into this? How is this my life?*

All signs pointed to the Storm.

I wondered what would happen if I just kept walking… out of the Marigny, through the Bywater, out of Orleans Parish. *Surely someone would pick up a sparkling hitchhiker? Could I make it on my own? In some new town? Away from all of this…* I opened my eyes and stared up at the changing sky. The sun was almost completely gone, which meant the vampires would soon come out to play. One of them already had. Goose bumps invaded my flesh.

I stood, brushing grass from my skirt.

Who am I kidding? My heart and soul is in this place. *They* need to leave. The vampires. And currently, there were only two ways to make that happen.

Kill them all, or close Pandora's Box.

A flame rose from my hand so I could take one last look at the Mardi Gras-masked statue. I envied her anonymity.

I hovered the flame over the ends of the thin metal mask, heating it just enough so I could pop it off.

"I'll return it later, promise."

I pulled one of the extra laces from my corset bow and used it to tie the disguise over my eyes.

When I looked up through the mask, I found my mother staring back at me, perfectly re-created in bronze.

What?

She had been hidden by a mask.

Frozen in time.

With me all of these years.

I had never known the ballerina was modeled after her.

Could anyone ever love someone as much as my father loved my mother?

40

night of la fée verte

I RAN BACK TOWARDS THE QUARTER. And when I say ran, I mean *ran.*

Like all magic, the elixir felt wholly natural and utterly unnatural at the same time. The effects were physically instinctual, but shocking to my psyche: the amount of weight my muscles could handle, the speed my legs could carry me, the depth of my vision. Every tree root splitting the sidewalk became an obstacle as my mind struggled to keep up with the supercharge.

I slowed down and paused from the sprint, bending over my knees to give my lungs a minute to catch up. The head-rush was exhilarating. When I waved my hand in front of my face, my eyes had trouble following the blur of motion.

In the next few minutes that all changed, too. My vision became sharper, and the pounding of the distant bass drums felt like they were deep in the pit of my stomach instead of half a mile away.

Is being a vampire like this? Times ten?

As I continued the trek back through the Marigny, my internal systems synched, my coordination became more natural, and my confidence grew. The music pulsed louder into the fresh dark of the night, and the scenery whipped by as if someone had hit the fast-forward button. A soft, billowy material hit my face. I stopped mid-stride, nearly wiping out.

"What the…?" I was surrounded by hanging fabric.

I waved my hand with the intention of bringing a small flicker of light from my finger, but a giant flame shot from my hand, setting one of the flowing linens ablaze. The light showed a sea of ghosts surrounding me. *So, this is what everyone in Ren's hood had been prepping their sheets for.* I strained my neck, looking up at the floating heads, which had been crudely made by stuffing tufts of newsprint in the center of the linens and tying them off with twine. They were strung across the useless power lines, creaking, dancing in the breeze.

The fire quickly flamed out, and the ashes of the singed ghost blew away into the damp night. I carried on my way.

The closer I got to the Quarter, the more of them there were: hundreds, thousands of ghosts casting oblong shadows, backlit by the tin-can fires in the street, the tiki torches on lawns, and the altars of candles on porches. Weaving in between them, faster and faster, I became paranoid by the shifting shadows. I pushed one sheet away only for another to fall in my face. Drowning in a river of ghosts, I broke into a sprint.

At the end of the street, I halted under a large spray-painted banner made from a molding quilt.

Blessed are the unnamed souls lost in the Storm.
You will never be forgotten.
Rest in Peace

I choked back tears, turning back to the army of ghouls floating under the moon. There were so many of them. Death. Death was everywhere. My own mortality suddenly became very comprehensible.

Am I really prepared to die tonight? My chest tightened, and my throat closed. I remembered Désirée's warning and threw my arms over my head, telling myself that the anxiety attack was just an effect of the elixir.

Breathe.

My chest loosened.

I began to move again through more ghosts, but this new batch was less anonymous. These were painted and adorned with scarves, Spanish moss, and photos, almost as if they were life-sized Voodoo dolls. They had descriptions and birth dates.

They were no longer unnamed.

I could feel a crying fit coming on, so I sped through the open-air homage, promising to come back later to pay my respects.

WITH ONE MORE TURN, I stumbled upon the *Krewe de Boo,* dressed in what might have been the most shocking costumes I had ever seen in my years of parading: every single man, woman, and child was sporting their Sunday best. I had gone from a river of ghosts to a sea of suits.

What planet am I on?

Feeling like I might have accidentally passed through some kind of vortex, I tapped the back of a man in a tawny tweed. "Sir, what exactly is this year's theme?"

He turned around, and I let out a short scream at the sight of his milky white eyeballs and rotting flesh. He buckled over with laughter, and I was back to breathing exercises.

"We're Marching on Washington tonight," he said, pointing to his float: a giant papier-mâché Capitol Hill, which peaked in a very, er, mocking manner. Their satirical response to the government's recovery efforts made my smile slip out. I gave him two thumbs up and moved on.

The marching crowd might have looked unusually corporate, but the noises of revelry reeled with familiarity. My soul sponged up the trumpets, trombones, and resonant tones of the tuba as if this was the last time I would hear them. There were so many things about this parade that were out of the ordinary, it was hard not to gawk. Instead of mule-hitched wagons, each float had been constructed from a Storm-destroyed car, truck, or boat whose top had been chopped off. Two long poles protruded from the sides, with drones of stiff-limbed zombies standing by to manually push them down the parade route. A short line of horses 'n buggies waited to carry the local celebrities who had made it back to New Orleans. Partially returned dance troupes clicked their fringed tap-boots and flipped batons to entertain the crowds. There was a twinge of lighter fluid in the air. I had never seen the Flambeaux out for any occasion other than Mardi Gras, but tonight the torchbearers were dancing wildly in the streets with their heavy flaming poles, and not accepting so much as a penny from the crowd for lighting the way.

The only things missing were the tourists, of which there were none. This was truly a night of celebration for locals, who were starting to pack the street, singing, dancing and shouting for the parade to start.

Through the mask, I watched the costumes become more crass and more nonexistent, until they were not much more than fishnets, pasties, neckties, and gobs of ghoulish makeup. I paused to laugh at a kissing couple dressed as a witch and a vampire. *Beh,* I thought, just as a hand grabbed my shoulder. Before I could protest, a second hand grabbed my arm and hoisted me into the air. Almost as soon as I started to kick, I was back on my feet, on top of the royal float.

"Your chariot, *Mademoiselle*," yelled Blanche, holding her hand out to the converted swamp boat.

"At your service, *ma chérie*." The king took a deep bow.

"Ren! Is that you?" His hair was slicked back and tucked. And with fake glasses, loafers, and a pocket square, he looked weirdly normal.

"Watch this!" he said, and pointed a large gold scepter towards the sky. A blast of funny money and doubloons whooshed out over the crowd, who instantly roared and scavenged the treasure in a melodramatic style.

"My King," said Blanche duGovernor, Queen of the Dead, as she placed a gold-sprayed crown made out of banged-up soup cans and chicken wire on top of Ren's head. Her own tiara of spoons was nestled in a tall bouffant wig that mocked the governor's outdated hairdo. Blanche was also nearly unrecognizable in pumps and a bulging fake ass underneath a red skirt suit. Only her signature glitter-swept eyelids remained in her usual style. "My little Addie," she shrieked, "I could just eat you up!"

"Or drink 'er up!" chimed Ren, laughing at his own joke.

"Hold this, baby," Blanche yelled, handing me a roll of wide red ribbon. She held the other end and twirled around. The crowd began to cheer as she became mummified.

"Ha!" I yelled. "Amazing!"

"I'm gonna die caught up in this red tape, baby!"

Behind the royal couple was a giant papier-mâché bobble head of the president, whose approval rating was non-resuscitable after the way he had handled the national emergency.

"How do you like our krewe of stiffs?" asked Ren.

"Pun intended?"

"Triple pun!" His eyes led me to the giant phallic symbols capping the pushing poles.

"Got it!" I was now thankful for the mask. "Everything is awesome!" I yelled. "How did you know it was me?" I gave my mask a quick flip.

"Honey, I've known you since you were born."

"Besides, who else would be running around the Marigny Triangle in couture and those nasty sneakers?" replied Blanche.

"Ha!"

"*Bébé*, you're all grown up! I'm getting a little teary." Ren gave me another twirl, and a breeze kicked up my wispy wings.

The float jerked forward.

"Ren, I need to get down! The parade is starting!" The words choked me, knowing that this might be the last time I ever saw him.

"You aren't going anywhere," Blanche yelled, pulling me back. "You're our little princess!"

Police sirens blared, and the drum major's whistle shrilled out the tempo for the marching band.

"Heave-ho!" roared the crowd, and the wheels jolted forward as the zombie krewe pushed the old swamp boat onward.

"Wave to your constituents," Blanche instructed, maneuvering one of her forearms from the tape to do her best impression of the Queen of England. The mask gave me enough anonymity to stand tall before the debaucherous throng.

High on the madness, I felt strangely like a princess.

The bleak populous of New Orleans squealed with schoolchild delight as the crowd of zombie drones pushed through them. I'd never stood in a parade before, nor had I imagined how fun throwing Tootsie Rolls at familiar faces would be. Maybe it was the times, or maybe Désirée had activated the wormwood, but everyone seemed extra crazy, or extra loaded, as they staggered about, pointing at things in the air.

Pointing at me.

Suddenly something knocked me off balance, and I nearly fell backwards – without the boost of the elixir, I would have. Esplanade Avenue. But this time it wasn't just a warble as we crossed the neutral ground to those old streets of the *Vieux Carré*; the protection ward was significantly stronger than before, which meant Dee was on track and should be passing the baton on to Isaac soon.

Ren wavered in place, mumbling, "I knew I shouldn't have sampled any of that moonshine."

"It's going to be a wild night," I said, to which he cried, "*Laissez les bons temps rouler!*" as if we were riding into battle.

We kind of were riding into battle. At least, I was.

As he continued to hoot and holler, my peripheral vision caught sight of a lonely figure on the street corner. Sébastien's face glowed pale under the light of a flood lamp that had been set up on the neutral ground. As the float passed him, I ran to the edge, clasped his hand, and yanked him onboard. The crowd cheered as the momentum nearly knocked us to the bottom of the boat, but I managed to hold us both steady.

"Adele, how did you do that?" he asked in disbelief, pushing his black glasses up the bridge of his nose.

"Do what?" I yelled, overjoyed to see him.

"You just lifted me into the air!"

Remembering the elixir, I scrambled. "Adrenaline!" But I could tell he was already mentally calculating weight, leverage, and torque.

I looked into his baby blues and felt a swell of happiness in my chest. My expression seemed to make him forget about the illogical occurrence and return my smile. Before I knew it, my arms were wrapped around him, awkwardly smushing his elbows against his sides. He turned pink as I rested my head on the side of his shoulder and yelled, "*Je'taime!*" squeezing him harder than I should have been able to. I couldn't help it; it was as if love was actually radiating from my arms.

"*Moi aussi, je t'aime, mon chou,*" he said, baffled, but he squeezed his left arm out from underneath mine and rubbed my shoulder.

Then the emotions swung, and I felt overwhelmingly sad. *I had killed Sébastien's grandparents. Jeanne is going to hate me forever. Forever might only be the next few hours...* The thought of never seeing the twins again became too much to bear. Concern washed over Sébastien's face; he unlatched my arms and turned me to face him.

"Adele, are you okay? Are you high?"

Adele, get a grip! It's just the elixir.

When I didn't respond right away, he shook my shoulders and yelled, "Did someone give you something? I think you've been drugged."

The thought of getting caught made my heart pound. We'd come so far. "I'm not high, silly!" I slipped my hand into his and turned him outward. "Wave to the crowd!"

His shy smile crept back with the warm reception, and soon he was lost observing the chaos of the streets. That's when I saw Gabriel slowly walking through the crowd, keeping up with the float. Our gazes locked, and he eyed me like a predator who enjoyed the hunt more than the prize. My head swung to the other side of the street, and I spotted Lisette pushing through the crowd with annoyance.

I twisted around.

About fifty feet behind Gabe, was the curly-haired woman from the bar, skipping along, who, if I was adding up Adeline's history lessons correctly, was Martine Dufrense, vampire diva. I assumed the others weren't far. My heart thumped.

Not only was I surrounded, but I had pulled Sébastien into the bull's-eye. *So much for giving me until midnight.*

Jackson Square was in sight. A high school band filled the amphitheater and went into an encore. The crowd chanted out the next ominous verse as the royal court came into the final stretch.

"And when the moon turns red with blood,
Lord, how I want to be in that number..."

I leapt off the float and made a run for it.

"When the Saints go marching in"

JUST LAST NIGHT, THIS SQUARE had been a private stage for me and Isaac to juggle fireballs long after the shroud of curfew. Now, everyone back in town from the Mississippi River to Lake Pontchartrain filled it. I tried to tail Lisette's blonde locks, pushing my way through groups of drag queens, gutter punks, and suburban invaders. The elixir helped, but every person who stopped to pet my costume or yell, "It's the Green Faery!" slowed me down. Then one caused me to come to a complete halt.

"Well, aren't you just the belle of the ball?" asked Annabelle Lee Drake in the guise of Jessica Rabbit. She was a knockout in the sparkly, formfitting gown, with her deep auburn locks swept across her right eye, but her ear-to-ear grin set my nerves on edge.

Why is the Queen of Uptown giving me recognition?

Thurston looked less than pleased to be dressed as Roger Rabbit. It still blew my mind how Annabelle so easily controlled everyone and every situation she came into contact with. The world just bowed down to her. Sexy Cop and Sexy Robber stood on her right, and Sexy Cowgirl on her left. Most of the lacrosse team was sneaking beers behind them, and the freshmen Little Sisters (a gamut of sexy) completed the group.

Everyone was looking at me, waiting for a response.

"Have you seen Désirée?" I asked, knowing full well they hadn't.

"Funny, I was about to ask you the same thing," Annabelle said. "I just texted both of you."

"Oh, sorry. Left my phone at home." I held up my hands in innocence. "No pockets."

"Don't you think Tinkerbell is a little childish?" asked Dixie.

I tried not to imagine myself clawing her eyes out. It didn't work. "I'm gonna go and look for her. I'll be back in a bit."

"No way. We're going to Le Chat Noir," said Annabelle.

Voilà. Rick must have cracked down on fake IDs, and now she needed me to get them in. And she was not happy about needing me. She forced a smile, which made me want to vomit on her Jimmy Choos.

"Umm..." I squirmed, frantically scanning the crowd for a glimpse of Lisette's head, trying not to panic over losing her. "I kind of have plans—"

"You can bring your friends!" Bri yelped like a little lapdog.

"You should definitely bring your friends," echoed Jaime before they both burst into giggles.

"Maybe we can meet up with you later." *At the rate I'm going, I'm not even going to be alive later.*

The freshmen's eyes bugged at my act of defiance, and Annabelle's jaw clenched. She floundered for only a second, confused, and then looked straight into my eyes and repeated the proposition. Only this time it didn't sound like an invitation. For a split second I almost found myself agreeing.

"Sorry, Annabelle, next time."

She looked baffled, but more by her own faulty power of persuasion than my defiance. "So, it looks like you really are the Queen of

Downtown." Her hand touched my shoulder in a gesture of false surrender – an electric shock shot down my arm.

"Jesus!" we both yelled in unison, scowling at each other with suspicion.

What the hell? My eyes lingered on her as she rubbed her fingers.

"It's not about controlling their minds, *ma fifille.* It's about controlling their hearts," came a familiar French voice.

"Freak," Annabelle whispered.

I turned my head and nearly jumped out of my skin when I saw Lisette's face only inches from mine. Her usual hostile expression had dissipated, and she was staring intently at Annabelle Lee. I feared it meant she was hungry. Not that I would have minded Annabelle getting taken down a notch. Or ten.

"Holy shit, she is *hot,*" yelled one of the moronic jocks, ogling the three-hundred-year-old, sole-surviving triplet.

Jessica Rabbit fumed, turning back to them. "Shut up!"

"*Voilà,* Liz! I've been looking all over for you. We're totally going to be late for that thing everyone has been waiting *so* patiently for." I put my arm on her chilly shoulder and felt another bolt of electricity shoot up my arm. My back stiffened. "Let's go, *now,*" I said in French, turning her away from my classmates.

"Bye, Adele! I hope we see you later!" yelled a freshman dressed as a cat (a non-Sexy Cat). My Little Sis. I attempted to throw her a smile over my shoulder as I pushed Lisette away from the beehive.

I dragged her through the square, past the park, and into Pirate's Alley, alongside the Cathedral. Away from the crowds, the volume level dramatically decreased, and the sudden darkness was a little too eerie for my taste – especially while I was alone with Lisette. Soon, flames were growing from the gas lamps hanging outside a Storm-abandoned bar.

"What are you doing?" I hissed.

"*Moi!* What are *you* doing? I thought you were following me, but zhen I see you decide chatting with your friends is more important zhan saving your life? Zhe lives of your friends? Maybe you really are a Saint-Germain after all?"

"What is that supposed to mean?"

"She put all of our lives at risk!"

"*Je ne comprends pas!* What have they told you, Lise? You're supposed to be on our side! The coven's side…"

She opened her mouth to reply, and then quickly shut it.

"I know this isn't just about a curse, Lisette. Tell me what the Medicis are looking for!"

She looked past me and said in French, "I don't know. They won't tell me."

My eyes squinted in suspicion.

"Adeline never told us either. We never knew the vampires were after anything other than blood."

"Adeline wanted to protect the people of *La Nouvelle-Orleans,* the casquette girls, her coven!"

"Adeline Saint-Germain wanted to protect herself! And the count!"

Had Adeline really used the coven to do her own bidding? My instinct was to rush to Adeline's defense, but the sides were already too off-balance. I didn't want to lose Lise – not that we really had her on our side.

"Either way, would it have mattered?" I asked. "Would it have changed anything? Would you have refused to join the coven, knowing the vampires had thrown your dowry overboard so they could use your *cassette* as a sleeping coffin?"

She looked at me with surprise, and her eyes glistened with tears. "Probably not. *Non.*"

"Adeline would never have betrayed the trust of her sisters by using the coven's powers for personal gains. Other than her father, she loved the coven more than anything."

"And do you?"

"Do I what?"

"Do you trust your coven? Do you love them over all else?"

I remembered the words chanted when we called upon the spirits to bind our circle.

> "*… Let all who enter the circle of the casquette*
> *girls under your guidance do so in perfect love*
> *and perfect trust…*"

We hadn't yet had the time or circumstance to bond in the same way the original casquette girls' coven had. Nonetheless, I responded with a resounding, "*Oui.*"

"And what if it came down to your father, *ma fifille?* Would you still stand so strongly next to your friends if it meant the life of your papa?" Lisette asked slyly.

I could no longer tell if she was trying to help me or just antagonizing me. Regardless, her question shook me, and she knew it.

"Adeline was never able to give her father up—"

"I would never betray my father," I assured her.

Her slow-spreading smile felt like a noose tightening around my neck. "That's what I thought you would say, *ma fifille.* Just like her."

Then she was gone.

I tried to forget her words, but I couldn't. *Am I putting Désirée and Isaac in unwarranted danger?* It wasn't the first time the question had entered my thoughts. And then, as if my feet had minds of their own, they rerouted themselves once again. My rational side instructed them to go back towards my post on the roof, but it was like the connection between my brain and feet had gone awry. Deep inside, I knew there was only one way to ensure we got *all* of the vampires into the attic, and it didn't involve me sitting in a cozy post or using passive magic. There was only one way Nicco was going into that attic.

I TURNED ONTO ROYAL STREET and into a web of yellow police tape. The two crime scenes: Café Orleans and Saint Anthony's Garden, were only fifty feet apart. I sped up, imagining Emilio sucking the life out of the old couple and defiantly hanging the Wolfman up. As I passed St. Ann, my fingers began to tingle – someone or some*thing* was near. I moved into a defensive position just as he sped out of the alley behind the Carter brother's house. Impeccable timing, as per usual.

Nicco rushed at me, grabbed my hand while still in motion, and tried to pull me along after him. The chill from his touch swept up my arm, but my feet didn't move as easily as usual, and he ended up aggressively jerking my arm.

He stopped and let my hand drop. "I'm sorry… I didn't mean to…"

"I know."

He looked at my unnaturally sturdy (albeit shimmery) legs and then back to my face. His surprised expression made me want to do something else to show off my newfound strength, but I refrained. I needed to keep at least some element of surprise on my side.

He circled me slowly. My back stiffened.

Note to self: he is the enemy.

I suddenly felt very exposed in my scanty costume, even though I knew that wasn't why he was examining me. I tried to appear confident, although I don't know why I bothered. Never in my wildest dreams had I thought I'd meet someone whom it would be harder to lie to than my father, but Niccolò Medici managed to be that person. His constant, not-so-innocent smile made me want to melt into the floor.

And it all scared the hell out of me.

I closed my eyes and tried to visualize the two innocent students he had killed, and *not* think about the love note in the DVD. *Enemy.*

When I opened my eyes, he was looking at me with pleading concern, and I knew my feet had made the right decision by not listening to my brain. *There was no way Nicco was going to step foot in that attic unless I was there too.*

"What are you doing, *bella*?"

"What do you mean?"

"You are changing your plans."

"What?" I stammered. "I haven't changed any plans."

"You're lying." He took a step closer to me.

"How could you possibly know my plans – old or new?"

"I don't know your plans. All I know is you are lying, and you are choosing a new course."

"I thought you said vampires couldn't read minds, only bend them?" I yelled, suddenly nervous about some, er, inappropriate thoughts I may have previously had about him. About us.

"Calm down, *bella*. I can't read your mind." He smiled at the ground. "Just the arrhythmia of your heart."

I aggressively twirled a lock of hair that had escaped my up-do.

"You see, heartbeats are like fingerprints. No two are alike, but the differences are so delicate, no human ear would ever be able to hear them, no matter how powerful an instrument he had. And you… just made a decision that is making your heart shudder. And I don't like it."

"Great, so my own heart is giving me away to all of you? Could the stacks be any more *uneven*?"

"Not to all of us." He took another step closer. "It only works with someone you've made a connection with. It's like pheromones, or what humans call chemistry." He inched closer. "Only you can allow a vampire to hear your heart."

My weight shifted from one leg to the other. "And we have that connection?" I took a loud, calming breath and reminded myself to bottle my emotions since they were not fully under my control, thanks to the coven.

"You tell me, Adele. I have been able to hear the cadence of your heart ever since the night in the bell tower." *At least there was one thing I wasn't delusional about.*

"That's intense," I choked out, trying not to smile even though my heart felt like it was going to burst.

"*Si.* Although it pales in comparison to other connections…" His not-so-innocent smile escalated to *most definitely* not innocent. He touched my fingers. I jumped backwards out of fear I might start ripping off his clothes.

Mentally cursing the elixir, I rubbed away a fresh glaze of sweat from my hairline, as my mood quickly swung. "Well," I spat, "I guess none of that really matters now, seeing how I'll likely be dead in a couple hours."

"Adele, just figure out a way to break the curse. I know you can do it!"

"It's not that easy, Nicco! Especially when I don't know the full story. Which, by the way, you could readily supply—"

"I'm *trying* to protect you." He grabbed my hands. When I tried to pull them back, his grip tightened. "I am sorry if it hurts," he said, pulling me closer to him. "I really am, but I would rather you be mad at me than dead. And..."

"And what?"

"And, it's complicated. I cannot betray my family—"

"Bertrand and Sabine Michel were *my* family!"

Each of us refused to look away from the other.

"Well, isn't this just a fairy tale," I whispered.

"I know." His fingers twisted into mine. "And I am sorry this has become your battle. I tried to stop them— I *am* going to figure everything out. You just have to give me time."

"Ha! Time? The other thing your family has stolen from me." I ripped my hands away. "Tell me what you were looking for in my house the night Isaac caught you breaking and entering."

He scowled at the mention of Isaac's name. "You really should just concentrate on breaking the curse instead of digging up skeletons from days gone by. Your ignorance of the past is the only thing you have going for you."

"Oh, really?" I whispered, and a tall flame rose from my hand, lighting up his pale face like a ghost's.

He curled my fingers closed, trying to not to wince as the fire touched his hand.

"That's not what I meant. They are going to kill you if you don't break the curse, Adele. We can figure out the rest later; just let the skeletons lie—"

"If the skeletons weren't sticking out of the ground trying to attack me, I wouldn't be trying to pull them out!" I shoved angrily at his chest. He staggered one step back, stunning us both.

His baffled gaze shifted from his chest to my hands. "How did you...?" he whispered under his breath. "Magic."

I was oscillating between a total meltdown and wanting to jump him.

I bolted before I could crack.

"Whatever you're doing," he yelled, "I'm not going to let you martyr yourself, Adele!"

I didn't look back.

But this time he caught up with me. I forced myself not to smile when I heard his footsteps behind me, and I swatted away his hand as it brushed my fingers. He linked my arm into his. The old-timey gesture sent a sensation though my body that I certainly shouldn't have been feeling just then.

"What are you going to do? Lock me up in chains?"

"Don't tempt me."

"You are worse than my father!" I yelled, coming to a halt.

"Just from a different time." His eyes dropped to my lips. "When things were far more simple."

My heart leapt into my throat. But then his gaze moved around my head, as if monitoring a circling fly. He blinked twice and shook his head before looking at me with momentary skepticism.

"Ha, you know chains couldn't hold me," I said pathetically, not wanting to lose the moment.

He squeezed my arm. The thought of running away together flashed through my mind. I wondered if he was entertaining the same idea.

The thought was fleeting; Gabe came crashing into us from behind, breaking our embrace. "What are you crazy kids up to, tonight?" He boxed his arms around our necks, and I immediately scooted out from underneath him. His freed arm resulted in a head tousle for his brother. They wrestled for a minute, and then Nicco wriggled away, annoyed. He ran his hands through his hair a few times, and it fell perfectly back into place. I hated my pulse for accelerating.

"Damn, I love this city!" Gabe yelled into the night. "It really hasn't changed all that much in three hundred years."

"Yet, you are so eager to leave." My words dripped with disdain.

His head rolled to me as if he was loaded. "I'll admit, if there was ever a city to get trapped in, this is definitely the one. There's just one little problem with that scenario." My fingers burned. Suddenly, he was smack in front of my face, fangs out. "I take issue with the whole being trapped part—"

Nicco knocked him to the ground, and they rolled around just like idiotic human brothers.

"How long are you going to keep up this heroic act, *fratello*?" Gabriel asked, landing on top.

Nicco flipped him over. "As long as it takes."

"Ha!" Gabe yelled, throwing his younger sibling up to his feet. "You'll crack in the end. You always were father's little pet." He sprang up next to Nicco with the grace of a gazelle.

I turned and walked away, fuming. I couldn't listen to them quarrel any longer as if they weren't referring to *my life*.

They quickly caught up, brushed themselves off, and continued to rattle on.

"I wouldn't have thought you'd be so drunk already on a night so important to you, brother," Nicco accused.

"Drunk? Who's drunk? I've hardly had anything to drink tonight. Lorenzo, my two girls, and I only had a couple rounds at Le Chat Noir."

My shoulders tightened at the mention of my father's bar, and I quickened my pace. So did they. Nicco gave Gabe a look that said, "Yeah, right," and then turned to me.

"Where are we going, *bella*?"

I stopped and looked at Gabe. "You want the curse broken?" I teased. "Then to the attic, of course."

Nicco knew I was lying about breaking the curse. His catlike eyes surveyed my face for the truth. When I gave him nothing, he sighed and held his hand out in the direction of the convent, letting me play it out.

"Back to where it all began. How poetic!" Gabriel shouted and danced and pulled us along with the exuberance of a recently flowered Titania.

41

plight of la fée verte

"THE THREE MUSKETEERS!" Gabe yelled as he continued to dance down the street half a block ahead of us.

Nicco looked at me, and I did my best to shrug in innocent confusion before we went after him. There was something about a vampire's erratic behavior that escalated the tone from crazy to dangerous; suddenly the thought of vengeful vampires not being in control of their minds seemed like a *very* bad idea.

"Isn't it amazing?" the beautiful blond asked with his neck craned towards the sky.

"Isn't what amazing?" I replied.

"The stars. The universe!"

Nicco smacked his brother's arm and yelled something in Italian. Gabe ignored him, took my hand, and spun me. My wings flitted up. I finished the twirl, but he didn't let go. His eyes continued to circle around my head. A small smile escaped as I wondered what kind of chaser he was seeing.

"I think you really are *La Fée Verte!*" he said with a goofy expression. Then he yanked me close to his chest, exposed fangs suddenly inches from my face. His grip became painful as he whispered, "What did you do to me, faery?"

"Stop being such a freak, Gabe," I muttered, trying to hide my fear as I pushed him aside. He was too loaded to think it strange that I sent him staggering, but his quick flash of fang had focused my mind on our mission. I began to walk again.

Gabriel quickly flanked my left side and Niccolò my right, playing their respective roles of the Fool and the Knight, but whether they were blinded by arrogance or worry, neither saw me as anything more than the Ingénue.

That was my first card to play.

Adeline or Cosette, with their feminine charms, could have more easily slid into the role, but even without their talents it wasn't too difficult, for my doe eyes were partially real. Even now, my fingers twitched because I wished Nicco would hold my hand – and I loathed myself for it. I might not have been able to hear the pattern of his heart, but I knew deep within my being that he was on my side. The thought made me blush at the stone sidewalk, but I quickly picked up my head, put on an expression as stoic as his, and quietly played my real role: the Pied Piper.

THE SOUNDS OF REVELRY, which could just as easily have been mistaken for the sounds of an insane asylum, began to fade as we marched further away from Jackson Square and Bourbon Street, until they were nothing more than ambient noise. A mild undercurrent of energy flowed through my body. A subdued state of electrocution, as if I had been continually licking a battery. Between the elixir, the magical wards, the close proximity of vamps, and the constant reality of impending death, I knew the feeling was not going away anytime soon.

Walking in between the two Medici brothers brought me a weird sense of both fear and excitement. I forced myself to stay in the present moment. Whenever my mind wandered, our amiable history gave me a false sense of security. One slip too far into the comfort zone could cause not just my demise, but also the coven's – or, God forbid, my father's.

I reminded myself that I still had two witches on my side. Even though I couldn't see them, I could feel their presence. The closer we got to the attic, the more overwhelming the sense of togetherness, strength, and power became. The medallion radiated warmth beneath my costume, making me sense that Adeline and the original casquette girls were with me in spirit, too.

WHEN WE ARRIVED AT THE CHURCH PROPERTY, the wrought-iron gate swung open before I had the chance to hide the magical action. I stared at the attic window that had started it all – one of the shutters was swaying and the other hung loose, just as Isaac had mentioned. The glass panes had been replaced, but the window arch was still bricked up from the inside. Nicco's gaze followed mine to the roof. I knew he was silently trying to figure out my plan.

Unable to contain his excitement, Gabe moved ahead as we silently weaved through the labyrinth of overgrown hedges. The stake burned through the fabric of my bodice, the enchanted metal longing to be back where it belonged.

The convent door creaked open. No more time to think. No turning back.

Nicco's lips quickly brushed my ear as he whispered, "You can do this, *bella.*" His hand went to the small of my back. I was too worried about whether he had felt the hidden stake to be encouraged by his unbridled optimism.

I stepped away from him and into the dank vestibule. My elixir-strengthened eyes adjusted to the darkness more easily than usual; nonetheless, I picked up a dusty oil lamp from a small marble table, turned my back to them, and passed my hand over the glass to produce a flame.

"After you, *mademoiselle*," Gabriel said, waving his arm toward a wide, wrapping staircase.

I took a deep breath and stepped ahead of them, once again trying to suppress that girl-in-attic horror-movie image.

You are the predator, not the prey.

The mantra turned over and over in my mind, forcing out any lame, romanticized scenarios I had gained from years of reading too many tales of unrequited love.

I passed the second floor and hurried on up to the third, fearful that I might turn back. Not that turning back would have been an easy option with two vampires at my heels. The staircase became less grand and eventually dead-ended at a simple wooden door with a rusty old padlock.

"Step aside," said Gabe. "Let's get this party started." He chuckled at his proper use of the modern idiom, and gave the wood a shove. To our surprise, the door didn't budge – Gabe did. His misjudgment sent him teetering on the top stair.

Nicco caught him before he could take a tumble. "What the hell, Gabriel?"

As they exchanged foreign words, presumably about Gabe's failed strength, I opened the padlock and attempted to mentally move the door, but there was little metal in the old wooden joinery, and said wood was severely swollen into the post-Storm doorframe.

Nicco moved past me and pressed his hand against the door. It slammed open. Gabe looked at his own hands with curiosity and then at Nicco, who was rubbing his wrist and looking at me as if for answers. The ripple of suspicion was soon lost when Gabe took off down the hallway, singing some kind of Italian folk song.

THE FLOORBOARDS HOWLED as I made my way with the lamp down the hallway of doors. The thin slats of wood that formed the old walls now hung loose, and the cracks between them revealed small rooms that must have served as simple living quarters at one point in time. I wondered who had rested so close to the sleeping vampires. *Orphans? Slaves? Ursuline sisters?*

The hallway led us to a dark room, where I immediately bumped into the keys of an old pipe organ. I raised the lamp so I didn't further injure myself before we even got going. The floor planks wobbled as I meandered through the sea of dusty objects stacked high upon Victorian furniture and salvaged church pews: ornately-framed oil paintings of generations of priests, boxes of Bibles and rosary beads, racks of holy vestments in clear protective bags that had long since yellowed, French maps, modern Christmas decorations, and statues of the Virgin Mary in different styles from different centuries.

The deeper we walked into the cave of holy artifacts, the thinner the air became until the smells of dust and mothballs poked at my brain. Nicco had followed his brother to the far end of the room, where they were both waiting for me. Generally their dispositions couldn't be any more opposite, but now they both seemed equally anxious. As I approached the seal, they parted, making room for me and also revealing a short door with a mélange of locks from a different era.

This is it. I slid my finger over the first rusty chain. Gabriel practically vibrated with excitement.

The lock released with a loud pop. I moved onto the next, first working open the intricate metal mechanisms, and then undoing the remnants of three-century-old spells. I felt the enchantments linger, not leave – just allowing us passage. In my peripheral vision, I caught sight of Nicco balling his fists with anticipation. The sound of the final lock dropping sent a wave of fear rippling through my body. With a lift of my hand, the rusty hinges slowly pushed the door open. An unpleasant creak warned: *this door has been kept shut for a reason. Enter at your own risk, fool.*

Once again, Gabe went ahead while we took a beat, knowing that whatever was going to happen on the other side wasn't going to be good.

AS SOON AS I STEPPED INTO THE DARK ROOM, flames burst around the walls in one quick whip, until each of the sconces was ablaze.

So much for the element of surprise.

Suddenly, everything felt right. I knew I had made the right decision – I couldn't let any more lives be put at risk. Now I just needed to stay alive until all the vampires were contained.

No problem, Adele. Just stay alive.

"I can almost smell the freedom!" Gabe boasted, which I found ironic given we were now in the room where he had been imprisoned for so long.

I quickly scanned the battleground-to-be. The room was gigantic, with an angular ceiling that peaked in the center. There were six dormer windows on one side and an asymmetric five on the other. The fifth window was bricked up. That was my target: the lid to Pandora's Box.

Thick floor-to-ceiling beams rendered the large room useless for anything but storage space, but it had remained fairly sparse. The only metal objects I had to work with were the crude, antique gardening tools piled in a corner. Each one was my weapon, but each one could just as easily be turned and used against me. I approached the first of a couple dozen long wooden boxes that resembled caskets. Some were stacked high on top of each other, and others were alone on the floor.

"The infamous *cassettes*," I whispered.

My foot nudged a heavy chain from the lid, sending squeaking mice scattering across the room, and a wave of supernatural energy through me. A vision flashed through my mind: *The open sea. A cassette about to go overboard. I heard a scream. Mine. No, Adeline's.* I was seeing the scene through her eyes. I could feel the rush of her heartbeat and her fear that it might be Gabriel in the box. She had been scared *for* Gabe just as much as she had been scared *of* him. But she hadn't entirely trusted him – the slave driver in the sugarcane field, the pirate massacre, saving her life after the lethal vampire bite – it was impossible to know whether those events weren't entirely self-serving. *Was he just protecting his food supply? Using her to get to her father?* The image vanished, and, as I came back to my senses, I realized Gabe was waiting on me. He had asked me a question, and my blank expression seemed to be frightening Nicco.

"Come on, Adele. Do it," Gabe said, his tone now serious.

"Do what?" I asked coyly, trying my best to invoke some of Adeline's allure.

He answered with a heavy backhand that sent me sailing across the room. I hit the northern wall with a loud thud and landed hard on the metal stake hidden in my corset. Inhaling sharply, I rolled to the side in pain, but when I saw Nicco's fangs come out, I forced myself to jump up.

"I'm fine, Nicco!"

It was exactly the reaction I wanted from his older brother.

"Don't bother trying to help your little girlfriend, Niccolò," Gabe yelled. "It will only make things more painful for her in the end." He launched at me again, but I quickly sidestepped, and he crashed into the wall. He fell back in a drunken stupor.

"It doesn't look like she needs my help." A little laugh slipped from between Nicco's lips as he jumped on top a shaky table and crouched in a pseudo-referee stance.

I'm glad this is humorous to him.

Unfazed, Gabe picked himself up and began to circle me. "There is something about you that looks a little like Adeline, I'll admit." His eyes seemed to have trouble focusing on me, so I bounced away like a boxer. He blinked and shook his head. "But you're nothing alike," he spat and took a swat, missing me completely. He looked baffled and forced himself to refocus. "You're so innocent, so sweet…"

It was just the provocation I needed to plant my feet. With a quick flick of my wrists, I pulled one of the chains from a *cassette* and sent it whacking across his chest, throwing him against the wall. The sound of his cracking bones made me want to rush to help him, but I forced myself still. He slumped down to the floor.

Nicco stood on the table, knowing my action would cause an aggressive counterattack.

"Nice shot," Gabe said with an almost genuine flair. He attempted to stand but stopped, holding his rib cage. His strength and speed weren't his only failing attributes – his bones were taking their sweet time to regenerate. "*What* did you do to me, *witch*?" He lunged at me, but the chain popped up, and he tripped back down, landing face first.

I took a few steps backwards, shocked by my attack and still uncertain of the extent of my powers.

He looked up from the ground, fuming, and then charged at me, yelling through the pain. The look in his eyes made me gasp.

Just before he grabbed me, the chain jerked up and lassoed him. I watched in astonishment as he was hurled back across the room into the wall again.

Holy shit, I thought, trying to hide the fact that I was visibly shaking. Before guilt could set in, I remembered that in this very room, he had forced Lisette Monvoisin to murder her own triplet, to literally suck the life out of her.

My fingers slowly twirled. The lasso tightened, and the chains wrapped themselves around him three more times as he yelled obscenities at me, in shock that his perfect body was failing. I forged the ends of the chain together, trapping him.

Confidence grew inside me with the defeat of one vampire. *Thank you, Désirée.* The moonshine had definitely kicked in. Without it, I wouldn't have stood a chance. I hoped they would continue to arrive one at a time.

I walked back to Nicco, who sat down on the table, making us nearly eye-level. "What are you doing, *bella*? How can I help you if I don't know the plan?"

"It's really better this way." I did my best to keep a wily smile from forming. "I'm just trying to protect you." My hidden grin transferred to his lips as he heard his own words used against him.

I took a deep breath. "And now we wait." The calm in my tone made my voice unrecognizable to my ears.

He gritted his teeth, knowing I wasn't willing to divulge the plan any more than he was willing to give up the past. At this point, I *was* trying to protect him. I rested my hand on his leg, and his jaw relaxed. The less he knew, the better, because things were about to get *beaucoup* awkward for him. The only way for him to not betray his family was for me to fall – a reality each of us kept pushing to the back of our minds.

"Little girl," Gabriel said with a strange mix of ecstasy and threat in his voice. "You are really, *really* going to regret this in about ninety seconds. And brother, when I get free, you'd better run."

"Chill out," Nicco said, pushing himself off the table, seeming to enjoy the humility that had been forced upon his older sibling. He traipsed over to Gabriel and stooped to his face. "She locked you in a chain, bro. It's not like she set you on fire." He tousled his brother's hair.

"And how do you think this is going to end for you, little *bro*? The two of you are going to ride off in the moonlight together?"

"Something like that," Nicco grumbled with a swift kick to his brother's foot. He walked back to the table in discontent. We tried not to let the question cripple us, but how quickly the energy in the room changed.

"Tick. Tock. Tick. Tock," Gabriel taunted like a broken record.

At first, the childish words escaped my ears, but soon I had to hold myself back from kicking him in the face to shut him up.

"Tick. Tock."

A spark buzzed from my finger.

"That's it, *bella.* Stay angry!" Nicco yelled, just as the girls burst through the door.

"Where is he?" shrieked Martine Dufrense.

Lisette whipped around the room and came straight for me. I underestimated her speed, and in a flash, her pale hand clutched my throat. "Have you no sense, girl?" she screamed in my face, lifting me from the ground. "Do you not remember what I told you about Gabriel?"

"Kill her now, Lise!" Gabe ordered from across the room as Martine frantically tried to release him from the magical chains.

"Gabriel, why don't you get Lisette to break the curse," I screamed. "She's the one who cast it, after all."

She squeezed my throat tighter, digging her sharp fingernails into my skin.

My vision spasmed; tears squirted out as she tried to crush my windpipe. I couldn't focus enough to cast magic, and I knew it was just a matter of seconds before I passed out. But then she became distracted by something next to me, and her grip loosened a tad. I turned my eyeballs as far as I could, but saw nothing. Her gaze continued to follow an invisible tracer as I clung to her wrists, supporting my dangling body enough to sneak half a breath.

One. Two. Three.

I shoved my feet into her chest and pushed against the wall with an animal-like grunt. She fell back, and I dropped to the ground on my tailbone, wheezing for air.

She wasted no time coming back at me, but this time Nicco intercepted and threw her across the room. Gabe shouted at him in the background. I rejoiced as my lungs sucked in large gulps of air, but just as I caught my breath, Martine grabbed my waist, scooped me up from the floor, and slammed me back down onto one of the *cassettes*.

"Dammit!"

The rotten wood collapsed beneath me, breaking my fall, but the stake pounded into my back a second time. My shout echoed through the room as Martine hovered over me, practically salivating. She had the same dopey smile on her face as Gabe. Unfortunately, I had no emotional strings to pull with her.

I eyed the spade. She saw the direction of my gaze and sprang for it. But, instead of attacking me with the iron tool, she took a dramatic spin, as if performing on stage, and began humming a French lullaby.

Without thinking, I lifted my hand to the heavy spade – it jerked to and fro, but she grasped it like a tango partner. I spun her around, faster and faster, but instead of becoming worried, she squealed in delight and began to sing the lullaby lyrics operatically, louder and louder. *Jesus, no wonder she and Gabe get along. So freaking dramatic.*

In her rapturous state, she didn't even notice the metal twisting around her wrists into a makeshift pair of cuffs. Adrenaline surged through my system as I stood up and focused harder on the metal. The spade began to float, spinning the singing diva into the air, until the old gardener's tool plunged itself into the ceiling beams. I was halfway across the room when the singing abruptly stopped and Martine realized she was now stuck hanging from the rafters.

Nicco was sparring with Lisette. Any human witness would have thought they were killing each other, but for vampires they were barely roughhousing. As I watched them more closely, I could see that they were both wavering, although Lisette far more than Nicco. They both seemed tipsy, while Martine and Gabriel looked like drunks flopping down Bourbon Street at dawn. Circus music started playing in my head as the insanity ensued, accentuated by Gabriel's foreign profanity and Madame Dufrense's intermittent shrieks of laughter.

"Lise, I see three of you!" Gabriel yelled. "How do I see three of you? It's like your sisters are back. What kind of witchy hex did you put on me?"

"*Je vois six!*" screamed Martine, swinging herself from the ceiling as if she was under the Big Top.

Lisette fumed at the mention of her sisters and hurled a ceramic statue of an unfamiliar saint at Nicco, who was staring in disbelief at Martine, the trapeze artist. It split over his head into large chunks, causing me to tense up.

As the pieces dropped to the floor, he shook them off with a dangerous smirk, and then cracked his neck twice, ready to pounce.

"Niccolò!" Gabriel yelled, growling beneath his chains.

Nicco looked back at his brother and then rolled his eyes and stepped away, as if deciding not to assert himself over a drunk girl who was acting crazy. The fact that Nicco wasn't slamming her into the wall made my chest swell with some bizarre sense of pride.

Gabriel continued to yell provocative things at both of them, easily switching back and forth between Italian and French. Between the languages and his slurred speech, I could only understand a fraction of his banter, but it didn't take a genius to fill in the blanks.

"You disgust me," Lisette sneered at Nicco. "How could you betray your brother?" Her voice escalated to a scream and, despite Nicco's gentlemanly showmanship only a moment ago, she snatched up another statue and lifted it over her head.

A lethal protective instinct flared inside me when she threw it.

Nicco dodged the flying saint and watched it smash against the wall. When he looked back at her, his jaw tightened, as did mine.

One of the thick rusty chains slid off a *cassette* and slunk to my feet, slithering like a snake as I moved towards her.

My empathy for the original casquette girl was wearing thin. "How could *you* betray your sisters?" I yelled back at her with what was left of my voice. The chain slid from my ankles to hers. "You make her death in vain!"

Her face darkened with rage. She jumped towards me, but the chain tightened and yanked her to the ground with a loud crack. I raised both of my hands, no longer hearing the words that came out of my severely bruised windpipe, and pulled her up into the air kicking and screaming for Gabriel like a little girl.

As the chains carried her past me, she swiped my face and her steel-like fingernails sliced the skin from my clavicle to my ear. Holding my neck, I winced in pain, but remained focused on driving the chain into the rafters, until Lisette Monvoisin – *la petite-fille de La Voisin Magnifique*, founding member of the Casquette Girls Coven, and eighteenth-century Medici-made vampire – was left hanging upside down like a bat.

"Look, Lise! We're flying!" Martine yelled in French as she rocked herself towards her blood-sister.

The hissing sounds coming from Gabe brought my mind back to reality. I removed my hand from my burning neck – blood dripped from my fingers to the floor. Gabriel violently thrashed about in his chains, hissing louder.

Breathe.

I looked up at the ceiling and sucked air through my nose. Warm liquid dribbled down my chest. Muscles in my back spasmed in pain. *Two more down. Two to go. Three, if you count Niccolò.*

Martine swung around in delusional glee, singing something about breaking the curse and finally going back to Paris, while Lisette spat lewd indecencies about the smell of my blood. The warmth that rose to my cheeks alerted me to Nicco's presence. Or lack of it.

My eyes quickly scanned the room. *Where the hell did he go?*

Then, the vibrations of a trembling voice directly behind me sent shivers down my neck. "Get away from me, *now*," he growled.

Without hesitation, I darted across the room and behind the table.

When I whipped back towards him, he was leaning over the tabletop. His fangs were out, and he was roughly biting his bottom lip.

"Just stay over there, Nicco!" I yelled, my voice cracking.

His knuckles were white from clutching the table, and I could see the trance-state coming on.

"I'll put you in chains, Niccolò. I swear!"

"Absolutely *not*!" His eyes were threatening as he snorted, "Adele, do not even *think* about it."

The idea of Nicco being chained up when Emilio and Lorenzo showed up was not exactly ideal, but I reminded myself of my number one priority: *survive.*

"Then stay on that side of the room!" I screamed, frantically ripping the bobby pins out of my hair, allowing the waves to cascade around my neck and mask the bloody wounds.

He blinked.

Gabe began to laugh hysterically. "Oh, this is too good, brother. How the irony of this tale will be remembered for years to come, when you end up being the one to kill your *bella*! It's almost too sweet." His laugh faded. "Almost," he added, exposing his fangs to me.

In a flash, Nicco was in his face. "*Silenzio!*" The aggression in his voice reverberated through my bones and echoed in the rafters.

42

flight of la fée verte

NICCO EXILED HIMSELF to a dark corner to cool down while I pressed my hair into the gashes and prayed to the coagulation gods. Never in my life had I thought I would look forward to the onset of scabs.

"Tiiiiiiiick. Tock. Tiiiiiiiick. Tock." Gabriel synched his taunts with Martine's swings.

I had banked on Lisette and Martine flocking to aid their troubled maker, but now it was up to Isaac to play a serious game of cat and mouse to get Emilio and Lorenzo here.

In the voice of a child, Martine slowly began to echo Gabe. "Tick. Tock. Tick. Tock."

My foot twitched. Désirée just might get her wish after all. Just as I was contemplating whether a kick to the crotch was worth risking the physical contact, in sauntered the middle child, fangs protruding.

"La Fée Verte," Emilio said, stopping in the middle of the room. "My, my, aren't you just stunning tonight?" He retracted his fangs and ran his tongue over his bright-red lips. His gums and teeth were also

stained crimson. *Who the hell had he just bitten?* A sudden chill passed down my spine. *What if the cat had gotten the mouse?*

Emilio ended his dramatic cleansing process, and then paused, looking my way. His teeth rested on his bottom lip, similar to the way Nicco's did, as if he was forcing some kind of self-control.

"That little redheaded friend of yours is so feisty," he said. Lisette began to thrash about from above. "But I had to settle for that blonde again." He rolled his head in annoyance. "She never *shuts up*."

As horrible as it was, I let out a sigh of relief.

"They *really* should stay out of the bars... you never know what kind of seedy characters you'll come across in this town." He smiled at me and his eyes dropped to my bloody cleavage.

"Now, what kind of trouble have you been getting yourself into?" He took a slow spin on his heel to assess the situation, stopping to shake his head at Gabe, who was stewing. *"Bravissima, signorina,"* he said with a round of slow applause. "Do we have a Heroine tonight? *Impressionnant, ma chérie.* I have to admit, I pegged you more as the Damsel in Distress."

"So everyone keeps telling me."

He took a deep bow in hyperbolic admiration. I wanted to drop-kick his head.

He continued to approach, but suddenly stopped and whipped back to the door. "How did you do that?"

"Do what?"

"Move that quickly?"

"Um... I didn't move at all, Emilio." He spun towards my voice. Now he was being just as weird as the others. And I wasn't the only one who noticed. Nicco was now lurking in the nearest shadow, his eyes fixed on his brother. Emilio spun around again and even swatted at the air.

"I'm over here, E." I whistled.

"Wormwood," Nicco muttered under his breath. "But how—" he started to ask and then quickly snapped his mouth shut. The word lit a fire in Emilio's eyes.

I braced myself for his imminent attack.

But he didn't attack. Well, not like I expected.

His gaze lingered on Nicco, and then he traipsed over to me and ran his finger over my left cheekbone. His cool touch sent a chill through my burning, magic-saturated shoulders. The contrast made me shudder. I took a few steps backwards, and he followed.

"My, how quickly humans grow up. It seems like just yesterday you were that little lost duck in Paris." He brushed my face again. My spine stiffened.

Now I had nowhere to go: I was backed up against the wall, exactly where he wanted me. The hanging vampire girls giggled in delight at my submissive position. I pinched their restraints tighter.

Emilio stole another glance at Nicco.

He was just trying to get a rise out of his little brother. I realized this was just the preshow. Knowing that Emilio was more concerned with pissing off Niccolò than hurting me gave me momentary relief.

He looked back at me through his dramatic lashes, and then his face came closer to mine until his cool breath tickled my flushed skin. "*Paris. La cité de l'amour...*"

Nicco snorted from the corner.

Emilio's fingers traced my jaw; my heart pounded against my chest, wondering how far he would push this little charade. Then his other hand swept the side of my leg through the flimsy feathers of my skirt. My whole body twitched upright.

He's just trying to irk his brother, I told myself. squeezing my fist to contain the sparks. *Lure him in.* And it was working. Nicco was inching out from the shadows, fangs exposed. My eyes begged him to stay back.

"We did have some good times, didn't we, *ma chérie?*" Emilio smiled salaciously as his hand crept through the fringe and grabbed my ass-cheek. My arm reflexively twisted, and I slapped him across the face with elixir-boosted strength.

He fell to the ground with his arms covering his face, yelling in what seemed to be an exorbitant amount of pain.

"You wish," I scoffed, breathing heavily, satisfied with my impulsive move even if it was a death sentence.

The room lapsed into silent confusion as Emilio writhed around on the floor – bright red peeking from between his fingers.

My hand burned with a sticky wetness. I looked down to find a gooey substance dripping from my palm in bloody chunks. I shook my hand dramatically, flinging his molten skin from my fingers, and a tsunami of nausea crashed into my stomach. My knees buckled, and I hit the splintered floor, forcing myself to choke back my own vomit.

Horror flooded Niccolò's face, and hoots from the peanut gallery encouraged retaliation.

Emilio jumped to his feet, panting like a rabid animal.

Pushing myself backwards on the floor, I stammered: "Why… why couldn't you have just given me more time, Emilio?"

"It's just skin, Emilio," Nicco yelled. I could tell he was nervous – unsure of what role to play. "It will grow back."

But Emilio was no longer concerned with his baby brother. He was only concerned with me.

I froze, repulsed by my own destructive actions.

A smear of his skin from his left eye socket, across his nose, over his right cheek, and down to his chin was missing. The wound, in the shape of my hand, left his facial muscles exposed and bloody, and the bone protruded where the ball of my hand had made contact with his cheek. Every time he blinked, it looked like his left eyeball might fall out.

Distracted by the bloody mess of veins and tissue, I didn't move fast enough when he came straight for me.

A silent scream escaped my wounded throat as he slammed me into a stack of *cassettes*, crushing the wooden tower and bringing a round of cheers from Gabriel's hanging progeny. Pain shot from my torso out to all of my extremities.

Lying in the pile of broken wood, I attempted to move my hands into an offensive position, but I could no longer feel them. My eyes fluttered open for a second – Emilio had straddled my chest and was kneeling on the creases of my elbows, cutting off circulation to my fingers.

"I am starting to think that draining you might be more satisfying than this whole curse-breaking business." He slowly licked the bridge of my nose, bringing me fully conscious, and reminding me that I might actually die tonight.

But then Nicco pummeled him from the side, and I rolled in the opposite direction, groaning in pain.

"Let's go, brother!" Emilio screamed like a total psychopath, blood flinging from his face. "I just fed, so let me know if I hurt you."

I hobbled to a dark corner as they tumbled across the room.

The floor shook as they pounded each other into the ground. Each held on with such tight grips, it was difficult to tell whether they were still just brothers wrestling or if they really wanted to kill each other.

Nicco landed on top and slammed his older brother's shoulders down, cracking the floorboard beneath. "The only part stronger than me after you feed, Emilio, is your mouth."

As they continued to spew sibling rivalry, the sound of creaking metal distracted me. I looked at the ceiling – both Martine and Lisette had started to sway slowly in the breeze.

Breeze?

My eyes shifted to Gabriel, who was smirking at his brothers with nostalgia. The blonde locks that hung in his face gently lifted in the air, but he was too engrossed in the fight to notice the inconspicuous whoosh.

At first I thought it was the sound of my own ears ringing, but when I strained, I was sure I heard a faint whistle. It rapidly grew louder until it howled like a derailed train.

The boys stopped scuffling, and everyone's attention turned to the door as a giant force of wind hurled a furious vampire into the room, blowing out all the lights in the process. He landed heavily in the dark, all the while shouting aggressive-sounding Italian words.

Lorenzo. This was the moment – and even better, Isaac had managed to push him in rather than being chased. *Nice one, bird-boy.* The last vamp was at the party. I knew what I had to do.

No one else would die.

I took off towards the door, arms pumping, ignoring the pain shooting from multiple points. Even in the darkness, I felt all eyes shift from the new vampire to me just before I hurled myself against the door, slamming it shut.

The building quaked as the hexed door joined the circuit of spells cast upon the building.

DUCKING BEHIND A WOODEN PILLAR, I leaned over my knees and sucked air into my lungs, relishing in the knowledge that Désirée and Isaac would now be safe. I braced myself for the Medici retaliation. *Breathe.* But no one immediately attacked me for sealing the exit of the now pitch-black attic.

Well, this is anticlimactic, I thought. The waiting caused a squeak of nervous laughter to slip from my lips. *Oh, God, I am losing my mind.*

When I stood up, I realized there was a distinctly fresh tension in the air – the kind of tension that only results from silence. I quickly relit all the sconces and peeked out from behind the pillar: Lorenzo was still on the ground, Emilio was hovering over him, and Nicco stood with his back to me.

And still no one so much as looked my way.

"What is she doing *here*?" Emilio yelled with strange urgency. "*Idioto!*"

She? Had Lorenzo rolled in with a hostage?

The high I'd felt after sealing the exit crashed as my self-sacrificial plan atrophied. The entire point of deviating from the coven's plan was to *avoid* putting any unnecessary lives at risk. About to transcend into a complete state of hysteria, I repositioned myself to get a closer look, but Nicco turned and then walked back towards me, purposefully obstructing my view.

I heard rustles, and then Emilio yelled violently, "You were supposed to be guarding her!"

"It was a cyclone, Emilio!" Lorenzo yelled back. "How was I supposed to fight the wind?"

"What happened to your face?" asked a new, dainty voice. A very female, very French voice.

I know that voice.

My chest heaved. I tried to move closer, but Nicco moved with me, so I couldn't see.

"Nothing that won't heal," Emilio assured her, trying to suppress his rage. The tender change in his voice alarmed me.

"Well then, I guess it's time for a family reunion," Gabriel teased.

Sighing, Nicco finally let me push him out of the way, revealing a sight that absolutely nothing could have prepared me for.

My heart seized.

My brain spun a million times, refusing to process the fact that I had just trapped my mother in an attic with two— no, three unrestrained vampires and a slim-to-zero chance of getting her out alive.

Hot tears began to stream down my face, blurring my vision. I was too paralyzed to wipe them. *Did I just sacrifice my mother for the safety of the coven? For the other innocent people in New Orleans? For my father?* I didn't even notice that Emilio was lunging towards me until I heard *ma mère* scream my name.

Maybe she does care—

I didn't get more than a couple steps away before Emilio roughly grabbed hold of my hips, and swung me in the air. I hit back-first against a wooden beam. The stake felt like it had become permanently lodged into my spine. Before I could fall to the ground, he smashed my palms together and pushed me back against the pillar. I gasped as his other hand wrapped around my throat. Nicco stormed towards us, only to be tackled to the ground by Lorenzo.

"Don't break the curse, then," Emilio jeered. "I'd rather kill you, hunt down all of those other brats, and break it myself." Blood spattered from his oozing wound onto my face, making me gag. "Niccolò's right. You don't know *anything*. You're useless to us."

I tried desperately to move my hands, but he crushed them tighter.

Breathe. Focus. Get hands free.

I willed my vocal cords to work. "I know you don't care about the curse, *Émile*."

His eyebrows rose with suspicious interest. "Aw, *ma chérie*, you know me so well." His faux-sexy, faux-French accent had suddenly returned.

Nicco might have wanted me to break the curse so Gabriel could go free, but I knew Emilio never truly cared about his brother's predicament. Since I didn't know what the Medicis were really after in the first place, the only thing I could do was negotiate. The first thing that came to mind was Gabriel's desperate fake-out, which had cost Lisette her life. *Focus on the things you do know: they are looking for something... something to do with Adeline's father.*

So, that was my second card to play – and it was a bluff.

"What if I could do something better than break the curse?" I choked out, trying hard to keep my poker face despite the lack of oxygen flowing to my brain.

All movement in the room suddenly stopped, and everyone looked our way. Nicco was not thrilled to see where this negotiation might go.

Emilio scoffed, but allowed my throat to open a little more. I nearly choked, sucking in air too quickly.

"Don't get any ideas, Emilio!" Gabriel yelled, fighting with the enchanted chains. "Tonight, we're here to break the curse!"

"*Oui, ma chérie?*" He leaned so close I could see the curls of his torn skin slowly beginning to regenerate.

"Adele...," excitement flickered in his Medici-green eyes, "did you bring it?"

"No, I didn't bring *it*," I lowered my voice, "but what if I brought *him*?"

"Him?"

A wave of shock passed around the room, landing with a wry smile on Emilio's wounded face. "And how can you be so certain *le Comte de Saint-Germain* would come to save you, *chérie*?"

I strained my neck forward against his palm until my lips swept his ear and whispered, "Because he's right behind you."

He released me as he spun around.

He was duped for only a few seconds, but when he turned back around, an enormous pair of sparkling spheres pulsed in the palms of my hands.

"Move the hell away if you want the other half of your face to stay pretty, Emilio!"

He sneered as I pushed the flames towards him and pulled them back again.

"Adele, stay away from him! You'll only get hurt!" my mother screamed. Nicco and Lorenzo were both restraining her, but she fought them like a lunatic.

It felt completely unnatural to listen to my mother, but hearing her voice brought an unfamiliar, yet welcomed comfort. My intuition listened to her and guided my feet away. I had almost reached the other side of the room when Emilio suddenly snorted like a bull and charged me. I had no choice but to release the perfectly aimed orbits in self-defense.

I didn't even contemplate *not* killing him.

Then it all happened so quickly.

My mother broke away from Niccolò, tore across the room in a blur, and leapt directly into the line of fire. The flames engulfed *her* instead of her assistant.

Exorcismlike sounds expelled from my raw throat as I ran to extinguish *ma mère*, but Nicco caught me mid-stride and dragged me away kicking and screaming. With my back to the room, he held my waist tightly against a beam until my muscles could no longer fight him and nothing but wisps came from between my lips. I sucked in air that reeked of burnt hair.

"Je ne comprends pas." I wiped my tears with the back of my hands like a child. "I don't understand… I don't—"

With a loud sigh, Nicco moved me to the other side of the beam so I could see my mother lying on the ground. "I'm sorry, *bella*." The flames were gone, and smoke now rose from her charred body. But what sent me into shock was seeing the middle Medici brother hovering over her with desperate affection.

Nicco caught me as I sunk towards to the floor in what felt like a million shattering pieces. “I don’t understand,” I repeated over and over.

The world as I knew it ceased to exist.

“I’m so sorry you had to find out this way, Adele,” he said gently in my ear.

I couldn’t take in enough air. I began hyperventilating, as my entire psyche unraveled.

Emilio was cradling my mother’s shoulders, gently petting her arms. Below his hands, her skin was charred and blistered… but as I watched, it began to shift back to perfect porcelain. It was regenerating.

I didn’t know which was worse: thinking I’d just killed my mother, or realizing what she really was. I slunk the rest of the way to the ground as the answers hit me like bullets from a firing squad:

Why she wouldn’t let me live with her in Paris.

Why she only saw me at night.

Her finicky eating.

Her unusual relationship with her “assistant.”

Her mysterious disappearance twelve years ago, abandoning my father.

Abandoning me.

It was all there in front of me, and most of it had been for a while. My mother hadn’t deserted us.

She had *died.*

My mother was a vampire.

I couldn’t breathe. I couldn’t talk. I couldn’t hear. She screamed something to me in French, but it was like I suddenly didn’t understand the language.

Nicco shook my shoulders, also yelling.

Everyone in the room was yelling. My head became very light, and then dizziness overwhelmed me. Heat radiated from every part of my body. I felt like I was going to spontaneously combust, like the light bulb in my bedroom.

But I couldn't stop gaping. The way Emilio held my mother's head made my stomach lurch. As if she was his child. *Is she his child? Had she killed people? Had she killed the man with the blue eyes?*

Then it dawned on me.

"Nicco?"

"Si, bella?"

"You didn't kill those students."

He looked down at me and gently shook his head.

My heart ached as I looked back at him in shock. For a split second, the chaos in the room seemed to freeze around us, and I regretted all of this. I didn't want to die. I wanted to be with Niccolò forever. And I wanted forever to be longer than the next five minutes.

What have I done?

Emilio yelled in Italian to his cousin, and Lorenzo twisted Nicco around straight into his fist, cracking his nose. Enraged, Nicco grabbed an old rake from the floor and went after him.

Now that I was alone, Emilio rose from my mother's side, snarling.

I didn't care. I didn't care about anything anymore. I didn't understand anything anymore. I wanted this all to go away.

No. I wanted to kill him.

My half-broiled mother leapt towards Emilio's feet, and he spun around in confusion.

"Stop it, Emilio! *Arrête!* She's my daughter!"

He bent down and yelled something to her in French, something about killing me. In response, she knocked him to the floor and jumped on top of him. *Ma mère* had apparently not partaken in the moonshine.

Emilio dug his hands into her charred chest. Flesh that I had burned.

She screamed in agony, but didn't budge. She looked directly at me. "I'm so sorry, Adele. Get out of here, now!"

"Break the curse, Adele," Emilio boomed. "Or I am going to kill you, and then your mother!"

"Never, Emilio! You're a monster!"

"Je suis désolée," my mother apologized to Emilio, despite still straddling him and baring her fangs in his face. *"Échapper-toi maintenant!"* She screamed to me, *"Get out, now!"*

I raised my hands, stole the rake from Nicco, and bent it around Lorenzo's neck, anchoring him to the wall.

"Grazie, bella," Nicco said, looking back at me.

Lorenzo laughed from beneath the shackle and spat, "*Chiaroscuro* worthy of a gilded frame the two of you are."

Nicco looked at him sharply, but retracted his fangs.

I ignored them and ran towards the door. If there was a chance of surviving this pit of predators, then I wanted it. If I could get the door open, I knew Nicco, my mother, and I could defeat Emilio and escape. It wasn't the original plan, but I didn't care.

"Niccolò Giovanni Battista Medici, you better stop her," Emilio commanded from across the room. "You shame our family's name!"

I looked back over my shoulder at Nicco, who was standing in the middle of the room, breathing heavily like he might implode. He was the only one left unrestrained. Gabriel echoed Emilio's command as I turned back to the escape route.

My hand touched the doorknob, and suddenly Nicco was pressed up against my back.

"Do you trust me, *bella*?" he whispered into my ear.

My entire nervous system felt like it was short-circuiting. Every primal instinct told me to fry him, but my intuition consumed me. There was only one thing I was sure of in this supernatural world where nothing made sense.

"Yes," I gasped, turning around.

Before the syllable was out, his hands wrapped around mine, and I knew something was wrong.

His grip was too tight.

A sharp edge pressed into my palm as he pulled me from the door.

"I knew you would crack in the end!" yelled Gabe. "You are a Medici after all!"

"Whhh... what are you doing?" I dug my heels into the ground, but he squeezed my hands and pulled, forcing me to stumble.

His eyes begged me for forgiveness, but I was unable to accept that I had made the wrong decision.

"What are you doing, Niccolò? Stop."

We were back to the middle of the room. He began to turn on his heel and spin me around.

This is not happening.

This is not happening.

"How could you?" I choked out with tears.

"Adele, please stop resisting; it will hurt so much less if you stop."

"What?"

"I'm so sorry, *bella*," his voice cracked. "But there is no other way." He gained momentum, and my feet left the ground.

"No, Nicco!" I screamed as he let go of my hands and flung me towards the ceiling.

Never trust a vampire.

My right shoulder crashed directly into the fifth window, and I went straight through the bricks, shattering the window for the second time. His pitch was so fierce, I continued to soar upwards.

I yanked the stake from my corset and hurled it back towards the window – my death was imminent, but I'd be damned if it would be in vain. Adeline's spirit stayed with me as the metal zipped through the air and snapped the shutter closed, just as it had been for the last three centuries.

My last glimpse had showed my mother attacking Nicco. He didn't resist. The entire building trembled, and I knew the curse was restored.

The moment of solace didn't last long. Nicco's pitch peaked.

The stars held my heart as gravity plunged my body back down to Earth, twisting, turning, faster and faster. Images from my subconscious flooded like waves crashing ashore: all those times I had used magic as a kid, every metallics lesson my father had taught me, every story Ren had told me, every clue that my mother was a vampire.

The signs had always been there. I just hadn't been open to them.

My vision blurred. I told myself I was getting what I deserved for being so *naïve*.

Knowing that it would all be over in a few seconds didn't make my broken heart ache any less.

Niccolò let go of my hands.

43

la fin de la fée verte

I JOLTED TO CONSCIOUSNESS as my back made contact. The sensation was strange. The impact was not as painful as I thought it would be. But then again, maybe my mind was so numb with shock that my body was impervious to pain.

Or maybe the impact killed me and I'm already dead?

Everything was peaceful and serene. Sleepy. So, so sleepy.

When my eyes fluttered, all I saw were thousands of stars in the pitch-black sky. That's the nice thing about no electricity. Stars.

I heard noises in the distance.

People.

Celebration.

Trumpets.

The deep brass tones had always brought me such comfort in the past, but now I worried they were being blown from Gabriel's horn – the Angel Gabriel, not the vampire.

Ugh, vampires.

My heavy eyelids slowly blinked open, making me very aware of the weight of my own eyeballs. I struggled to focus on a new shape coming into view.

A big triangle.

No, a cone.

A big ice cream cone.

Maybe I am in heaven?

I squinted to sharpen my focus on the giant ice cream cone, and pressure flooded my head. My neck turned slightly to try to release the tension, and the outline of another object appeared. I stared at the lines that separated the negative and positive space until a church came into focus.

Something was wrong.

It was upside down.

Why is there an upside church on top of a giant ice cream cone? The church looked like the Cathedral. Once more, I tried to refocus my eyes. My head fell to the side, and the ice cream cone suddenly reminded me of the bell tower.

Our bell tower.

Nicco let go of my hands.

Nicco tried to kill me.

Maybe Nicco did kill me?

I gasped for air and was struck with a wave of vertigo. My hand slapped for something solid to ease the spinning, but I just ended up swatting air. The pressure was building in my head because I was upside down.

I was not, in fact, splattered on the concrete.

A focused stream of wind was pushing the arch of my back up towards the sky like a geyser while my body hung limp like a rag doll. I was no longer falling, but floating upwards. Up, up, up towards the looming crescent moon that hung low over the Crescent City.

My city.

I quickly dropped as the jet of air morphed.

The gust caught me again, this time like a mitt. I wheezed as the wind flipped me around. Right side up, the vertigo eased, and I extended my left arm to help navigate. My wings whipped up to the celestial sky, and I felt like I was flying up to the heavens.

Is this the way to heaven?

My blood-caked hair blew behind me, and the night air began to cool my dangerously feverish body temperature, sending ripples of tickles to the tips of my toes. The strength of the gust held me tight, and the thickness of the wet air wrapped a comforting familiarity around me that almost made me smile.

Fear abandoned me as the gale carried me closer to the glistening Mississippi and back to the *Vieux Carré.*

THE RENDEZVOUS POINT came within my line of sight, and the gentle twister slowly began my descent onto the cupola of the *Presbytère*, the historic building adjacent to the ice-cream-cone steeples of the St. Louis Cathedral. The wind dissipated, and I fell the last six feet without much grace, but despite the lack of magic, Isaac moved underneath me to break my fall.

He held me steady by my left elbow while examining my other arm. Emotions pummeled me as I tapped my foot on the stone floor, reveling in the sensation of stability. Solid ground.

"He tried to kill me," I choked out, not quite able to look Isaac in the eyes, overridden by the need for some kind of confession. An admission of guilt. "You were right all along."

"What?" he asked, pulling me closer. "Who? What the hell happened, Adele? You're covered in blood."

My wild eyes locked with his, which were filled with worry. "He let go of my hands. He threw me into the bricks."

Isaac went to hold my hand, hesitating briefly to pry something out of my palm. I felt instant relief not having the sharp points pressed into my skin anymore. He laced his fingers with mine, and his touch brought immediate comfort.

"Actually," he said, "we kind of pla—"

My head felt like it was still floating. I didn't hear anything he said. My toes elevated my trembling legs as I tried to throw my bloodstained arms around his neck. Only my left arm moved. My right hung limp, its wing drooping on the floor. But with the aid of his arm slinking around my waist, it was enough to hoist my face close to his.

"Adele, you're blee—"

My mouth brushed against his.

Just inches away from mine, his heart pounded, but he didn't stop talking. He asked questions my ears didn't hear, forcing my kisses into birdlike pecks.

"You're hurt, Adele," he said sternly, imploring me to stop.

Ignoring his concerns became futile, so I refrained from kissing him and leaned my forehead into his. My recession brought his nose nuzzling against mine. He didn't really want me to stop.

"What happened in there?" he asked me again.

It all rushed back.

"We won," was all I whispered as my eyes fell shut.

My mother. Emilio. Nicco. Each flashback made me want to melt into him more.

His lips swept the thin skin of my eyelids, sending a wave of shivers through my shoulder blades. I didn't have to open my eyes to know he was smiling. He kissed my cheekbone and jawline and then pushed my hair aside to continue down my neck.

"What the hell?" he said, suddenly alarmed. "Adele, we need to get you to the hospital."

"No!" I yelled, beginning to panic. "It's too overcrowded. They would just turn us away." The truth was, I was scared to leave this moment. I quickly pressed my lips to his cheek, letting them linger. His body responded to my touch, and I felt him let the thought go.

I knew that every part of him wanted me. Wanted to protect me.

And I wanted to drown in that feeling.

The heightened sensory experience caused my aching body to squirm into his, and with that, his lips crashed into mine, finally giving in to me.

Giving in to the elixir.

My hand moved to his face; I 'd never wanted anything so badly in my life. His arms pressed tighter around me until I could barely tell where I ended and he began. Dizziness overwhelmed me again.

I could feel his heart race faster. This time it was me who broke our embrace out of concern. He didn't release me so easily, forcing me to arch backwards so I could see his face. His lips tried to follow me, but I held his jaw at bay. "You're shaking," I whispered.

His eyes searched for something to focus on before dropping to the ground.

"I...," he fumbled.

He pushed his face back to mine and roughly pecked my lips. Then took a deep breath and looked me in the eyes.

"Before... I was so scared that I was going to drop you." The shaking caused a slight vibration in his voice.

"But you didn't." The scratchy stubble of his otherwise baby face scraped across my cheeks, and my lips parted his. His vulnerability sent me into another manic tizzy. My pulse raced.

Too fast.

The electric feeling expelled from my body as a breeze rushed around us, but this time it wasn't from the wind-powered witch in my arms. It was simply Mother Nature.

Although, there's nothing simple about Mother Nature.

Her knowledge. Her beauty. Her power.

Cold.

My arm wrapped around Isaac until it wasn't possible to hold him any tighter.

And that was it.

Everything I had left inside me.

I was drained.

Blackness.

Orbs of color flashed beneath my eyelids. Blindness only exacerbated the pain searing every inch of my body. My muscles cramped and convulsed. Someone was hovering above me. Aggressively cursing. Panicking.

Isaac.

I tried to raise my hand to comfort him, to no avail.

"Jesus, what's wrong with her arm, Isaac?" asked a female voice. Maybe Dee's? "Keep trying to wake her up."

"Adele, wake up." He frantically shook my dead weight.

I winced.

"Isaac, watch her shoulder!"

Definitely Désirée.

"Sorry. Adele, it's time to wake up. Please," he added, as if it might have been his lack of manners keeping me in the semiconscious state.

"What happened?" Désirée demanded with a hint of accusation. Her pitch was a little higher than usual.

If Désirée's worried, should I be worried?

"I don't know... we were just... and she... she just blacked out." His voice warbled.

Through the slits of my lashes, I saw Désirée leaning over me, dragging her hands down my torso, lips moving quickly. My body burned as if I'd been struck by lightning.

I blinked slowly. Everything was fuzzy, but I could tell we were still on the roof of the *Presbytère*. The stars were gone. A dense fog now bridged the gap between the clouds and the small cupola. Chills swept over me.

Isaac yelled something to Désirée.

I tried to move my mouth, but nothing came out.

"Adele, can you hear me? Please, say something."

I had a strong desire to answer him, but couldn't seem to remember how to do that. How to make words. I blinked again, willing my eyes to stay open this time, but they drooped shut.

"She's alive."

"Of course she's alive, birdbrain, she's breathing!" Totally unsatisfied with Isaac's efforts, her head rushed above mine. "Adele, open your eyes, NOW. Tell me who I am."

My eyes popped open as if attached to marionette strings. "You're Voodoo Queen Dee."

The puppet master leaned back and breathed a sigh of relief. "Jesus, Adele."

I tried to sit up on my own, but fell back. Isaac caught me. "What happened?" My throat felt like it had been clawed raw both inside and out.

"You passed out," Isaac said from above me. His upside-down head hovered so close to mine, his eyes looked giant, like a prehistoric bug's. "I was about to take you to the hospital, but Désirée rolled up with her juju. For the record, I still think we should go to the hospital."

"There's only one open hospital," Désirée told him. "Unless you want to put a bullet in her, she'll never be seen. We're better off waking up Gran if we need help."

"Thaaaaanks, Dee. No hospital. My dad'll freak." I smiled, not recognizing my own voice. She was rubbing something cool and minty into my skin. "Wait, why might we need Gran?"

"We don't, Adele. I can handle it."

"Are you sure you know what you are doing?" Isaac asked.

"All Voodoo is based on the art of healing."

"I'm a little inclined towards science at the moment. No offense."

"Well then, it's a good thing Adele has me."

The minty rub was soothing on my feverish skin. "I'mmmm gonna go back to sleep, guys."

"No!" Désirée yelled. "Isaac, switch places with me."

Suddenly she was gone from my sight. My eyes drooped closed.

"HEY! NO SLEEPING, TINKERBELL!"

My eyes flew open again. Isaac was straddling me on all fours. His outline was blurry, but I could sense his frazzled nerves. I focused on him until I could finally make out his expression – intense concern. Despite the pain, my stomach did a small somersault.

"I'm not Tinkerbell."

"I know. I know. *La Fée Verte.*"

"Ha, ha. Your accent is terrrrrrrible."

Désirée snickered in the background. Isaac leaned over my head to whisper to her. His black leather vest hung open, and his bare chest hovered over my face.

"Where's your shirt?" I slurred.

My words brought his face back, and he shot me a short, nervous smile. He didn't answer, but his eyes fell to my neck, and I realized there was something tight and damp wrapped around it.

"Isaac, you have to hold her down!"

"I *am*."

"No, don't be a wuss. Sit on top of her. If she tries to fry me, I'm using you as a human shield."

She pushed the hair from my shoulder. I cried out in pain as his knee moved into my open palm, pressing it against the stone floor.

"Do it, Désirée!" he yelled.

"Do what?" my loopy voice asked. I stared at his chest. "You're hot…"

He let his hair fall in front of his face to hide his blushing cheeks.

Désirée snickered. "Don't flatter yourself, Isaac, it's just the elixir talking."

He leaned in, crushing my left shoulder and right hip. "Do it!"

A bolt of pain surged.

The scream that came out of my mouth sounded more like the pathetic whimper of a dying animal. My body tried to lurch into a sitting position as Désirée rammed my arm back into socket, but Isaac kept me pinned down. My eyelids fluttered in shock as my brain registered that my arm was now reattached, and the pain was actually a good thing. He shifted his weight off, and everyone was silent for a minute.

I curled the fingers on my right hand, and Désirée let out a loud sigh.

"Breathe," Isaac whispered, brushing my hair off of my face.

I nodded, inhaled deeply, and the convulsions slowed.

"*Merci beaucoup,* Dee." I sucked in a few more breaths, utterly exhausted. "Now can I take a nap?"

"Not if you want to avoid the hospital," she snapped.

"*Ça va! Non hôpital!*"

"We still need to torch the convent, Désirée," Isaac said. "If she's too weak to light the fire from here, I can go down and do it myself."

"No fire!" I rasped. Suddenly, consciousness was not an issue.

He squeezed my hand. "Don't worry… we can handle it. We're almost mission complete."

"We are *not* burning the attic!" I yelled, jerking my hand away.

They stared back at me with wide eyes. The surprise on Isaac's face slowly morphed as he drew his own conclusion about why I didn't want to burn the attic.

He was only half right.

I didn't want to kill Nicco, even if he *had* tried to kill me, but, more importantly, my mother was trapped in that attic, thanks to me. I had already nearly burned her to death by accident; I couldn't do it on purpose – even if she was a vampire. Even if she had killed those two students twelve years ago.

"We are not burning the attic," I repeated and looked at Isaac, expecting him to cave and take my side.

He didn't.

There was no way I could tell him about my mother; he hated vampires. There was no way I could tell *anyone*.

"If she says we aren't roasting the vamps, then we aren't roasting the vamps. I mean, arson is a little seventeenth-century witch-hunty, anyways."

Thank you, Dee.

"This is *not* the same as dark-ages witch hunts. Those witches were innocent. These are cold-blooded *killers*. Vampires!"

I gave Isaac a look, letting him know there would be no forgiveness if he took matters into his own hands.

"Fine," he said through gritted teeth. "But we have to do something. It's not safe leaving them like this."

"He's right," I said. "They'll die, not being able to feed—"

"That is *not* what I meant."

"We can cast the same Slumbering Spell Cosette Monvoisin did back in the day," Désirée suggested.

"Do you think we're strong enough?" I asked.

"We're only three, and they're now six," Isaac said. It took all of his strength not to gloat. "That's two additions to the original bloodsucking attic crew."

Seven, I thought.

"There's only one way to find out." Désirée grabbed our hands forming a circle.

My fingers slid around Isaac's. I rubbed his thumb, begging him not to be mad at me. He attempted to crack a smile, but barely glanced at me for a second.

Désirée began to chant the French words of the long-since-dead triplet, and soon Isaac and I joined her, repeating the ethereal phrases over and over again until they felt as natural as saying our own names.

The pain in my body began to subside as the wind swirled around us in a swell of paranormal excitement. I don't know if it was the elixir, or the delirium, or the magic, but I swear a harmony of girlish voices began to sing a lullaby from the sky. I smiled, knowing that either way, *les filles aux la cassettes* were with us in spirit.

The air stilled, and everything felt totally peaceful.

"How do we know if it worked?" I asked.

"We don't. Unless you want to open the attic door and—"

"Not happening," Isaac said, just in case she wasn't joking.

She smiled deviantly, causing his chest to puff, and then she started laughing.

I unwrapped Isaac's bloodstained shirt from my neck, ripped a strip of fabric from my wings, and tied it into a bow around my neck. "I have an idea," I said, poofing my hair to further conceal the herb-packed slashes. "Let's go."

"SO THIS IS WHERE EVERYONE RAN OFF TO," Isaac said as we turned the corner into the *Faubourg Marigny*. Jackson Square had become desolate, but Frenchmen Street was filled with zombies, screaming children, and revelers of all levels of intoxication, drinking and laughing under the sea of ghosts. Musical scales tooted from horns as musicians warmed up the Second Line.

Two old geezers chased each other down the street with sparklers, squealing with glee. "Looks like the wormwood is still active," Désirée murmured. We all let out a short laugh.

"Dead Green Faery?" a placid voice said. "Awesome costume." I turned to find Theis approaching, with Ren on his heels.

"Merci beauc—"

"Oh, thank God, *bébé*!" Ren cried, bending over me, but Isaac intervened.

"No hugs."

I chuckled.

Ren understood and made a crack about Isaac's hunky chest, who in turn quickly fastened the two buttons on his vest, while Theis wolf-whistled.

I spotted the twins passing out small white candles in red Solo cups.

"I'll be right back," I said and walked over to them.

"Adele!" Sébastien yelped, his lit candle fumbling to the street. "You disappeared. You scared me half to death!"

I picked up his candle and sniffed a tear away. "Sorry about that."

"Why are you covered in blood?" Jeanne asked, genuinely concerned.

"Oh… this stupid girl from school thought it would be funny to have a *Carrie* moment and dumped corn syrup on me." *Did I really just lie to a chemist about blood? I am an idiot.* She looked at me with doubt and opened her mouth to protest, but then let it slide. My smile beamed in gratitude. Despite being covered in actual dried blood, I wrapped my good arm around her. *"Je t'aime,"* I whispered.

"*Moi aussie*."

"Can I get three candles, *s'il te plaît*?" I asked Sébastien, wiping my eyes.

"*Oui, mon chou.*"

"*Merci beaucoup.*"

He smiled.

I walked back to Désirée and Isaac, who were both still mesmerized by the ghoulish tribute, and handed them each a candle-poked cup. We all watched a flame magically grow from my candle, and then I kissed it to each of their wicks, lighting theirs the old-fashioned way.

Other than the specks of a thousand candle flames, the street was totally dark. A solo accordion started squeezing out a song, and then a woman in the middle of the block slowly began to belt the first phrase of "Cryin' in the Street." The horns followed, and the crowd started moving together back towards the Quarter.

Listening to the beautiful alto voice, tears rolled down my face. I thought of Brooke, Klara, and Alphonse Jones. I closed my eyes and wished for them to come home soon.

At least my mother is home, I thought, surprising myself. In a weird twisted way, I really *was* glad she came back. I finally knew the truth.

I looked at Désirée and found her crying too. Everyone was.

We all linked hands and walked down the street. Our voices singing together gave me the confidence that my city was going to get better.

Our city.

WHEN WE CROSSED ESPLANADE AVENUE, both the warble and the close proximity of the convent made my pulse climb. Désirée signaled to me – I placed Jeanne's hand into her brother's – and our trio peeled off as the crowd continued its procession to St. Louis Cemetery No. 1.

For the second time that night, I entered the iron gate and walked through the overgrown hedges, this time flanked by two witches. Nestled into a weed-covered hedge was a large metal bucket filled to the brim with the long carpenter nails that had rained down on the strange morning everything went haywire. The original nails the Ursuline sisters had sealed the shutters with, blessed by the Holy Pope himself.

The convent's front door was wide open, but all that mattered was that the attic was secured. Both Isaac and Désirée breathed a sigh of relief to see the windows still sealed, but I swear that *one shutter* had a slight vibration. As I stared at it, my heartbeat echoed in my chest until it felt like my whole body was reverberating to the beat.

I could still feel the elixir coursing through my veins.

I closed my eyes, and all I saw was Nicco and his not-so-innocent smile. *I am such an idiot.* My heart beat faster as I remembered that morning I first stepped foot through the convent gate. *Why? Why? Why?* Despite all the fires, all the hurricanes, all the crimes, hauntings and magic in this city, somehow the shutter had stayed shut tight over the centuries, until right before *I* got to it. *What was so special about this Storm? Is there such a thing as a coincidence? Maybe so?* I felt the metal stake rattling high above us. *Maybe not?*

Breathe.

"Are you okay?" Isaac asked.

I nodded, sucking in a big breath through my nose.

"Are you sure?"

I opened my eyes to find him standing right in front of me. All the chaos stopped.

"I locked the front door," said Désirée, walking back to us. "We all good over here?"

"*Oui. Tout va bien.* All good."

I smiled at Isaac, and his hand went to my face. "Just don't go opening any more shutters, okay?"

"*Oui.*" I knew he was only half-joking. I glanced back at the attic, and for an instant Emilio flashed in my head—

"*Il ne faut rien laisser au hasard!*" I yelled, and with a flick of my wrist, the old nails rose from the rusty pail and hammered themselves back into the wooden shutters.

They both stared at me.

"Why leave anything to chance?" I asked, looking straight at Isaac.

He smiled at me without worry for the first time since we parted ways on Bourbon street, and then he fell in beside me as I walked by.

And I knew he would always be there. Beside me.

IN A SUBDUED STATE, THE THREE OF US crossed the railroad tracks to the Moonwalk and kept going to the river's edge, where we sat under the star-swept sky. With everything along the riverfront obliterated by the Storm, I wondered if our view was closer to how the landscape had looked for Adeline three centuries ago. I wondered if she ever left *La Nouvelle-Orléans*? *Did her father ever make it to the city?* The number of unanswered questions was maddening, but the one that bothered me the most was about my mother: *Was she just a casualty in the Le Moyne's insanely magical lineage? Had I been wrong about her my entire life?* She was the only person who could answer those questions, and I had locked her up for eternity.

Désirée finally broke the silence.

"I'm glad we didn't torch them," she paused, rolling her eyes. "I kinda miss Gabriel."

Isaac groaned and leaned back on a small tuft of weeds.

I tried my best to contain my giggles as I lay back next to him. "I miss ice cream."

"Mmm… pralines and cream," she agreed, lying back.

"These other two descendants better be dudes," Isaac said, and we all burst into delirious laughter.

"All right." Désirée leaned towards me, propped on her elbow. "Time to spill it, sister. What the hell happened in the attic?"

"Yeah." Isaac mirrored her elbow-prop on my other side. He fiddled with the silver feather resting on my stomach.

I took a deep breath and thought about where to begin. "Well, in essence, *le Comte de Saint Germain* saved me."

"Your dead great-great-great-something-grandfather *saved* you?" Isaac asked.

"Yeah… although, now, I'm not so sure that he's dead."

"Oh, lord." Désirée sighed.

After I finished telling my version of the night, Désirée told hers and then Isaac his. And when all was done and all was said, we sat silently staring at the moon's reflection on the rippling river, soaking it all in. The differences between people, cultures and times.

The monsters. The myths.

The heroes.

The victims.

The love and loss.

Loss and love.

epilogue
la toussaint

November 1st

"WELL, DAD... YOUR WIFE IS LOCKED in an enchanted attic a few blocks away on the property of the Catholic archdiocese, forever or until further notice," I explained to my jabbering reflection in the toaster. "Last night, I nearly killed her by way of fireballs exploding from the palms of my hands. Also, she has a strange familial relationship with this total psychopath from the seventeenth century, who I used to have a massive schoolgirl crush on. That was before he tried to kill me, by the way. Oh, and those murders that Mom was accused of twelve years ago? Totally guilty. So, in a nutshell, you sent me away to Paris to live with a bloodsucking vampire. At least Mom had enough sense to send me away to boarding school."

The toast popped, startling me.

"You're right," I told the toaster. "That is not gonna work."

Too bad Hallmark doesn't make a card that says, *Sorry, your wife is undead.*

I sipped my lukewarm *café* sans *au lait,* wishing I could magically turn stale bread into beignets, when I heard the front door heave open. I quickly buried the idea of ever telling my father any of this nonsense.

"Adele?"

"Kitchen!"

His boots clacked quickly on the wooden floor, and a few seconds later, he threw his keys on the table, hurrying to the chair next to me. His hair was messy, a blue and red lightning bolt was painted down the right side of his face, and his eyes were slightly bloodshot.

"Why didn't you call me? Are you okay?"

My heart skipped. *How does he know?*

"Call you about what?"

"Ren just came by the bar and told me about a cat attack knocking you off the King's float and nearly getting run over by a drunk on a mule?" he said with a smidgen of disbelief.

"Wha? Oh, yeah, um. I'm kinda banged up." I stretched the collar of my black turtleneck to show him the bandage.

"Do you need a doctor?"

"No, Désirée's mom patched me up and gave me some kind of herbal tea for the bruising on my back." *It was a little more than herbal tea, but whatever, it was more than a little bruising.*

"Well, let me know if anything gets worse," he said, not thrilled with my choice of treatment.

If he bought that load of bull from Ren, he must think I'm an even bigger spaz than I realized.

"What's with the lightning bolt?" A flash of Emilio's scorched skin whipped through my memory.

"Oh, sweetheart, we still have so much David Bowie immersion to do." He kissed my cheek and reached for my coffee mug. "Are you sure you're okay?" he asked taking a sip.

I nodded.

"No school today?"

"Nope. It's a Catholic holiday. All Saint's Day, not to be confused with All Soul's Day, which is tomorrow." I took back my mug.

"Well, speaking of miracles, I have more good news."

"Hmm?"

"Once this semester is complete, you won't have to return to Sacred Heart in the spring."

"What!" I shrieked, sloshing coffee onto the table. "NOSA is reopening?"

"Not exactly." He extracted a newspaper from his interior jacket pocket. "This, by the way, is the first post-Storm issue of the *Times Picayune.*"

"Well, things are looking up."

I unfolded the thin newsprint and found a photo of Morgan Borges standing in front of the convent. I read the headline and quickly set down the mug so I wouldn't drop it on the floor.

OLD URSULINE ACADEMY
TO REOPEN HISTORIC FRENCH QUARTER CAMPUS

Mayor Morgan Borges and Ursuline Prioress Sister Angela Rouen are pleased to announce the reopening of the Ursuline Academy's historic French Quarter location, which miraculously received little damage from the Storm.

"I am so proud to make this announcement. The Ursuline Academy is almost as old as New Orleans herself. I look forward to the Ursuline sisters carrying on the traditions of the school and its mission to provide education for students of all walks of life in the French Quarter area," says the Mayor.

"What the…"

My pulse started to crawl back towards the danger zone as I thought about attending class inside a vampire catacomb. I dropped the paper on the table.

A loud noise erupted, and the lights flickered. We both jumped from the table, clutching our chests.

"Damn, we're back on the grid!" He smashed a kiss against my cheek. "See, sweetheart? I told you things were gonna be all right."

A small laugh escaped my throat as I realized the noise was just the air conditioner revving up after being dormant for so long. A gentle rap at the door interrupted the celebration. My stomach tightened when I saw Isaac's silhouette through the thin white curtain.

"I hope he doesn't think we're working the day after Halloween," my father said, going to the door. "Morning, Isaac."

"Good morning, Mr. Le Moyne."

The switch in formality made my father immediately suspicious. He looked at me, then back to Isaac, and stood his ground, barricading the entrance. "Just remember that I have a gun, okay, son?"

"Dad!" I cringed.

"I'm just putting it out there, that's all."

He grabbed the paper, my mug of coffee, and exited the kitchen.

"Does your dad really own a gun?" Isaac asked as I took my father's place in the doorway.

"Yeah, I know. It's surprising."

"I also have half the Parish Precinct on speed dial!" my father yelled from the other room.

"Dad!"

"And don't forget that everyone in this town owes me a favor. Or ten. I've got dirt on everyone!"

Isaac's confidence was wavering, so I stepped outside, shutting the door behind me.

He hopped down the stairs, but I leaned against the door, suddenly nervous.

"Hey," was all I managed to get out.

He repeated the greeting back, but then just stood there.

"What are you doing up so early?" I asked.

"Early? I'm used to rising before the sun. What are you doing up? I just dropped you off a few hours ago."

"I don't know. Couldn't sleep. I guess it was the excitement, or the elixir." I left out the part about the severe anxiety brought on from locking Nicco and my mother in an attic to rot for eternity. Then there was, of course, our mini makeout sesh.

"Yeah, I know what you mean." He nervously spun something in the front pocket of his jeans.

"So… what's up?" I asked with the feeling we were teetering on a no-going-back moment.

"Oh, I just wanted to see if you were okay… and, uh, tell you something."

"Well, if by 'okay' you mean 'feel like I got hit by a truck,' – *a truck called Niccolò Medici* – then yes, I'm okay."

He frowned.

Nicco let go of your hands, Adele… Nicco let go of you.

My feet moved out of the doorway, as if they knew my mind was about to downward spiral, and stopped on the last step to make up the gap in our heights. I was surprised to feel my best ingénue eyes peering at him in admiration.

All I got back was awkward silence. It felt, strangely, as if it was the first time we'd ever been alone.

"I still really think you should see a doctor."

I groaned internally. *Maybe everything between us last night had just been due to the elixir-adrenaline cocktail?*

"I'm fine." *I'm an idiot.*

Just as I began to feel self-conscious about my aggressive rooftop behavior, his two index fingers hooked the front belt-loops of my black jeans.

My head stopped spinning.

"Did you just come here to lecture me?"

He tugged the denim near my hips, making it difficult to balance on the edge of the step. My eyelashes batted nervously as I looked into his golden-brown eyes.

"Oh, I am never kissing you again, if that's what you are wondering," he said.

I bit my lip to keep the shock from sprawling all over my face.

He did his best not to crack a smile. "Do you realize that, after the first time I kissed you, you started crying, and then after the second time I kissed you, you *blacked out*?"

"Third time's a charm. Maybe I'll burst into flames next?"

"Oh, so this is funny to you?" He struggled to keep his serious demeanor, but didn't budge.

"Fine," I said, lightly sweeping my fingers over his cheekbone. "Glitter."

"No matter how long I stayed in the shower, I couldn't get it all off."

"So, what were you going to tell me?"

"Nothing...," he whispered nervously. He repeated the word again with more authority. "Nothing."

I pulled back. "If you have something to say, you'd better just spit it out."

"It's nothing," he reassured me, gripping my hips.

I didn't totally buy it.

"It's just that..." His fingers crawled together at the small of my back, and he pulled me close again. "It's just that I can't believe after everything we've been through, you ended up with me."

"Oh, did I?"

His head bobbed as it came closer to mine.

"*Oui*, you definitely did."

It became difficult to hide my smile.

"Isaac..."

"Hmm?"

"*Merci beaucoup* for catching me."

"I'll always catch you, Adele, I promise." His lips gently touched mine, breaking his short-lived vow.

No wind. No fire. Nor magic. Nor elixir. Just the warmth of his hot-blooded heart. When he pulled a tiny bit away, he took my breath with him.

"I can't believe it either," I said, trying to contain a giggle.

"Oh, really? Is this still funny to you?"

"Mm… hmm," I said angelically, which he returned with devilish eyes that could only mean one thing.

"No. No!" I tried to leap back to the kitchen door, but there was no chance of escape. He easily pulled me back and attacked my ribs first. "No, stop, please!"

I deserved it, but still, I hated being tickled. Although, it was impossible to really hate his touch. Buckled over, I did my best to wriggle away, but the attempts were futile because I was laughing so hard I could barely breathe.

"Isaac, stop it!" I screamed between gasps.

A scream that brought on another kiss. And a scream that resonated for six blocks and slipped into the slumbering subconscious of the Knight, whose trust in the Heroine trumped all.

la fin.

ACKNOWLEDGEMENTS

Hello there.

In particular, I want to thank my bestie, Jennifer, who always listened attentively as I explained complicated threads about French triplets as we ran along the Hudson day after day. My editor Marissa van Uden, who has reset my bar for creative collaborators. Lucas Stoffel for working through ten thousand graphic revisions with me and for running around New Orleans with my manuscript to read all of the scenes "on location." Liza and Ana for giving me such detailed feedback early on. ALL of my beta readers, but especially Sarah and Zee. Caitlyn and Zoë for convincing me to write a book. Hellvis for her amazing map! *Merci, Coralie!* Lisa, Alex, and Charlotte. <3

I want to thank the tens of thousands of people who read *The Casquette Girls* while I wrote it in real-time online, both the conspiracy theorists and the silent readers. *Merci beaucoup!*

I want to thank all the people who believe in magic. Most of all I want to thank the people who believe in New Orleans – the people who've had to eat Hurricane gruel for months, who've suffered the smell of Bourbon Street on a late July afternoon. To the coffee slingers, beignet friers and omelet beaters. To the street artists, jazz boys, and coke-bottle-tap-shoed dancers. To the Cajuns, to the Creoles, to all those who have dreamed and suffered on our stone "streets." I want to thank the drag queens who raised me to think wearing costumes is a nightly affair. To the tarot card readers, and Nosferatu-ring-wearing-blood drinkers. I want to thank every person who has cleaned mold, bailed water, or seen a Nutria on the neutral ground. I want to thank the people who have rebuilt after every fire and every flood.

Love,
Alys

ALYS ARDEN grew up in the *Vieux Carré,* cut her teeth on the streets of New York, and has worked all around the world since. She still plans to run away with the circus one day.

WANT TO STAY IN OUR WORLD?

@alysarden
www.alysarden.com
www.thecasquettegirls.com
www.facebook.com/TheCasquetteGirls
#nola4life

Laissez les bons temps rouler!

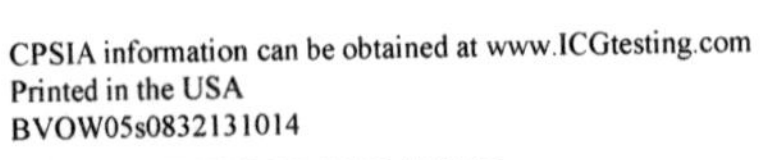
CPSIA information can be obtained at www.ICGtesting.com
Printed in the USA
BVOW05s0832131014

370451BV00001B/22/P